The
PALACE
DRESSMAKER

JADE BEER

HODDER &
STOUGHTON

First published in Great Britain in 2024 by Hodder & Stoughton Limited
An Hachette UK company

This paperback edition published in 2024

1

A CIP catalogue record for this title is available from the British Library

Paperback ISBN 978 1 399 74417 1
ebook ISBN 978 1 399 74418 8

Typeset in ITC Galliard Std by Nancy Resnick

Printed and bound in Great Britain by Clays Ltd, Elcograf S.p.A.

Hodder & Stoughton policy is to use papers that are natural, renewable
and recyclable products and made from wood grown in sustainable forests.
The logging and manufacturing processes are expected to conform to the
environmental regulations of the country of origin.

Hodder & Stoughton Limited
Carmelite House
50 Victoria Embankment
London EC4Y 0DZ

The authorised representative in the EEA is Hachette Ireland, 8 Castlecourt
Centre, Castleknock Road, Castleknock, Dublin 15, D15 YF6A, Ireland

www.hodder.co.uk

The Palace Dressmaker

'A moving exploration into how clothes make up the layers of our lives, as well as a wonderful insight into the worlds of dressmaking, royalty, and friendship across generations. I loved it.'

Jessica Fellowes, international bestselling author of
The World of Downton Abbey

'This is Jade Beer's most delicious novel yet. Romantic, intriguing, and emotionally compelling. Missing *The Crown*? This glamorous love story will fill that space in your life.'

Adele Parks, international bestselling author of *Just Between Us*

'Gorgeous . . . There are fabulous frocks and sumptuous descriptions, but also emotional depth, friendship and romance. It's glamorous, heartwarming and poignant, with a fascinating backdrop for anyone interested in fashion and royalty. A real page-turner – both escapist and satisfying, as all good books should be.'

Veronica Henry, bestselling author of *Thirty Days in Paris*

'A beautiful and deeply moving book about love, loss, and found families . . . Tender, powerful, and healing . . . Meredith and Jayne will stay with me forever. I loved this book.'

Daisy Buchanan, author of *Careering*

'An endearing story of loss and recovery, mystery and memory, heartache and love – and dresses . . . Completely captivating.'

Shelley Noble, *New York Times* bestselling author of
The Tiffany Girls and *The Colony Club*

'In glimmering, sumptuous details this exquisitely imagined novel unfolds in a wa   .'

                                                                    ers

Praise for
The Last Dress from Paris

'A delightful fashion treasure hunt . . . Paris is resplendently depicted.'

Natasha Lester, *New York Times* bestselling author of
The Disappearance of Astrid Bricard

'A rich exploration of the power of female friendships and the true meaning of family. Moving and utterly enjoyable.'

Fiona Davis, *New York Times* bestselling author of
The Spectacular

'An absolute delight! . . . Original, elegant, and romantic . . . Beer delivers intriguing, complex characters for her readers to really care about.'

Hazel Gaynor, *New York Times* bestselling author of
The Last Lifeboat

'With breathtaking prose and a stunning Paris backdrop, Jade Beer offers a tender, heartfelt look at love and friendship, and the sacrifices we make for both.'

Lori Nelson Spielman, *New York Times* bestselling author of
The Star-Crossed Sisters of Tuscany

'Jade Beer's gorgeous prose brings Dior's fashions to life as she deftly weaves together a novel that is part homage to fashion and part romance, as well as a celebration of mothers and daughters.'

Renée Rosen, *USA Today* bestselling author of
Fifth Avenue Glamour Girl

Author photograph by Holly Clark Photography

Jade Beer is an award-winning editor, journalist, and novelist who has worked across the UK national press for more than twenty years. Most recently, she was the editor in chief of Condé Nast's *Brides*. She has written for other leading titles, including the *Sunday Times Style*, *Harper's Bazaar*, the *Mail on Sunday's YOU* magazine, the *Telegraph*, the *Daily Mail*, the *Tatler* wedding guide, and *Glamour*. Jade lives in the Cotswolds with her husband and two daughters.

ALSO BY JADE BEER

The Last Dress from Paris

To Dad,
who is always memorable,
with love x

The farther backward you can look, the farther forward you are likely to see.

—WINSTON CHURCHILL

You are not something that you need to become to be loved.

—CHARLIE MACKESY

She wanted to see the world, but she never wanted the world to see her.

—CLARA BEER

PROLOGUE

❧

There is a red carpet outside 502 Park Avenue tonight. The auctioneer wears an expensive dinner jacket and bow tie, his glasses balanced low on his nose, chin dipped, surveying the crowd, slowly inhaling the energy in the room. Soon he will hold it in his hands, take the crowd where he wants them, roll his immaculate British vowels over their heads, wielding his authority, driving the values higher, sometimes in leaps of $5,000 at a time. There are no reserves and it is all to play for.

This audience is here to see the world's most glamorous working wardrobe. More than one thousand men and women take their seats. Countless others will bid by telephone. Museums, investors, private collectors, famous fans. They've had a chance to view the lots. They know what is coming. Favorites have been selected. Financial ceilings have been set. Now they eye the competition. Who are they up against tonight and who will be the last to raise their paddle victoriously?

One reserved seat on the very end of a back row remains

empty, filled only in the final moments before the bidding begins. A slim dark-haired woman, alone, elegant in black tapered wool trousers and a single-breasted, red knee-length blazer, her lipstick perfectly matching the shade. She lacks the one identical characteristic everyone else in the room shares. The weighty, glossy white catalog in their hands, revealing the briefest glimpse into the private life of a royal. A handwritten note that simply states, *The inspiration for this wonderful sale comes from just one person . . . our son William.*

The woman in red doesn't make a single bid tonight. She sits motionless until the very end, smiles and leaves ahead of the crowd, no interest in claiming her souvenir catalog.

One single image graces its cover. Diana is posed, a pearl dangling at each ear, half smiling directly into the camera, wearing lot number 80. In its former life this dress sat at the banqueting table at the Élysée Palace in Paris. Tonight, as it slowly rotates on the turntable, the oyster duchess satin warms under the lights. It comes to life once more, so familiar now you might expect its owner to appear next to it, to share an anecdote from the night she last wore it. The embroidered carnations that spread across the bodice in simulated pearls and white and gold beads are beautifully spotlit against a backdrop of rich green velvet drapes.

But it is not dress number 80 that is causing a stir through the crowd. Another gown is struck through in the catalog and now causing a ripple of intrigue to float among the first to notice it. Number 19 was listed in the original lineup, but it won't go under the gavel tonight when every other dress will be given its chance to live a second life.

Eighty dresses, but only seventy-nine will sell. One is missing.

ONE

Meredith
LONDON
1988

She's barely slept. Not last night and not much for the previous ten, the number of days since she was offered the job she will start this morning. But she knows adrenaline and coffee will power her through whatever lies ahead. Meredith's stomach flips. She takes a deep grounding breath and hopes with all her heart that they will be kind. That she will be able to add something, to answer any questions directed at her. But more than anything she hopes that she will love this job every bit as much as she's always dreamed she will.

She checks her bag for the final time, ensuring everything she needs for the day is there before she leaves her small apartment. She arrives early and circles the block several times. It may inconvenience others if she arrives too soon. They won't be ready for her and it will cause a disruption.

At eight a.m. on the dot she presses the doorbell and waits. Another deep breath, smoothing her hands down over her brown wool coat, which now feels lacking, given what she knows is created behind this door, which is at this very moment opening to reveal a man.

"Meredith?"

She nods, nervous anticipation not yet allowing her to smile or offer a *good morning*. She reaches out a hand to shake his but the tall man ushers her inside a cramped narrow hallway and misses it.

"You can hang your coat there"—he nods toward a rail that runs the length of the small space—"and ideally your bag. We try to keep as few personal belongings in the workroom as possible. No drinks, obviously. Staff room and the bathroom are one floor up." He nods skyward. "I'm Peter, the sample cutter."

"It's lovely to meet you, Peter. I'm really looking forward to getting started."

"That's great to hear because there is a mountain to do," Peter adds with all the weariness and none of the enthusiasm of first-day Meredith. "This is the workroom where you'll be based." He pushes open a door to another room that is again much smaller than Meredith anticipated. Everything she would expect to see is here—and nothing else. Everything is in its place, just as she likes it. There is very little color, no plants, no personal effects, no packed lunch waiting to be eaten later.

"It's all pretty self-explanatory. That's your seat." Peter nods toward the one vacant spot close to the window, not that there is much of a view through its frosted glass. It's one of the lower ta-bles and, she can see, has enough space for her to neatly display all her own essentials. "I'll leave you to make your own introduc-tions if you don't mind. I've got to get on."

"Absolutely, no problem at all." Meredith casts a broad smile around the room. She takes her time introducing herself, ensuring she makes eye contact with everyone, eleven of them in total, mostly women. Everyone nods, taking the briefest moment to acknowledge her, to assess how she will fit into their tightly ordered regime.

All except one.

A man in a pristine long white coat leaning over a high table, a small sharp pencil in his right hand. Meredith refuses to be ignored so she waits. She sees the faintest frown pinch at his eyebrows. He doesn't want to pause. Doesn't want to raise his head from the work he is doing, breaking his concentration, but understands that he should. His eyes move a fraction toward her. He senses her continued presence and eventually straightens. Surprisingly, his eyes are kind, not challenging. Shy perhaps, or unassuming, thinks Meredith, rather than rude.

"Hello, I'm Meredith," she says directly to him, then watches as his face remains motionless. He's going to ignore her. She can see his head start to dip back toward the white shapes in front of him on the table.

"And you are?" She tilts her head, searching out eye contact again. She allows her smile to deepen. Now is not the moment to be intimidated by anyone, least of all someone she is about to have a close working relationship with. Their eyes reconnect for a second or two longer than she suspects he has awarded anyone else so far today.

"William." There is the subtlest curve upward at the corners of his mouth. She's reminded of the efficiency of Peter's smile earlier. It wasn't friendly. It was intended to communicate something else altogether, his doubt about how much she might enjoy being here, perhaps. William's smile is different, more genuine.

"Well, I'm looking forward to working with you, William."

Meredith hears the door open again behind her and feels the faintest shift of energy in the room. She looks over her shoulder just as Catherine enters, instantly recognizable with her dark

shoulder-length hair and an immaculate jet-black trouser suit, the
jacket open, its sleeves pushed a little up her arms, ready for work.
Meredith didn't imagine she would meet her so soon. She's con-
siderably more beautiful than the few images of her in the press
suggest. But it isn't her looks that impress Meredith. Here is a
woman at the very top of her game, whose creativity and work
ethic have ensured the kind of meteoric rise that might give birth
to a giant ego in some. Not so, in this case. Meredith has read
enough to know this is where she wants to be and whom she
wants to learn from.

Catherine extends a hand. "A pleasure to have you with us.
Meredith, isn't it?"

"It is, yes." The two women exchange a firm handshake before
Catherine makes her way to the back of the room to chat with
Peter.

Meredith turns to take her seat and notices that William is yet
to return to his task. He is watching her, a subtle curiosity in his
eyes, and apparently feels no need to hide the fact.

TWO

⁓⁓⁓⁓⁓

Jayne
BATH
JULY 2018

Margot is so much like me. Hates unnecessary noise. Prefers to be alone. Very happy just to sit, as we are now, side by side, her weight leaning into my right arm, watching the early-morning mist lift off the grass, the city far below us starting to stretch and wake.

The realization that I have more in common with a scrappy Jack Russell than I do with most people always makes me smile. A smile that is 80 percent genuine—this dog has a lot going for her—and 20 percent denial, but at least I can admit that. I am okay with the fact that Margot and I share a love of peaceful solitude, but I have some awareness that others think I shouldn't be.

It's eight a.m. and we have just completed the two-hour skyline walk of the city, as we do at least twice a week together. Her at my heel, fiercely obedient until her nose lifts, she catches a whiff of something she likes, then she's gone. I learned early on not to panic. Unlike some of the other dogs I walk, Margot always comes back. I don't even have to pause for her to catch up. She will find me again. Loyalty is everything to her. Plus, she knows I'm carrying tripe sticks.

As I stretch my long nettle-scratched legs out in front of me, I feel the heat of the new day starting to burn away the last of the clouds, and the sharpness of the scorched grass on the back of my knees. It's going to be another brilliant blue-sky day. Margot's owner, the highly impressive Davina, will be manhandling her two children off to school by now, while I sit here, surely the lucky one, feeling a deep contentment. I have made this dog happy and I didn't have to say a single word. That's the great thing about dogs. The more you get to know them, the better they are. I can't always say the same for humans.

We didn't see anyone on our walk this morning. Too early for the tourists who always get lost in the network of fields and trails and need redirecting, or the grumpy older men determined to make me solely responsible for every poop bag thoughtlessly left behind. Not even a text from Mum. Two hours of uninterrupted isolation with just a series of kissing gates and stiles between me, Margot, and the space we both crave. Would the air have smelled any fresher, would my lungs have expanded any further, would this dog like me any better if I was something more than just me, doing what I love? If I was more boldly striding through this life with great confidence, as the world likes to remind me that I should be in my final year before I hit thirty?

I look down onto the rooftops of Bath, the honey glow spreading across its network of famous Georgian terraces, already warming in the early sunshine. Just the odd spire, construction crane, or church tower asserting itself above the other buildings. I notice the city's beauty first, but while Margot is loudly crunching on her well-earned breakfast, I think about all those people packed into those buildings. Beautiful town houses just like the one I live in, that have been converted by ambitious landlords keen to see the best possible return on every square meter. Every day the same. Up. Commute. Work. Repeat. What confrontations, negotiations, problems might they face today? Will they feel energized at the prospect of it all or intimidated by it? Are they making themselves live a life someone else convinced them they should desire? Am I too?

I was always the quiet, awkward one. The girl not to sit next to. The girl whom everyone loved to talk about rather than to. Most people understood why I was quiet, the sadness that had written itself through my family history. All it took was one careless mum to lower her voice over coffee and retell our story to others, forgetting that a hushed tone was the quickest way to pique the interest of the children in the room next door. Unfortunately, as a kid, that made me intriguing, the focus of the last thing I wanted: more attention. For some I was just that strange girl who never talked much. For others I presented a challenge. Could they provoke me enough to *make* me talk?

I hear a siren, a police car or an ambulance some way off in the distance, and its urgency reminds me that I also have the second part of my own working day to get to at a local florist, Bouquets & Bunches.

I wait until the last possible moment to slip Margot back onto her lead and then we walk the thirty minutes or so back to Lansdown Crescent, her home and mine. My eyeline never dipped on the walk, I was taking everything in, absolutely reveling in the landscape and all it has to offer. But once I'm back on the streets of the city, it's my walking shoes I see, my gaze lowered, not wanting to interact or be seen but knowing that my height, a lofty five foot ten, will always make me visible in a crowd. Margot seems to share my discomfort, too, and she picks up her pace, keen to return to the comfort of her dog bed and an empty house.

When I finally plucked up the courage to leave Mum's place, this address was an easy choice. Lots of people wanted it. Mum and Dad's money helped. It's the best terrace in Bath, the estate agent said, you'll rarely see a **FOR SALE** sign. He was right about that.

But it was the sheep that sold it to me. I can look out the window of my top-floor apartment at the sweeping view over the city skyline and at the livestock that roam the private patch of land directly opposite—with no idea quite how lucky they are to have claimed this space in the middle of an overcrowded city.

It's also sufficiently far enough away that Mum or my older sister, Sally, has to call before visiting, they can't risk a casual drop-by. Mum gets it, but Sally, always the loudest of us two, still doesn't understand why I don't fancy the improv comedy night at the Theatre Royal, or the live debate at the Assembly Rooms on the city's relevance to modern architecture. Why is it considered somehow lacking to want to sit alone with your thoughts or a good book?

Margot's owner, Davina, an overworked event planner who keeps the kind of hours that would kill me in less than a week, will be at her office by now. I let myself into her ground-floor apartment and immediately trip on a trail of odd shoes that includes a stray flip-flop, a filthy trainer, and a scuffed school shoe, its sole flapping open. I follow them like breadcrumbs down the hallway into the kitchen, where Margot's bed is and where domestic chaos reigns. Whoever paid for this kitchen obviously has very good taste, and if you took away the dog and the lived-in family mess it's exactly the sort of room you might see under a Pinterest search for stylish family living spaces. It has chalky coffee-colored walls, impossibly high ceilings, and a central island that this morning is barely visible under the clutter. The sink is piled with breakfast dishes and half the cutlery didn't quite make it that far. There are opened pots of jam and peanut butter, their lids discarded, littering the counter—I can't help myself, I wipe them off, close them, and pop them back in the fridge—and a saucepan on the hob with porridge crusted around it, which won't be the most appealing welcome home later on. I can't leave that either. I wash it up and pop it back in one of the bespoke wooden cupboards, the sort I know I'll never own. No one thought—or had time—to turn the radio off and I can see tiny greasy fingerprints all over the low lights that hang above the island. It's Monday so the usual stack of Sunday papers sits on the kitchen table, still cellophane-wrapped and unread. An optimistic attempt at some weekend downtime that never came.

Davina's must be the largest apartment in our town house, with uninterrupted views of the shared rear garden from the floor-to-ceiling sash windows in the kitchen.

I stand for a minute and take it all in, as I have many times before. It's staggering how much you can learn about people from the space they inhabit. For a start, there are never any men's shoes. Willow and Maggie, Davina's daughters, claim the lion's share of the apartment and its air space. I've heard the unbridled laughter and the shrill arguments that can erupt at any time of the day or night. I first met her elder daughter, fourteen-year-old Willow, when I moved in about a week after the new year. Small talk doesn't exist in Willow's teenage world. She speaks only when she thinks she has something worth saying. I could tell the day we met that the excitement of Christmas had already receded. Davina was back at work and Willow's handwritten Post-it notes had begun to build up on the kitchen work surfaces, her preferred, perhaps only, means of communication. Just as I am letting go of my own mother more, Willow is trying to claim a larger stake of hers. Sometimes they're reminders that *I've run out of toothpaste* or *Have you signed the school forms yet?* But occasionally they tug at my heart a little stronger. *Will you be home for dinner tonight, Mum?* or *Will you have time to finish watching the movie with me this evening?* The really sad ones—*I've forgotten what you look like!* or *Remember me, your daughter?*—I am tempted to dispose of to save Davina the hurt, but I know I mustn't. I just do a bit of extra tidying or make it clear I am available for more dog walks if she needs me, anything that might give her a little more time with her girls.

This morning I notice the full lunch box that's been forgotten— right next to the empty bottle of Sauvignon—and I wince at the problems it's going to cause Davina later when someone realizes. The younger daughter, the energetic eight-year-old, Maggie, gets collected from school by a childminder Monday to Friday—I've seen it marked on the family planner on the kitchen wall—and I think this might be her tea. Then I see a note for me. *Jayne, would you mind picking up my suit from the dry cleaners next to the station? I know you'll probably walk that way and I haven't got time. I've put the extra money with the dog walking fee, next to the microwave. Also, we're out of dog food. Sorry!* There is no money there, just a potted fern, dehydrated and desperate for resuscitation. I want Davina to be pleased with the job I do, so I pour a half-drunk glass of water on it, make a mental note to collect the suit later, and give Margot a quick ruffle on the head to let her know I'm off but I'll be back with something for her to eat. I let myself back into my place on the top floor, the smallest apartment of the four in the town house but with priceless views from my little roof terrace.

My alarm went off at five forty-five this morning and that's when I laid out my clothes for the day—a plain dark navy linen dress, a gray tee underneath, and a pair of flat sandals. I set up my usual breakfast in the kitchen last night before bed so I can be back out the door in under thirty minutes. It's Monday, there will be the week's delivery of fresh flowers arriving at Bouquets & Bunches for me to arrange and a stack of orders from the weekend to process. I get ready then wait ten minutes until I hear the front door downstairs bang shut.

That will be Jake, the man who lives in the coach house at the bottom of our shared garden, checking his postbox in the hallway on his way out to work. He's one of those people who's impossibly handsome, late thirties, I'd say, a bit of gray hair peppering the outline of his face, the kind of casual good looks that don't appear manufactured by expensive face creams and hours in front of the bathroom mirror. The sort of guy who'd look all wrong in a suit and someone I actively avoid. From what I've seen he has plenty of admirers, he doesn't need another.

THREE

It's 5:42 a.m. and I wake to silence. Just the way I like it. While I'm waiting for my milk to warm on the hob my eyes find the grainy Polaroid baby photo stuck to the fridge, my faded birth date written in pencil just below the image of a small bundle held in my mother's arms. My birthday is approaching. Mum will call but I won't celebrate it. I haven't since I was a small child. This morning I'm walking Margot and Teddy together, the latter a high-energy springer spaniel owned by Olivia, a digital designer who lives on the second floor. Not long after I moved into the building and she heard I was walking Margot, she knocked on my door and begged me to do the same for her.

Olivia is someone who locks herself out of her apartment at least once a week, adding to her peaked stress levels. She'll often be heard cursing loudly outside her front door until she remembers I also now have keys to her place. I've seen the very long to-do lists she writes for herself to push back missed deadlines and cancel drinks with friends. I've seen the half-finished plates of food, the coffee gone cold, the laptop and page proofs that are permanent fixtures on her kitchen table, the blanket that doubles as a duvet on the sofa. I suspect she might never hit a deadline if I didn't walk Teddy at least four times a week. Sometimes, if she looks extra stressed when I collect him, then I may "forget" to charge her. Knowing that I'm giving her the breathing space to make a dent in her workload and keep her miserable boss at bay makes me far happier than the money would.

I remember the first time I met her. It was early morning. I could hear a commotion in the hallway downstairs, all the way from my sofa, where I was checking emails. Voices were raised and I felt I had no choice but to investigate.

"I'm not sure how many times I can say it. I am *not* your milk thief." Olivia was conducting this conversation with Davina and Jake while on the phone to someone else, presumably a work call.

"Well, *someone* is nicking it from the hallway and now there is no milk for the girls' breakfast cereal again. I just wonder if we could all stop behaving like impoverished students, please!"

"I'll grab you some from the coach house, I've got plenty." I could tell Jake was trying not to laugh, despite Davina's exasperation.

"Maybe *he's* nicked it all," shrieked Olivia. "Did you consider that? Or it could be her!" She points in my direction, making me a suspect too.

"I haven't taken anyone's milk," I added weakly, immediately feeling guilty for a crime I had not committed.

"This sounds like a job for me!" Maggie appeared, wearing a pair of bright pink knickers over some sparkly leggings, a bikini top decorated with slices of watermelon, and a giant magnifying glass pressed to her right eyeball, trailing Willow behind her.

"Why are adults so tragic?" Willow shot a withering look at us all. "Maybe the wrong number of bottles got delivered? Maybe it was the old couple on the first floor? Maybe we could all just have toast for breakfast this morning?" She made some valid points.

"Maybe you should all get out of my crime scene!" bellowed

Maggie, and everyone started to laugh, despite the confrontational start to the day.

"D'you wanna put some proper clothes on, Maggie?" Willow turned her sharp tongue on her younger sibling. "Seriously, have you got no shame?"

Maggie looked down at her perfect little body and stunning outfit, confused. "What d'you call these?" She adjusted her stance, legs wide apart, hips thrust toward Willow.

Willow flounced back into the apartment and we all dispersed.

When Olivia eventually answers the door this morning, she has her mobile in one hand, a bowl of cereal tucked into the crook of the same arm, and the lead draped over her right arm and not yet attached to Teddy. An earbud from her usual accessory, noise-canceling headphones, is jammed into one ear, explaining the long delay in her opening the door.

"I'm sorry," I say for the interruption even though this is my regular day and time to collect Teddy.

I lean forward to take the lead off her and she lets me without once making eye contact. Not even a cursory nod. She just continues with the conversation she's having and moves to close the door. I can tell by the alarm in her eyes that this caller is not happy with her. Something has been forgotten or missed and tears are not far away. The fact Teddy's tail is wedged between his legs tells me he senses it too. He is desperate to get out of here and starts jumping up at me repeatedly, which results in me dropping Margot's lead. I immediately regret collecting Margot first, but I know it helps Davina to have her out of the house as soon as possible in the morning so she can focus on getting the girls ready for school.

While I'm fumbling to get Teddy under control, Margot bolts down four flights of stairs and I can hear her jumping up at the front door, knowing freedom lies just the other side. I can also hear Jake trying to control her. I pick up the pace, taking the stairs two at a time, praying no one is foolish enough to open the front door. Without me there, she'll bolt. There's a nighttime's worth of energy inside her that needs unleashing. And I am almost to the bottom when I see the door to the first-floor apartment creak slowly open. The face of a small older lady appears. It must be Mrs. Chalis, who, along with her husband, are the only residents in the building I have yet to meet, despite the fact I pass their door several times a day.

Davina said I should keep my distance. Apparently, Mrs. Chalis is a bit . . . eccentric. She's been spotted wandering about barefoot, sometimes in just a nightie, regardless of the time of day or night. Olivia says she hears her singing through the walls and Jake's reported the lights stay on in their apartment all night sometimes. What can the elderly couple possibly be up to? I wonder. I know they don't own a dog, so there's no potential business there, but still, it seems odd to live in such close proximity to someone and not ever have set eyes on them. I guess I'm about to find out if they live up to the intrigue. The apartment door is wide open now, and Mrs. Chalis is watching me with an air of confusion.

"William?" she asks over the commotion of Jake still trying to restrain Margot downstairs. "I thought I heard William's voice."

She looks a little swamped by the blue-and-white cotton dress she's wearing. Her face looks friendly enough, she has a broad smile that radiates in lines out across her cheeks, and as she smiles her small eyes almost disappear. But not entirely. I can see the distress sharpened there. She looks alert, more than she needs to be. She has a mass of gray hair that looks unbrushed and, I notice, she is wearing only one earring, the other missing from her right lobe. She's barefoot.

Margot bolts back up the stairs from the hallway with Jake in pursuit, sees the open door, gets confused, and before I can reach out a hand to stop her, she charges into the apartment, causing Mrs. Chalis to stumble slightly against the doorframe.

"Oh my goodness," she half laughs, half shrieks, and I can see I've got no choice but to follow Margot in.

"Sorry, Jayne." Jake has caught up now. "She wouldn't listen to me, I'm afraid. Shall I take the other dog while you grab that one?" He nods toward the Chalises' door.

Margot must be the only female immune to Jake's charms and I admit the idea makes me feel a little proud of her, especially as I can feel my own features softening at the mere sight of him. It's his half laugh that gets me. Despite his best efforts, Jake has failed to get Margot under control, and the realization amuses him greatly.

I recall the first time I ever set eyes on Jake. The weather had just turned warm and he was hosting drinks in the garden one evening. An invitation had been pushed under my door a few days before, but I'd ignored it, easily convincing myself it came out of a sense of obligation, invite the new neighbor or it might look rude. What kind of man, I wondered, goes to the effort of dotting lanterns among the flower beds, hanging more from the trees?

The soft sound of laughter had drifted up to my roof terrace. There had been about thirty guests in all—women wearing long floaty floral dresses, beautiful and carefree, some of them barefoot on the grass. The men looking casual yet fashionable as they circulated the garden, seeking out their host. They'd all exuded perfection, radiated confidence, drinking freely of the champagne Jake was generously offering. Since then, it's been a constant rotation of new faces in our back garden but mine has never been one of them.

I should have gone. I could have shown him not everyone is

like that. Some people are more earthy and natural, some have legs covered in bruises. Some like to be coaxed into the conversation, not dominate it.

Jake finally clocks the older woman standing in the doorway. "Oh, Mrs. Chalis," he says, and then when she shows no sign of recognizing him, Jake adds, "It's Jake, from the coach house. I haven't seen you in a while . . ."

The silence is becoming awkward, so I fill it.

"I am so, so sorry," I splutter. "I will have Margot out of there in one minute. Don't worry, Jake, I'll take Teddy too. I've got this." I give him a firm nod to convince him I will not be outdone by a wayward dog.

"Are you sure, because it doesn't look like . . ." He's smirking at me, finding the whole thing highly amusing, and I wish there was a moment to pause and take in the beauty of him, up close. There is no other word. He is beautiful in a *slightly disheveled, totally oblivious to it* way. But at the same time, quite put together. The shirt is ironed. The socks match. But his hair is unbrushed, he's unshaven, and a golden chain at his neck is caught on his collar. He hasn't looked in the mirror this morning and yet he is easily the most attractive man I've seen—although perhaps quite incapable, too, otherwise I'd now be on my way out the door with Margot.

Jake gives me another amused smile before tucking his hands into his jeans pockets. "If you're sure. Have a good day."

I watch him nod to Mrs. Chalis, who is still standing by the door, before he turns and heads back down the stairs. I decide to limit the possibility of more upset by tying Teddy to the banister before I dart into the apartment, calling for Margot and searching my pockets for something that might entice her back to me.

But as soon as I am inside, I struggle to see anything. All the wooden shutters are closed across the windows and the whole place is in near darkness. Then I hear the door shut behind me and I am aware that Mrs. Chalis has followed me back in. I feel the faintest tingle of nerves travel up through me and shout Margot's name a little louder.

"Oh dear, oh dear, where is he?" I hear the older lady mumble.

"It's a she actually, Margot, I'll find her, don't worry. Is it possible to put a light on, please?"

Mrs. Chalis pauses behind me and makes no attempt to reach for the light switch I assume must be somewhere on the wall near one of us. She just stands there, her eyes flicking from left to right. I pull my mobile phone from my pocket, and with the minimal light that offers, I find the switch and flick it on.

"Do I know you?" asks Mrs. Chalis, and I turn to see how confused she looks.

"I'm Jayne, from upstairs." I needlessly point toward the ceiling. "I live on the top floor," I say. But she stands, motionless, and none of what I'm saying seems to land as it should. Then finally, she asks, "Remind me of your name?"

"Jayne," I say again as I turn and start to take in the rest of the apartment, hoping Margot will appear voluntarily any second now.

I can smell something overly sweet, ripe, that doesn't seem right. Nothing awful but something that feels like a warning to act. Perhaps something has bubbled over in the kitchen during all the commotion. I begin to walk deeper into the apartment and the corridor I entered through leads into a large drawing room. "Would you mind if I open the shutters?" I ask. "It might help me find Margot. She lives with Davina and her two girls on the ground floor, so she's very used to hiding from drama."

"It's not Margot I'm looking for," she replies calmly, and I decide at this point to open the shutters anyway.

As I do, Mrs. Chalis squints into the light like she hasn't seen it for some time, and I can immediately see what is causing the smell. There is a fruit bowl full of blackened bananas that should have been thrown out days ago. She notices that I've seen them. "He likes them that way, they mash easier, on toast for his breakfast."

I want to ask who, but I am completely distracted by the mess I can now see around me. Every surface is covered. There are newspaper cuttings, randomly placed stacks of hardback books, some so high they have toppled over and been left where they fell. Old photographs, pieces of fabric thrown indiscriminately over furniture, a huge box of buttons has spilled all over the floor, and under a small desk in one corner of the room I can see writing paper, balled and discarded around the wastepaper bin, like Mrs. Chalis has made multiple attempts to write something difficult. The desk lamp has fallen on its side and been left that way.

The room, the entire apartment from what I can see, is overflowing with belongings. In the center of the room are two yellow sofas piled so high with cushions that it would be impossible to sit down. The fact each one is covered in a different fabric only adds to the chaotic feel of the place. The sofas face each other and around them four armchairs are grouped, not one clear enough of clutter to sit on. The wall above the fireplace, which runs the length of the room from where we entered to three double-height sash windows, is covered in drawings, mostly of flowers, some framed, some not. There is barely an inch of free hanging space. I notice a bottle of furniture polish on one of the shelves, its lid discarded, a thick rim of dust settled around its nozzle.

It's the same brand my grandmother used, and it reminds me of a terribly sad story my mother once told me. How my grandmother was so lonely after my grandfather passed away that she would routinely polish his bookshelves. He had hundreds of books, but she would take them off the shelves, dusting the jacket of each one, just to pass the hours in the day. To distract herself from the loneliness, the feeling of being no use to anyone anymore. When she put the last book back in its place, she would start all over again. On and on it would go. Anything to avoid sitting with her thoughts. Pretending to have purpose.

"Is everything all right, Mrs. Chalis?" I ask, because clearly, it's not.

She stands perfectly still, staring at me, still smiling and, it seems, comfortable in my company, despite the fact the two of us have never met before.

"I can't remember what I was going outside to do." She's shaking her head and getting a little frustrated with herself, trying to shuffle a thought back to the surface. Then the phone rings. Again, she makes no effort to move, like she hasn't heard it at all.

She isn't that old. I'd place her maybe in her late sixties. I'd imagined a hunched, slow-moving, little old lady from the description the others gave me. By contrast, Mrs. Chalis seems quite young, but something obviously isn't right.

"Do you need to answer the phone?" I nudge as it continues to ring.

"No. I don't like the way it makes me feel." Her smile drops.

"The phone?"

"Yes. It's never good news, is it?"

"Leave it then," I say. My heart tugs in my chest as I look at her. She appears so small in this vast apartment. So lost. I never reacted to the constant sight of that furniture polish at my grandmother's house. I remember seeing it, much later being told why it was there. And yet, I don't remember it sparking a change. I didn't suddenly spend more hours with her. I didn't offer to take her out more and, standing here now, I can't understand why.

"Would you like a cup of tea," she asks eventually, "while we search for . . ." Her face looks blank.

"Margot." I'm reminded that Teddy is still waiting for me outside.

"No, thank you, but let me make you one," I offer.

The kitchen feels very dated. There is a bright red Aga instead of a modern cooker, which strikes me as not very practical when it comes to cooking a simple meal for two. The walls are lined with densely patterned wallpaper, there's a large farmhouse-style dining table and a plate rack dominating one wall, but it's awkwardly jammed with utensils rather than crockery. There is a microwave, its door hanging open, revealing a bowl of what I think is tomato soup, so old a thick skin has hardened on the top of it. It must have been there for days. I open the fridge next to find a line of single-pint milk bottles—eight of them I count—and very little else. Davina stuck *another* notice up in the hallway last week asking whoever is helping themselves to the milk intended for other apartments to stop it. I think we have our culprit.

I lift the kettle and flick the lid open, ready to refill it. As I glance down inside of it, there are three eggs swimming in the water there. Mrs. Chalis is next to me now.

"I keep forgetting them and they boil dry in the saucepan, so I cook them in there," she says with a satisfied smile, and I have to agree that's quite a clever solution to her problem.

Then we're both distracted by the sound of Margot's low whimper coming from a room we haven't entered yet. I follow Mrs. Chalis through to her bedroom to find Davina's dog sitting at the foot of the bed, probably wondering what's caused such a lengthy delay to her daily walk. But it's not Margot who has my attention now.

In the corner of the room, casually thrown over the back of a chair, is the most incredible strapless evening dress. It's pink, silk I think, floor-length, and the bodice, which seems to drop lower to the hips rather than the waist, is covered in the most detailed pink-and-white floral embroidery. It has what looks like a matching cropped jacket, too, which has been discarded on the floor. There is a faint familiarity to it that I can't place.

"We have to wash our hands," says Mrs. Chalis. "If we want to touch it. It's raw silk."

"Is . . . is this *your* dress?" I ask.

"No." She seems very sure of that. "It's dress number nineteen." She nods her head, happy that this fact is correct.

"Number nineteen? I'm not sure I understand. If it's not yours, whose dress is it?"

"I don't know, but William will."

"William is your husband?"

"Yes. He's put it there to be helpful."

I'm not sure what she means by that, so I try again.

"Are you looking after it for someone? Or did you borrow it?"

"I probably don't have long left with it." She raises the fingers of her right hand to her lips and taps them gently there, thinking. "Oh gosh, I don't know. There is a reason why it's here, but . . ." She pauses, casting her gaze back toward the dress. "I know it's important to me and William and . . . someone else." Which tells me very little. It's clearly a very beautiful dress, quite at odds with the manic snapshot of the Chalises' life the rest of the apartment has offered up this morning.

"I won't touch it, but do you mind if I take a closer look?" I start to move toward it.

"I don't mind." Mrs. Chalis has taken a seat on the bed next to Margot and is gently smoothing the top of her head.

This is obviously not your average evening dress. It's far fancier than the sort of thing Mum used to splash out on to accompany Dad to his work events, before he started going to them alone. The intricate pattern of flowers, jasmine and cherry blossom, some miniature orchids and calla lilies, I think, green and star-shaped sequins, gold glass beads and braid has surely all been stitched by hand to perfectly fit the occasion it was worn to. Maybe that's it, I simply recognize the flowers. It seems very specific. I look at Mrs. Chalis for any hint of understanding, but she is far more interested in Margot, who is offering up her belly for a rub. I check the label at the top of the dress. *Catherine Walker.* A name that means nothing to me. Then I see the small handwritten note that has dropped under the chair and I bend to pick it up, reading it aloud.

Dearest Meredith,

Please accept this dress, she wanted you to have it and so do I. She says it will make her very happy to think you will gain as much pleasure from it as she once did.

Yours with love,
Catherine

"Meredith? Is that your name?"

"Yes, hello." She says it like we are meeting for the first time again.

I can't shake the feeling that I have seen this dress before. I just can't think of where. As I look up at Mrs. Chalis—Meredith—who is still happily stroking Margot's head, I make a mental note to google Catherine Walker as soon as I get the chance.

The note is dated June 1997. I look back to Meredith. Who was so keen for her to have this dress? And why? Why did they believe it would make her happy?

Then, as I watch, Meredith's demeanor changes abruptly. She shifts away from Margot, her eyes flare, her arms fold protectively across her lap.

"Such a rush," she breathes. "Such exhaustion. I'll never feel like myself again." She's shaking her head, looking weary. "He is tired too. We all are. But what choice is there? I can't let her down. I never will."

My thoughts and Meredith's are interrupted by the sound of Teddy barking outside in the hallway.

"I need to get going, Mrs. Cha—Meredith," I say as I pull Margot from the bed. She follows me and again I notice the furniture polish on our route back to the front door. Clearly no one in this building has been inside of Meredith's apartment, they would have helped her if they had, I'm sure of it. But it is the image of the polish that brings this realization into sharp focus. I know what it meant once before. I am convinced it, along with everything else I've seen, indicates much more now. Just as I am lifting my arm to open the door, I feel Meredith's gaze on my back. I turn to face her, and all the happiness has drained from her features, but she doesn't say anything.

"Who likes the bananas, Meredith? Can you remember?" I ask.

"My husband, William," she answers. "Have you seen him? He's missing. I wonder if you might help me find him, please?"

FOUR

❦

Meredith
1988

"Well, you must be doing something right." There is an edge to Peter's tone this morning that suggests a degree of trouble is on the horizon. "William doesn't normally bother to get to know anyone new until they've really proven themselves." Peter is standing over Meredith's desk, *again*, distracting her from a deadline she must hit by lunchtime today. She lets the pale blue silk slacken in her hands, knowing that unless she indulges this conversation, Peter will linger and waste more of her precious time. "And what are you? Six weeks in, barely into your trial period and already he's requested you for one of his *special commissions*."

Now Peter has Meredith's genuine attention.

"What do you mean?" Meredith looks toward William's workstation, but he isn't there. He was called to Catherine's office about an hour ago and is yet to reappear.

"A dress for *her*. A very special one this time. She wants something a little different apparently. More dramatic. Naturally William will be working on it, but the strange thing is he wants *you* on it too. I'm sure he'll fill you in when he's back. Ah, here he is."

William comes back through the door of the workroom, registers the devious look on Peter's face, ignores the pair of them, and returns to his desk. Realizing William has no intention of being drawn on the subject now, Peter retreats to his own table, leaving Meredith wondering whether any of what she was just told is accurate or not.

William waits until everyone has left the workroom that night before, finally, he asks to speak to Meredith.

"Do you have a moment?" He waits alongside her table.

"Of course. How can I help?" Meredith stands.

"I'm sure Peter has already filled you in on whatever half details he has managed to scrape together by hanging around unwanted in various corridors . . ."

Meredith can't help but laugh. It's exactly the sort of juvenile thing she has already witnessed Peter doing.

"I'll take that as a yes." William cracks a small smile. "He may have told you that I suggested you work on this next piece, and if he has, I'm afraid he's wrong."

"Oh." Meredith can't hide the disappointment in her face.

"I would have asked for you, but I didn't need to," William quickly corrects himself. "Catherine beat me to it. She specifically wants you on this one and, well, I couldn't agree more."

Meredith is shocked that such an endorsement of her work has come so soon.

"Wow. I mean, obviously, I would be honored, but do you really think . . ." She trails off, all of a sudden realizing she shouldn't undermine his obvious confidence in her.

"I've seen your dedication. You've been the first one into the workroom every morning since you started. I like that you care as much as you do, and so does Catherine. It hasn't gone unnoticed.

And . . ." Now it's William's turn to hesitate. He breaks eye contact. "It will give me the chance to get to know you a little better too." By the time he finishes the sentence, he's already walking away from her, not waiting to see how his comments land, trying to play them down, even as he's saying them.

Meredith isn't sure why William credits this decision solely to Catherine. She may have sanctioned it—Meredith's sure she would need to approve it—but the idea can surely have come only from William, the person who sees the quality of her work, day in and day out, in the workroom.

"Thank you, William. That means a lot, really it does. Can I see it?"

"See it?" He turns to face her again.

"I mean, is there an early sketch that you can show me? Perhaps just to give me a hint of what's to come?" She looks toward his table, knowing it will be there somewhere.

"It's already on my wall." The two of them step toward his workstation and Meredith's eyes follow the line of dress silhouettes hanging in chronological order on the wall behind his desk. "It's the last one."

Meredith leans in for a closer look. "I'm going to be working on *this*? With you?" She swallows down the weight of expectation already building within her. In less than two months she has graduated from the newest recruit to working on what will undoubtedly be one of the most talked-about dresses of the year.

"You will." William allows himself a deep smile now. "It's going to be covered in thousands of simulated pearls, not a dress that will be forgotten in a hurry, and a chance for you to add your name to the history books." He looks directly at her, knowing he is delivering the best possible news, enjoying the fact.

Meredith glances around the tiny hidden workroom in the center of London where this will happen, with paint peeling from its walls, not even a potted plant to break up the unexceptional blandness or add even a hint of personality or color to its foundations.

No one could possibly guess what goes on in here. The thousands of footsteps that pass by every day on the street outside, people with no reason to question what could be happening in that unassuming room.

Meredith's eyes find the noticeboard on the wall to the left of her table, filled with the kind of images she hopes one day will bear her name, despite the anonymity there must always be. That unforgettable black dress worn in Rome, that had William's expertise written all over it. Finely corded lace over a black silk bodice, long sleeves, an Elizabethan collar, cut at midcalf length and scalloped at the hem, the only accessory a mantilla. An image that was published around the world, and now here is William giving her the chance to claim a little of the private glory on the next dress.

Meredith understands the spotlight is not hers to seek. Far from courting the press, Catherine has sought to evade them, avoiding the theater of the fashion runway unlike so many of her contemporaries, letting only a very small handful of trusted press into her studio. Even then, in the minutes before their arrival, she turns any photographs of her with her most famous client to the wall. There are strict instructions never to throw anything relating to this client away. Some of the less principled press will go through the bins if their news desks demand it. Catherine must trust Meredith, which can only mean William trusts her too. Funny, it's the second thought that makes a swell of pride fill her chest.

They are interrupted by a loud knock at the front door, and

when William returns from answering it, he's clutching a discreet posy of flowers. "They're from her, for Catherine. A thank-you for the last dress, I expect."

"How do you know who they are from?" Meredith can see the card is still wedged unopened among the blooms and there isn't even any obvious branding to indicate a favored florist.

"It's forget-me-nots. She always sends forget-me-nots. They're her favorites."

FIVE

Jayne

I never set out to be a dog walker. Does anyone? It was a job born out of not knowing what else to do. I've always been honest about that. I don't tell people I'm a business owner. I say I walk dogs. I'd tried all the obvious choices. Office work—with its terrifying reliance on last-minute presentations given while a circle of faces stared expectantly at me—had never been for me. Waitressing had its moments. The tips alone eclipsed what I earn now, and it was fascinating to watch couples eating together. I could tell immediately who really cared, who didn't let their phones trespass out of their bags or pockets, who had to be reminded of the specials more than once because they were interested in only each other. That was Alex and I once, fleetingly, before . . . Well, I'm not quite sure who ruined it, me or him.

Then there was a brief spell nannying—the children were truly wonderful but the parents I had a hard time satisfying. Not long after that I saw a man walking a tangle of five dogs through the park, the name of his business—*The Dog Father*—printed across the back of his T-shirt. It made me laugh and I thought, why not? It's time to make changes that I know will be good for me. Then the only person I would have to rely on would be *me*. There would be no one waiting to be impressed. A couple of well-placed online ads was all it took.

Dogs are glorious. You love them and in return they ask so little of you. Okay, some of them have taken a bit more persuading—there is a three-year-old labradoodle whose owners have never invested any time in training him who hated me for a while—but most can be won over with a good long walk, a firm cuddle, and plenty of treats for good behavior. And seven months in, there have been some wonderful upsides. I've never been fitter. My legs are toned, and I feel physically strong. I can eat whatever I want in the course of a day and never put on an ounce. Interacting with the owners is minimal, since most are at work when I collect and return their dogs.

But neither can I ignore the downsides. Spending another Friday night alone like this, living on the outskirts of expectations, is a strange place to be. I suppose I should be used to it but I'm not. I love the solitude, but I wonder what it might do to me in the long run. Already I know I could never return to the *working world*, to wear its uniform, to keep its hours, to play its games. But so many hours on my own means a lot of time questioning myself. I know Mum worries about me. Thankfully my sister, Sally, is too busy to, but that's fine. One sister attacking life, the other one observing it. Oil and water.

I learned from a very young age to let her go first. Sally wanted someone to compete with. I wanted to let her win. Most people would look at her now—the beautiful, happily married, and respected physiotherapist with a waiting list over a month long—and they would agree, she wins. I'm not so sure. I'm not a slave to the business world but I paid a very different price for my freedom. It wasn't in lost weekends and evenings glued to a laptop but something far more valuable, a missing piece of me, which is why I'll always be grateful for what I *do* have. But it's also what makes me feel a little lacking sometimes. I'm not everything I should be.

My childhood, even my life now, wasn't one Mum expected or planned. I know for a long time she grappled with that, but there is acceptance and a deep love laced through our relationship today. She said I rarely cried as a baby. Even then I didn't want to draw attention to myself. Like any mum might, she viewed my shyness initially as a problem that needed to be fixed. There were excruciating summer schools of drama and dance classes for show-offs that I typically lasted a day or two at, never to the final performance at the end of the week. This is when I should have been laying down the groundwork for friendships that would last me a lifetime. But I didn't like parties. I rarely asked to have friends over. Wouldn't it have been wrong to fill the house with little girls in pretty party dresses and not a care in the world? It would have made Mum cry, I'm sure of it. She might be able to kiss the bad dreams away or to patch up a rough day at school with a favorite supper. But she couldn't—wouldn't ever be able to—fix this. I didn't know how to tell her then that I didn't dream of a *different* me, I dreamed of being left alone to *be* me.

It felt like it took a long time before she was able to accept that. I don't know if she saw it as giving up, failing to bring me out of myself, or truly conceding to what was in front of her, but eventually she let me slip into the background, seep into the shadows.

And I was so comfortable there. I could watch and listen, unseen. I could absorb everything I wanted to without ever having to contribute, to offer an opinion or face a confrontation. I'm not built for it. I don't like to be challenged. Honestly, I prefer to hide.

Stepping into the light is exposing. It's home to the overconfident and single-minded. Those with a skin much thicker than mine.

The downside is there are no old friends to lean on now, just the occasional face in the crowd that seems familiar. I didn't go to university. I finished school, then I hid at Mum's place for far too long while I tried to work out what to do with my life. Eventually I realized I had to leave. The hiding had become too obvious.

"Are you sure you should be getting involved, Jayne? I don't want to sound callous but is it fair for anyone to expect you to take this on? To help Meredith." Mum places a steaming mug of tea in front of me. We're sitting at the small wooden table in her garden, parasol up. It's the place I feel most naturally at ease, but I know this conversation is going to be tricky. "I can already tell from the determined look on your face that you're not going to leave it alone, are you?"

I take a sip of tea, scorching the roof of my mouth. "No."

"Jayne . . ."

"I think if you'd seen her, the state she is living in, you might feel differently. And no one is *expecting* me to take anything on."

Mum sits back against the chair, drinks her own tea before responding.

"That's not entirely why you're doing it, though, is it?" She half smiles at me.

I knew this was coming. That we couldn't just have a basic conversation without Mum understanding the deeper meaning in it. The annoying thing is, she's right.

"You don't have to do this. It's not going to change anything. You can't rewrite history," she says gently.

"I know that." I feel my cheeks warm. Are my motives really

that easy to see? "But it's not going to be forever. A couple of weeks, maybe three, just until I can get Meredith the help she needs and try to understand what's happened to her husband."

I have so much of what I need in life. Two jobs that I love. The chance to help people who I know have come to rely on me. A better relationship with Mum than ever. A beautiful apartment that I own. But Mum and I both know the deeper sadness that sits behind it all.

"All I'm saying is just think things through properly before you take on something that you won't easily be able to walk away from." Mum takes my hand. "Meredith isn't your grandmother. You were so young when she passed away, Jayne, I wish you'd had more time together, I really do. But . . ."

"I know, Mum. You don't need to say it."

Her body language shifts, she looks uncomfortable all of a sudden. "You should be making more time for *you*, for . . . new relationships." She can't meet my eyes.

"Leave it, please, Mum." The last thing I want is a discussion about my love life. "And just in case you're thinking about it, I would rather not have another reminder of how lovely you think Alex is."

"Well, it's funny you should bring his name up because he called again." She opens her palms to me, indicating this shouldn't be surprising news but also that it's not her fault.

"Mum, no." I harden my tone. She should know by now that this subject is off-limits.

"He's asked for your new address. Again."

"Oh, Mum, you didn't?"

"No, I didn't"—she sighs—"I know that chapter is closed for you, but he seems pretty determined not to give up."

"He dumped *me*, Mum, in case you have forgotten that crucial detail!" I can't help sounding a little outraged at her ability to feel sympathy for a man who asked me to move in with him before Christmas and then ditched me when he didn't get the answer he wanted. But I can't dwell on it. I don't want to be reminded of the excruciating moments leading up to the end of a relationship I was once so hopeful about. I don't want those images filling my head, especially not when I am sitting here with my mother. I know her intentions are good, but she has no idea how the mere mention of his name sends a spike of regret up through me, making my jaw tighten.

"I know what he did at the time felt heartless and cruel, but I think it was an act of self-preservation more than anything else. He adores you, and when he didn't believe the feelings were mutual, he couldn't face it. It seems clear to me he still loves you."

"Is that what he told you?" I scoff at his glossing over of the uglier facts, ones that I'm reluctantly grateful he chose not to share with Mum. "Well, you haven't given him my address and that's all I need to know."

Mum is silent for a moment. "I just worry about you, darling, that's all. I want you to be happy and fulfilled. To have someone special in your life. A true partner." And I feel deeply for her then because we both understand this is something we share. There is no one for her to confide in late at night either.

I tighten my grip on the small posy for Meredith, a colorful mix of wildflowers that I hope she'll like, before I knock on her door. She takes an age to answer, and when she does, she just stands there staring at me. Something is wrong. Her hair looks flat, like she has coated it in product, she's repeatedly scratching at it, and there is an overly sweet smell coming from her.

"Have you found William?" There is urgency in her voice, she's wringing her hands together, rocking back and forth toward me.

"I haven't, not yet, but I brought these for you." I hand the small posy to her.

She takes the flowers and looks into the bouquet. "Forget-me-nots! Oh, how perfect."

Her eyes come back up to meet mine. She's scratching again.

"I do know you, don't I?" She's smiling, her face warm and trusting when perhaps it shouldn't be.

"We've met, yes. It's Jayne, from upstairs. I live in this building, on the top floor," I say. "Can I come in for a moment?"

"Yes, I like you. You're kind. Where's your dog?"

I decide not to confuse her further with an explanation about who actually owns the dog and settle for "Just having a rest."

Meredith's hallway is covered in floral wallpaper, a pattern that seems far too intricate and repetitive for such a small area, it shrinks the space, and I think she feels it, too, because she stops and stares at the three doors, all closed around us. I watch as her hand rises to her lips and she runs her index finger across them, like she's struggling to solve something.

"The drawing room." Her eyes move between the different doors, but she stays rooted to the spot. "Oh, for goodness' sake." Her chin drops to her chest.

I take her arm and lead her forward before she has a chance to get more annoyed with herself. I clear some space on one of the sofas for us to sit. She's still scratching so I ask, "Your hair looks different today, Meredith. Did you do something with it?"

"I washed it," she says proudly, and I have to stop myself gasping. It's shampoo that is weighing it down, not a styling product. I think she has attempted to wash her hair, without actually getting it wet. I don't want to distress her, so I turn away from her for a moment, breaking our eye contact, and when I look back, her shoulders have crumpled like she has collapsed in on herself. Her hand rises to her head again, and this time, she seems to understand she has done something wrong. She's connecting my reaction with the smell and the itching and it makes me want to help her, to reassure her it doesn't matter, we can fix it. Why is no one else doing this for her?

Again, my thoughts are pulled backward to my own grandmother. How Mum's grief became hers, only amplified because she was powerless to take away her daughter's pain. The weight of the sadness was too much for her old bones, Mum said. Even when I was small enough to sit on my grandmother's lap, feeling her arms close too tightly around me, her body shuddering to the sound of muffled sobs, I knew it was the sight of me that was the cause.

I clear my throat before lightly saying, "I think a little of the shampoo might still be in your hair, Meredith. Just a little. Shall I wash it out for you?"

"Oh yes, please," she says, and I can already see the relief soften her face.

We find the bathroom together and I drag one of the chairs in from the kitchen. I drape a towel around her shoulders, then I get her to sit and lean back while I support her neck with my left hand and hold the showerhead with my right, letting the water loosen and rinse away all the crusted shampoo into the bath. She closes her eyes and a beautiful smile breaks across her face. I sense her whole body relax into the chair and her arms go limp at her sides.

"William only puts conditioner on the ends," she says.

As I look around, I realize there is no sign of a husband in this bathroom. I remember how Alex had more grooming products than I ever accumulated. I sit her back up and towel-dry her hair as best I can, annoyed that thoughts of Alex, and Mum's sympathy for him, have intruded on this moment. Taking a look around, I notice just one robe hangs on the back of the door, a single toothbrush in the cup on the sink. There is nothing to confirm the presence of a man. No larger coat hanging in the hallway. No discarded shoes. No second bowl of soup in the microwave. Is Meredith waiting for someone who has no intention of coming home? I kneel in front of her.

"Is it ever a good idea to go back, Meredith?" I realize once I've asked the question, I'm not entirely sure what I mean. Back to the source of my problems, back to a former love, back to the child whose juvenile attempts to make her grandmother happy always failed? I'm expecting a look of detached confusion from Meredith, or at least a flat *no* from a woman of her generation. Shouldn't it be shoulders back, head high, looking forward, never inward, to whatever challenges we face? So, her response is surprising.

"Back is the only place you can go if you want to make things better, if you want to make sense of things. It's much braver, much harder, don't you think? Not going back is like picking up a book and starting to read halfway through, expecting to love and understand the characters. You won't. You can't. You don't know them yet. So much good can come from going back. Everyone should try it."

We both smile at each other. She looks warmed by the fact she's said the right thing. And I feel cheered. She may have forgotten how to wash her hair properly, but she's still got a firm grip on what's really important in life. How could anyone walk away from her without helping?

"What are *you* looking for, Jayne? What gives you a need to go back?"

The bathroom walls seem to shrink around us then. There is

no obvious diversion to avoid such a direct question from Meredith and I struggle for something to say.

"Do you need a friend?" She asks it in such a gentle way that there feels like no shame at all in admitting that, yes, I probably do.

I nod.

"Friendship comes in all shapes and sizes." Meredith seems surprisingly coherent on the subject. "But the golden rule is it has to make you feel good. Don't spend time with people who don't do that for you, who won't allow you the luxury of total honesty. The freedom to say whatever you need to, knowing you will always be supported, if not agreed with." We move back into the sitting room and she throws some of the cushions off the sofa and takes a seat.

"If you need a friend, I'd be happy to be it." She taps me on the thigh. "We might be very good for each other, you know." She bumps her shoulder into mine and we both laugh—me at the strangeness of the situation, her because I think she remembers what it feels like to be happy and she wants to be back there, even if it is with me and not William.

"Yesterday, you asked me to help you find your husband, William. Do you remember?" I turn to face her.

"Yes, have you seen him?" It's said with such enthusiasm, like she truly believes I might have bumped into him at the supermarket this morning, despite me telling her half an hour ago I haven't seen him, and I wouldn't recognize him even if I had.

"I'm afraid not. I've lived in this building for seven months, Meredith, and I don't ever recall seeing him. Was he living here with you?"

"Oh yes, he lives with me here." She sounds cheerful at first but then her tone changes, becoming heavier, wearier. "We used to

live in London before. But he's gone now. I don't know where."
Then she's optimistic again. "He'll come back, won't he?"

I nod gently. "I'm sure he will. When was the last time you left
the apartment, Meredith?"

"I don't know," she says, looking around her for a clue to the
correct answer. "Quite some time, I think."

SIX

❦

Meredith
1989

What a commission! It's everything she hoped for when she took
the position. The chance to see her work sit across the front pages
of every national newspaper around the world.

Now she would work around the clock with no complaints if
she needed to. Day after day. Night after night. She knows she
owes William a great deal for giving her this opportunity.

Twelve days is her assessment. The time needed to transform
the precisely cut silk crepe fabric into something worthy of the
woman and the occasion. But William takes longer than anticipated. Cutting and recutting, mapping and remapping, on and off
the stand, solving one problem, then creating another, not entirely
satisfied with the dummy calico. Now he has remade sections of
the jacket in a softer crepe, allowing him to get as close to the real
look and feel as possible before the point of no return, when the
fabric will be cut and there will be no way to reverse the slice of
the scissors.

No one can approach his bench. His head is bowed and all
anyone will hear from him in the course of a day are muttered

frustrations that they know better than to try to understand or interrupt. Whatever it is, it can wait. The clock is ticking over him. The immovable date is approaching. The world is waiting. And his tension is absorbed by everyone else in the room.

When his pattern is eventually ready, there is no celebration in the workroom. It is passed to Peter, who studies it before the fabric is rolled out along a huge smooth-surfaced table. The assembly of the jigsaw puzzle can begin. Meredith watches with fascination. How to get the greatest number of pieces from the most economical stretch of fabric? The only acceptable interruption comes from Catherine. Another commission, very last-minute, can it be done in time? she needs to know. Then back to the table to cut. The fabric yielding easily under the fall of steel blades.

The following morning, they are ready for Meredith. She looks at the pieces; she studies William's notes on the paper margins; she looks at the calendar. Ten days until the dress and jacket are due to be delivered, well in advance of the date they will be worn, as requested. She looks again, sensing there is a mistake. That the pieces of the right sleeve will not fit together as Catherine intended them to. This is the very first dress and jacket she will work on for this special client, her first chance to impress everyone. There cannot be mistakes. It's unthinkable.

William's mood has lifted. He is lighter, more bearable to be around now that the task has left his table. She feels comfortable questioning him.

"William, can I speak to you about the jacket?" she ventures.

"Of course, what about it?" He's almost dismissive, not expecting any issues.

"Something isn't quite right with the sleeves. I think there is an error. One is coming up short."

She feels the atmosphere crackle around her. A hush falls and she isn't sure what people are more worried about: that she is right and what that will mean, or William's reaction to being publicly questioned by her. She suddenly feels she has betrayed him.

"It's correct." He lines the paper pattern pieces up on the table in front of her. "They are perfect."

With every stitch Meredith makes, she feels more confident in her assessment, more concerned that every moment she continues to work is time wasted. Time she cannot get back.

In the end, she is right. But it will be weeks before their professional relationship recovers from that fact.

It's nearly two weeks since William has spoken to Meredith, beyond what is absolutely essential for them both to perform their roles. She remains professional. Arriving early. Responding urgently to every request made of her. She smiles. She's pleasant. She is not going to allow the bruised ego of one man to ruin this opportunity for her. She also knows he can't feel slighted forever. Surely no one has the energy for that.

But why has he been so silent? Nothing about the way William conducts himself in the workroom—brief in his exchanges with others but always polite, never condescending to younger members of the team, always considerate of how the speed he works at impacts everyone else—would suggest there is an insecurity under his calm exterior. And yet, Meredith's comments have clearly knocked off-balance what had the potential to be a solid working relationship. Is he too used to keeping his vulnerabilities to himself and her comments shone too bright a spotlight on them? Maybe she could have been more subtle in her approach?

She's been watching William. There is an underlying distraction to his work since she pointed out the mistake. Occasions when he appears deep in thought, concentrating on something beyond the paper in his hands. He will walk over to Peter's table when he's not at it, determined apparently to work something out. Maybe she is simply reading too much into it and this is him— although Peter's tactless comment one morning that "You're no longer head girl then" would suggest not.

Then, almost as quickly as he froze her out, William softens. Meredith is making an early-morning cup of tea in the staff room and there he is beside her. At first, he says nothing, goes about making his own hot drink, but she can sense from his body language, angled toward her, closer than he needs to be, that he wants to talk.

"Do you feel settled in now?" he finally asks, just as she is lifting her mug to leave the room.

She is unsure how to respond. This is the first vaguely personal approach he has made, and it feels premature without an apology for how deliberately and unhelpfully distant he has been. But she can also see a nervousness in his eyes, like seeking her out today has taken some courage. Has he been waiting for her to leave the workroom so the two of them can speak?

"I think settling in could have been made a little easier for me." Meredith doesn't allow her tone to sound cross or bitter, just matter-of-fact. He can hardly disagree, and she's not going to pretend everything has been fine between them when clearly it hasn't been.

William nods, appears at a loss about what to say next, so she puts her mug down, a clear signal that she is happy to wait and hear whatever it is—presumably an apology is lurking somewhere beyond his immediate reach. But then he changes tack entirely.

"Are you married, Meredith?"

"Oh, um, no I'm not." She smiles, slightly bemused at how

they've gone from zero personal contact to such a direct inquiry into her private life.

"Sorry, that's a bit blunt, isn't it?" William smiles too. "I suppose I was just wondering how you might be juggling the hours here with family life."

"It's not an issue for me right now. How about you?" She wants to be friendly, but she also feels a little bruised by the way he has treated her for pointing out a fault that needed to be corrected. It was unfair of him.

"No, me neither. Not the marrying kind, I suppose."

Meredith considers his age. Late forties to her late thirties perhaps. Old enough to have come to that conclusion, but the words don't sit comfortably on his lips, he doesn't say them with total ease—or conviction.

"Really?" She offers him the chance to be a little more honest.

William doesn't respond immediately but opens one of the white wall cupboards and pulls out a small tin. "Custard cream?"

"Yes, thank you." Meredith takes one, then leans her back against the work surface, hoping no one will interrupt now that the two of them are finally talking. She waits for his answer.

"I think it may be more to do with a lack of nerve, if I'm being really honest." He places the tin back and takes up the spot next to her, the best position to avoid direct eye contact.

"What are you so nervous about? Women aren't that terrifying, are we?" She feels confident that she isn't at least.

"Honestly, Meredith, I could never understand why a long-term relationship or marriage is the place where people believe they'll feel safest. The stakes are so much higher, aren't they? There is so much more to lose."

Meredith contemplates this for a moment. "Yes, I can see what you mean. But that is also assuming there will be a sad ending.

It's quite a negative view, isn't it?" Or maybe one that has been shaped by a previous hurt. "You never wanted children?" Since he's being so direct, there seems no reason for her not to be.

"No." This time there is no ambiguity to his response. "It's not that it was never an ambition, just that that ship has sailed and I'm okay with that." He shrugs his shoulders, it's something he feels is beyond his control. "Anyway, I better get back to it, but I just wanted to say thank you for saving the jacket. Someone had got it wrong. I knew it wasn't me and I was confident it wasn't you either. But someone was happy for it to look like your mistake. That's what I needed to be sure about."

"Okay." She's surprised he has devoted so much thought to it.

"It was a mistake to underestimate you, Meredith. I won't ever do it again—and I won't let anyone else either. You deserved my support—and now you've got it."

It isn't an apology, but it feels like so much more. It's clear recognition of her talent by someone who has a great deal of it himself. It's a promise that he is now on her side and will stay that way. That her days here will be happier, protected. And despite Peter's prediction, perhaps this is just the beginning, not the end.

SEVEN

∽❦∾

Jayne

I spend the evening going through work emails and trying to confirm the dog walking slots for the week ahead, eating a sandwich I grabbed on the way home. But I'm distracted, worrying about what Meredith might be doing downstairs. I think about all the closed doors on every floor of our building, the close proximity the tenants share but how shut away we all are from one another. I try to help everyone where I can but there is no sense of community. A whole house full of adults who might be alone and perhaps might prefer not to be. Even at this moment, Davina will either be wrestling Maggie into bed or charging home from an event to relieve whichever babysitter is on duty tonight. I bet Olivia's working, too, mopping up the missed deadlines from the week or heading out again for another late night. Meredith is alone, trying desperately to remember how she came to be that way. I'm alone too. By choice, I know, but I hope it won't always be this way. Is it only Jake who enjoys the closeness of good friends? Are they good friends, I wonder, the people who fill our shared garden on balmy evenings? I've never seen him sit with just one familiar face, losing the afternoon to close conversation and shared secrets. Is there someone special? Or does he prefer the anonymity of a group, where he can hide among the banter and the polite chitchat, never needing to reveal too much? Where he can flit from person to person, never offering an opportunity to see deeper than the handsome face and the relaxed smile, the chilled champagne and the desirable address?

I take a tea up to the roof terrace and sit there for a while, absorbing the last heat of the day, in my own private walled garden where no one can see me. And in one sense it is heavenly, everything I ever wanted. I can sit high above the city, feel its energy, my proximity to its people, without having to respond to any of it. And in another, which I reluctantly and quietly acknowledge, it is desperately sad because there is no one to share this peace with. Perhaps if there were, I wouldn't feel this way.

Spending time with Meredith today reminds me of how I learned to distance myself from my own grandmother. It felt kinder. I lacked the words to make things better. All I could offer her was affection, but that didn't work. I was a visual reminder of everything that was wrong in our family. "Some walls are just too big," Mum said once. "You can climb so high up them, but you never reach the top." She told me when Granddad passed away it seemed like the final excuse my grandmother needed. The loss of a love so intrinsic to her life was insurmountable. Home wasn't home anymore, and no task, however hard she tried, could hide the fact. So, she stopped trying. But should *I* have stopped trying?

I remember one afternoon, I couldn't have been much older than seven, Mum had trusted me to drop something off at her house, something she had borrowed that needed returning. My grandmother looked like she had been crying—her mascara had traveled down her face in two wonky lines—and was doing a valiant job of pretending otherwise. It was impossible to miss but I ignored it, knowing the act of intimacy involved in offering a tissue, or merely asking about it, would have brought fresh tears. So I left that afternoon without mentioning it, glanced back over my shoulder at my grandmother waving at the front door looking like a circus clown. She'd told me there was a man coming that afternoon to fix the TV aerial, and I knew if she didn't see herself in the mirror first, he would be greeted by the same sight. He might even point it out. I felt awful for days, weeks even. Maybe I have never stopped feeling bad.

Perhaps it's because my birthday is coming that all these feelings are surfacing again. Dad will send a card. Mum will call and we'll sit together in the small memorial garden she created at the back of her house. It seems almost inconsequential now, just a few neat beds of pansies and petunias and a discreet heart-shaped stone plaque with the words *We will love you forever, grateful always that we had you at all*. When I was a child it seemed to engulf the whole of Mum's garden. When we weeded it together, she used to test me on the names of all the different flower varieties, in a desperate attempt to make it more bearable—for me and for her. Back then, the memorial garden seemed to expand and creep across everything, just like her grief. As I got older, Sally and I would watch her from the kitchen window, sitting motionless in a chair, like she'd fallen asleep with her eyes open. "We'll make dinner tonight," Sally would say. Then we'd take a plate of sandwiches out to her, some roughly cut cherry tomatoes and slices of cucumber on the side of the plate "for color," Sally said. "It will cheer her up." Back then, we truly believed it would.

Sally and I saw the physical strength it took Mum to heave herself out of bed or off the sofa. Eventually the accompanying groans stopped.

Tonight, the enticingly warm glow from the lights inside Jake's

place forces a change in my thoughts. I wonder whom he's enter-
taining tonight.

They might come out into the garden later like they do sometimes. Then I can watch them and imagine what it might feel like
to be down there with him. Before Alex there were plenty of
missed opportunities to get close to someone, when my answer
could have been yes but was always no. Because it was easier that
way. The disappointment with myself brushed aside far swifter
than the piercing nervousness that would hold me in its grip all
day until that first date. They rarely made it to a second one.

My past feels like a hard, full stop in the conversation. How
can I show a man who I am without talking about it? But who
wants to have that unloaded on them on a first or second date?
Too many normal, expected questions quickly revealed the hole
in my story. I could always see him trying to work it out. She's a
dog walker and part-time florist, and yet she lives in one of the
fanciest addresses in the city? I guess most people would simply
skirt over it, but I never can. It makes me feel dishonest.

Alex was much easier at first. He was just a stranger on the
bench, reading last summer's instant hit. The same one everyone
lying in the park or sitting on the bus seemed to be reading. The
choice made him immediately accessible. I liked the obviousness
of it. As I walked past, I glanced at the pages, wondering if he'd
gotten to the big twist yet. Our eyes met and he said, "She's not
seriously going to say yes, is she?" I opened my mouth to respond
and he shouted, "Christ, no! Don't tell me!" We laughed. People
looked. He apologized for shouting and then there was an offer of
a coffee. It was all so easy, until it became much more difficult.

Maybe it's the money. People look at me, see the height first,
the lack of eye contact second, and would never guess. Then it

feels like a secret I'm deliberately keeping. It makes me feel like a fraud. I didn't do anything to earn any of it.

I toy with the idea of knocking on Meredith's door again, inviting myself in for a cuppa and perhaps finding out if there is a family member I can call. Maybe no one is aware of the way she is living, the help she clearly needs. But is it too intrusive? Will she feel patronized? I decide instead to write a note to each of the other house residents asking for their help. Do any of them know any more about Meredith or her missing husband? Has he ever even been seen? Has she, unbelievable as it may sound, invented the whole thing? Surely someone can shed some light on it. I push all the individual notes into the wooden postboxes in the hallway downstairs and hope for the best.

By Monday morning not one person has responded. Not even to say they know nothing and can't help.

I have forget-me-nots for Meredith, bunny tail grass and dried white gypsophila for Jake, sweet peas for Olivia, and garden roses for Davina. It's the only idea I have to wrestle some interest from them all, so I'm banking on it working.

It's four o'clock when I knock on Davina's door. I can hear Maggie singing on the other side of it. Something unrecognizable that I think she's making up as she goes along but with total conviction. It's Maggie who opens the door. As soon as she sees me, she lowers her head disapprovingly, frowns, raises her eyebrows, then tells me off. "You're late for rehearsals. This is not what I call professional."

"Actually, Maggie, I was wondering if your mummy is in?"

"I seriously doubt it!" she cackles. "Do you think I'd be wearing these if she was?" She nods toward her feet and I see she is struggling not to topple in a pair of Davina's skyscraper heels, her chubby ankles wobbling back and forth.

"Oh, they are lovely," I gush.

"Jimmy Choo," she informs me. "Mummy puts them at the top of the wardrobe so I can't reach them." Then she winks at me. Maggie the rulebreaker.

I'm considering handing the flowers to her when I hear the front door swing open and Davina comes tumbling through it with two supermarket carrier bags, her laptop, a giant bag of dog kibble, and a Tupperware box filled with fancy-looking cupcakes wedged under her arm.

"Coming through! I can't hold this lot for much longer. Oh no, did I forget to pay you again, Jayne?" She clatters past me. "Get those shoes OFF, Maggie! I guess that's you not getting one of these delicious cupcakes then."

Maggie shoots her the sort of death stare a sixteen-year-old would be proud of and I have to laugh.

"No, you've paid me," I say to the back of her head as Davina just manages to place the Tupperware box on the floor before it slides from her grip. "I just wanted to give you these." I hold the bunch of nectarine-colored roses toward her and suddenly feel very unsure of my strategy. This must look very odd and I can feel the warmth in my cheeks betraying my awkwardness.

Davina's eyes widen as she takes in the flowers, before her face softens with a small smile. "Well, I'm popular today. A client insisted I bring these cakes back from an event we had this morning and now this. Thank you, Jayne. I don't know what I've done to deserve them, but it's very kind of you. Now, I'm sorry but I have to be out the door again in one hour, so I must get on." I can see Maggie over her right shoulder. She's put the shoes back on and is catwalking her way through the apartment, peeling the paper case off a cupcake as she goes, making zero attempt to hide either transgression.

"I just wondered if you had seen my note, was all." I feel like such an irritation, I wish I hadn't bothered her now.

"Oh yes, but not much I can add really. Her husband does live here but I haven't seen him for ages, must be months. But I'm probably not the best person to ask. I'm rarely here myself, and when I am, I'm constantly harassed." I'm not sure if she's aiming that comment at me; Maggie, who is singing at full volume again; or Willow, whom I can hear pleading with her younger sister to *shut up for once.* But I take it as my cue to leave and head up the stairs to Olivia's front door.

Teddy nearly knocks me off my feet when Olivia opens up. "Oh my God, you couldn't take him, could you? I'm about an hour away from missing *another* deadline. Just an hour?" Olivia's face is tight, the face of someone who knows that deadline isn't going to be hit whether I take Teddy or not. I wonder if she ever smiles. *Genuinely* smiles.

"I actually came to give you these," I venture. "I'm not sure if I told you but I work at a florist as well as the dog walking and . . ."

"Oh cheers, that's great they let you help yourself to the flowers at the end of the day."

"Actually, I did buy—"

"So, d'you think you can? Take Teddy, I mean? Sorry to spring it on you but I'm working again tonight so I'll have no time to catch up then." Her mobile starts to scream on the table behind her. I look at Teddy sitting by her ankles, tail wagging, and I know he probably hasn't left the house this afternoon.

"Of course I can," I say, smiling. "But did you get my note, Olivia? Do you know anything at all about Meredith?"

"No, never spoken to her. She always darts back into her apartment whenever she sees me. I would avoid her if I were you. Not sure she's quite all there."

"Have you ever seen her husband?"

"Jayne, I am *always* working, every day all day and at least three nights a week too. There is very little time to hang out with the neighbors or take a view on how weird or not their behavior is. But if you are chatting to her it would be great if you could ask her to turn the TV volume down a bit. They watch the same film over and over again. It drives me nuts when I'm trying to work. Speaking of which . . ." She nods back over her shoulder, then hands me Teddy's lead from a hook near the door as her phone starts to ring again.

Next up, Jake. Teddy and I head into the garden and he bounds around while, with little enthusiasm, I make my way to the back. The garden is surprisingly small, given the size of the house. It has a neat stone patio filled with potted plants that I've only ever seen Jake water or weed. There are two deep borders either side filled with all the usual stuff—rosemary and thyme, fragrant lavender bushes and cheerful chamomile flowers, a couple of apple trees providing some shade to the one metal bench. It looks like this is where the garden ends. But a narrow path breaks off to the right, picking its way under a plum tree, before you reach another small stone terrace and the door to Jake's coach house.

The exterior is covered in climbing roses, some shedding their petals to form a floating pink carpet below. I recognize the yellow cone-shaped flowers of a hop that is filling the air with its appley scent. A Virginia creeper vine, which will turn a brilliant red and orange come autumn, has tangled its way along the garden wall and is fighting for space on the exterior of the coach house. The door is framed by a heavy arch of roses drooping over it.

I knock and ridiculously hope he won't answer. I feel stupid holding the flowers. Despite my prediction, no one else seemed to appreciate their flowers and now it feels over the top. I don't bother to knock a second time before I leave them on the step with a hurriedly scrawled note on the paper they're wrapped in and my phone number.

I head back through the main house and out with Teddy, pausing as I look toward Meredith's door. Should I ask her to join me? Might it help? To blow away some of the cobwebs that are hanging heavily over her. The sun is still shining and will be until well past nine o'clock tonight; surely it will do her good. I order Teddy to sit, and tap lightly on the door.

Meredith, wearing a nightie and three cardigans despite the fact it must be eighty-two degrees outside, answers. I feel my heart rise into my throat as she looks at me, her face full of sadness, but still she's polite enough to smile.

"Hello, Meredith. It's Jayne, from upstairs." I return the smile.

She stares at me blankly and her eyes slowly drop. "A different dog today." She says it with no feeling, no energy.

"This is Teddy. I'm taking him for a walk, and I was wondering if you would like to join us? Not far, perhaps just a couple of streets, if you like. I can keep him on the lead."

"Forget-me-nots too." This raises more of a smile.

"Oh yes, these are for you. I know you like them."

"Always a favorite. From the gardens." Her smile deepens as she reaches for them. "I'll have to put my lipstick on. William always buys me the same red from Estée Lauder, the pinky one, you know, it's called . . ." She searches for the name of the shade, but it escapes her. "Anyway, I'll do that and then we can go."

I can't let her out of the house dressed the way she is, so I offer to help.

The apartment is even more of a mess than before. I struggle to push the door open and have to poke my head around it to see why it won't budge. Wedged between the door and the wall is a pile of unopened post that she must have let collect in the box, then retrieved but didn't open. I tie Teddy to the inside door handle, wondering at the unpleasant smell in the air. Sour this time, not sweet, and definitely less appealing than the overripe bananas or the dried shampoo.

I lead us through to her bedroom, where the bed is unmade and there are clothes strewn everywhere. The Catherine Walker dress is barely visible now below a mountain of clothing she seems to have taken out of the wardrobe, then discarded.

I find a light silk skirt with an easy elasticated waist that she can pull on over the nightie and I help her out of two of the cardigans, doing up the final one across her chest. She just stands there, arms limp at her sides, and lets me. I rummage for two matching shoes and leave her to put them on while I head to the kitchen to investigate the smell.

The surfaces are lined with opened half-empty milk bottles, the contents of which have curdled in the heat. I watch a fly teeter on the rim of one and then fall in, sinking into the thick band of cream. None of the bottles were here before. It looks like she has got a fresh one out of the fridge every time she wanted a cup of tea, then failed to put it back again. I push open a window that looks onto the garden below and inhale some fresh air. This all feels so much worse than just a few days ago. I look over my shoulder to check that Meredith hasn't appeared behind me, then I start to open some of the kitchen cupboards that line the walls.

Nothing is where it should be. She has teacups and saucers in with saucepans, and cutlery has been placed loose on a shelf instead of in a drawer. A colander is filled with jars of spices and another cupboard has a random collection of items—a bottle of washing-up liquid that's open and fallen on its side, leaking everywhere, a bag of flour, two pairs of black tights, and a bag of cotton wool balls. There is no logic to any of it and I realize she must have to search behind each door every time she needs something. I remember my own grandmother's kitchen cupboards, how everything was spotlessly clean and ordered despite the private battles she was fighting.

I open each cupboard and not one of them contains any food. My God, when was the last time she ate a proper meal? My eyes fill with tears and I take a slow, deep breath to stop them overflowing. Why is no one looking after her? Where is William? How can we all go about our business while this lady sits alone in this mess, unable to even feed herself? I don't understand it and, perhaps more important, neither does she.

"Shall we go then?"

I turn to see her standing in the doorway, lipstick expertly applied, smiling, like no one would ever guess the state she's really in.

Teddy will have to wait a little longer. I want to try to understand more about what's happening with Meredith.

"Yes, we should go. But can I use your loo first, Meredith?" I have no intention of using it. There is one more room at the end of the corridor that I have yet to see inside of. Every other room in her apartment has helped to paint a picture of the life Meredith is living. Perhaps whatever lies behind that door will offer more clues too.

EIGHT

❧❧❧

As I step inside, I immediately see a network of strings crisscrossing a wall to my left, and attached to it with tiny wooden pegs are a collection of images, many of them dress sketches with what look like locations scribbled in pencil on the bottom of each one.

"This is not the loo." Meredith is standing beside me, laughing, like she's enjoying someone else getting something wrong.

"No, it's not, sorry. But it looks fascinating. Do you mind if I take a peek? Perhaps we can look together?" I venture.

"This is my memory room," she whispers. "William knows I need it."

I move closer to the images, the dimness of the room making it hard to see them fully from a distance. Meredith—or perhaps William—has strung them up in date order. I trace the line along, reading aloud the locations and dates and noticing the distinct silhouette of each dress in sharp pencil outline. There is a sentence with each, a prompt that appears to relate to whatever was happening in Meredith's life at that time.

1989: The Royal Albert Hall. It's a full-length, textured, body-skimming dress that's strapless with a high collared jacket with three-quarter-length sleeves. *The start of our golden period. Remember the mistake only you could spot.*

Could the prompts have been written by William? What Meredith just said about him knowing she would need this room could suggest so.

1989: The Dorchester Hotel. Another full-length dress with folds of fabric that climb up around the neck but this time with a much looser skirt that's scattered with tulip-shaped flowers. *A dress made in reverse and the first time you cooked me dinner.*

"Did William write these notes, Meredith? It sounds like he's reminding you of things you did together." I lean in closer, my eyes scanning the next one in the line to see if it fits my theory.

"That's it, yes. He makes a bit of a fuss of doing it quickly, after he collects me from the Fashion Museum, yes, and when I point that out, he says I'll thank him for it one day. I can't think why."

Meredith has buried her face in a large hardback book and isn't really paying attention to my interest in the sketches and their notes anymore.

1990: Odeon Leicester Square. This ensemble looks heavier, more regal, a long-sleeved coat with dense embroidery that covers the bodice, then drops away at either side of the hips to reveal a straighter-cut dress beneath. *No one guessed our secret. They were blinded by your talent.*

I glance at Meredith to see if what I'm reading aloud is prompting any reaction in her too. But she's taken a seat now and seems almost disinterested; perhaps because the notes are so familiar to her, they hold none of the excitement of my initial discovery.

1991: Launceston Place. A detailed long-sleeved bodice is finished with a wide sash tied at the hip before it drops delicately down over the skirt. *Soon we will be three.*

I say William's prompt aloud again, feeling sure that will spark a reaction from her, but she simply reclines her head against the chair wing and closes her eyes.

1992: Spencer House. This time a complex-looking dress with a high jeweled collar, a sleeveless bodice cut more daringly under the arms to reveal the shoulders, then a section of tightly folded fabric across the hips before a very full skirt falls to the floor. *The happiest day of our lives and a dress that had to grow.*

1993: Sandringham. Something much simpler this time. It's a straighter column dress with some detail running around the neckline and up over the shoulders. *Days without you and long sleepless nights.*

Sandringham? What could Meredith possibly have to do with a royal residence? And why would William be without her? I can't immediately guess at a logical answer, so I read on, alert to any more clues.

1994: Home, Northamptonshire. The only shorter dress with a sharply angled, square-cut neckline. It has large buttons drawn in two perfect rows down the front, a striped skirt, and deep cuffs at each wrist where two more buttons sit. *It was the straight lines that gave me away.*

This feels much more cryptic. "Did you ever live in Northamptonshire, Meredith?" She studies my face like I've asked her a very complex question before simply saying, "Never," and returning her gaze to her lap. I can only assume the words must mean much more to Meredith than they do to me, or anyone else who may read them.

1994: Venice. A classic evening dress this time with what looks like a band of sequins running across the neckline and up around the neck. The skirt is wrapped and there is more detailing on the left hip. *An ocean apart but not for long.*

1995: New York. The final dress is drawn low at the neckline and dips at the back below the shoulder blades. It feels very modern. *Now it's you without me.*

Is this the point when he left her, or they parted? Surely not, given it is dated more than twenty years ago. I search Meredith's face, knowing that she is not about to fill in the many missing blanks this display has presented. Her eyes are open. Her smile is back. She looks safe and happy in this room.

"This is a lot of dresses, Meredith." There are nine in total, ten if you count the pink one still discarded in her bedroom.

Meredith is nodding enthusiastically at me, like their meaning should now be perfectly obvious. "William says it will all make sense when the time comes."

William, I fear, may be wrong about that. Surely the time is now.

"Do you mind if I open the curtains a little more?" I ask her.

She nods her approval.

As light fills the room, a lifetime's worth of Meredith—the treasured and the everyday—reveals itself. All the fractured pieces of her. The story of her past on postcards, maps, handwritten letters, sepia photographs, concert invitations and RSVP cards, newspaper cuttings, piles of sheet music, programs, recipe cards, a stack of old CDs missing their cases, pages torn from old school reports, guides. In among it all are prompts she seems to have written to herself. *Trauma steals memory* has been written in capital letters on a bright pink Post-it note, then attached to the bottom of a photograph of a man leaning on his elbows over a high white table. The lettering is indenting the paper, perhaps the pen was pushed too harshly or too quickly. There are larger blobs of ink across some of the letters, too, and the tail of the *y* trails off like her hand slipped.

Trauma steals memory.

Did something happen to Meredith? Something that caused so much upset that she is no longer able to process or recall it?

She picks up an image of who I assume must be William, discarding a letter that has got stuck to the back of it, then holds it up for me to see as her eyes fill with tears. "I forget names and places, sometimes even people. But I never forget how they make me feel. I feel close to him when I'm in here. For a few seconds some days, it's like he isn't missing at all."

"Have you seen a doctor, Meredith? Has anyone been able to tell you why this might be happening to you?"

"Oh yes, we've done that. A waste of time though. William says it's better for us to handle it ourselves, so that's what we do." She sounds definitive. "I protect him and he protects me, that's it."

"But maybe it's worth another try? Maybe—"

"No." She cuts me off. "I trust William. He knows what's best for me." Her faith in her husband is unwavering, absolute.

I look back at the string of sketches of dresses on the wall and the letter she has discarded. Something about the bold letterhead, the string of surnames, holds my gaze. Delaney, Abbott & Curtis. It's a firm of solicitors, based centrally. I must walk past their offices three or four times a day. I step closer, my intention merely to check the date. Is this something she's been sent recently? But it's addressed to William and dated 15 January 2017, well over a year ago.

Meredith's focus is lost to the dresses, so, despite the obvious intrusion, I read on.

> Dear William,
>
>   It was a pleasure to see you looking so well last week. I am delighted to be able to tell you that your affairs are now all in order. As agreed, everything is updated and finalized and the necessary paperwork is ready for your signature. We have also set the letter you dictated to Fiona.

You can have a final read through this before it is sealed
and we will hold it on file for her here, as discussed.
Please call the office when you have a spare moment
and we will find a time that suits you.

With very best wishes,
Andrew Curtis

"Who is Fiona, Meredith?" I have to repeat the question before she drags her gaze from the dress sketches, looks at me, and smiles warmly. "That's her. Isn't she beautiful?" She nods toward an image of a young woman I'm guessing is in her late teens. She's standing on the stone steps of an arched entrance to an imposing redbrick building, a sense of pride flooding from her eyes.

"She's my daughter," adds Meredith casually.

Now we are three.

"And where is Fiona now?" I hesitate to say the words. Is Fiona connected to the trauma Meredith may have suffered?

Meredith's head turns back to the photographs on the wall like the answer must be there somewhere.

"In London?" she asks me. "She doesn't talk to me. She doesn't love me anymore." The severity of what she's saying isn't matched by the casualness of her tone.

"When was the last time you saw each other?"

"Oh goodness." She lowers her head. "It's been a very long time. She's very busy, always practicing." Meredith smiles again and nods her head, reassuring herself. "William says everything I will ever need is in this room. All the answers, all the clues, all of *me*, he says. It's a map." She stands and starts to shift her weight from foot to foot and I sense her panic beginning to build again.

"It's okay, Meredith. We're going to find him. I promise you." I cast my eyes along the list of locations scribbled onto each dress, noticing again the deliberate date order. A clue perhaps, laid down by William and Meredith together when she was more able? I think again about the lack of response to my appeals for help from everyone else in this building.

Then I take a surreptitious snap on my phone of the legal letter. If Meredith has a daughter, she is surely the best place to start at unraveling this. And if nothing else, the solicitor must be able to help with determining William's whereabouts.

Meredith believes she and William once lived in London. She also seems to believe Fiona is based there. The first dress in the sequence on the wall is annotated with the Royal Albert Hall in London. So many pieces, but no clear picture.

"Come on, Meredith, we can't keep Teddy waiting all afternoon for his walk, can we?"

"Absolutely not!" She's as keen to get going as he is.

As we pull the door closed behind us, a thought begins to emerge. Perhaps the search for answers that will help Meredith has to extend well beyond the four walls of this house.

NINE

❦

Meredith

1989

It is an almost impossibly complicated series of drapes and pleats, woven together across the bodice before rising high around her neck, falling away to a long streamer down her back. Shoulders exposed. Meredith studies William's every move. It's like watching a mathematician work his equations with the patience and precision of an origamist.

He must work in reverse at the mannequin. This time it's the fabric first, the paper pattern comes second. Pleating, refolding, calculating, pinning, marking every placement of the material between his fingers until finally he is satisfied. There is a network of pins that he lifts from the stand, removing them one by one, when he is sure he has marked their individual positions. Only now is he confident the fabric can be unfurled and laid flat over the paper. He begins to score, running the small tracing wheel back and forth to re-create his work on paper so it can be shared, bringing to life the two-dimensional drawing that took shape in Catherine's imagination. In the weeks to come it will float along the red carpet, then travel around the world in the newspapers and on the TV screens of millions.

Meredith can see his discomfort. Day after day on his feet, never sitting. Needing to be bent close to the fabric or angled over his table, connected to his tools, seeking precision.

Tonight Meredith stays late, even though her own work is done and she could leave.

"Can I help, William?" She approaches the table where he has worked all day with only short breaks to eat.

He doesn't hear her, so engrossed in his passion. What should have taken ten days has already taken twelve, and she knows when the fabric is delivered to her, Meredith will have to work quickly herself to finish on time.

"William?" She knows she is risking his irritation by interrupting him.

He looks up, surprised to see her there. "Oh, Meredith. It's late, you should go home. I'll finish tonight and tomorrow you can start. Get a good night's sleep." He smiles and she can see the relief starting to soften his features. He knows he is nearly there. His brows are more relaxed than they have been in days. His shoulders slightly lower. He rubs the back of his neck with his hand, then stretches out his shoulder blades, cracking the tension away. He squints into the harsh lighting.

"Are you sure?" It's been dark for hours. She doubts he's given any thought to what he will eat tonight.

"I appreciate the offer, Meredith, but no thank you. I'd rather you feel fresh tomorrow for when it comes to you. I'm sorry I've made the timing so tight." There is a kindness in William's eyes that she noticed the very first day they worked together. Others miss it, too intimidated by his sharp skill, his quiet confidence. They back off when, she suspects, he would rather they didn't.

There is an openness to William, a willingness to share his expertise, if you choose your moment wisely.

"It's okay, we'll manage, we always do." She checks everything is in her bag. The small Tupperware box of last night's leftovers that passed for her own lunch, an uneaten apple, a bottle of water, barely touched. She would prefer to stay and keep him company. Once she leaves there will be no one left to insist he calls it a night.

"I'm cooking lamb and there is plenty for two. I'm happy to wait, if you'd like to join me after you're done?" She's not sure what prompts her to extend the offer—they have never spent time together beyond the workroom. It's a presumptuous invitation but one she is willing to risk. Does his admiration for her exist beyond the skill she demonstrates at her table? She finds herself curious to know.

He raises his head and holds her in his gaze.

"Lamb? I can't resist—it's my favorite. How did you know?" he finally says, allowing himself a small laugh.

They walk the half an hour back to her apartment and sit at the small table in the kitchen, covered in a plain oilcloth, mopping up the juice from the lamb with hunks of white bread that will be too stale to eat tomorrow. They share the last of an opened bottle of red wine between two glasses.

"I never actually apologized to you and I should have," he says when they have finished the last of it.

"For what?"

"I never told you, but it was Peter who made the mistake with the Albert Hall jacket, he was just never going to admit it. It took me a while to work it out, but that day, he was distracted. Do you remember? Catherine came into the studio to discuss a very last-minute commission. She was talking to us both about it and it threw him. When he turned back to the cutting table, he mistakenly cut a lining piece for the sleeve from the real fabric. It was never going to fit together with the other half of the sleeve, the proportions were slightly different, of course. But you were the only one who spotted it—and I've since made sure everyone understands that."

"Well, thank goodness there was enough fabric left for us to rectify the problem quickly and easily," Meredith responds as she stands and clears the plates from the table to the sink.

Suddenly, William is behind her, his hands on her shoulders. "It was that moment I realized quite how brilliant you are."

He turns her gently and places the softest kiss on her lips. She's only dared to hope before this. William is a consummate professional—he's given no hint to his feelings before, but there is a tenderness and intent behind his touch that tells her he has wanted to do this for some time.

As they approach the workroom together the following morning, they share a look that passes as an understanding between them. No one else needs to know. But Meredith knows. And the memory of it will burn inside her all day long. How this man, so professional now in his white coat, so economical in the way he speaks to colleagues, so reserved and respectful, was a different man last night. There were no boundaries between them then and no restraint, until the final frantic, passionate moment when he took her breath away.

TEN

～⊛～

Jayne

The second we exit the building Meredith comes to life. She lifts her face to the late afternoon sun, inhales deeply, and starts to stride alongside Teddy and me, easily keeping pace. I link my arm through Meredith's, encouraging her to slow, and together we let gravity propel us down toward the river.

"Will we be stopping for egg sandwiches for tea?" asks Meredith as we pass a small café.

"If you like," I say. "Are you hungry now?"

"Not yet, but we usually pack them."

"All right. Well, there is a little place in the park at the back of the Holburne Museum, we can stop there for a bite to eat. Then I can let Teddy off for a run before we head back. How does that sound?"

"It sounds lovely, Fiona, thank you. I wish we did this more often."

I decide not to risk confusing Meredith by correcting her. She seems to be genuinely enjoying our outing and I don't want anything to ruin it. There is a lightness to her that I want to preserve.

We make our way up the wide stretch of Great Pulteney Street, flanked on either side by an unbroken terrace of Georgian town houses, their grand uniformity imposing an air of ordered calm on us both.

As we enter the grounds of the museum, she loosens her grip on my arm, then she lets go, relaxed. She pauses at the building entrance, admiring the stone archways and columns that dominate its facade while I'm accosted by two tourists brandishing a huge map.

I turn to redirect them back toward the Abbey, one of the city's most famous landmarks, and when I turn back, Meredith is transfixed on a poster advertising a temporary exhibition of paintings by the Italian artist Canaletto. There's been a lot of local excitement about this exhibition, as the private collection is on loan for the first time in decades. It's on display here for only a few weeks before it returns to its owner and thus the flow of people trying to get inside is significant. But Meredith barely seems to notice. She doesn't remove her eyes from the poster. She's rereading it, her face pressed far closer than it needs to be. As I approach her, I can see her shoulders are shaking, and I can't imagine what she might be finding amusing about it. But as I draw level with her, I am horrified to see she isn't laughing at all but struggling to contain her sobs. I look from her distraught face to the words in front of her and read:

A LOST VENICE

"Memory's images, once they are fixed in words, are erased," [Marco] Polo said. "Perhaps I am afraid of losing Venice all at once if I speak of it. Or perhaps, speaking of other cities, I have already lost it, little by little."

—Italo Calvino, *Invisible Cities*

"Is that what I am?" she asks quietly. "Lost? Is William lost too?"

And it is so heartbreaking to watch a woman whose anchor to this world has disappeared. Who can no longer make sense of who she is and where she is, how everything fits around her. Just living her life through the fragments of information her mind indiscriminately throws at her.

"You can't be lost, can you, Meredith?" I reply just as quietly. "Because I have found you. I am here with you."

She places her hand on my shoulder, smiles gratefully. "But what about William? He's still out there somewhere." She looks back at the poster that prompted her tears.

"Did you go together once? To Venice?" I ask.

"It's part of our story," Meredith says hesitantly, like she is trying to piece a memory together as the words are forming on her lips. "I want to remember. I *need* to remember. Perhaps my pictures will help me to?" Meredith is more agitated than she has been all afternoon, her eyebrows painfully pinched together.

"In the memory room, Meredith. Is that what you mean?" I can't think what other images she could be referring to.

She doesn't answer me but turns and starts to retrace her footsteps back out of the gardens toward the main road again. I take my place beside her, studying her face, seeing in the fresh lines on her forehead the strain of trying to find the words and the images that will make sense of what she has glimpsed. I don't want to deliver her back home in this confused state, so I take us the slightly scenic route back across the river, breaking right, past the Abbey and up toward the Assembly Rooms. Far from disorientating her, the crowds of shoppers and sightseers serve as a useful distraction. Gradually, Meredith's face softens and relaxes. Whatever she found upsetting about the Canaletto exhibition has drifted away, beyond her reach now. As we begin to walk past the

Assembly Rooms, she pauses briefly before turning into their
courtyard.

"The Fashion Museum!" she announces. "We must go in!"

"I'm afraid you've only got ten minutes, ladies, until we close,
fifteen at a push," says the doorman, eyeing Teddy. "And I can't let
him in."

Meredith has already walked in through the entrance doors
without me. The doorman spots the slight panic on my face as I
look from Teddy to where she has disappeared, and he relents.
"Here, as you won't be long, give him to me"—he holds out a
hand for the leash—"but don't be any longer or you'll get me in
trouble with the missus if I'm late home for my tea." I see a treat
immediately appear from his trouser pocket; clearly, he's a dog
lover too.

Meredith places her fingertips lightly on the glass cabinet directly
in front of us and leans in as close as it will allow her to. Her
features are pained. Like she can't bear the necessary separation.
She looks like she wants to press through the glass to touch the
fabric on the other side, to feel it pass through her fingers.

"Such an incredibly difficult dress to construct," she whispers
into the glass. "All those different elements to get right. All cut
separately and then mounted together. The draping and the con-
cealed seams, so tricky but I think it's just right."

"It's beautiful," I say.

"See how the layers of the skirt fold in reverse? It has William's
hands all over it. There are triple layers of tulle and silk petticoats
too. All needed, of course—it was heading for Buckingham
Palace."

I make a deliberate effort not to let my eyes flare wider at her unexpected knowledge. I want her to keep talking. Any interruption from me now might be all it takes to shut her down again.

"It's a banquet dress, very grand and formal. The duchess silk satin is from Hurel, and the bodice is overlaid in cream silk lace, embroidered with pearls, crystals, and mother-of-pearl sequins."

I read the information card mounted next to it. None of this information is here.

"I came to see it. When it arrived in Bath." Meredith steps back from the glass now and faces me.

"You've seen it here before? You remember that?"

"Yes, 2016. There was quite a fuss made about its arrival, I remember that. I came alone. William had a terrible headache."

It's this mention of William that seems to dampen her interest in the dress. Her eyes have grown sad again. She's trying to smile for my benefit but there is a shift in her mood that she can't hide.

We start to trace our steps back out toward the door we came in through and Meredith's demeanor slowly changes the closer we get to the exit. She's agitated, wringing her hands together. There is something else about this place that is making her feel uncomfortable. She didn't feel it inside when we were close to the dress, but now she does.

"You'll have to call William," she says when we step outside. "I can't remember the way home. Please, do it quickly."

"It's okay, Meredith, I'm here. I will get you back, don't worry."

"No, that's not what happens." She's shaking her head, getting annoyed with me for wanting to change her plans. "William is going to come and get me because I can't remember. He'll make everything okay again."

Before I have a chance to comment, Meredith fixes me with a determined look.

"It's the dresses. William says the dresses will help, when the time comes." Her face fills with enthusiasm now. "That's what he means," she adds triumphantly. "The dresses will help me find him. That's it!"

Olivia smiles, very broadly, when I return Teddy, well over an hour after I collected him. But Meredith isn't happy at all. She looks confused and agitated when she was so pleased with herself earlier. Now her entire body seems tight from the sheer frustration of not fully understanding something.

"What is it, Meredith?" I place a hand on her shoulder as we pause at her front door.

"The pearls."

I try to understand the significance this one word holds for her.

"On the dress we were looking at together at the museum. Is that what you mean?" I remember it was embroidered with them across the bodice and the sleeves.

"Those ones are pink. But the other ones are white. They come first. That's important, isn't it?" She searches my face expectantly for any hint of confirmation that she is right.

I simply have no way of understanding the meaning of what she's saying, so I smile at her, trying my best to reassure her that we will get there together, somehow, before I watch her turn and walk through the door, her face lowered to the floor, still trying to connect the dots as they drift too quickly away from her.

I return to my own apartment. On the doorstep is a brown paper bag with *Baked fresh this morning* written on the side, along with a phone number and instructions to *come have coffee with me Wednesday if you can. 11 a.m., Margaret's Buildings*. It's from Jake. He will have to wait. I put the bread on the counter in the kitchen and slump onto the sofa, at a complete loss as to how I am going to help unpick Meredith's story.

With no other ideas springing to mind I tap the words *Catherine Walker* into my laptop and feel my breath catch in the back of my throat. One or two images of an elegant dark-haired woman appear on-screen, but they are completely eclipsed by hundreds of another, far more famous woman: Princess Diana.

Image after image fills the screen, a never-ending scroll, but amidst the splendor, it is impossible to miss Meredith's pink dress—number 19, as she called it—with its colorful smattering of jasmine, cherry blossoms, orchids, and lilies, worn by Diana on a tour of India.

I need to speak to Carina, my boss at Bouquets & Bunches. I remember her mentioning Diana's wedding bouquet before. Carina said she was only thirteen the day of the wedding, but she can still recite every flower it contained. She may know better than I what all this means.

ELEVEN

❧

Carina and I have just finished setting up for the day and now the entire shop smells like the most exquisite floral perfume. It is impossible not to be happy in here. The clean, green youthfulness of the lily of the valley; the powdery sweetness of the freesias; the denser earthiness of the orange blossom and violets; and the lighter freshness of the white lilac that reminds me so much of my mother's garden. They all combine and blend with the strong, warm myrrh fragrance of the David Austin roses, their pale blush petals an immediate magnet for anyone who enters the shop.

In my first week here Carina told me it was very important that we serve the whole community, not just those who can spend £40 on a whim as they pass by on a Friday afternoon. "I never want anyone to feel intimidated coming in here," she told me. "However much someone has to spend, even if it's just a couple of pounds, we should be able to help them. Always make sure there are £5 posies outside. It will make people feel welcome."

I think she does it because she knows how it feels to be excluded. The deeper shade of her skin, the wiriness of her hair, and the fact she's petite and female have resulted in customers talking down to her at times. Not that she has once stood for it. A woman came in last week and before she had even said hello, she took issue with the fact Carina was watering the orchids, openly criticizing her for not knowing they need very little moisture. Carina politely corrected her, pointing out they originate from the tropical rainforests of Asia and so are, in fact, very used to being wet. The woman looked down her nose, shocked that she'd been contradicted, while Carina held her ground, smiling, offering to help but allowing the woman to make her own decisions. It was only after she left empty-handed, because she didn't have the gall to ask for the assistance she needed after insulting Carina, that I could see the effect it had on her. She made us both a cup of tea, and when she returned, she simply said, "For some people it will never be enough, Jayne. I will never be enough. The years of study it took to get here, the financial risk of setting up this place, the hours and sacrifices it takes to keep it open, and all she sees is a dark-skinned woman that she thinks she knows better than."

It made me realize just how different our approaches to life are—how she wants to be embraced and accepted and valued while I want to make as little fuss as possible, to have the spotlight shine on someone else. She's my boss and there's a line drawn between us, whether we like it or not, but this makes me want to know more, to get to know her better.

"Would you mind doing some deliveries this morning, Jayne? There are so many bouquets to get out. They're all local, so you can walk them, take a few at a time. It's a nice morning for it."

What I really want to do is ask Carina about Princess Diana and see if she knows anything about her relationship with Catherine Walker, but there is too much to do. Besides, if responding to customers' whims in the shop is my least favorite part of this job, then the deliveries are something I could spend all day doing. I love the reactions, standing there in that couple of seconds, watching someone guess why the flowers have been sent and by whom. I love that as I walk the flowers through the city, people involuntarily smile at them. I can pretend they are smiling at me.

The first bouquet is a luxurious mix of peonies, spray roses, astilbes, and white orchids. One of the most expensive arrangements we offer, and it is heading for an apartment that sits above the shops on the main high street. When Lucy answers the door, I can tell she has been crying. Her eyes are puffy and sore. Perhaps she didn't sleep well last night. Her hand is at her forehead like there is a headache blooming there. When she sees me and what I'm holding, the corners of her mouth lift gently, but she doesn't commit to the smile. She's guarded, not wanting to believe they are for her. "Lucy?" I say, hoping they are indeed for her.

"Yes." Now her smile deepens fully, she can't hold it back.

"These are for you." I hand them to her and watch as her face, her whole body slacken with relief. I'm quite sure these flowers are from a lover, not a friend. Maybe she argued with a partner last night, waking this morning believing it was all over, until this very moment. They're extravagant, designed to change someone's mind about something. Force an impact. Something half the price would have been an adequate apology. I watch her shoulders rise and fall. These flowers will change the course of her day, how she will feel for every second of it. And I love that I got to witness it. She thanks me and closes the door, and I imagine her rushing back upstairs to make a phone call that will make someone else happy too.

The second bunch are more rustic, softer and looser, less showy. They're designed to say *I care* and nothing more, and when Janet opens the door, clocks them, and cackles, "Oh, the silly sod, I told her not to bother with a thank-you!" I am happy to be right again. I laugh to myself as I walk back down the garden path. But it's the third delivery that has the greatest impact on me. The house is on Daniel Street, back across the city and in another beautiful row of Georgian town houses.

As I approach, I see the curtains are still drawn, and there isn't one part of me that wants to knock on this door. I wish I could take the basket of white lilies back to the shop.

When the door eventually opens, it's an elderly woman I'm guessing must be in her late seventies. She's pale and drawn, her lips cracked. Her hair is gray, her skin is gray, her eyes are gray. It's like she's drowning in grief in front of me.

"Mrs. Matthews?" I ask gently, because she'll always think of herself that way, won't she? She nods and I watch a tear fall onto the woolen cardigan she has let fall open across her bony chest.

"I hope these might bring a little comfort to you today," I say, because there is nothing more I can offer her.

These flowers will have no impact at all. They will sit on a table, unwatered, until they wither and brown before someone throws them out.

"Thank you." She doesn't smile but in the depths of her despair she remembers her manners and it makes my heart break right there on her doorstep.

"There is a card with the flowers, Mrs. Matthews, if you needed to call the shop at all. For anything." I hope she understands my meaning, because I have to back away—my own tears are threatening to come, and I don't want her to see them.

I walk back past the row of houses on her street, watching people come and go with their grocery shopping, their dogs, throwing bags into the back of the car, about to head out for the day. I wonder if they are grateful for the mundanity of their actions. I hope one of them will think to check on her. I hope they'll notice that the man who might have accompanied her to the park each morning no longer does.

Will I ever have someone like that in my life? I almost envy Mrs. Matthews her grief because it means she has had a great love. I buy a coffee and sit on a bench in one of the residential parks on the way back to the shop, taking five minutes to gather myself. I have tried so hard to force Alex from my thoughts in the months since we split. And I was succeeding.

But now the image of the two of us in bed together the night before he said it wasn't working is brought back to me with searing clarity. My body stiffens, just as it did then, when my mind was racing with a thousand disconnecting thoughts that didn't belong among our tangled limbs. He had been searching my body for a deeper level of intimacy, trying to take me to a place that required total abandonment, to be there with him and shut everything else out. And I couldn't do it.

How could I explain that I needed emotional closeness first without hurting his feelings? It all just needed to be slower. I needed to see vulnerability, to know he was human and we shared the same emotions. Just the tiniest chink would have been enough. If just once he had questioned himself, paused to ask if I was okay, if I needed less or more or something different. I didn't have the words and he didn't have the intuition or patience—it was clear in the way he sulked off to the bathroom while I stared at the ceiling, desperate to be at home in my own bed, not feeling like a disappointment in his. I shudder at the memory of it because I know now Alex didn't end our relationship because of one awkward night in bed. He ended it because he didn't care enough about me to uncover *why* it was that way.

I drain the last of my coffee, check the time on my phone, then head back to the shop, grateful that my afternoon will have Carina in it.

"Here comes a woman on a mission," laughs Carina as soon as I enter the shop. "You look surprisingly decisive today!" She's at my side before I know it. "Fancy a cup of tea and a chat?"

There is kindness poured right through Carina. She is nearly at the end of another manic morning and who knows what stresses and rudeness she may have encountered along the way. But she will always find the time and energy for anyone who needs it. Today that's me. I've always been mindful of the fact she's my boss and kept my personal life out of the small boutique we work in together. There have been times when she has invited closeness— I don't think she can help herself, she's the kind of person who won't ignore someone's upset because it's easier not to ask or through fear of prying.

So, I fill her in on the latest with Meredith, the very large task ahead of tracing not just William but Fiona too. Everyone in the building's lack of interest in helping. Alex, I keep to myself.

"Does the name Catherine Walker mean anything to you?" I ask as she is putting the kettle on for a refill.

"Catherine Walker?" She shifts her gaze toward the ceiling, as if she is running through a mental Rolodex of client names. "She's not a regular customer, is she? The name doesn't feel familiar enough. Why? Is there a problem? We haven't missed an order, have we?"

"No, no, not at all. She's not a customer, I think she's a dress designer. Have you heard of her? She has some pretty famous clients." I take my mug of tea and we both perch on the stools, just out of sight of customers if any pop in.

"Oh, *that* Catherine Walker! Well, she had the most famous client of all, of course. You might not remember because it was all in the very late eighties, early nineties. I would have been in my early twenties and you were . . ."

"Born in 1988."

"My God, were you really? Well, you missed the glory days. I vaguely remember reading about Catherine, but she famously never gave interviews. The press were obsessed with the fact that she never courted publicity when she so easily could have, given who she was working with. She dressed Princess Diana for years."

"I know," I say. "I've seen all the pictures online. But do you want to know something really intriguing?"

"Go on." Carina shifts more upright on her stool. Now I'm the one with the power of knowledge, patchy as it may be.

"There is a dress in Meredith's apartment, a very detailed one. The label confirms it's a Catherine Walker."

"That must have cost her a fortune."

"Actually, I don't think it cost Meredith a penny." I smile, enjoying the lack of understanding on Carina's face. "There is a hand-written note accompanying it, gifting it to Meredith. It's signed by Catherine and it says, 'Please accept this dress, she wanted you to have it and so do I.'"

Carina lowers her mug of tea. "She? Are you kidding? You don't think it could seriously be . . ." She trails off, not believing this is a possibility. "But why would *Princess Diana* gift a dress that's worth a small fortune to your neighbor?"

"That's the mystery, isn't it? But it definitely belonged to her. I've seen images of Diana wearing the dress that right now is thrown over a chair in Meredith's bedroom. She has no idea how it got there or what she is doing with it. Somehow, I've got to work it out. I think I'm going to need your help, Carina."

I don't need to ask twice.

"Of course, yes, I'm in! Try to *stop* me! Just give me a job." She's off her stool to emphasize her enthusiasm. "Something I can fit around what I have to do here."

I try to determine a logical starting place. "I'm not sure many leads will come from Meredith herself but perhaps her daughter is the next best bet? I think we need to find her. How about you take on the social media search for Fiona? We know she's Fiona Chalis and we think she lives in London. That should get you started at least."

"Do we know for sure she's Chalis? She hasn't married?" Carina grabs a discarded till receipt and starts scribbling on the back of it.

"No, it's an assumption, I'm afraid. But Meredith has never mentioned a son-in-law, that much I do know."

"Okay. Any chance I can have a recent snap of her? That might help to narrow it down a bit."

"Yes, I'll see what I can do. But are you sure, Carina? You could be wading through thousands of possible Fionas, it won't be a quick job."

"I'll get in a little earlier each morning so I can devote some proper time to it. We'll find her, Jayne, I know we will."

"I hope you're right, Carina, because I can't help but feel that Meredith is running out of time with every day that passes." I know Carina is excited about the dress and who wore it and so am I, but my bigger concern is how long Meredith can realistically remain in her apartment without proper professional help, the kind none of us can be expected to provide.

"You need to get the others in the house on board, Jayne. Whatever it takes, get them interested. They must have seen or heard things that can help. This Fiona may not want to be found so we can't rely on that avenue. We need other ideas, everyone's input." The bell above the shop door signals that we have customers.

Carina calls out, "Hello," to acknowledge them, then notices the doubt on my face.

"You can do it, Jayne." She takes hold of both of my shoulders. "You persuaded me easily enough. Everyone will have their reason to get involved. You just need to work out what it is."

I guess this means I'm having coffee with Jake tomorrow.

TWELVE

❧

I look at myself under the stark lighting of my bathroom mirror, making a silent promise I know I can't keep to not overanalyze this coffee with Jake. Why is it I can function perfectly normally in Meredith's company and somehow not in Jake's? I open the door to my wardrobe, then close it. I brush my hair, then pull it back into an elastic.

Finally, I force myself to sit on my sofa and think about what exactly it is that I want to say to him. What am I asking him for? How might he help Meredith? As much as the idea of spending more time with Jake is appealing, I also think about how quickly I can drink a cup of coffee. I try to determine the minimum number of minutes before it won't be considered rude to leave. Fifteen? Why am I feeling all this pressure to make this meeting go well? It's just coffee!

The frontage of the shop is painted a cool jet black, its windows stuffed with an impressive dried flower display that I know Carina would love. The bright yellow metal chairs that sit on the terrace outside are full of the kind of Lycra-clad mums I see building up a sweat speed-walking with their tribe around the parks every morning.

Inside, it is magical, the kind of place I could linger for hours. It opens up to double height, and as I step inside my eyes are pulled upward to a galleried balcony where I can see rows of colorful books, quiet spots to sit, and more bunches of dried flowers hung upside down. There is a strong smell of aged wood and expensive hand-milled soap.

To the right, there is a solid wooden counter that runs the length of the shop all the way to a small coffee counter at the back. It's thoughtfully dotted with things I want to touch. Pretty stoneware pots filled with vivid green ferns, smooth handmade ceramic bowls that I want to run my fingers over, folds of softly colored linen, willow baskets stacked with pale tapered candles.

Behind the counter is a glass-fronted cabinet that stretches all the way to the ceiling, its shelves lined with huge white china jars with stenciled lettering on each telling me they are full of loose-leaf tea, and an array of different herbs and spices. Behind me, the opposite wall is devoted to an impressively large wine collection.

And there is Jake, at the very back of the room, sitting astride a high stool, a woman opposite him. I pause. Should I interrupt? Perhaps he's forgotten he invited me. Perhaps it was one of those invitations that's offered but not meant? As I'm mentally racing through my options, he sees me and immediately he's up and off his stool.

"Jayne!" he calls as I fail to stop a huge smile breaking across my face. His female friend spins around on her stool, sees my face, and smiles, too, like she recognizes me as well and is pleased I've come. It is the loveliest welcome, from both of them. I head their way.

"Jayne, meet Aurora. She's . . . Oh, it's a long story." They share a small laugh. "What can I get you? A coffee? Tea?"

I nod without saying a word, too distracted by Aurora's dress. It's pale cream and scattered with faded lipstick prints, like someone has kissed her all over. It has an elasticated neckline she's pulled down to expose her tanned, smooth shoulders—skin I find myself wondering if Jake has kissed.

"Which?" Jake raises his hand to the barista. Both of them are now waiting for me to confirm my drink order.

"The coffee here is the best," Aurora offers.

"Coffee it is then!" Jake orders it.

While he does, Aurora stands and offers me her stool while she pulls another into our now-tight little trio.

"So, *you're* Jayne." She laughs, like she knows she looks even more beautiful that way. But the laugh is warm, not mocking.

"Oh, thank you, Aurora!" Jake is laughing, too, now, raising his eyebrows at her.

"Sorry! I promise he hasn't spoken about you the entire morning, Jayne . . . just most of it," Aurora directs my way, before she erupts into giggles, knowing full well she has put Jake on the spot, but she doesn't particularly care. They're like two siblings winding each other up.

"Christ, Aurora, *really*?" Jake ruefully shakes his head, his cheeks getting a little pink. "Okay, time for you to go, please. Didn't you want to investigate the new French linens that have just arrived? Now's your chance."

"No, no, I'll stay." Aurora is obviously enjoying herself teasing him.

Jake laughs, bumps her shoulder with his, and mouths "unbelievable" at her, something he seems happy I've seen too.

He hands me the coffee and dismisses my attempt to reach for my bag and pay.

"So . . ." They both look at me, faces full of expectation. Right, this is the bit where I need to explain why I am here. Why I need Jake's help.

But I hadn't anticipated explaining everything to Aurora, too, and it's thrown me. I'm not sure how much to reveal.

Jake sees I'm struggling and tries to ease me into the conversation. "I'm so glad you came, Jayne. We never get a proper chance to chat. I often look out for you but, well"—he falters, like he's revealed more than he intended—"I guess we must be on very different schedules." He briefly drops eye contact. Aurora notices it, too, and I see something flicker across her face, the slightest raising of her eyebrows. She silently slips off her stool, reaches for her wicker handbag, and says, "I'll leave you both to it." She kisses Jake on the cheek, and I watch as his hand naturally squeezes hers in return. "Lovely to meet you, Jayne," she adds before she heads toward the linens.

After she's gone, Jake turns back to me. "Work has been a bit crazy for me and you always seem in such a rush, but I hope everything is okay, with you, I mean. I hope you're okay?"

There is such a softness to Jake, a willingness to draw you closer to him. I wonder if he grew up surrounded by sisters, encouraged to talk about everything and anything, nothing ever off-limits. "Everything is fine, thank you. The house is great, I love living here." I nod enthusiastically, I can do this. "How long have you lived in the coach house?"

"A few years now. I wouldn't want to be anywhere else. It's close to work and everything I need in the city but, really, I love the sense of having room to breathe, beyond the madness, to escape when I need to."

I smile, because without my saying a word, he has identified exactly what I love about living at Lansdown Crescent.

"Anyway, you asked about Mrs. Chalis in your note. How can I help with that?"

"So, she is definitely married?" I figure we should start with the basics.

"Yes, to . . . William! Lovely guy, very friendly. Although, I haven't seen him for a while, now I think about it. But nothing unusual there, I can go weeks without seeing any of the neighbors when work is manic."

I stiffen a little in my seat, knowing I can definitely eliminate the possibility that William is a figment of Meredith's imagination. The solicitor's letter was convincing, of course, but hearing from Jake that William lives in the building, has been seen there, is more reassuring.

"I see. The things is, I don't think she's very well. Meredith, I mean," I say hesitantly.

"Oh, I'm sorry to hear that. Is it serious?" Jake nods to the guy behind the counter, points to one of the cakes in the glass chiller in front of us, and holds up two fingers. "Forks," he mouths.

"It's hard to say. I think it might be." I'm trying to think how to summarize what has happened, what I've witnessed in Meredith's apartment, and beyond it, in the past few days.

"Do you think she needs to see a doctor?"

I need to tell him more. He obviously thinks we're in the territory of a sore throat or a raised temperature. But I don't want to sound alarmist or like some awful nosy neighbor. Or like I'm making much more of this than there needs to be.

"I'm sure she does but, well, it's not really a physical condition. She seems to have trouble remembering things."

"What sort of things?" Jake smiles like a child as a huge swirl of custard-filled, chocolate-covered pastry is placed in front of us.

It looks delicious but also like the kind of thing that needs to be eaten in private. I won't be risking it.

"Simple, everyday things. Like where items are in her kitchen, what day it is . . . whether she has eaten or not."

He frowns and there is genuine concern in the creases of his face. "That doesn't sound good, does it?"

"It's much more than that too. The apartment is a mess. It's far too big for her to manage. It doesn't seem like she's able to look after herself and . . ."

"William has always struck me as a very capable sort of bloke, one that would stay on top of all that kind of thing."

"Well, that's just it . . . Meredith says he's missing." It sounds so sinister when I say it aloud.

"Missing? But he lives there. Unless of course she means he's left? Left her?"

"There is no physical sign of a man living there. No personal belongings that would indicate she is not living alone. But she speaks very fondly of him. It doesn't feel like they split up—and coupled with the way she seems so confused about lots of things, well, I'm worried."

Jake responds immediately. "I think you're right." Then he pauses and shakes his head. "I mean, obviously, they could have separated, but whenever I've seen them together, they've been so . . . physically close. There is a solidness to them, you know?"

I think of the effort poured into creating Meredith's memory room, how William may have been right by her side helping her do it. How she may be entirely incapable of re-creating it again now if she had to.

"Jake, she can't even dress herself. She gets lost in her own apartment. It's filthy and cluttered. We chat one day and the next she seems to have no idea who I am." I take a big breath and swallow down the emotion that's making my words ragged.

Jake's face has lost all its lightness. But just as I am feeling reassured that he cares, that he is going to help, his features shift, his eyes are dragged off behind me.

"Hello, mate, I was hoping I'd bump into you!" a voice says from behind me, and I watch as the man approaches, extending a tanned arm toward Jake, who has stood to greet him.

The man pulls Jake into a deep hug but it's brief, the sort men do when they want to be casual, not meaningful. Jake's hand finds my shoulder, so I don't feel forgotten, and I'm grateful for it. Only now does the man seem to acknowledge that he is interrupting something.

"David, I had no idea you were back in town. How long are you here? Long enough for us to catch up, I hope?"

"Sadly not. Back to London tonight. I should have known there was no chance of finding you alone. But if I'm not interrupting anything"—he looks to me for approval—"I have a few minutes now for a quick coffee?" He's already looking toward the barista.

My gut reaction would usually be to jump up from my seat, let him have it, and ease any awkwardness. But Jake, apparently, isn't going to let that happen.

"I can't, sorry. I'll call you later though. Maybe I'll catch you next time?"

I register David's disappointment. He tries to hide it with a quick wave of his hand and a shoulder shrug, but the way his eyes flash over me tells me he was not expecting to get a rebuttal. From the corner of my eye, I spy Aurora, who's noticed it, too, and is smirking to herself, which makes me warm to her a little more.

"Sorry, Jayne, David's an old colleague. I had no idea he would be dropping in today." Jake waits until he is out of earshot before he fills me in.

"Oh, don't worry about it, seriously. But are you sure you don't want to . . ." I motion behind me, where David is heading for the exit.

"No, this is important. I'll catch up with him another time." Jake's hand settles on my elbow and I feel the effect of it ripple up through me. "From everything you've said, Meredith obviously needs help."

I'm reassured that Jake has heard the kindness behind what I'm saying and not mistaken me for some sad curtain twitcher with nothing better to do with her time.

"I truly think she does. But I'm not quite sure what to do for a woman living all alone in a big apartment who seems to be losing herself a little bit each day." This is exactly what I didn't want to happen. Me getting emotional in front of a man who always seems so together, like drama knows not to bother with him.

"We just need a plan." He clasps his hands together. "You've spoken to Davina and Olivia too?"

"Yes. They weren't unfriendly but I don't think they want to be bothered. I get it, they're busy, but if we all put our heads together, maybe we might get somewhere. I can't leave her wondering every day what's happened to her husband, Jake, I just can't. She deserves to know there are people who care."

"Well, we are *long* overdue for a residents' meeting. They should happen every six months, basically an opportunity for everyone to have a moan about rates and draw up a list of everything that needs fixing. It's my turn to organize the next one so I'll do it this week. They will come, I'll make sure of that bit. Then when we are all together, that's your opportunity to convince them to help."

"I'm not sure I can," I stammer.

His face softens into a smile that I can't help but find reassuring. "You can, Jayne. You've convinced me. I know you can do it again."

As I'm leaving, I notice a list of names etched into a wooden noticeboard on one of the walls near the door. It dates back to *1780: Mr. Bond, Coach Builder*, it's a list of the past owners. I scan down, through cabinetmakers, wine merchants, grocers, and antiques dealers until I get to the final name at the very bottom, which is *2013: Jake Gilmore, Baker*. "Wait, you actually own this place? It's yours?" I ask.

"I do," he says sheepishly. "But don't be too impressed, Jayne. I'm just the one who bakes the bread—and I don't do that very often or perhaps even very well!"

I can't help then but look at his hands. They're lightly tanned with baby pink nails that are clipped short and spotlessly clean. Hands that make something as basic and nourishing as bread but that have also sustained this business, created this beautifully welcoming space. Hands that are going to travel across his keyboard this afternoon, inviting the residents to a meeting that may just help Meredith force open some locked doors. Whether she will like what she finds behind them, I cannot say. But I am glad Jake has said yes. He notices my gaze and must see something of my troubled thoughts in my eyes, because he gently sets a hand on my shoulder, squeezing it reassuringly.

"It's going to be okay, Jayne. I'm here to help."

We say our goodbyes and I head back to the house feeling inflated with . . . what? Hope that there will soon be some answers? Yes. But excitement, too, one that has nothing to do with Meredith and everything to do with the man I just left. After I arrive home, I cut myself a slice of the bread he baked for me. It's beautifully crisp on the outside and soft and doughy in the middle—and absolutely delicious. I send him a quick text to tell him so, which feels like the least I can do for him.

His response is immediate.

> I hope you'll let me make you some more. Anytime. It would be great to get to know you better, Jake x

By the time I crawl into bed, I've reread it several times but can't think how to respond.

THIRTEEN

Davina is the first to arrive at my place, unexpectedly trailing Maggie with her. "Okay, iPad on, watch the movie, and don't cause any problems, please, Maggie. There is a trip to the cinema in it for you this weekend if you can manage that."

Maggie already has her headphones on, and I doubt she's even heard the incentive. Would it make any difference if she had? She heads straight for the kitchen, where she has presumably spied the snacks, and then we both smile as she bellows, *"I live for peanuts!"*

"Strange that we're meeting here?" Davina says to me. "It's usually at Jake's place when it's his turn."

I don't get a chance to respond as there is another knock at the door and Olivia and Jake arrive. Everyone knows one another in that basic *we share an entrance hallway and recycling facilities* kind of way, so they all quickly take a seat on my two sofas, filling the room for the first time since I moved in. Everyone looks expectantly at Jake, assuming, of course, he is about to run through some standard maintenance updates. He does, but I'm not listening to a word of it, too preoccupied with the thought that soon all these eyes will be directed at me.

Davina thinks the security measures in the building should be upgraded after hearing one of the other town houses had a break-in last month. Olivia suggests a key lockbox for one of the external walls at the back of the property to avoid any future lockouts, and Jake volunteers to see to it that all the communal walls and halls are repainted by the end of the year before he readily agrees to get quotes for the other requests. He is very giving of his time considering the large chunk of it running a business must take. His phone lights up continually with new messages while we're all chatting but he doesn't respond to a single one of them. There is no sense that he feels hassled by everyone else's reluctance to put their name to a task—he's happy to oblige—but I sense he is rushing through the practicalities so we can get to my part.

"Fantastic!" says Davina. "That's us done for another six months then. Maggie!" She stands and Jake moves quickly to intercept her.

"Actually, I think there might be something Jayne wanted to add?" He looks at me encouragingly.

I shuffle forward on the sofa, gripping my hands in my lap. "Yes. Um. You all saw the note I sent you recently?" There is no ripple of recognition from Davina or Olivia. "About Meredith, our neighbor on the first floor." I continue.

I immediately see Olivia's shoulders drop, like we've dealt with this issue already and there can't be anything more to say. Davina slumps back into her chair, disappointed by the unexpected extension to the meeting. There's not much she can do, though, seeing as Maggie has failed to appear.

"I know you are all incredibly busy."

"That's a major understatement," scoffs Olivia. "I'm not sure I can actually recall the last time I had a full day off. It's relentless."

"I know, and I'm sorry to ask, but I do think Meredith needs our help."

"In what way?" asks Davina. "What can we realistically do that her own family can't?"

"Well, she's struggling and doesn't seem to have any help. Her apartment is incredibly untidy." But I can see this isn't going to persuade them.

"Worse than mine?" asks Davina flippantly.

"It's different, Davina. Your apartment is lived-in. It's a home for a busy family. It would be odd if there wasn't some clutter, things to put away. But Meredith's is *chaotic*. There is little, if any, logic to where things are placed, except in . . ." I'm not sure whether to expose her memory room, it feels so personal and not really my information to share. "It's messy. And she's the same."

"She's still playing that movie on loop," adds Olivia. "It's the one with Julia Roberts. She gets sick and falls out with her mother, can't remember the name of it now, but why does she watch it so many times—and so loudly?"

"I don't know, but I just hoped as a building we might find a way to come together, to make sure she's okay. Maybe there's a rota for when we can all check in on her. Could we help her with some food? What if we all cooked an extra portion of what we are having for our dinner each night. That would really help."

"Correct me if I'm wrong," asks Davina, "but she's not even that old, is she? What, late sixties, perhaps?"

I flick my eyes to Jake, whose attention is focused squarely on me. He's nodding reassuringly.

"Yes, probably, but I've seen a lot that doesn't add up," I continue. "Margot darted into her apartment one morning and that's when I started to get a sense of quite how bad things are."

"In what way?" asks Davina.

"She'll wear the same clothes over several days, despite the fact they are obviously dirty. There are piles of unopened post, no food in the cupboards, burned-out saucepans. I think I need to get in there and give it all a really good tidy-up for her."

Olivia has started to shake her head. I've lost her already.

"Please, Olivia, there's more." I look to Jake to see if he might step in and help convince her, but he seems to feel this needs to come from me. "If we could just give a little bit of our time, of ourselves. Maybe we would all benefit from it?"

"Tidying up is probably the last thing you should do," Olivia says urgently. "Don't tidy anything. She needs the mess. The point is, it's not a mess to her."

"What d'you mean?" I wonder for a second if Olivia has seen Meredith's apartment for herself.

She takes a prolonged deep breath, looks at each of us, and then begins to speak, much slower this time.

"My mum was diagnosed with dementia three years ago. She died last year." She says the last bit mechanically, without much feeling at all.

My mouth drops open. Jake's gaze shifts for the first time from me to Olivia.

"Oh, Olivia, I'm so sorry," says Davina. "That must have been incredibly hard."

"It was. It still is, to be honest. She was about the same age as Meredith and it just feels far too young. I wasn't ready for it at all but keeping busy helps me . . . avoid . . . wallowing in it, I suppose."

I watch her swallow hard. She wants to continue but she's worried the tears will come if she stops focusing all her energy on preventing them.

"My point is, she was doing all the things you are describing. If Meredith is the same, then she needs to be properly diagnosed.

That's what will help her, not a bunch of ill-qualified neighbors dropping their leftovers off at her front door a few times a week. I mean, has she even seen a doctor?"

"She says so, yes. But I'm not sure it was recently. I feel she'd have more help in place if it was."

"Well, she needs to. We can't responsibly help someone when we don't know what we're dealing with, can we? And besides, I'm sorry to be so blunt but I don't have the time. I work every day and some nights, too, and I can't add anything else into my week. As you know, I don't have the time to walk my own dog."

I feared this would be the response. But I am also a little shocked. It feels like such a cold reaction. I know now this will be especially hard for Olivia, but she has so much knowledge to bring that will help Meredith. Surely, she can see that.

Davina doesn't say a word, but I watch her studying Olivia's face, drawing her own conclusions.

I have no choice but to plow on.

"I can contact her GP, that's a good idea. I'm pretty sure I saw a doctor's card stuck to the fridge door."

"Even if you can just arrange for them to call her, that would help. If she's as bad as you say, they will pick up the signs, I'm sure." Olivia starts to gather her things again, readying to leave.

"But it's also everyday assistance she needs from us. Maybe we can all do a bit of that too?" I cast my eyes around the room, trying to convey I don't think this all has to come from Olivia.

She shakes her head.

"Mum's decline was very rapid in the end. She'd be a constant danger to herself if she was left to it. She'd go out at night without telling anyone and would be gone for hours, or forget she left the bath running. It was frightening, we couldn't trust her to care for herself. None of us can be responsible for that."

"I'm sorry, Olivia. I can't imagine how hard that must have been to watch. But I'm not sure Meredith is quite at that stage yet." I plead, "Maybe we can all help to make sure she never gets to it?"

"You can't stop or cure dementia, Jayne. That's not how it works." Her tone is harder now. She's getting annoyed with me, irritated by my lack of understanding of the subject. "Look, I'm no expert, but if that's what she has, then she will only get worse, not better. Mum got very angry with everyone too. She was convinced people were conspiring against her, making plans for her behind her back. She hated feeling left out of those decisions. It made everything worse, so I think you need to be very careful about deciding what may or may not be best for her."

I notice she is placing all the decision-making on me, determined not to be a part of it.

"I saw a letter, when I was in her apartment." I was hoping not to have to admit I've read Meredith's mail, but if I stand any chance of persuading them all, I need to explain everything. "It was addressed to her husband, William, from his solicitor. It references their daughter, Fiona. I got the sense from Meredith that she isn't around much, but if we could track her down and make it clear how Meredith is living, then surely, she will help. Carina at the flower shop has already agreed to help with that. But has anyone ever seen Fiona? Does she visit at all?"

I look at a room of shaking heads. I shouldn't be surprised. Jake is a busy entrepreneur. Olivia is a workaholic. Davina is juggling highly irregular work hours with the needs of two young girls. Why would anyone notice anything beyond their own daily to-do list?

"Couldn't it just be that William and Fiona are together?" Davina looks like she's stating the obvious, but honestly, this hadn't occurred to me. "That he's left and is staying with her?"

"Perhaps?" It seems unlikely but possible. "Either way, Fiona wouldn't be hard to find, would she, if we all put our heads together?" I prompt. "Meredith led me to believe she is in London, and if her surname is the same then we're halfway there already."

No one offers any other suggestions, so I say I'll also make contact with the solicitor if they can all just please think about how else they might help Meredith day to day, however small, a suggestion that is met with no clear sign of commitment from any of them beyond Jake, who kindly adds, "You've got my full support, Jayne, whatever you need."

I am about to mount a robust final plea when there is a very gentle knock on the door. We all sit still, looking at one another, all slowly thinking the same thing.

"You didn't invite Meredith to this meeting, did you, Jake?" I whisper across the room at him.

His hand is over his mouth. "I just sent the email to the usual residents' chain without thinking."

"She was definitely on it," confirms Davina. "I saw her name."

"It won't be her," I say confidently. "I don't think she is exactly checking her email inbox every morning."

But when I open the door it is Meredith standing there, her face wet with tears. "Is *this* my apartment?" she asks as she starts to shuffle inside. "I've tried my keys in some of the other doors and none of them will open."

"Oh no, it's not." I falter. "It's where I live. It's Jayne, Meredith. Do you remember we took that lovely walk to the park together?"

She looks closely at my face, her own completely expressionless. "I don't know a Jayne," she adds. "Is William here? I think we need to get back to London."

Jake steps in. "Mrs. Chalis, I can take you home. I know exactly where your apartment is." She doesn't respond at first, like she hasn't registered the sound of her own name. But then Jake's decisiveness seems to put her at ease. "If that's okay with you, Meredith? I'll walk you home now."

Meredith's eyes travel across every one of the faces in the room, waiting for a glimmer of recognition, I think. When none comes, she relents. "Okay. But can you let William know I've gone home?" she says to me.

As the door is closing behind them, I hear Meredith plead with Jake not to mention this to Fiona. "She doesn't know, and we don't want to upset her. That's what we agreed."

I look at Davina and Olivia, appealing to them to do something. Neither of them says a word for a minute. "She needs us," I urge them both. "There are dress sketches in her apartment that are laid out in a very specific date-and-location order. Each one has writing on it that I'm pretty sure is from William. I could be completely wrong, but their placement seems very deliberate, like he or they wanted them to be found, to be seen like that. I think they're intended to help." I hold back on mentioning Diana for now. Carina may have found the connection exciting but I'm not so sure Olivia or Davina will. It may just make Meredith sound even more detached from reality.

"Add to that the fact that her husband appears to be missing and we have a daughter who never visits. How is Meredith ever going to unravel any of this without our help?"

"I can carve out some time in my week," Davina finally says. "It won't be much, but something. Food won't be a problem, there's always something I can bring home from events." Her face drops. "We should have done this a while ago by the looks of it. Olivia? If your suspicions are right, you're the only one of us with any direct experience at this."

"Maybe, but seeing Meredith only makes me more convinced

that this is not a job for us." Olivia is making no apology for her lack of commitment. "I think it's really admirable that you want to take it on, Jayne, but that doesn't mean I'm going to join you. I've spent a lot of time trying *not* to think about this horrible illness. I can tell you what I know when and if it's relevant, but that's as far as it goes for me. There are reasons why I fill my days and nights with an insurmountable pile of work. And I do help. Just not in the way you think I do. I cannot, in good conscience, say yes to this when I think it's a mistake." Olivia is very measured, seemingly not at all moved by the sight of Meredith in tears, unable to remember which door in this house leads to her own apartment, and I know I have no option but to relent.

I look to Davina, who is giving nothing away. "Fair enough, Olivia. That's your decision and we will respect it. But please, if there is anything that you think we need to know, it would be incredibly helpful if you could share it with us. We won't ask any more of you than that."

"The dress sketches sound interesting—and important if Meredith has made a point of displaying them in the way you describe, Jayne. I haven't seen them, so I don't know, but they sound to me like a good place to start." I sense that Olivia is trying to be helpful in the best way she can. "There is lots of assistance out there, I know that from the helpline shifts I do at the Live Well Center." And then when we look blankly at her she adds, "You've probably walked past it a million times, it's just behind the Abbey. I've put business cards in the hallway if anyone ever needs one."

We all exchange glances. I'm not sure anyone knew this about Olivia. I recall seeing the cards offering *an unjudgmental ear*, but have never given it much thought. She senses our surprise and answers the question before anyone has a chance to ask it.

"I volunteer there, helping people build an action plan to get out of whatever trouble they're in. It might be helping someone get on the road to clearing their debts or supplying a woman with contact details for all the local refuges and making her aware of the support she's entitled to. Supplying the practical information is the easy bit, but what a lot of people need is a voice at the end of the line, an opportunity to say what they may not be telling anyone else."

"Wow, I had no idea you do that." I am genuinely stunned this is the same woman who lacks the time for eye contact when I collect Teddy some mornings. Then I think about how much I love delivering flowers to people, getting that glimpse into their lives on the sad as well as the happy days—and how unsatisfying it can be when the brief transaction on a doorstep prevents me saying everything I'd like to. How sometimes I would dearly love to offer them my ear for an hour or two. I make a mental note to take one of the business cards from the entrance hallway.

"There's probably a lot you don't know about me." Olivia says this like it bothers her, but she has always seemed so preoccupied and busy, like making time to get to know her neighbors was never exactly a priority. "I guess we could say the same for all of us. Anyway, we're always looking for extra volunteers if anyone ever fancies it. Maybe listening is your superpower, Jayne?"

"Well, it may not be a bad thing Meredith saw us all together tonight," Davina says, bringing us back to the task at hand. "If we're going to help her, we need to include her. We need to be led by *her* and what she needs."

At this point Maggie strides back into the room, her lips covered in a bright orange powder from the cheese puffs I also left out.

"I feel *really* sick," she groans.

"Which sounds like my cue to get going," says Davina. "Jayne, why don't you let me tackle the solicitor? You can't do everything yourself. And while you only ever see me failing to control my children, believe it or not, I can be very charming and persuasive when I put my mind to it."

"Thank you, Davina, that would be wonderfully helpful. Okay, let's meet again in the next couple of days," I suggest. "Olivia, maybe you can let us know what did and didn't work for your mum ahead of our meeting?"

"Okay, there's lots I can share just as long as you understand I won't be at the meeting."

"We can all meet at the coach house if that works for everyone?" Jake is back with us.

"Is Meredith okay?" Davina asks.

"I think so, but very confused. And you're right about the apartment, Jayne, it's in a shocking state."

The others say good night and leave as Jake gathers the empty coffee mugs and takes them through to the kitchen for me. When he returns, he's smiling.

"What?" There can't be much in my kitchen to amuse him.

"Nothing, that's just a very cute baby snap, that's all."

He's obviously seen the Polaroid on the fridge, and my heart sinks.

"Good night, Jake."

I watch his smile fade as he turns to leave.

FOURTEEN

❦

Meredith

1990

She'll be photographed from every angle. The dress and coat must reflect that. Metallic embroidery sits at the nape of the neck, the back vents where the tailcoat meets the slit of the skirt, the elongated shape adding to its femininity, lengthening the waist, achieving the right degree of formality.

By now, Meredith appreciates the role Catherine must play, why her diplomacy is so legendary. She understands the clothes are a line of defense to all the scrutiny Diana faces, down to the color of the nail polish she chooses. Catherine never once bows to it. Her loyalty is solid. She won't trade even the smallest morsel of a valued friendship for a quick compliment from the fashion press, words that could bring more business through the door.

Her research is meticulous and lengthy. The team have got used to her regular trips abroad.

A dress cannot be designed until she absorbs the function it will perform, the cultural sensitivities it needs to negotiate. And Meredith has seen enough now to know there is no better woman for it, one who combines directness and patience with the determination of a self-made businesswoman and the protective resilience of a genuine friend. They grew together. That's what drew them close. It was a slow evolution. Catherine discovering her designs. Diana finding her voice. Now Meredith realizing her dreams.

Can it really be that the little girl who used to sit next to her mother, inches from their tiny black-and-white TV screen, watching the royal family wave from the balcony of Buckingham Palace, will make a dress to be worn by that very royalty? As that small girl she longed to see the clothing come to life in full color. She remembers how her own mother, so close in age to their young monarch and a proud royalist, would sit motionless, never saying a word until the footage ended. Then the two of them would loudly debate the merits of one outfit over the many others they loved, Meredith reaching for her sketch pad, making childish scribbles to show her mother what improvements she would make. Her mother helped plant the seed of ambition in the mind of young Meredith. She saw no reason why her daughter couldn't be the one who reached the top.

It became the thread that bound them together. When Meredith returned from school in the early afternoons, they would cut out easy patterns, bringing them to life on her mother's sewing machine. By the time she was ten years old, Meredith could make basic garments and alterations to loved-but-outgrown clothes she couldn't bear to part with. The greatest compliment of all was being trusted to rehem one of her mother's favorite slim-cut skirts or her tapered capri pants. She knew then this was all she ever wanted to do. Maybe one day she would share her love of fashion with her own daughter.

She may have dreamed of a career in fashion, but Meredith couldn't have predicted what it would also bring her. The long nights she and William are sharing in the workroom, hours after everyone else has left. When they dim the lighting and Meredith feels his soft lips whisper across the back of her neck.

Still no one knows. The thrill of the secret they both keep is almost unbearable in the daylight hours when they professionally negotiate their way around each other, knowing how they held each other last night and will do again tonight. This man, so respected at work, so privately passionate with her.

Meredith feels she will explode some days from the strain of avoiding eye contact, fearing her reaction, the way he lights her up, giving them both away. It isn't that their closeness would be frowned on by the company, not when their work is as exceptional as it is. But neither of them wants to share what they have with anyone else. They don't want their every word listened to with a new intensity, every meaningful look belittled to workroom gossip.

But even they can't resist fully, and Meredith cherishes every accidental brush of William's finger against hers. His every snatched opportunity to touch her when they find themselves briefly alone, their bodies pressed tightly together in the narrow stairwell before footsteps force them quickly apart. The moment when the door has closed behind their last colleague and it is just the two of them again, and he gives in to the overwhelming temptation to lift her onto one of the worktables, to direct his total dedication and passion to every inch of her, his hands moving with a devotion even he has never known before.

Meredith's work is incomparable. Better than it has ever been. She holds her needle more confidently, she feels the tension of the fabric in her fingers more astutely, as if every emotion, every sense has been heightened. They collaborate in a way no one else can match. He may write his instructions in full in the margins of his paper patterns, but she barely needs to look at them, knowing instinctively what is required. Now it is William who will ask her advice on the construction of a complicated design, and later she may ask him to check the pitch of a sleeve before she progresses. Only they know what lies between them and how it has made everything better now they are together. Their love feels deep-rooted already, moving through each of them every day, flesh and blood.

Neither could predict what it might become, how something born of so much love could twist and turn and change, eventually ripping them all apart.

FIFTEEN

❧❧❧

Jayne

When Meredith answers the door, I can tell immediately that my face is unfamiliar to her. She's looking at me expectantly, her eyebrows lifted, waiting for an introduction. I predicted this might happen, so before I left the shop, I grabbed some more forget-me-nots for her. They seem to help and reassure her that, even if she can't place my name or my reason for being at her door, I am someone kind and friendly. It forms the thinnest thread of trust between us.

"Hello, Meredith, it's Jayne from upstairs. I was wondering if you feel like joining me on a bit of an adventure this afternoon?" I haven't mentioned this to the others. I don't want to be talked out of it and I have a feeling Olivia may have tried.

"Are we going somewhere nice?" she asks.

"I thought we might take a little train ride if you feel up for it?"

"With egg sandwiches and the red flask of tea?" Her wonderful smile is back.

"Why not! I'm taking you somewhere I hope will remind you of William."

"Well, that makes me very happy." She beams as she reaches

out and gives my hand a tight squeeze. "You always were such a kind girl."

I don't feel entirely kind as I am noting down the name and number of her GP from the card on her fridge.

The dress in Meredith's apartment, her reaction to the gown at the Fashion Museum, the personal letter from Catherine Walker, and the deliberate lineup of sketches in her memory room are the most significant clues I have to the life Meredith has lived. And perhaps the first of those dresses chronologically is the most obvious place to start. I remember the dress was full-length, it had a short, high-collared jacket with it, and the words *The Royal Albert Hall, 1989* written at the bottom. It was, according to William's note, *the start of our golden period.*

"Give me thirty minutes to get everything ready and I'll be back." I race up the stairs to my apartment.

What other choice is there at this point? There is no word from Davina yet on her call to the solicitor. Carina's task won't realistically get started until I get her that snap of Fiona, and I can't call Meredith's GP until they open again tomorrow. I have a free afternoon and nowhere to be. The same is certainly true of Meredith. So, really, what's stopping us? It is perhaps the nagging doubt that this is not my business to interfere in and whether I have the right to take a woman from her apartment when she has shown herself to be not entirely capable of sound decision-making. Olivia made it clear she thinks the whole thing is a terrible mistake and yet . . . I pause, the butter knife still in my hand. Will Meredith even notice if I don't go back downstairs to collect her? I think of my grandmother's mascara-stained face and the many small ways in which I could have helped but didn't. The problems I chose to ignore. It was forgivable then perhaps, but not now.

I make the sandwiches, fill a flask with hot, sweet tea, and head down the stairs. There is a train to London in forty-five minutes. Meredith is standing in the hallway waiting for me with a black canvas utility bag looped over her right wrist.

"What's in there?" I ask, nodding toward it.

"All my essentials," she says, smiling. "Obviously I can't go without them."

We sit in the quietest carriage I can find. I settle Meredith into a seat facing the direction of travel and get the flask and sandwiches out onto the table so she can feel some sense of familiarity.

"Oh, a new flask."

What she means, I think, is that it's not the red one she is expecting.

"Is this a work trip?" she asks as I feel the tug of the train leaving the platform.

"No. It's just a bit of fun. Think of it as a girls' day out."

"Now that we're friends?" She leans her weight into me, emphasizing the closeness I am so pleased she feels between us.

"Exactly!"

She keeps her gaze on me for longer than necessary and asks, "I have my William, but who is looking after you?"

It throws me a little and she registers my lack of an immediate response.

"Well?" She's not going to let me wriggle off the hook.

"I'm not sure I need someone, really. I'm happy on my own."

She smiles and nods in a way that suggests she doesn't believe me at all. Like maybe there was a time when she used this excuse too.

"I'm sure you've had offers, you're very beautiful."

I try to bat away the compliment, but she sits, staring at me, waiting for a response, so I make a better attempt to be honest.

"The thing is, Meredith, I'm sort of happiest in the background, you know? I'm not sure it's in me to get out there and compete for attention."

She nods slowly, considering her response.

"I see. But doesn't that mean you're missing out? Opportunities are passing you by? Someone else is claiming what should be yours?"

"Maybe." The thought is not a comfortable one. "But if they are, I don't know about them, so it's not like I can regret them, I suppose." It sounds so weak, so defeatist.

"You may not regret them now, but what about further down the line when you'll have less time to do something about it? Sometimes going after what you want is uncomfortable and exposing, but doesn't that just make getting it all the more satisfying?" She hugs her arms around herself, perhaps remembering a time when she did just that.

I love the way she smiles and raises her eyebrows at me. Her silent way of saying, *You know I'm right.* It makes tackling the subject of my reticence a lot less challenging. It opens up a little space for me to consider what she's saying, rather than mentally running away from the idea. I think she can see that, because she continues.

"You don't have to be the loud voice in the room. What those people never work out is that they are tolerated, not loved. You can be the sunshine, not the north wind. Didn't your mother ever read you the Aesop fable? Gentleness and kind persuasion win where force and bluster fail."

Once again, Meredith has managed to distill my complex

thoughts into something far simpler, more relatable. Considering the jumbled state of her own mind most days, it's quite a skill.

"If there is something you want, I'd reach out and grab it if I were you, before it's too late."

The only image filling my head then is Jake. How much I would love to give it a try. To see where it may take us. But does he feel the same?

"I thought so!" chuckles Meredith. "What's the worst that can happen? He says no. So what? We've all been there."

I'm sure the color of my cheeks is all the evidence Meredith needs that she has called this one exactly right.

Then she opens the flask and happily pours herself a tea. When she's drained half of it she asks me where we're going, and I realize I've forgotten to enlighten her on that point.

"To London, Meredith. There's something I want to show you."

"St. James's Park? We like to eat our lunch there on warm weekends, on one of the benches near the palace."

The park is a very short walk from our destination so I promise her we will go if there's time.

The bold redbrick and terra-cotta curve of the Albert Hall is impressively silhouetted against a bright blue sky, its glass dome blending into the feathery clouds above as our black taxi pulls up outside on Kensington Gore. The sheer size of it immediately dwarfs us both. We're too early in the day to clash with a performance time, so despite the heavy traffic nudging its way slowly toward Hyde Park Corner, it is relatively peaceful. I help Meredith onto the pavement and watch as she immediately clutches one hand to her mouth, then straight to her black bag, reassuring herself that it is still there.

"Do you remember this place, Meredith?" I prompt.

"Oh, the sparkle." She smiles and closes her eyes. "All those flashbulbs bouncing off all those oyster pearls. Twenty thousand, they say. So many photographers here. They are all penned in over there." She points off to the right. "And not one of their cameras is still. They can't hide their excitement. I suppose most of them would normally just prefer to be getting off home to their wives and children. But not now." She looks back over her shoulder toward the park.

"It's October, the leaves are turning, there is a chill." She waves a hand across her face. "She makes us all forget that the second she arrives, looking so radiant." Meredith raises her hand to her collarbone. "Nothing at her neck. She lets the dress do all the work. I am so pleased about that."

Meredith looks down at her watch, taps its face.

"Bang on time, as always, exactly as they said she would be. No waiting around. I stay here." She starts to follow the curve of the building around to the right. "The only unmarked door, not numbered like all the others. She has her own staircase too. Can you imagine it?"

It's the most coherent I have heard her talking about the past, perhaps because she isn't placing the memory in the past. It's as if she is reliving it all now, as we walk around the building together. It's obvious Meredith has been here before, on an occasion that feels rooted in her memory through all the detail she observed.

"The effect is almost blinding. And the noise the second she appears is like nothing I have ever heard before." She raises both hands and covers her ears briefly. "People are shouting for her attention. *Really* shouting. They lose themselves around her. I can feel the joy as it sweeps through the crowd, traffic is at a standstill."

Meredith is smiling in a way I have not seen her do before, it's full and infectious. Her entire face is animated. She's almost laughing. "People are waving from the tops of buses. Faces are pressed into the windows of the mansion blocks." She points up to those same windows now. "I am so happy to be a part of it. I stand in the gallery, so high above everything, and watch. I feel special, too, but . . ." She trails off, losing her thread, like she's suddenly hit a blank spot. Her eyes have found the upper windows of the neighboring Royal College of Art, the lifeless, armless tailor's dummies silhouetted there.

"What is it, Meredith?" I keep perfectly still, not wanting to break whatever train of thought she is trying to follow.

"Something isn't right. I've done something wrong. I'm annoyed with myself."

"Take your time, there's no rush."

Her gaze drifts back toward the entrance.

"William. He's cross with me." I can see how much the thought upsets her. She has dipped her head, breaking her connection with the building, not wanting to see any more.

I let my hand find hers and lace our fingers together.

"It nearly ruins everything." She gives up trying to force the memory forward. Her eyes darken, like clouds covering the sun.

"It is the slight flush of her cheeks that gives away her nerves. Nothing else. I keep my eyes on the hem and those heels. And the high collar, Elizabethan, so close to her earrings. No one else could wear that dress like she does."

Meredith takes a long thoughtful pause, allowing her eyes to travel up to the windows above. She steps back and looks up at the domed roof.

"But what did any of this have to do with me? Why are we here?"

I study her face. The pained expression that has settled there. The deep, deep frustration that her mind will let her go only so far. But it's a long way, isn't it? Just being here has ignited something in her that I don't think was there before, or at least she hasn't shown me before.

"That's what we're going to work out together, Meredith." I smile to let her know that we are a team now. It's no longer just her problem to solve.

We both hear the music at the same time. There is an intensity to it that rises and falls. Melodic strings, then the delicate, unrushed sound of featherlight fingers on piano keys. Both our heads lift and tilt in the same direction, around toward the main entrance of the hall. We walk together slowly, following its faint trail.

"Chopin. Piano Concerto Number 1 in E Minor." Meredith comes to a stop, her face lifted to the sky, her eyes closed, as the music softly peters out.

"Do you know this music, Meredith?" It seems highly unlikely that most people could name it from the little we have heard. I don't recognize it at all.

"I've heard it many times. But never live, as I should have. It's my greatest regret." She shakes her head and pulls me on, not wanting to linger or discuss it further.

There is plenty of time before we need to think about our train home, so we cross the main road and enter St. James's Park, joining the network of paths up toward Kensington Palace. There are dogs galore, and I know Margot would love it here.

As the imposing redbrick outline of the palace takes shape, Meredith's pace slows.

"The gardens are always stuffed with forget-me-nots," she says. "Masses of them clustered in the flower beds of the formal gardens."

I watch as her eyes move across the exterior, taking in the uniform rows of paneled windows.

"It's where Princess Diana lived for some time, isn't it?" I nudge. "They've had some wonderful exhibitions here over the years."

She looks back over her left shoulder toward the Albert Hall.

"Have you ever been inside, Meredith?" I try to keep her focus on the palace now.

"Yes, I must show you the photograph. William looks so handsome in it." Then she looks at her watch. "We better get going. It's Sunday, I always cook his favorite lamb on Sundays."

By the time I deliver Meredith back to her front door, it's nearly nine o'clock. I'm shattered, so she must be exhausted. I hope what I did today was the right thing. She is happy to go in alone, but before I let her, I remind her of the photograph.

"The one of you and William," I prompt her. "You told me about it today when we were in front of Kensington Palace. You said he looked very handsome in it."

She laughs at me then. "You do say some very funny things. I think you need an early night."

SIXTEEN

Jake's place is every bit as cool as I imagined it would be. The second he opens the door to me I can smell the comforting waft of freshly baked bread. The smell of contentment. He sees me register it.

"Delicious, isn't it? Come on in."

The ground floor, where the horses and carriage would originally have been kept, has been converted into a large open-plan kitchen that's dominated by an enormous dark wood island. I can see the remains of flour scattered across it and I like that Jake hasn't felt the need to make the place spotless for us.

At one end is a deep-inset butler's sink with a central golden tap arched over it. On either side are huge wooden chopping boards and at the opposite end is what must be the hob, its sleek silver hood pulled down over it. A glossy black cooker sits beneath. A low chandelier creates a soft light, just enough to illuminate all the copper pots filled with a staggering array of utensils and knives and a giant marble mortar and pestle. All this for one man? One wall has an open fireplace, the other is lined with shelves that are filled with cookbooks. I'm not sure I own even one.

I'm relieved to see the others are here already, including Maggie (but no Willow, who is "pretending to do her homework," according to her younger sister). Carina has already arrived and has introduced herself to everyone rather than coming to get me first.

"You had to duck to fit through that door." Maggie giggles, characteristically direct.

"Thank you, Maggie, you are far from the first person to ever point this out," I reply as she hurls herself toward me.

"I like it. It makes you look strong." She raises an arm and flexes a bicep to demonstrate her point. Without realizing it, Maggie is the ultimate icebreaker. She's probably exactly the kind of girl my mum hoped to raise. She achieved it once, but not twice.

I smile at the nerve of this little lady, wondering how long she might stay this way before self-consciousness descends and wraps its firm arms around her. Before a thoughtless or ill-timed throwaway comment might pull the rug from underneath her, her foundations never quite recovering from the shock or hurt. There were countless times when I got off the bus home from school one or two stops too soon so I wouldn't have to listen to the boys in the back row shouting my name and loudly debating whose turn it was to come and sit next to me, to goad me into talking. It's hard to imagine this for Maggie, watching her cheeks fill with color, but I know it's possible.

"Would you like me to set you up with a movie upstairs, Maggie, while the adults have their boring chat?" offers Jake, extending a hand to her. "Help yourself to a glass of wine, Jayne." The two of them disappear up an exposed wooden staircase to the first floor.

Before I have a chance to question where the fridge might be hiding, Davina kindly jumps up and pours me a glass. I plonk myself onto one of the empty stools and look around, taking in the understated but undeniable luxury of the home Jake has created.

"He must be loaded," says Olivia, echoing all our thoughts. "Have you seen the gold tap?"

"He's obviously got a few spare pennies but he's very nice with it, in my opinion," adds Davina.

"Okay, that's Maggie sorted." Jake is completely comfortable with the fact that she is now unattended upstairs where she could, and probably will, wreak all manner of damage. I suspect there is a velvet sofa up there that will never recover from a soaking in strawberry smoothie. He might be finding chocolate finger marks on the walls for weeks to come. But he looks like the thought hasn't even occurred to him.

I watch as he moves confidently around his own kitchen. He pins a large focaccia bread that's dotted with olives and sun-dried tomatoes with one hand to a chopping board. Then he carves generous slices and slides it down the work surface so we can all reach it. I think about how his hands would have tenderly kneaded that dough this afternoon. His patience waiting for it to proof. The satisfaction of watching it rise in the oven and now the joy of carving something he made for us all to enjoy.

"I am available for lessons," he quips, noticing the attention I am paying his small actions. "For bread making, I mean, if you ever fancy it?"

I really do fancy it. But just the two of us? I suspect Jake has never had a similar doubt in his life. His confidence is both impressive and a little baffling.

"We've got lots of different olive oils here. I can highly recommend the Sicilian, very fruity with a hint of almond nuts if you like that. Just help yourselves to whatever you like, plates are here if you need them."

I try not to think about the cheese puffs I laid out the other night. Another reason to love Maggie, who kindly hoovered them all up before anyone else saw them.

Jake takes the stool closest to mine. "Okay, Jayne, where shall we start?" His eyes linger on mine and there is a beat or two when I don't—or can't—break away. He's so easy to like. Everything about him is designed to entice you closer. The open body language, the kind eyes, the warmth and ease of him. A man apparently totally comfortable in his own skin.

"With me, please." Olivia ignores the fact Jake's question is aimed at me. "I can't stay long." I was hoping she may have softened since our last meeting, that there may be a shred of willingness to embrace and join this challenge. But clearly, there isn't.

"You mentioned before that Meredith seems to be worse in the mornings. More distressed and confused." Olivia takes the vocal lead, not waiting for a response. "Well, if you think about it, that makes perfect sense. It's like any of us who have some form of regret or hurt, isn't it? Everything is fine for the first few seconds when you wake up in the morning, and then you relive it all over again."

I watch as everyone reconnects with their own dark cloud, gently nodding in recognition of Olivia's assessment. I wonder if she is thinking about her mum's final weeks. Then there's my mum again, pricking at the corners of my conscience. Her loss, mine, too, but also my gain, the horrible guilty mess of it all.

I look at Jake—even he has mentally left the room, and I can't imagine what his Achilles' heel might be.

"Maybe she is reliving the absence of her husband?" offers Olivia. "If she is suffering with some form of dementia, then typically short-term memories are not laid down and stored in the same way as longer-term recollections. Every morning she might relive him packing his bags and going, or the last time she saw him. Mum could remember the most detailed stories from her childhood. She could describe the stitching on a dress she wore to a birthday party, the pattern of markings on her first kitten, the flavor of the ice cream she was bought at the end of the pier one summer. Her storytelling was vivid and specific, and seemed to come so easily to her. But, if I asked her about a conversation we'd had the day before, she wouldn't remember any of it."

"That's why most days I have to reintroduce myself to Meredith?" I had guessed as much.

"Exactly. While she might be able to visualize scenes from her life with William from decades ago, what happened in the past few months may be completely lost to her or at least very disordered. Think about it from her point of view. Every day she wakes up and sees the bed empty next to her. That could trigger huge anxiety. She might feel abandoned all over again and that level of continued trauma could be affecting how her broader memory functions. Everything might have got very fragmented, thrown up in the air. She might have what I've heard referred to as an *emotional residue* to an event. She knows how she felt at that time, but she won't necessarily remember key facts or the part she played in it all. Mum managed to set off all the smoke alarms in her kitchen once when she forgot she was baking a cake. She couldn't remember the incident, the fact there was smoke billowing out of the oven, but afterward she couldn't listen to Radio 2 without getting upset because that's what was playing at the time. She associated the presenter's voice with the panic of trying to disperse the smoke and the knowledge that she had done something dangerous." Olivia sighs heavily and I wonder at the silent questions she may be asking herself while we all digest this information.

"Okay, this is a lot more complex than I imagined." Davina suddenly looks a lot less confident about our endeavor and I can't lose her too. I decide to inject the conversation with some good news about our trip to London yesterday. As I start to explain, Davina's eyes widen. Olivia looks horrified. Jake mildly and Carina highly impressed.

"Why did you do *that*?" Olivia's voice is laced with a hint of accusation that doesn't feel quite in the spirit of why we're here.

"Okay, let me explain," I start.

"Actually, I'm sorry, I really do have to get going or I'll be late."

"Late? But I thought we agreed we were meeting tonight?" I can't help it. I'm annoyed Olivia has made other plans.

"Actually, I wasn't going to come at all, remember? But my conscience got the better of me. But there is somewhere else I need to be. Add me to the WhatsApp group if you're setting one up, and I'll drop in anything else that feels useful." Olivia waves a hand around the room, offering a collective goodbye, and leaves.

Davina notices the slump of my shoulders.

"You can't make her care more than she does, Jayne. Besides, there is plenty else to focus on." Davina's logical approach to life makes a lot of sense, I just can't replicate her pragmatism. "It's not that she's an unhelpful person, I think she's shown us she's not. This just isn't something she wants to commit to."

I open my mouth to complain but she's having none of it. "Tell us about London."

My mouth suddenly feels very dry, so I take a decent glug of wine before I go on. "As you know, Meredith believes her husband, William, to be missing and both you and Jake have confirmed he was once here and hasn't been seen for some time, probably several months, from what I can gather."

"Would it be too mean to suggest that maybe her erratic behavior just got a little too much for him?" suggests Davina. "If it's as bad as you say, then we could hardly blame him, could we? Things may be much worse than we realize. I still think William and Fiona could be together."

"Perhaps." But I can't believe it's true, not from the tender way Meredith talks about him, the detailed visual record she has kept of their love story and the way I believe he may have helped her construct it.

"Actually, let me just jump in and tell you what I know from the call I made to the solicitor yesterday," adds Davina. "As I should have perhaps predicted, he was reluctant to tell me anything as I am not a client and specifically not *the* client in question, William. But what he did say is that if I were able to prove that William is deceased, he would be able to release details of his will and, although he didn't specifically state it, one would presume the letter that is being held there for Fiona."

"But we don't know if William is deceased or not, do we, even if it is a possibility?" Much as I don't want to consider that option, logic dictates that we must, although *surely* Meredith would remember that.

"Actually, we do. I checked the death records after my call with the solicitor and there is no record of a Mr. William Chalis of this address dying in the past two years. I went back a little further than the solicitor letter was dated to be extra sure."

I imagine Davina then, masterminding one of her events with a detailed running order, a call sheet and timeline accounting for every minute of setup and pack down.

"Busy as we all are," she adds, "I'd like to think one of us might have noticed an undertaker or a visit from a coroner, the arrival of sympathy flowers, something. I also checked with the local police station and there is no missing person report filed."

I'm not so sure. I often have to shout Olivia's name through her letter box before she answers the door, and Davina, the girls, and Jake are very rarely here in the daytime. Something significant could very easily be missed.

"I can check back over the orders at Bouquets & Bunches," adds Carina. "If William did pass away, then there is a good chance flowers will have been sent to Meredith and every chance they could have come from us, since we're the closest florist to this address."

"Brilliant," says Davina. "Let's cover all bases." She pulls a small notebook from her bag and starts to bullet-point our action plan.

This is exactly the kind of cold logic this process needs. The kind that I have been incapable of, so caught up in the emotion of Meredith's story, incomplete as it is. "I think it might help if we make sure someone visits her every morning to check she isn't too distressed?" I lightly suggest.

"Perhaps we just need to get her to a doctor?" asks Jake, his voice more concerned now.

"It's a good point," Davina says, scribbling in her notebook again. "Even if she has seen a doctor, she still seems quite young for de-mentia to be the obvious or only diagnosis. It could have been dismissed as depression or something else, particularly if her hus-band has left her. Anyway, I'm not sure a GP will speak to any of us on her behalf. That would have to be done through her family."

"Actually, I spoke to the receptionist at her doctor's surgery this morning." I'm pleased to tick another action off our long list of jobs. "Meredith is on a waiting list for a telephone call from the doctor. They slot them in between physical appointments in the sur-gery. I didn't go into too much detail, but I explained that she seems confused and forgetful. I'm hoping that she may say something on the call that will alert a GP to her needing more help."

"Let's just hope she actually picks up the phone when they call," adds Davina.

"There's more too. I asked how Meredith might be able to access her medical records and she told me if she makes an appointment, they will have them ready for her."

"Very interesting." Davina nods her head enthusiastically. "Those records won't necessarily lead us to William, but if she has a daughter, they will show when and where she was born. We would have Fiona's confirmed full name and a date and place of birth, which would surely make finding her a lot easier."

"That will certainly be quicker than relying on social media," adds Carina.

Davina throws her smile around the room, but I am uneasy with the suggestion we march Meredith in there and, what? Peer over her shoulder while she reads her records, perhaps not really understanding why she is there or what she is looking for?

"How would I even explain to Meredith the reason she is at the doctor's? Would she even be capable of making the appointment in the first place?" The last thing I want to do is remind them all of the difficulties we face, but this is an obvious practical hurdle.

"You could just explain that it's best she goes and gets a professional assessment. This could give us a real breakthrough." Davina has more confidence in my abilities than I do.

"I could. But she has specifically told me she doesn't want to go, that William said they will handle it together and she trusts his opinion. I need to think about it."

Jake refills our glasses and offers the bread around. As I bite into it, I feel the silkiness of the olive oil slide down my chin and he offers me a napkin. "Messy but worth it, I hope." He smiles.

"We got a little sidetracked, Jayne, tell us what else you know." Davina's hand is still poised over her notebook.

I tell them more about our trip to London, how we visited the location the first dress was worn, the Royal Albert Hall, and the effect it had on Meredith.

"You're forgetting the really exciting bit," shouts Carina, and I wince as I realize I never told her I was planning to keep that detail to myself for a little longer.

Everyone's head turns to me.

"What!" Davina is impatient to know everything, especially this.

"Well, it's not just sketches. There is a very luxurious-looking dress in Meredith's apartment. The dress itself is impressive but there's a handwritten note to Meredith along with it."

"Go on . . ." Davina leans over her notebook, pen still poised.

"It's signed from Catherine Walker."

Silence.

"Sorry to be dim but should that name ring any bells?" Jake looks baffled.

Carina beams, ready for the big reveal.

"She's a fashion designer. That's most likely a very expensive dress and probably completely bespoke," Davina jumps in before I have a chance to respond to him. "The label is a real favorite with mothers of the bride at certain society weddings. They've been dressing royalty for years, the Duchess of Cambridge more recently, and of course . . . hang on . . . you're not suggesting . . ."

"Yes, the label is most famous for dressing Diana and the note from Catherine makes clear that *she* wanted Meredith to have it." I try to keep my tone factual so everyone will take this seriously. "I've done some digging and Diana is pictured wearing this dress. It was made for her—and now it's Meredith's. We just don't know *why*, what the connection is between the two women."

"Wow." Davina puts the pen down like there aren't the words to turn this into an actionable bullet point.

"Quite something, isn't it?" Carina looks thrilled to have this fact known among the group.

"Well, there is clearly a lot more to Mrs. Chalis than meets the eye." Jake looks almost proud of her and I love that he seems every bit as invested in this story as the rest of us are.

"Meredith told me that this dress is connected to William in some way, that he is also part of whatever story we are trying to uncover here—and there's something else. We ended up in the Fashion Museum together the other day and she saw a dress there that was worn by Diana back in the nineties. She knew it, every little detail about it. She was able to tell me facts that were not on display."

"There is a lot to work out." Davina bites down on the end of her pen. "But here's what I'm thinking. If Meredith felt closer to William and more connected to her past when she was standing outside the Albert Hall, then it stands to reason that if you visit the other locations, more could be revealed."

I want to breathe in Davina's optimism and make it my own.

"She might recall more of their relationship and how she has got to where she is today. She may remember enough to help us find William, to work out what exactly has happened to him, and to answer why she has a daughter who never visits her."

Jake nods his agreement. "And we all take care of her as best we can in the meantime until we can trace one or both of them and get her the professional help she needs. Where were the other dresses worn, Jayne?"

"Quite a few were around London, then some further afield. Northamptonshire, Sandringham, and abroad in Venice and New York."

"You could start with the London ones, Jayne, and see how you get on? It might just be enough to reveal some of the missing parts?" Davina is definitely the ideas person in the room, and I love her for it but I'm not sure I can put Meredith through that again.

"She was fine while we were there, but I think that much travel to and from London is going to be too hard on her. Her apartment is really the only place she feels entirely safe. It's her lifeline."

"Okay, let's park that problem for now," determines Davina. "There will be a way round it but in the meantime, from what everyone has said, we have a good hit list of interventions we can put in place." She flicks back through her notebook, ready to remind us all. "What about a laminated checklist for Meredith that we attach somewhere in the bathroom, perhaps even inside her shower? It should list the number of steps in her morning and evening wash routine, in the order in which she needs to perform them to ensure she gets washed and dressed properly."

"Yes, that's certain to help," I say, feeling immediately encouraged. "I also love the idea that we number the internal doors to each apartment, too, and make sure Meredith has a numbered key ring that reminds her which floor her apartment is on."

"Brilliant. Anything else?" I can tell from the sparkle in Davina's eyes that this is her at her problem-solving best.

"Perhaps we should ask the milkman to place the bottles for each apartment on a numbered or named place mat so Meredith can more easily identify which are hers," suggests Jake. "Might ensure we all get our latte in the morning too."

I'm less sure about this one. If the visual reminder of all those opened bottles in her kitchen didn't force a change of behavior for Meredith, then I'm not convinced this will, but I keep my skepticism to myself for now.

"What about the morning checks?" I ask. "Do you think you and I might share that task, Davina? Could you take two mornings a week and I'll take three? Then we tackle the weekends according to whatever commitments we have. I'm not sure it's right to include you in this, Jake. I'm not sure Meredith will be comfortable opening her door to a man she doesn't know when she's not dressed properly."

"She might not be comfortable with us either," says Davina. "But I agree, for now let's keep it to us two, if that's okay, Jake?"

"Sure."

"But I am worried about this bit." It's the first practical concern Davina has voiced. "I can check on her, of course I can, but I'm not sure how much time I will have each morning to react to what I might find. I won't be able to keep clients waiting if she needs help getting dressed or she's spilled food down herself and needs cleaning up."

"Then you'll need to call me," I offer. "I'm only in with Carina a couple of mornings a week, the rest of the time I can be more flexible than you can. I have more time to pick up some of the cleaning as well. I know we've agreed not to tidy her apartment, but some of it really does need cleaning. Does that all sound okay?"

"It sounds perfect. We have our jobs." Davina draws a sharp line under her notes and closes her book. "Shall we meet at my place Monday night, same time? We can see how it's going and add any more jobs we think are needed?"

"I'll be there," I say, gathering my things.

"Absolutely." Jake jumps off his stool just as Maggie lands in a heap at the bottom of the stairs, having attempted to slide down the banister. Davina looks surprisingly calm. She's seen this sort of stunt before, no doubt, but moves to gather Maggie up. I see Maggie's trying to keep the tears in, so I tell her it's fine to cry.

Suddenly, it's my waist her arms are looped around, not Davina's. Patting her on the head, I offer to get her a plaster while Davina gathers their things.

Jakes takes the two of us into a small utility room off the kitchen. There's no obvious sign of injury, he's just trying to make her feel better.

"Have you ever been to the fairy forest?" she asks me through a very wobbly bottom lip.

I smile, reminded that despite all the bluster she is still just a fun-loving eight-year-old, flitting between her imaginary world and the very sore bum she's going to have from negotiating the real one.

"There's no need to look like that," she says, offended. "I'm not talking about the stupid pretend ones you see on TV. I'm talking about the one right here, in Bath. If you're going on one of your dog walks tomorrow, I could come with you and show you it? Your boyfriend can come, too, if you like?" She nods toward Jake, her face full of hope.

"Oh, no, Jake's not my . . ." I watch as Maggie's face crumples in confusion while Jake's sparkles with amusement.

"He should be. You look nearly perfect together," she adds, "although he should be taller."

"Well, there's not much I can do about the height, I'm afraid. But I'm working on the other one, Maggie," Jake says, amused.

Mercifully, Davina has appeared in the doorway, registers the color of my cheeks and the delight on Maggie's face, and immediately understands it's time to get her home. Maggie repeats her invitation while Davina shrugs her shoulders as if to say it's up to me, if I can bear a couple of hours in Maggie's world.

"You can ask them anything. They love solving problems. If you leave them a note, they will answer you."

"Well, as we need all the help we can get, I'd say we have a date, Maggie. I'll pick you up at ten a.m."

I'm the last to leave, and as I approach the door, Jake stops me. "Would you like to stay for supper?" he asks. "There's enough for two. I prefer not to eat alone and, well, seeing as I'm your boy-friend now"—he chuckles—"it might be nice." Is the concept a massive joke to him? I feel instinctively he wouldn't be that cruel but I've no idea how to respond.

I waver on the doorstep, the seconds stretching between us, all my usual excuses readily springing to mind, then wonder why there isn't already a date booked into his diary tonight. The reasons to stay filter in too: I could spend a little more time getting to know this generous man, to show him I'm not as awkward as and hopefully more likable than he may think. But it is easier to say no, so that's what I do. "I better not. I've got an early start but thank you," I say before I head back upstairs, regretting my decision with every step I take. Jake will eat alone, and so will I.

SEVENTEEN

Meredith
1991

Meredith is late again, and people are starting to notice. It was another terrible night's sleep. William moved to the sofa in the lounge in the end, for her sake rather than his.

"It's the third time this week," Peter is moaning, encouraging one of the other seamstresses to do the same. "I'm not sure why she gets to roll in late when the rest of us are working all the hours we can."

William takes a deep, slow breath, keeping his head low, focused on the pink chiffon in front of him. He's not going to bite. It won't do any good. But he's tired and facing a mountain of work that will mean at least a twelve-hour day.

"Well, maybe I'll leave early tonight." Peter won't let it rest. "It can't be one rule for her and another for the rest of us. I'm not sure who she thinks she is."

William almost manages to ignore it but Peter mutters something else under his breath that he suspects is personal. It causes a nasty ripple of laughter that makes something in William snap.

"Why don't you just concentrate on what you've got to do,

Peter? Meredith's not holding you up, is she?" If Peter backs down, William will let it go. He's not looking to fall out with anyone. Just an end to the sniping will do. But Peter's pride gets the better of him. He won't be spoken down to in front of more junior members of the workroom.

"I'm not saying anything we're not all thinking. She's taking the piss and I'm not afraid to point that out. Ahh, here she is, nice of you to join us, Meredith."

Meredith's eyes are puffy. She ignores the comment and heads straight for her table, peeling off her coat and sitting down. Her back is to everyone, but William can see the jagged rise and fall of her shoulder blades as she tries to breathe her way through it.

"Must be lovely to flounce in whenever you fancy it."

"Leave it alone, Peter." William's voice is hard, a firm warning not to take it further, which is ignored.

"No explanation then? Sure, don't worry about us, we're only your colleagues. Why would we matter?" Peter is appealing for support from the others, but he is on his own now. Everyone else has more astutely felt the edge in the room and returned their focus to their work.

Meredith turns to face Peter and immediately William sees the upset held in her face, the tears swelling behind her eyelids. It's not like her. She's not easily rattled but it's the tiredness. She's not equipped to deal with the petty sniping this morning.

William forces his chair back from behind him, causing an abrasive scrape of metal against the hard floor, and raises his voice. "What is it, Peter? You've never forgiven her for pointing out how your work is lacking? Is that it? You're so unsure of your own ability that you have to try to undermine other people's? She's more talented than you'll ever be and everyone in this room knows it."

The comment hurts. Peter tries to laugh it off but can't. His smile is forced. He can't hold it for long enough to look genuine. And it has shocked Meredith, who immediately rises from her seat and heads back out the door she arrived through. William follows her.

"Oh, I see, it's like that, is it?" There is a lewd tone to Peter's voice that he's happy for everyone to hear.

William catches up with Meredith on the stairwell.

"Don't worry about that idiot," William tries to reassure her.

"I'm not, he's not important." Meredith is hesitantly smiling now. She takes William's hand and places it on the soft center of her belly. "But this is."

William falters, not sure if he understands her correctly. He says nothing.

"I did a test this morning, after you left."

"You're pregnant?" he whispers. His eyes flare wide open.

She waits for the smile to break across his face, but it isn't coming.

"I thought we were being careful." He immediately registers the hurt streaking across Meredith's face and understands this is not the reaction she needs. Before she can pull away he quickly stops her.

"Wait, I'm sorry, I didn't . . . It's just, this is a real shock. Did you have any idea?" He tries to gather himself.

Meredith looks down to her belly, where she is still holding William's hand.

"A feeling, nothing more until this morning. I'm sorry, I wasn't going to tell you until this evening, but Peter forced my hand a little. At least I know why my sleep has been so disturbed. We can talk more later." Meredith nods her head, trying to rally her emotions. She's never been one to cry at work.

"Okay." William runs both hands through his hair. The shock has made him pale.

"I know this wasn't part of the plan. Not something you saw in your future. But perhaps not everything that's great *can* be planned? Maybe this will prove to be the most wonderfully happy accident?" Does her voice sound convincing? She's not sure.

William pulls her toward him and rests his chin on the top of her head so she can't read his reaction, but she can feel the frantic beat of his heart.

"Let's talk more later. I need to get back to the dress. The Snowdon shoot is next week, and it can't wait."

EIGHTEEN

❧

Jayne

Maggie is waiting for me in the hall as I descend the stairs, dressed in a way that makes laughter bubble up inside me. Silver knee-high glitter wellies, despite the sun that's already blazing high in the sky; a multilayered strappy pink dress that is ruched on the body and then explodes into a frothy skirt that is so full it juts out from her tiny waist like a tutu; a pair of white wings that extend far beyond her shoulders so that she'll have to negotiate doorways sideways; a baseball cap with a bright blue letter *M* on its peak; and a pair of aviator-style mirrored sunglasses.

"You're going in *that*?" She lowers her head, allowing the sunglasses to slide down her nose, surveying my blue shorts, gray T-shirt, and Converse like I'm the one who's got it all wrong.

"I was planning to," I say, trying very hard to stifle a giggle.

"No wings?" She looks so disappointed in me.

"Awful as this sounds, Maggie, I don't own any." I offer a smile by way of apology for my pathetic lack of preparedness for this trip.

"Okay, well, that's odd, but why didn't you just say so? I've got loads of spares." She drops her unicorn-shaped backpack and disappears back into the apartment, ignoring my plea not to waste her time, I can do without.

Davina appears in the doorway.

"Don't let her boss you around too much," she says in a defeated tone that suggests that's exactly what Maggie has been doing to her since she opened her eyes this morning. "I've no idea what she's packed in that bag, but it weighs a ton and I fear you will be the one left carrying it. Which dog are you walking today? Shouldn't it be a day off?"

"I'm not. No one's booked."

"Oh, I thought you said last night that . . ." She trails off, understanding that the walk is for Maggie's benefit alone.

She drops her head to one side and sighs. "Jayne, you really didn't have to do that." She looks extra tired today, like she could do with the rest. "You know where this place is, don't you? Up near Claverton Down. It's the Family Discovery Trail through Long Wood. We usually drive up there but Maggie much prefers to walk through the woods and wildflower meadows."

"Yep, I know it, and as I'm going anyway, shall I take Margot too? Consider it a freebie."

"Are you sure? That really would be amazing, thank you. I can spend a bit of time just with Willow. She could really do with it. We both could, actually." I see the gratitude in her eyes, like this might be the first time all week, perhaps all month, that the two of them have a few hours that aren't dominated by Maggie's constant need to play.

Maggie returns with a not-subtle pair of white feathered wings and insists I put them on immediately.

"Shall I just carry them until we get to the forest?" I don't know why I bother to say it, she's never going to let me get away with it.

"Jayne . . ." I see she's about to launch into a lecture on show-ing the fairies the respect they deserve, so I quickly comply.

"Much better!" she shouts as I feed my arms through the far-too-small elasticated straps.

"Well, don't you two look like twins! You look amazing, Jayne," chuckles Davina, handing me Margot as we all head for the front door.

Maggie slips her hand into mine and looks up at me with such admiration that I can't respond. There is suddenly an enormous lump in the back of my throat.

"Right, we need to lower our voices from here on," instructs Mag-gie. "And get Margot back on the lead. If she pees on one of the fairy houses, I will never forgive her."

"Good point," I agree, slipping Margot a few treats by way of apology.

We pick our way through the towering trunks of the beech trees, Maggie tiptoeing now, the sun bouncing off her sparkly wellies as she dips in and out of the shadows. Margot and I enjoy-ing the relief from the sun's heat.

"We need door number five," she tells me as she ignores all the wooden play equipment, the rope swing, and even the seesaw. "This way."

The place is deserted, too early on a Sunday morning for ex-hausted parents to make it up here.

"Here we are." Maggie bends down at the base of one of the trees. "Look." There is a roughly cut wooden plaque attached low to the trunk, the number 5 and a beautiful dragonfly etched into it. A folded piece of paper has been wedged between it and the trunk and I can see the name *Maggie* is written on the front. "She's written back to me. I knew she would."

Maggie sits on the floor of the forest and pats the ground next to her, encouraging me to do the same, then she opens the note and reads aloud.

> *Dear Maggie,*
>
> *It sounds like your sister needs a hug. Please give her one from me and tell her the fairies are always watching over her. How lucky she is to have a little sister as special and kind as you are. And how is your mummy doing now? I will send someone magical to keep an eye on her and make sure she is happy.*
>
> *Write to me again soon,*
> *Trixie x*

Maggie starts to pull pens, pencils, glitter crayons, stickers, colored stamps, and sticky tape out of her bag. "I'm writing back to Trixie now because I don't know when Mummy will get time to bring me up here again. Why don't you choose a fairy to write to? Have a look at all the doors and see which one you like," she says. "Here." She tears a piece of paper from her pad and hands it to me with a bright red pen. "Don't forget to ask her something. Remember I said they love solving problems."

I leave her to her letter writing and wander through the dell with Margot at my heel. Every tree with a fairy door on it has a note stuck behind it and the kindness is so overwhelming. All these children, having their imaginary friends brought to life through the kindness of strangers they'll never meet.

My note is short and simple. *Am I doing the right thing?* I scrawl, before I wedge the paper behind door number 8. Then my thoughts wander to Jake, a veil of regret still hanging over my decision not to have dinner with him last night. Will he ever bother to ask me again? And if he does, and I actually pluck up the courage to say yes, won't it just end in tears?

By the time I have circled the trees and returned to Maggie, she is putting the finishing touches to a picture she has drawn on the back of the letter. It's of her, Willow, and Davina, all relaxing on a beach together eating ice creams, disproportionately large smiles on each of their faces.

"Can you fold it and put it behind the door for me, please?" asks Maggie. "I want to check the other doors all have their letters too."

"Okay, but don't go too far, only where I can see you."

I watch from a distance as she visits every tree trunk, satisfying herself that there won't be any disappointed customers today. My fingers hesitate on the letter in my hand. As I unfold it, I can see her uneven lettering, the giant capitals in the middles of words, the childish punctuation and spelling. I start to read.

> *Hello Trixie,*
>
>   *Thank U for helping my MuMMy and trying to take away her tears. I know she is very lonely and I do'nt want her to be. can you bring back the days when she used to laugh a lOt? and work less? when DaDDy was hear to make her Happy. I tell her U CAN sleep in my bed with me if U like and I will keep U warm and safe. Thank U for sending help! She is hear already and I like her <u>very</u> much. Shes a GIANT. Not like U at all!*

Lots and lots and lots of love
Maggie xxx

PS I hope U like the picture. I used my new pens. The red
one smells like straw berries. DO NOT lick it. I tried and it
is not nice.

When I drop Maggie back home, I kiss her sweaty forehead. She puts her arms around me and squeezes me with surprising force.

"When were you going to tell me?" she whispers.

I smile and think about all the sensible things I probably should say to her. But I like the invitation to be part of her little world. It seems simple and kind and completely without agenda.

"I'm popping back tomorrow night, Maggie, so I will pay close attention to how your mummy is then."

She nods and looks impressed. "It was very clever to pretend you don't have wings. That threw me right off the scent."

Then Davina opens the door, just as Maggie is tapping the end of her nose and winking at me.

"See you tomorrow," I say as I hand over a worn-out Margot.

NINETEEN

Davina is dropping dried biscuits into Margot's bowl, emptying some ready-made Marks & Spencer canapés onto a plate for us, and trying to scoop some ice cream out of a tub for Maggie. Lovely Carina has joined us in Davina's kitchen, and the two of them have spent the past fifteen minutes sharing floral contacts. Jake is yet to arrive and I worry that he's interpreted my decline of dinner as a sign that I don't need or want him involved in our plans when the complete opposite it true—I'm just struggling to let him know it.

"Okay, let's get down to business." Davina is in proactive mode, as usual. "Given the success you had at the Albert Hall last week, I think the greatest help we can offer Meredith is to continue that memory gathering, don't you? To help her rebuild her life story. I know it sounds ambitious and daunting, but have you given any more thought to taking her to some of the other dress locations, Jayne? Giving her the best possible chance to reconnect with those times in her life? To find William again, if only through her story-telling?"

Carina is nodding enthusiastically at Davina's suggestion.

"It's a great idea, but it would be a huge amount to organize," I say. "I'd have to reassign the dog walking . . ."

"Willow can help with that," offers Davina. "The school summer holidays are about to start and she's desperate to earn some money, aren't you?"

"I'd love to," Willow pipes up from her keyboard.

"Obviously I can't let Carina down either," I say, looking in her direction. "She's incredibly busy as it is." I feel Davina needs a reminder that Carina is still my boss and we can't assume she'll be happy for me to disappear, leaving a gaping hole in the staff rota.

"I know lots of great freelance event florists, Carina, they are always looking for extra shifts." I wonder if there has ever been a problem Davina couldn't solve.

"That's very kind of you, thank you. And to reassure you, Jayne, you can take as much time as you need. You know I am fully on board to help, and if that means a few days short-staffed or with someone new for a few hours, then it is a very small price to pay."

Maybe I don't look convinced enough, because she quickly adds, "And once you've revisited the London locations, maybe you can go to the others too? Northamptonshire, which is of course where Diana lived as a child at Althorp, such a magnificent country house. I went with a girlfriend one weekend when we fancied being tourists in our own country. We were there most of the day, it was so captivating. It has an incredible library and private art collection. And Sandringham, which I assume must mean the royal residence there? You know you can stay in the holiday cottages on the grounds, like you're an actual guest of the royal family? You should go, you'll have the best time."

Before I get a chance to thank Carina for filling in some of the missing blanks I have yet to research, Davina jumps back in, refocusing us on the to-do list.

"What about the other practicalities, like her food? You said there was very little in her apartment when you checked. We can easily organize a weekly supermarket delivery for her, but we don't know what she likes, if she has any food intolerances, and I hate to say it, but who will pay for it all? We know nothing about how she is managing her finances."

"Well, judging by the amount of milk she's getting through, I'd say she doesn't have a problem with dairy," I say, noticing that everyone's eyes have moved over my shoulder to the doorway behind me.

"I'll pay for it." Jake spills through the door. "I'm so sorry I'm late, everyone, just a few problems that I had to iron out at work. I hope I haven't missed much?" His smile bounces around the room and I watch as everyone mirrors it, even Willow, whose affections strike me as hard-won. I watch as Carina's eyes widen in appreciation and then move to me, checking if I am enjoying the view as much as everyone else is.

"No, no, come in, take a seat." Even Davina's speedy efficiency seems to mellow and slow in Jake's presence.

And I'm not sure why entirely but I'm irritated. He's late. But because he's made the over-the-top offer to pay Meredith's food bills, no one is going to mention it. Isn't it us, our time, and attention, that Meredith really needs? Not just someone to pick up the bills?

"Obviously I can get a lot of produce at cost price through the business but, well, that doesn't matter. I'm happy to cover anything she needs while we sort everything else out for her. Hello, trouble." He ruffles the top of Maggie's hair, slides a canapé between his lips, and allows his eyes to find me, as if he's asking my permission for this great act of generosity.

While I flounder, my mouth moving but no acceptance, unnecessary as it is, forthcoming, it is up to Davina, the master of being direct without ever sounding rude, to secure the offer.

"Wonderful, thank you, Jake, that beautifully solves that issue. Christ, we're on a roll!"

"You shouldn't say that!" chastises Maggie. "That's basically a swear."

"Yes, it is," says Jake, nodding with a smirk.

"Quite right, Maggie, darling. I can only apologize. But I for one feel incredibly optimistic about all this, don't you, Jayne?" It strikes me that Davina is one of those people who is at her very best when she is up against a challenge. She rises to it, motivating the rest of us, who might understandably shrink from it. But is it all a front? Is this the real Davina, all of her? Where is the one Maggie described so eloquently in her letter yesterday afternoon?

I look around the room at everyone, feeling for the first time since I arrived at my little apartment on Lansdown Crescent a growing sense of promise, and the power of this important common goal we all now share, our little community edging closer together to ease Meredith's problems and hopefully some of our own too. Even Olivia, helping at arm's length, hasn't entirely rejected what we are trying to do.

"Yes, I do." I'm so grateful that everyone has seen the value in what we are setting out to achieve together. "But there has been one small setback. Meredith mentioned that the GP called. She had just made herself some boiled eggs and soldiers for lunch, which she said the doctor seemed very impressed with. They had a lovely chat apparently, about the eighties back in London. She seemed very pleased with herself, so I suspect the call came at one of her more lucid moments. I can't see a medical task force swinging into action off the back of it, is what I'm saying."

"No matter," says Davina, who is not about to have the wind knocked out of her sails. "It was always a long shot, but how about this trip? Are you up for it, Jayne, if I can cover your dog walking commitments?"

If she can then there seems very little reason not to give it a go, with the exception of perhaps one thing. "I'm not quite sure Meredith can cope with all the travel. She was wiped out when we got back from London late on Friday."

"It's a good point," says Carina. "The last thing we want to do is make things worse for her."

"Maybe that is something I can help with," offers Jake. "You said a few of the locations are in London. I have a small place there and you'd be very welcome to use it. It would mean you wouldn't have to keep coming back and forth on the train every day. I use it as a crash pad when I'm there for meetings, it's nothing flashy—just a little mews house—but it's big enough for you both. I'd really like to do this for you, Jayne. And obviously for Meredith, too, of course," he quickly corrects himself. Jake looks at me hopefully, waiting for the smallest sign that I approve of the idea, that I appreciate the effort he is making.

"Or we could just stay in a hotel?" It's only once the words are out of my mouth that I realize how incredibly ungrateful they sound. "What I mean is . . ." Jake's ability to swoop in and cover the cost of everything is annoying me. I don't want my or Meredith's affections to be so easily bought. I look at the other faces in the room. I register my rudeness in the arch of Willow's eyebrows and the way Davina has folded her arms across her chest. Only Carina, whose head has dipped to hide her smirk, seems to understand what I am driving at. "It's very nice that you have that at your disposal, Jake, thank you but, well, it's not necessary."

I watch as Jake tries to slow the collapse of his smile and I know I have offended him. Of course, it's up to Davina to say something that will scorch the awkwardness I've created.

"I think we should ask Meredith for her opinion. Let's not allow this to be something that happens *to* her, that she has no control over or say in. Let's include her in the decision-making from the very beginning. This is *about* her and *for* her and in many ways needs to be led by her. Let's simply ask her where she would prefer to stay."

"I completely agree." Carina's smile is so broad, she is clearly not anticipating a rejection from Meredith to the idea of a mini adventure, staying at Jake's no doubt gorgeous mews house.

"Shall I knock on her door now and see if she would like to join us, to hear what we have to say?" I'd love an opportunity to leave the room and gather myself. "If you're all agreeing to help, then she needs to meet you properly and start to learn to trust you, doesn't she?"

"Exactly right," agrees Davina.

"I was just looking through some photographs in my memory room," announces Meredith as she opens the door to me.

"Would you like to show me?" I ask, adding, "It's Jayne from upstairs," in case she needs the reassurance.

"I found one of Fiona. My Fiona. Would you like to see that one?"

"I'd love to, Meredith."

The image, when she hands it to me, is immediately unsettling. Fiona's smile isn't genuine. I've forced a hard grin enough times to feel it instinctively. It's painted on, almost clown-like. A long way from real anyway, of that I'm sure, even if Meredith doesn't recognize it. She's cut off just below the shoulders, her hair scraped back into a tight, low ponytail, facing the camera straight on in a way that also seems overly posed. I turn the image over in my hands and see it's dated 15 July 2017 with a brief note in pencil: *I hope you are proud of me now?* How strange. When was Meredith not proud of her? The thought seems entirely at odds with the woman I am slowly getting to know. She certainly seems proud of Fiona now.

"This is lovely, Meredith. Thank you for sharing it with me. I came because some of the other residents are all together having some drinks and nibbles, and there is someone else I would like to introduce you to, if that's okay?"

Meredith nods, although I can tell her thoughts are still with the photograph, rather than my invitation. "Bring the picture with you if you'd like. I'm sure everyone would love to see Fiona too."

My arm is looped through Meredith's as I lead her into Davina's kitchen. Someone has had a quick tidy-up in the ten minutes I have been gone. With the exception of the remaining canapés, all the clutter has been swiped from the island surface, making the place look a lot calmer and more welcoming. Far from looking nervous or intimidated, Meredith is beaming from ear to ear, thrilled to be out of her apartment and among friendly faces. Davina extends an arm to shake her hand and makes all the necessary introductions, including to Carina, who dispenses with formalities and immediately asks after the photograph Meredith is still clutching.

"Oh, who is this?"

I see the hesitation in the flare of Meredith's eyes. She knows it's her turn to speak but the word, or the name in this case, one she remembered so easily just a few minutes ago, has escaped her.

"Jayne?" She looks toward me and there is such sweet sorrow in the fact that she can remember my name and not her daughter's.

"This is Meredith's daughter, Fiona." I aim my response directly at Carina. Now she knows the face she is searching for online.

Meredith turns it around so everyone can see it, her deep affection obvious.

"Oh, she looks happy," says Davina, understanding that's what the photo requires of Fiona. "Where was this taken, Meredith?"

"I wasn't there." The smile seems to cool on Meredith's lips until she is the exact opposite of Fiona's forced jollity.

The moment passes and we all take our seats again, Carina sneaking a quick snap of the Fiona picture after Meredith places it on the worktop.

I explain our plan while Meredith sits absorbed on the small green sofa at the end of the kitchen, taking it all in. It's the area of the room that Maggie has commandeered as her own. The sofa faces a TV that's mounted on the wall and there are shelves underneath it filled with all her art and craft materials, open jigsaw puzzle boxes, board games, and playing cards that have escaped from their packs. Maggie always seems to greedily fill the space, making it look inadequate for her needs. But Meredith looks tiny in it. Shrunken and losing the battle against the rogue clothing and toys that no doubt Maggie has ignored all requests to put away.

"It will probably take us a few days to make all the arrangements, but if you are in agreement, Meredith, I say we depart nice and early next Monday morning. And our first stop will be the Dorchester."

"I like the sound of it very much. I'll bring my essentials bag."

"You can bring anything you need," I reassure her. "So, do you like the idea of staying at Jake's house, just you and I, or would you prefer a hotel?"

She shakes her head. "I don't like hotels. They always make me feel so far from home. They're always so full of other people's memories, traces of the people who have passed before you. It's confusing."

"That's decided then." Clearly, for Davina, it was never in doubt. "Thank you, Jake, for making this possible."

He ignores her comment and looks straight at me. "I just want to make this as easy as possible for you. For both of you."

Maggie reappears, spies the abandoned canapés, and starts stuffing a selection into her pockets before she flops down on the sofa next to Meredith and introduces herself, spraying pastry crumbs everywhere.

"Have you eaten, Meredith?" Davina asks.

"Not yet. I'm waiting for William to get home," she answers with a smile. "We always try to eat together." I watch as Davina pauses, unsure whether to correct her or not, and then turns away, clearly moved by Meredith's inability to accept the facts in front of her.

We all know that William isn't coming home tonight, that she will sit alone for another evening, the same questions speeding through her mind, then relive the panic again tomorrow morning when she wakes and feels the untouched coolness of the sheet next to her.

"William protects me," she suddenly adds. "He's the legs and I'm the brains, that's what he says. My other half. One can't work without the other. I'm cooking a lovely stew for him."

The words tumble from her so casually, and she has no awareness of the ripple of concern they cause around the room.

Davina's head flicks urgently back toward me. Jake's settles into both his hands. Carina and I share the same sorrowful look. Only Maggie is immune.

"You know he never gets jealous of Diana and me?" Meredith's face lights up again, a sweeter memory filling her now.

"Sorry? What was that, Meredith?" Davina stops brushing crumbs from the island and walks around toward where Meredith is sitting.

"He's very proud of me. Isn't that lovely? I don't suppose all husbands would be. I'm lucky. Sometimes I have to put her first, before everything else. She always requests me." A flutter of pride crosses her face. "It makes her feel better, knowing I am waiting in the wings. And he has never once complained about it."

"What else can you tell us about Diana, Meredith? What exactly was—*is* it that you do for her?" Davina takes a seat next to her on the sofa, reaches for Meredith's hand, and draws her in a little closer.

"Whatever she needs. She's fascinated that I'm having a girl. She always has so many questions about how it feels and how my planning is going. She checks I'm eating the right things and looking after myself, despite the long hours. She is missing William."

There is a sharp moment of connection between everyone in the room that Meredith is blind to. *Missing William.* Diana's elder son, Prince William. Was Diana seeing a lot less of the princes than she would have liked to? Did she confide those feelings to Meredith? Has Meredith confused another woman's sadness for her own?

"But I can't talk about the rest, that would be such a betrayal of trust, wouldn't it?" She smiles at Davina, acknowledging the gentle way Davina has tried to extract valuable information that is not about to be freely shared. And Meredith's right, it would be valuable, just not in the way she thinks.

"Let's get you back then," I say, and take Meredith's hand and guide her up and off the sofa. But Maggie takes her other arm and holds her back, leaning into her to keep her weighted there. Now is not the time and all I can think about is the stew. How long has it been cooking? What temperature is the oven set to? Did she remember to peel the vegetables or take the meat out of its packaging? Has she even thought to put it in the oven?

Maggie whispers something in her ear that I just catch. "She's a real-life fairy, you know. She's going to help my mummy not be lonely anymore."

"Another angel on earth. Whoever is in distress can call on me. I will come running wherever they are." Maggie is absorbed by Meredith's words.

Davina hears them, too, and looks at Meredith quizzically as we say our goodbyes.

"I'll walk you back to your door if that's okay? I've got some more calls to make and need to get going myself." It is testament to how trusting Meredith has quickly become that she immediately drops my arm and loops hers through Jake's. We all say our goodbyes and I promise I'll see her again in the morning, although this is one visit I am honestly not looking forward to. Meredith may believe it to be as innocent as the others I have made, but this time, there will be a purpose to it that I'm not particularly proud of.

"What's the theory then?" Carina asks as soon as the door closes behind Meredith and Jake. "That she worked for Diana in some capacity? Managing her social diary or as a member of her private household?"

"No." My mind is racing back through all Meredith's previous references to William. Has she said anything that would point more to Diana's William and not her own? Not that I can recall. "I could be completely wrong, but I don't think so. Her strongest

memories center around the dresses themselves and not the occasions they were worn to. I think she and William were part of the
team who helped to make them, although I'm not sure what exactly their roles were. But the point, I think, is that Meredith has
to get there herself. I can't tell her what I think, she needs to remember it. If I simply share my theories, there's no reason for her
to hang on to any of it, is there? She has to relive it so it's more
meaningful. If I can prompt her to revisit those times, then it may
also lead her back to William, and to Fiona." Willow reappears in
search of leftovers and picks up the photograph Meredith has left
on the worktop.

"It's a shame she couldn't remember anything more about it."
Carina takes it from Willow and starts to study it again, but it's
such a tight crop, there is very little in the background to provide
a clue. "Because I have started the Facebook search, have a guess
how many women are called Fiona Chalis."

"Hundreds!" shouts Willow.

"Possibly thousands," adds Davina.

"Well, in theory the list is almost endless because there are a
surprisingly vast number of ways to spell both her names, complicated by the fact that some use a profile picture and some don't.
We knew this wouldn't be a quick search but, honestly, it could
take me months."

"It looks like a graduation photo to me." Willow casually
swipes a handful of canapés and heads for the sofa.

"What?" I step closer to Carina, both of us scouring the image now.

"Look at what she's wearing over a blazer. You can't see it
clearly, but it looks like a graduation stole, doesn't it? That would
be my guess."

Davina joins us for another look. Willow could be right. I didn't see it before, but there is fabric—blue and gold and what might be white fur edging—draped over Fiona's shoulders, but it's hard to be sure. I turn the image back over to reveal the date again: 15 July 2017.

"Well, that certainly places it in graduation season," adds Davina. "And the idea that she wants her parents to be proud of her fits with that idea. If Willow is right, we need to work out where she graduated from. We have her name and the date, so if we knew the university, then she should be very easy to contact from there. Well done, Willow, you clever thing!"

"Let me see if I can trace it," offers Carina. "We'll have to assume she studied in the UK, and if so, there must be a gown supplier who could identify it if Google fails us."

Everyone is ending the evening with a renewed sense of enthusiasm, everyone except me, and Davina can see it.

"Jayne? You don't look happy, what's wrong?"

"I'm worried about tomorrow."

"What's happening tomorrow, have I missed something?" She glances down at her notebook, knowing it's unlikely she has. I just haven't shared this with the group yet in case I change my mind and cancel the appointment. Now I have no choice.

"I'm taking Meredith to see her medical records at the doctor's surgery."

"Well, that's great news, isn't it?" asks Davina. "We could be really closing in on Fiona."

"I had to pretend to be Meredith on the phone to make the appointment. All they asked me to confirm was my address and that was it, booked. I got a slot quickly because we don't need to see a doctor. But Meredith knows nothing about it. I've no idea how she will react when we get there."

I wait for everyone to leave, deliberately hanging back to have a private word with Davina.

"Is everything okay, Davina? Are you okay?" I ask as she's throwing the last of the dirty dishes into the dishwasher.

"Absolutely fine, yes, all good, thank you." She says this as she's sweeping a hand across the work surface, collecting stray dirty cutlery and using her hip to push closed a drawer of pans.

"It's just that something Maggie said yesterday afternoon made me wonder if perhaps . . ."

She freezes, mid-tidy, and I watch her sigh, irritated. Her head cocks to the right, her hand wedges at her hip. I open my mouth to head off any offense I may have accidently caused but she cuts me off.

"Don't say it! I can see you're about to and I don't want to hear it."

"Sorry, I was just going to—"

"You've lived in this building for months now, Jayne, and done so much for me in that time—and do you know how many times I have been able to help you?" She looks right into me, not waiting for an answer. "None. Doesn't that feel just a little bit unfair to you? I can lean on you, but you can't lean on me?"

"I don't expect you to do anything for me, really I don't. I don't help you to get something in return." I'm really sad if this is what she believes.

"I know." Her tone softens again, the way it does when she is trying to take the sting out of a row with one of her girls. "And I know my workload means I'm not around much to be that helpful. But that's not how friendship works, is it? Is it because I pay you to walk Margot? Does that complicate things? Because I can always find another dog walker." It's not a threat, it's more of a concession. Finding another dog walker gives Davina another job to add to the hundreds she already juggles but I know she'll do it if it makes me feel more comfortable with her.

"I really don't want you to do that. Please don't."

"Then why is it so hard for you to accept help but you can give it out to anyone and everyone who needs it?" She looks genuinely confused by this.

"It's not hard for me, it's just—"

"In that case I don't want you to offer to walk Margot for free, to take Maggie off my hands for *another* afternoon. Don't clean my kitchen for me without even being asked to or paid for it. Not unless you are prepared to let me help you in return." She uses both hands to push her hair off her face, looking exasperated—by me. "Otherwise this isn't a friendship, is it? And I'd like it to be."

I stay silently rooted to the spot, then I try to excuse myself so I can leave, but now she's started, Davina isn't going to stop until she feels her point has been understood.

"What I need is a friend, Jayne. Maybe you do too. Have a glass of wine with me one night. I just want to spend an evening with an adult who isn't a client and not because there is something that needs doing."

"I'd love to." I feel the smile slowly blossoming across my face again.

"Great, because I'd love to listen to you." She leans forward on her elbows on the worktop, drawing me back closer to her. "I want to know why you are not responding to every effort Jake is making to impress you—we all saw how you reacted when he offered to cover the cost of Meredith's food bills and make his place in London available to you and, well, it doesn't make any sense. Not to me anyway." She shakes her head, her eyes searching mine. "I'd like to understand. I might surprise you, Jayne, and actually be able to help you work out why you won't let this amazing man get a little closer to you. There is something stopping you, isn't there?"

I can feel my entire body recoil from the suggestion. Davina takes a seat. She's not done yet.

"When you're not busy caring for everyone else, what is it that *you're* worrying about before you close your eyes at night?" She raises a hand. "And don't tell me it's Meredith."

I don't know where to begin with it all, so I stand there opening and closing my mouth, until finally she saves me.

"Do you know what they used to call Diana? Her nickname in some corners of the press?"

I shake my head, wondering where she is going with this.

"The Trust Fund Cinderella. She had the means not to do the relatively undemanding jobs that she drifted through when she was younger. But she was drawn to them because they were roles that allowed her to get close to people without ever having to reveal much, if anything, about herself. They never challenged her emotionally. Does that remind you of anyone?"

Suddenly that drink together sounds a lot less appealing.

TWENTY

꧁꧂

"Hello, Meredith, how are you this morning? It's Jayne from up-stairs," I chirp.

"Is it time to go to London? I'm not quite packed yet."

I'm relieved that she has remembered our plan from last night.

"Not quite, but I was thinking we could write down our itiner-ary this morning. Would you mind if I take another look in your memory room so I can be sure I'm getting it all right?"

She nods but doesn't move, so I lead the way.

Everything is exactly as it was the last time I was here. Com-pletely untouched, like a shrine to the missing, the departed, and the almost forgotten. How long might it be before none of this makes any sense to Meredith? I wonder when she will take her own place on the wall, one of the lost. Less of an observer, more one of the silent figures, her edges frayed, her stories incomplete. Fading to nothing.

My eyes travel over the photographs again, these snapshots of time that were once so strongly felt, that might now instantly con-jure an occasion, a person, a feeling, fully formed, as if it were being lived out in the present. Vividly documenting a life, a ro-mance, a family, a career, but also the mundane and the everyday. A favorite jumper. A freshly painted front door. Wind-lashed faces and silly poses. Another time, another life. Everything that has been lived and passed and cannot come again. Images she can hold in her hand and travel to again at a speed of her choosing. Perhaps now they float at the very outskirts of her memory, less defined, their colors no longer as sharp, their stories less reliable. Will there be a time soon when she can't name the man, or the little girl sitting on his lap smiling back at us? When these scenes live no deeper than the cork they are pressed into?

Fiona, the little girl, is very present in this room, preserved as the smiling ball of energy she once was, playing on a black keyboard, whizzing by on a bike, streamers trailing from its handlebars. The teenager slightly less so, the young woman barely. Fiona's story, with the exception of the graduation photo, seems to shear off abruptly. She was here—and now she's not. It all makes me wonder what might appear on my own wall in my own memory room. Would it show such happiness? Such a breadth of experience? A family? A life lived? The thought is uncomfortable, and suddenly it feels like I'm the one missing from my own life.

"Why such a large sigh?" asks Meredith.

"Oh, sorry, I wasn't aware I had." I'm so absorbed in Meredith's life that I'm not registering what's going on in my own.

"It's your third, in fact, since you got here. Why don't you have a seat and you can tell me what's on your mind?"

Normally I would run a mile, but today, in the company of someone so open to absorbing my problems, I yield easily, flopping down into one of the winged armchairs, ready to unload.

"How do I know if he's the right one for me? If I can trust him with my heart? I mean, when I've got it so wrong before, why would this time be any different?" I release the questions like they've been lodged painfully between my ribs for years.

"Well, okay, we're getting straight to it." Meredith laughs in a way that suggests she's summoning all her best life experience for this one. She settles into the seat beside mine, her eyes gliding across the walls surrounding us, pleased, I think, with the responsibility to provide an answer. She stays that way for a good few minutes, not uttering a word until I start to worry that she's forgotten what I asked her. Then finally she adds, "It's actually surprisingly simple when you really think about it."

"Can you explain it to me then? Because I'm not sure I want to keep spending every night on my own." I immediately wince at my insensitivity. Solitary evenings are a forced habit Meredith and I have in common.

"I think it's the wrong question to be asking yourself. I think it's more about how he makes you feel when you're with him. Is it easy? Is he thoughtful? Is he prepared to show you more of him, to encourage you to do the same?"

I think of the day I left Alex's apartment for the last time. How he never even rose from the chair to help carry the few boxes I had packed. How the awkwardness was eventually just too much to bear so he left, with hurried instructions to push the keys back through the letter box when I was done. None of this was done with my feelings in mind.

Meredith leans in a little closer to me.

"I think you owe it to yourself to let people show you the best of them, and a little of the worst." She nods. "No one is perfect, not even William, but he does things for me that he doesn't want to do. Big things. Things he said he never would. That's when you work out how you really feel, when the imperfections are in plain sight and you can really see them."

I think about Jake. The hand to my shoulder in the coffee shop to let me know I was his priority. The fact he was the first to sign up to help Meredith. His confession that he hates to eat alone and the offer to join him for supper but also the parties, the safety in numbers but the lack of closer friends, at least as far as I have seen. His suggestion that he could cover the cost of Meredith's groceries. The invitation to stay at his place in London. Yes, a lot of this comes with Meredith in mind, but they all make life easier for me too. Is that the point I've been missing?

"What are William's worst bits?"

Meredith takes a large breath, holding it inside her until she is ready to answer.

"He thinks he's protecting me, not leaving things to chance, trying to preempt everything. But if you tie everything up neatly, it's much harder for others to come along and surprise you or help you. It might be more difficult to undo than you imagine." She pauses, her eyes focusing on a shot of the two of them on the wall in front of us. William has a protective arm around her shoulders, the other draped across the front of her, so she is enveloped by him. "I wish he didn't have to try so hard. I wish I could stop that . . . I just don't know how," she whispers.

It's the thought of Jake that makes me wonder if I am asking myself and Meredith the wrong question. Perhaps it should be if it's ever right to willfully stop yourself from falling for someone, for no better reason than you can't predict the outcome or how much of a mess you may be at the end of it.

"More than anything"—Meredith clasps her hands together in her lap and tilts her head toward me—"you owe it to yourself not to live a lukewarm life. Where is the fun in that?" She smirks in a way that suggests fun is one thing not lacking from her story. "Feel the intense heat of great passion, let it burn you up inside. Let it rage a little out of control. But be prepared to welcome in the searing, icy cut of rejection too. Only once you have experienced the bitter sense of drowning in your own disappointment can you start to soar again, only this time with the glorious knowledge of what you are aiming for."

I think she can see the shock on my face, because she adds, "And so what if you get it wrong? We all do at some point. Does it really matter? What's a little heartbreak in the search for your one great love? No one loves a know-it-all anyway." Then she chuckles at her own surprisingly brutal conclusion.

It's the kick I need. That a woman in Meredith's position, in a brilliant moment of clarity, can still endorse the pursuit of *great passion* is so inspiring. If she can, then why not me?

I check the time on my phone. We need to get going. I make a note of the four locations we will visit together in London and the order in which we will do them: The Dorchester Hotel on Park Lane. The Odeon cinema in Leicester Square. Launceston Place in Kensington. And finally Spencer House in St. James's. Northamptonshire and Sandringham may come later. For now, if I plan for us to stay two nights, I think that will be long enough. I don't want to take Meredith away from home any longer than necessary, especially when there is every chance that her time at home is already running out. The clock is ticking, loud enough that I fear even she can sense it through the fog.

I realize she's not going to be able to cope in London without her memory room. I can't pack it up and take it with us, that would be too great a job and too unsettling, she may never get it back in the order she has it in now. I pull out my phone and, with her permission, take a short film scanning around the room.

That's when I see the photograph she told me about the day we took our first walk together, the one she later denied any knowledge of.

"What's this?" I prompt her.

She lets her eyes take in every detail of the image before she responds. "It arrives already framed and carefully wrapped in navy blue paper, tied with a silk bow. She's signed it, too, see."

I lean in toward the image and she is right. In the bottom left-hand corner is a neat signature, the name instantly recognizable. It's dated May 1997. Diana is seated on the floor, wearing a black suit jacket, her lower half hidden under a huge swath of buttermilk satin. I think it might be the dress we saw at the Fashion Museum. Next to her on the floor is a dark-haired woman I now know is Catherine Walker, also wearing black. Behind them are twelve others, identical in pristine collared white coats that button down the front and fall to midcalf—eleven women and one solitary man.

"William." She confirms. "And wonderful Catherine, also gone." Her right hand settles on her heart.

"Can you remember anything else about it, Meredith? Why you were there?"

"There are so many nationalities among our little team," she giggles. "It's like a meeting of the United Nations, someone says. Brazil, Jamaica, Thailand, Portugal, Germany, Italy. Somehow, we all make sense," she says wistfully. "The very happiest of days." She nods slowly. I see the remembered joy in the faint sparkle in her eyes, the unrushed way she is reconnecting with the younger woman she sees before her, the one with the luxury of not knowing what was to come. "There are terrible nerves, but everyone feels so proud. And all those beautiful dresses. Sixteen years' worth worn to meet emperors and kings, gowns that floated along red carpets and to private dinners, tours, and galas, some much more difficult than others. And a chance to say goodbye to them all before they are off to America." She trails off again and a blank detachment glazes over her eyes. "You will bring the flask and egg sandwiches, won't you?"

"To London? Of course I will, if you'd like me to. But there is somewhere else I would like to take you this morning. Do you fancy a little walk into town in the sunshine, Meredith?"

She nods enthusiastically, which only makes me feel worse for the deception I am allowing to unfold.

It's such a nondescript building. Probably built in the sixties, it looks bland and functional but tired. White paint is peeling from the window frames. I can see last winter's leaves still stuffed in the roof guttering. Meredith and I pause on the steps outside. I watch as the flicker of recognition crosses her face—she knows this building—then her annoyance. Does she already understand that I've ignored her wishes?

I am rigid with nerves. Torn by the deception it took to get her here and our need to move her story forward—to do everything we can to trace Fiona.

"Why are we here?" Meredith's words sound cold and uncompromising. She is staring directly at me and I can't bring myself to look back. "I don't want to be here."

"I thought it might help," I offer weakly. I turn to face her. "Inside this building are all your medical records, possibly right back to when you were a child. I thought you might like to take a look."

"Help with what?" She's not smiling and there is a skeptical edge to her voice.

"Your memory. I hoped it might trigger some thoughts that you may not have had for a long time, that maybe it would help to—"

"I said no." She cuts me off, her voice quiet but firm before the volume builds.

"William doesn't want me here. I want to leave. What right do you have to . . . ?" Her own outrage prevents her from finishing the sentence.

"Yes, of course, I'm sorry, Meredith, we'll leave right away." I try my best to ease the panic she's feeling before it escalates further, but then she gathers herself. Her annoyance replaced by something far worse. Disappointment.

"I thought we were friends. Why would you do this? I don't understand why I'm here—and why *you* need to be here. What is it you want from me?" She's questioning my motives, how kind I might really be. Whether she feels safe with me or not.

Only now do I privately acknowledge what I could have intruded on, if my plan to get her inside had succeeded. Prescribed medications, surgeries, known allergies, her entire family medical history. Everything that is intrinsically personal to her. Information that should only ever be seen by those absolutely closest to her.

With every word she utters, I regret my decision to come and trample on this woman's privacy like it doesn't matter, like the end result justifies the means—and it doesn't.

"I'm so sorry." Far too late I acknowledge this invasion of her private life. I take a step backward, conveying my agreement that we should leave. "I thought today might help us, maybe throw up some clues as to where William or Fiona might be. That's all."

"She'll be playing the piano"—she sighs—"that's what she's always doing, I can almost guarantee it. You could have just asked me that."

"Can I take you home please, Meredith? Let's go and put the kettle on. We'll grab some of those custard creams you love on the way back."

"Marvelous!" She is happy again. "We can chat some more about your love life and I'll show you a picture of my wedding dress!" She winks at me and starts to laugh to herself in the same way I've heard Maggie do when she thinks she's being hilarious.

I'm touched that she's remembered our earlier conversation, but more than that, I love the look on her face, the invitation to an afternoon filled with gossip, hot tea, and favorite biscuits. What could possibly be better—for both of us.

TWENTY-ONE

I'm sitting on the sofa, wondering if I can possibly summon the courage to knock on Jake's door and ask if he fancies an early-evening walk or a glass of wine together in the back garden, when the WhatsApp group comes alive.

DAVINA: Problem.

JAYNE: Oh no, what? Did you forget you're on dinner duty?

DAVINA: No. I dropped it off to Meredith, as arranged. Some lovely roast chicken with all the trimmings. She looked delighted, she said she was starving.

JAYNE: OK, then what?

DAVINA: I just went back to collect my dish and it was still sitting on the side in the kitchen where I left it, untouched.

JAYNE: Do you think she needed help warming it up?

DAVINA: No, I delivered it warm and ready to eat.

JAYNE: So, why hasn't she eaten it? Was she able to say?

DAVINA: She told me she couldn't find a plate. I found some eventually, all stacked in the airing cupboard in the hallway, next to the pillowcases and towels, and more milk bottles. Honestly, Jayne, it was heartbreaking.

I slump farther into the sofa, feeling the enormity of the task ahead of us. Olivia is right, none of us is qualified for this. What if we are merely prolonging Meredith's agony or giving her false hopes?

DAVINA: Don't get disheartened, we've only just started.

OLIVIA: Maybe you could label the kitchen cupboards so she can see at a glance what's inside?

JAYNE: That could work. But we are giving her lots of extra things to read already. Will she remember to do that?

OLIVIA: We went one step further with Mum and took all the doors off her kitchen cupboards in the end. It saved her so much time each day, not having to root through every one of them until she found what she was looking for. It was all on display for her to see.

JAKE: That's a great idea. I can arrange for someone to come and do that, and we can store all the doors downstairs in the laundry room.

OLIVIA: While you're at it, you may need to look at the color of her crockery as you start to understand her food preferences.

JAYNE: Why? What difference does that make?

OLIVIA: Mum found it very difficult to distinguish certain foods if
they were on a similar-colored plate. You couldn't serve her
chicken or mashed potatoes on a white plate. The plate would
just look empty.

JAYNE: Okay, let's add that to the list too. Thank you, everyone.

Then Davina messages me privately, out of the group chat.

DAVINA: Fancy that glass of wine now? I could really do with it.

The second I start to descend the stairs toward Davina's ground-
floor apartment, I can hear them arguing. Davina and Willow,
driving the volume higher and higher with every insult they hurl
at each other, doors repeatedly slamming inside their apartment.
I try to turn and retreat back to my own front door, but Davina's
door flies open, and a teary Willow spills out screaming, "I hate
you!" as loud as her lungs will allow. I consider trying to stop her
but then I see Davina in the doorway and realize she's the one
who needs my help. This row must have been brewing while we
were all messaging one another.

Maggie is challenging herself with a five hundred–piece jigsaw
puzzle upstairs and I ask Davina not to tell her I'm here, so we
might stand some chance of a proper chat.

"What was it this time? Too much homework? Not enough
pocket money?" I hazard a guess at the cause of tonight's friction.

"If only. A much harder one to solve, unfortunately. Not enough
of me." Davina is already emptying most of a bottle of white wine

into two large glasses. "The tricky thing is never knowing quite how honest to be with my children. Do I lay it out for her—if I don't work, you don't get that laptop—or should I be protecting her from the worry of single-parent finances? I just don't know, Jayne."

"Does any parent?"

"Probably not, but I do know it would be a damn sight easier to negotiate if I was sharing the load. If her father were playing his part as I always imagined he would be."

We each take one of the stools.

"How do I explain to a fourteen-year-old that I just . . . need some understanding, some appreciation for the things I *am* getting right, while I work harder at the things I'm not. I know this is difficult for her, but can I burden her with the fact that it's difficult for me too?"

"I think you're doing a great job, Davina. She's a teenager. You'd be arguing regardless, wouldn't you? Even if there were ten of you here to share the load." I'm aware I have no direct experience with raising teenagers, but I do remember how fierce the rows could get between Mum and Sally.

"Maybe." She takes a long, indulgent mouthful of wine and I watch the almost instant effect it has on her.

"Honestly, it's the loneliness that kills me. It's partly why I work as hard as I do. When I'm busy, there's less time to dwell on it." She lets out a sad laugh. "I'm so absorbed by the never-ending list of jobs, I can forget that I'm in this on my own."

"Oh, Davina . . ."

"I know it will get better." She waves a hand across her face, not wanting to wallow in self-pity. "One day they'll be grown up and then I'll be forced to make the changes there aren't time for now." She considers expanding on her point, then I see her change her mind and her focus switches back to me. "But what about you, Jayne? What's your excuse?"

"My excuse for what?" I feel like I am massively missing the point.

"You spend more time alone than I do. You don't have children to absorb every spare moment of the day and every last drop of your mental energy, every beat of your heart. Unless I am wrong, there's no partner on the scene. Why is that? What's your story?"

She is so direct, but it's done with kindness too. I understand that she wants to get to know me better. She's not looking for gossip or secrets to trade with neighbors or colleagues.

"That's a big question." One I'm not sure I want to fully answer.

"Is it? Only if you think of it that way." She casually shrugs her shoulders.

I try to give her the top line only, my usual approach, except this time I include Alex.

"I get it. You don't want to be alone forever, but if you were one of my daughters, I'd tell you to run a mile from this Alex. Maybe he's not a bad man but he sounds like the wrong man for you." Another large gulp of wine disappears.

"Thank you! And, yes, I know that now." I love that Davina seems able to understand something my own mum can't—or won't.

"But, Jayne, too much solitude will unravel you eventually. We're not made to be alone too long, no matter how comfortable you are in your own company. Too much of it makes you vulnerable—too much space to pick yourself apart and you end up overanalyzing life rather than living it. My goodness, if I didn't have the girls there's a very long list of things I would beat myself up about night after night. My health, my level of success, where my time is being spent, what my future will look like . . . Can you see how this amount of self-examination is never going to be helpful?" she says ruefully.

"So how do you decide what to say yes to, when to take the risk, and when to allow yourself the kindness of not facing it? I like helping others, but, as you've already said, it's so much harder to let them help me."

Davina thinks for a minute, slowly nodding her head.

"I can see that's exactly what you are doing, and the thing is you're very good at it, Jayne, it's your natural state of being. But you can't be what everyone else needs you to be all the time— believe me, I've tried and it's impossible. You will eventually crack. Maybe you're starting to already. Why not just agree you're going to be ten percent braver, say yes to something you may have said no to before. It can be as simple as that to start with."

"Well, it sounds simple, yes, but . . ." I don't want to reel off lots of excuses why I can't do it, so I delve a little deeper into Davina's backstory instead. "What happened with you, when you were trying to be what everyone else needed?"

"Oh, Jayne, I used to love the hustle." Davina smiles deeply as she transports herself back to a time when there was no husband or, hard as it is to imagine, Maggie and Willow in her life. "The feeling of cracking through this life on my wits and my ability to shake every opportunity out of every day. I had such focus and drive, I achieved so much with the time I had. It was the last time I felt genuinely impressive. It's what got me up in the morning." I register the faintest quiver of her bottom lip. "But then I had the girls, and after Jonathan left, all that got very diluted. I couldn't compromise on the children, so I compromised on me, while he moved out and on to a place where he could always put himself first. Imagine the luxury of that!"

I'm not sure I've ever imagined it, actually.

"But what you've just described looks exactly like what you do now, Davina." I also allow the cold crisp wine to mellow me, to embolden my counterargument. "Every day you solve problems, for clients, for your children, and now for Meredith. You're not exactly underachieving, are you? Every time I see you, I think you're impressive." I raise my voice, trying to convey how ludicrous the suggestion she is anything less than brilliant really is. "You've simply transferred your skills. You apply them differently to the life you now live."

Davina looks at me, slowly raises her eyebrows like this is the first time the idea has even occurred to her.

"I'm not sure why, now I think about it, but Jonathan was always the hero in my story. I seemed to give him all the credit for the good things that happened in the course of a week. I awarded him that status. Perhaps it was simply because we had been together so long, he felt so solid back then, or because he had an amazing ability to make Willow laugh at herself, which, as you've seen tonight, doesn't always come naturally to me." Davina allows herself another large gulp of wine, then follows it with a second. "And Maggie adores him. On Friday nights, when we would let her stay up a little later, she would glue herself to him on the sofa and I would become invisible. When she eventually nodded off, he'd carry her up to bed, stay if she stirred." She smiles at the memory, there is no bitterness in recalling it. "There's rarely time for that level of indulgence these days and I think they miss it. I hope they know I miss it too."

"By the time my sister was fourteen, she was sneaking out of the house at night, meeting up with friends, and scaring the living daylights out of Mum. She was so bored at school—an affliction of the very clever—that most weeks Mum was sitting in front of one teacher or another trying to explain why Sally was so disruptive. Willow isn't doing any of those things, is she?" I'm determined to make Davina see all the good she is doing. How it could be a lot worse.

"No, that's true."

"I've seen the way you are with them both and I think you're a wonderful mum." I don't elaborate, I want her to feel the weight of these words.

Davina's eyes mist a little. We both know it's a compliment she would never pay herself.

"Thank you, Jayne. That means a lot. I know you wouldn't say it unless you meant it."

"No, I wouldn't. Give yourself more credit, I reckon. There are plenty of things you have to say no to, right? And they won't like it but maybe they're not supposed to. Imagine what they would be like if you said yes to everything, if they always got their own way."

We both laugh then.

"Can you even imagine?" howls Davina.

"Maggie would live her life in sequins. Willow would quit school and start her own business. I bet it would be a massive success too." I have so much admiration for both of Davina's girls, tackling life in their own unique ways.

We clink glasses and Davina refills us both.

"Okay, here's to the end of false modesty then," she says. "Recognizing my own strengths and running with them, just as I'm encouraging my girls to."

I can see the wine has fortified her somewhat, but it feels so good to hear Davina say this out loud tonight. I really hope it will mark a turning point.

"You're staying for dinner, right? Willow will flounce back in here in about twenty minutes and she'll be a lot nicer to me if we have company. Plus, I'd love to chat some more."

"I'd love to stay, thank you."

The next thing I know, Maggie has crept up behind me. Without warning she karate-chops her hands on either side of my waist and shouts, "Boo," which sends half my glass of wine across the work surface.

"Got you!" she yells. "Get me back later. Shave my eyebrows off while I'm asleep!"

The three of us collapse into laughter, then Willow is at the door laughing along, too, despite her best efforts not to, and I feel nothing but total gratitude to share in their messy, all-consuming familial ups and downs.

While the girls are laying the table for dinner and I'm filling a water jug, Davina places an arm around my shoulders and hugs me.

"Since you're so good at giving advice, will you take some too?" She smiles and I know what's coming.

"Give Jake a chance." She says it quickly, before I can cut her off. "It's obvious to everyone that's what he's hoping for. Whatever has gone on before with you, Jayne, he's not responsible for it. He's not Alex. He wants to get to know you and I guarantee he won't be disappointed with what he discovers."

TWENTY-TWO

❧

We're all back in Jake's kitchen, eating bread of course—this time a walnut-fig-and-date loaf. It's our last chance to get together before Meredith and I head off after the weekend.

"I'm pleased to report Meredith never nicked my milk this morning, so that's progress!" Everyone laughs at Davina's bluntness, then we get busy tearing into the bread, smothering the slices in a thick coating of butter and, on Jake's suggestion, fresh lemon curd.

"Just trust me on this, it works." He's right, of course.

"She was watching that movie again this morning. The one that's always blaring." Davina fumbles for the title. "You know, it has Dolly Parton in it?"

"*Steel Magnolias*!" shouts Carina.

"That's it!"

"Blimey, that's got to be nearly thirty years old." Carina laughs. "Maybe we need to add a Netflix subscription to the list of things Meredith needs? Although I understand the appeal. All those brilliant women helping one another in their own special ways. And the love story with Shelby and Jackson. *I would rather have thirty minutes of wonderful than a lifetime of nothing special.*" Carina has gone very uncharacteristically breathy.

While they're critiquing the script, I think for a minute. "One of our locations is the cinema in Leicester Square. Can someone google the movie? I wonder if it was shown there while Meredith was living in London. Maybe the dates overlap?"

Carina taps the details into her phone, and we all wait for the answers to load.

"Well, it wasn't just shown there, it premiered there. And it looks like Diana attended that night." Carina flicks her phone around so we can see all the images.

"That's the dress," I confirm. "The one that Diana is wearing, it's one of the sketches hanging in Meredith's memory room. It's very distinctive. Can I can take a closer look?"

I scroll through the images, looking for Meredith. Was she there too? Might William be with her? Is there any detail that I can use to prompt her? But all the shots are focused tightly on Diana and just one or two other official-looking types who are leading her along the red carpet. I keep going, loading several more pages, but there is nothing.

"What exactly are you looking for, Jayne?" asks Davina.

"I just wondered if Meredith might have been visible somewhere in the shots too. But she's not. Too much to hope for, I suppose."

"That's a shame, it would be brilliant if we could show Meredith herself, back at the time that seems to be so evocative to her," says Carina.

"Hang on, look at this." I pause over an image of Diana, stopped on the red carpet in front of a bank of photographers, the overhead lights reflected back into hundreds of lenses creating a backdrop of perfect bright white circles. I point to a small black object that has swung into the shot. It shouldn't be there. Everyone leans in for a closer look.

"What is that?" asks Davina.

"I know exactly what it is," I say, beaming. "It's Meredith's essentials bag. She brought it with us on the first trip to London and insists it has to come with us on Monday too."

"I'd love to know what's in it," says Davina.

"I have a reasonable idea," I add, "but I'm waiting for the right moment for Meredith to open it. I don't think she will until she feels she needs to. Maybe I should watch this film before we go? It might help if I can reference it to Meredith in some way."

"That's a great idea. So, besides the movie, are you all set for Monday, Jayne? Is there anything else we can do to help at this stage?" Davina asks.

"I don't think so. All the dog walks are scheduled. Willow is going to earn a nice chunk of money while I'm gone. Carina is covered and the itinerary is in place."

"You know how to get to Park Garden Mews?" asks Jake. He moves around the kitchen island, placing himself right next to me. "I'd be happy to take you and Meredith if that's easier? I mean, I could get away from work, if you need me to." He's lowered his head, fidgeting nervously. A quick glance at the others shows that Davina's eyebrows have shot skyward, and Carina is nodding furiously. I ignore the pair of them.

"Yes, it's an easy walk from Paddington station, isn't it? So we'll probably do that if it's not raining." I can feel the disappointment radiate across the room from Davina, it must be taking all her willpower not to shout at me.

"Absolutely." Jake's voice is louder again, and he takes a step back from me. "I just wanted to check you are comfortable with the arrangements, that's all."

"Thank you." I step toward him, closing the gap again. "I know you do, and I really appreciate it. It's very kind of you." It's the first time I wish I was alone with Jake. I want to take his hand. I want to let my eyes linger on his face far longer than I can in front of an audience, to let him know that I see everything he's doing and I hope he can see how it is pulling me toward him.

"I've sent you the security codes and a few pointers on how things work but call me anytime if you need to. You've got my number?"

I try to ignore the very loud exhale of breath from Davina and keep my focus firmly on Jake. "Yes, thank you." Maybe her unsubtle commentary is actually having the desired effect. I can feel myself wanting to let go of my inhibitions.

Our meeting wraps up rather quickly after that. Jake waits until everyone has left the coach house before he stops me.

"Jayne, do you have any other plans tonight? I thought I could give you that bread-making lesson we talked about. Only if you'd like to, of course?"

I hesitate, giving him the opportunity to add shyly, "And at the risk of sounding unmanly, I don't really fancy being on my own tonight. I'd prefer some company. Your company, I mean."

I'm surprised that someone as outwardly confident as Jake would say this. It makes me drop my defenses a little. Perhaps there are greater depths to Jake than he's been willing to show any of us so far. And I know it's daft, but I want to impress Davina. I want to be able to show her I don't just dish out advice and not take it from others, so I nod.

"What are we making?"

He immediately starts moving around the kitchen, pulling out a wide metal bowl and a brown paper bag of flour.

"Let's start you off with a basic recipe."

"Sounds easy enough. Why does this excite you so much?" I laugh.

"It's the ease of it." He casually throws flour into the bowl, unbothered by how much of it is cascading down the front of him. "Four ingredients, that's all it is. Flour, water, yeast, and salt. It's so simple. But if you treat it right, you get something at the end that gives such pleasure. It brings people together. It helps them enjoy each other. That is the miracle of bread, Jayne!"

Everything he does is instinctive, he doesn't pause to measure anything, he feels his way through it, holding the bowl in place with his left hand, using his right to dig into the mixture and combine the ingredients together. He never picks up a utensil.

"Pinch it, it shouldn't feel wet or sticky." He tilts the bowl toward me.

"Perfect." I'm not sure what else I'm expected to say.

When he's happy that I'm happy with it, he turns the dough out onto the wood and begins to fold it in on itself, pinching the sides inward.

"You try." The fact he trusts me with his precious dough feels like quite an honor.

While I'm doing my best to mimic his movements, he grabs a metal loaf tin from one of the low drawers and lightly greases it with his fingers. Then he takes the round of dough from me and cups it, balling it, smoothing its sides, holding it like you might a baby's head.

"Perfect. Now it just needs to proof. We can check it in a couple of hours, but it will need overnight for a really crisp crust that's tender inside. What shall we do in the meantime?"

It feels like an incredibly loaded question. What is he imagining we might do?

Jake and I are very different people, it seems unlikely he has thought of us beyond the safe borders of friendly neighbors, even if I have. But he edges closer to me and his smile softens. I've rejected him once before and he's trying again. Davina's comments are ringing loudly on my ears. Should I stay? The evening has been lovely, I can leave now, and it will remain that way.

I smile despite the nerves. I know that if I stay any longer, it's going to get personal. We won't have the distraction of the bread making, which means there will be no alternative but to really talk. As keen as I am to get to know Jake better—and there are so many unanswered questions surrounding him—I'm not sure I'm ready for this. I'm not sure I want to be on the receiving end of all his questions. He's a neighbor, and when it all goes wrong and gets awkward, there will be no avoiding him. This already feels like too much. I'm alone in his apartment with him. I'm about to go and stay at his house in London. Where is he imagining this is all leading?

"We could watch *Steel Magnolias*?" He laughs. "There can't be many men who have used that as a tactic to get a woman they like to stay a little longer. Help me, Jayne, this is getting embarrassing and I've got nowhere else to go now I've offered you that!"

Now I'm laughing.

"You're prepared to sit through that movie with me?" I raise my eyebrows at him.

"Yes, I am. And you shouldn't assume I won't love it every bit as much as you might." I love the way he can laugh at himself. To feel ridiculous and just go with it, knowing that he may just get what he wants on the other side of a little discomfort. I'm not going to think about the fact he also just said he likes me. He likes everyone. He doesn't know me. Only what I have chosen to show him so far, which is practically nothing.

"Let's see about that, shall we? I'll stay, but I need to be home by midnight, or I'll be useless tomorrow."

"All right, Cinderella, follow me."

We climb the stairs to the upper level, another large open-plan living space that is divided in two by a central stone archway. The ceilings are sloping up here, some brick walls are exposed, others painted a deep green that immediately reminds me of English hedgerows. It feels cozy and relaxed as opposed to the symmetrical elegance and formality of the rooms in the main house. It feels very Jake. We walk through his bedroom, my eyes disobeying me, lingering on his bed. It's huge, low to the floor, perfectly made with all white linen, chunky gray woolen blankets, a stack of books on the side I assume he sleeps on. A freestanding circular slate-colored tub is placed directly in front of a double-height sash window. A dull brass showerhead that must be a foot wide is suspended above it from the ceiling and it takes all my will to stop myself visualizing him in there every morning. I know tomorrow, when I am less under his gaze, I will imagine what I might look like sunken into that tub.

As we move into the sitting room, visible from Jake's bed, I smile as I see I called it right. A deep blue velvet sofa runs almost the entire width of the room, big enough for two people to comfortably sleep on. The wall facing the sofa is given entirely to bookshelves, the TV attached to the front of them. I see him then on Sunday afternoons, lying here, a coffee in front of him, scattered newspapers, probably a cookbook, dozing, looking every bit as beautiful as the surroundings.

"What would you like to drink?" Jake asks. "A glass of wine? There's some champagne if you prefer, or gin and tonic, beer? I have pretty much everything."

"A glass of white would be lovely, thank you."

He disappears back downstairs to grab it while I grapple with an overly complicated TV remote, give up, and then wonder where I should sit, grateful that any spot means my back will be to his bed. I decide on one end of the sofa—it's big enough for eight people, so we won't be on top of each other.

Jake returns, hands me the glass of wine and a small bowl of pretzels, then sits so close that our legs are touching. I use the act of placing my glass on the low wooden coffee table in front of us to create some space.

"Okay, Meredith, this better be good," he says as the opening credits start to roll and he stretches his legs out, placing them on the table—a level of relaxed I know I won't achieve before I leave tonight.

We go deep into the world of women: extravagant hairdos, irritating men, disappointing husbands, babies, weddings, mothers and daughters, lots of cooking and fussing and gossiping. I almost forget where I am, I'm enjoying it so much. It's the devoted kindness that sits behind everything the women do for one another that sucks me in. Halfway through, while Jake is refilling the pretzel bowl, I text Mum and Sally and arrange to grab a quick lunch with them both one day next week. Jake laughs genuinely in all the right places and especially loudly when Dolly Parton announces, *"When it comes to suffering, she is right up there with Elizabeth Taylor."*

But the ending is crushing. I try so hard to keep the tears in, but I just can't do it. How I wish I was watching this movie alone at home so I could sob loudly and allow the tears to pour out of me unguarded. The effort of keeping them in produces a loud sob from deep inside me that I'm not capable of disguising as a cough. I shuffle forward on the sofa, ready to make my escape. Jake can't ignore it.

"Jayne, anyone who didn't cry at this movie would be subhuman. I'm not far off myself. Come here." He gently pulls me toward him, wraps me up in his arms, my head on his chest. Then I feel his lips on my hair as he kisses the top of my head, and I don't know what it means.

"Oh, I'm ridiculous. Sorry, Jake," I mumble, pulling away from him. I wish I was one of those women who could genuinely laugh this off.

"Don't be." He's completely comfortable with a woman sobbing all over his sofa, but one look at my face tells him I'm a lot less at ease with it.

"Listen, Jayne," he says, his face now more serious. "I don't know your story. But I would like to. And I'm here if you would ever like to share it with me." He's shifted back a little on the sofa, giving me some space.

I say nothing. I want to answer him. But too much practice at saying nothing prevents me. Talking means I'm explaining myself and I'm afraid of what may come pouring out once I start. How unrecognizable it will be from Jake's own experience of the world. But the way his face is searching mine, the way he has created a respectful distance between us but continues to lean toward me indicating he's ready to hear whatever I have to say, has me teetering on the very edge of revealing everything to this man I barely know.

I want to let him in. I want to show him exactly who I am, but I've been here before with Alex. It's all wonderful, until it's not.

My silence and hesitance must be written on my face, because after a pause, Jake softly says, "You have so few expectations, Jayne. You never enter a room determined to leave with something—anything—do you? My God, that's so rare, do you even know that? It's so honest and uncomplicated, and I like that about you. I like *you*. I just wish you would show me more."

I open my mouth to respond but my breath is so ragged. Not

from the emotion of the film anymore but because of him, every-thing he's saying. I hadn't dared to imagine he might actually . . .

"I know the idea frightens you. I can see that. And to be honest . . . I'm nervous too." He gives a rueful shake of his head. "There's plenty you don't know about me."

He just needs the slightest sign. An intake of breath that tells him I want to give more, a flicker of longing in my eyes, a shift of my body weight toward him, something.

"If not with me, Jayne, then someone you think is special enough. You deserve to be happy and to feel loved. You do so much for everyone else. I just—I hope you don't think you are worthy of any less yourself?"

I am so close to letting go. I attempt to explain myself because I owe him that at least. "But it's not as easy for me as it is for you."

"Tonight hasn't been easy for me, Jayne. Not at all," he says, eyes soft.

"Oh?"

"I've spent five hours wanting to tell you just how much I like you but worried that I'll scare you off, doubting whether it's the right thing to do. Believe me, that's not easy." His eyes look heavy. "None of this comes naturally to me."

I sense he wants to expand on this, so I wait, hoping he will.

"You know, it was a really big deal for me to offer you my place in London." He leans back on the sofa, the closeness between us loosened.

"I know. And I'm sorry I seemed so ungrateful at the time, it's just that . . ." I can feel my cheeks warm at the memory of how I reacted.

"No, not in the way you think." He sighs. "The last person who used it really abused the offer. She was someone I thought cared about me, and actually, as it turned out, she liked the house more than she liked me." His smile is sad, I can see the admission still hurts.

It's also incredibly hard to believe. "What happened?"

He clasps his hands together and lowers his head, perhaps not wanting to expose his full emotions to me. "We'd been seeing each other for a while, I had a key cut for her, and then discovered on the weekends she told me she wasn't free, she was staying there with friends—and then another man."

"Oh, Jake." I feel the betrayal, the shock Jake must have felt.

"Yeah, she would have got away with it for a lot longer, but she got too casual about it, left things out of place, and eventually Sandra, my lovely cleaner, said something that gave her away." He shakes his head, then looks back at me. "I felt so stupid. Idiotic that I could put my trust in someone who clearly didn't deserve it. It happened last year but I still ask myself how I could have misjudged someone so badly."

"I really have no idea how someone could do that. The lies it must have taken to pull it off." I feel calmer, my tearstained face forgotten now that we are talking about someone other than me.

"It's the money, Jayne, it makes people weird." He allows himself a small smile at that observation. "I've realized it can change how some people think and feel about me. Like I'm somehow immune to hurt. That I wouldn't care because it's only a house and I have more than one of those." He pauses, checking I still look interested in what he's sharing. "I've worked really hard to build the business and it's doing well. I don't go out of my way to hide the fact, but I don't broadcast it either."

"I think I do understand the money thing," I say before I realize it needs explaining.

"You do?"

"I just mean, what you're saying makes sense." But it's too late to wriggle away from this conversation.

Jake leaves a silence for me to fill and I can't.

"I'm being presumptuous, I know, but you're a dog walker, Jayne. A *wonderful* one, obviously, Margot adores you. I bet they all do. But you also live in one of the most expensive addresses in Bath. Those two facts don't quite add up, do they? I know there could be a really obvious explanation for it but, well, I'm also wondering if there is more to it."

The way he says it, so confidently, not fearful of risking offense, makes me feel like he knows there is more to it. It seems unnecessary and insulting to deny it. If I'm going to share my story with anyone, Jake feels like the safe choice. Now feels like the right time when he has opened up so willingly to me.

I turn to face him. "The money was given to me by my parents." I pick through the words slowly, not sure what I'll say next.

He nods, encouraging me.

"It was a payout. A really significant one. From the hospital where Mum gave birth to me . . . and my sister." I let my eyes find his again. Just saying that one word makes my chest feel tight.

"I've heard you mention a sister, Sally, isn't it?" I love that he has listened, paid attention when I've been talking. But I need to correct him.

"Sally is my older sister, yes. But this was my twin sister, Emma." My eyes mist. Not just for a lost sister but for everything that's happened since that one pivotal moment at the very beginning of my life. The devastating effect it had on my mother, the breakdown of my parents' marriage, my darling grandmother and the grief she never came to terms with, the shy child I became, the relentless bullying I suffered at school in the years I retreated into myself. All the ways in which the loss of this other half of me has shaped everything. How I have allowed it to. How I've buried the hurt and hidden behind it, let it grow and never shared it, until now.

I look into Jake's eyes and I know he is already there. He understands exactly what I'm saying.

"The photograph on your fridge?" he asks quietly, respectfully. "Is that Emma?"

"Yes. You knew?" I know there's no way he could possibly know but he seems so definite.

"Only now, but your reaction when I first saw it seemed so closed off, I understood it wasn't something you wanted to talk about. I think I knew there was more to it."

We sit for a few minutes in an easy silence while I gather my thoughts. There is more I want to say, and he senses that, too, but he doesn't rush me. Neither of us feels the need to force our way through this conversation.

"I would hand all the money back in a second if I could go back to that hospital room, the one Mum should have left with two baby girls." My mind races back to the legal battle she told me she fought through her grief, the contradiction of her relief and her disgust at the payout when it came, something I am reminded of every day when I think about what it bought me. Mum didn't want the money, but she did want it to help me. She said my loss would prove greater than hers.

"I know you would, Jayne. I think everyone in this house understands there is a depth to you that most people don't possess."

"I thought the sadness would simply lift as the years moved on. But it has morphed into this heavy guilt and a deep-rooted insecurity." I want to tell Jake everything. I want him to understand how it feels to have this money, what it has done for me but also *to* me. "I am incomplete. Not everything I should be." I ask myself again, Was it my fault? What happened in that small dark world that we shared for those months? "Maybe it's why I'm so determined to help Meredith. I understand how it feels to lose your other half. It's exactly how I feel living without a part of myself that should be here. I miss her." I look into his eyes. "Does that sound really odd?"

"It doesn't sound odd at all." I feel Jake's hand slide into mine, the weight of it sitting there, telling me I am not alone now.

"I just wish I had some memory of the closeness we must have shared, you know, just the smallest shred of a shared love to balance out all the negative feelings I haven't been able to shake, even all these years on. All I have of Emma is the Polaroid image of my swaddled sister, the one others readily assume is me. But I was safe, wrapped in another pink blanket, sleeping soundly. The baby in Mum's arms was never going to wake up again."

He hasn't interrupted me once. Jake has held my hand and let me share thoughts and feelings I haven't voiced to another living soul. Not even my own mother.

"Thank you for telling me," he says as he wraps both arms around me and pulls me closer to him, tightly, in a way that says he understands what it took to let all that out.

We stay like this, I'm not sure for how long. I hear the timer beep in the kitchen to signal the bread has finished proofing. We both ignore it and eventually it stops. I drift off to sleep, enjoying the sensation of my body sinking into his, his breath deepening. When I stir, Jake has pulled a blanket across the two of us. He's still holding on to me like he never wants to let me go.

"You can stay if you'd like to, it's no problem." He runs his hands across the top of my head, smoothing my hair.

I don't want to but for the best possible reason. Tonight has been enough. I feel better, lighter, than I have done in a very long time—because of Jake. I want to go home, slide into bed, and think about just how lucky I am that this incredible man is in my life.

TWENTY-THREE

❦

Jake's house looks beautiful for our arrival. There are vases of forget-me-nots dotted around and the beds are freshly made with clean linen. The fridge is stocked with everything we need and a fruit loaf is sitting underneath a white muslin cloth on the kitchen counter accompanied by a handwritten note.

Something lovely for your breakfast tomorrow morning.

—Jake

I feel my heart expand a little. Jake must have come over the weekend to get the house ready for Meredith—and for me.

His place is halfway along a narrow cobbled mews, on the left-hand side, painted a bright white with three identical sash windows on the first floor. Each has a Juliet balcony, too small to stand on but filled with boxes of trailing red begonias. There is a wooden picnic table outside surrounded by pots overflowing with multicolored cosmos.

"I feel like I'm in the countryside," says Meredith.

She's right. We are a five-minute walk from Hyde Park, bordered by Park Lane and Knightsbridge, and yet it feels like we have

landed in a peaceful, secret pocket of London. It's the perfect retreat. It feels very Jake. Beautiful but not shouting about it.

"Let's get unpacked," I say, "because we have a date at the
Dorchester that we can't be late for."

I finish long before Meredith and sit in the small kitchen cradling
a cup of tea, gloriously reliving the scenes at Jake's coach house, surprised by the intensity of my own feelings, how much I have missed
seeing him since then. But I've got to stay focused on what we're
here for. Something that Davina said about her last visit to Meredith's
apartment has been niggling away at me. Apparently, Meredith was
humming along to a piece of classical music, one she seemed to
know well. I remember it because Davina found it upsetting—
Meredith had kept stopping, burying her head in her hands before
she'd start humming again. "There was clearly a memory attached to
it," explained Davina, "but I don't think it was a pleasant one."

I think about the stack of CDs I've seen in Meredith's apartment, the concert invitations, the sheet music. She hasn't said a
single thing to make me believe she is personally connected to the
world of music. But what about Fiona? There is the photograph of
her at the keyboard, Meredith's recollection that she was "always
practicing" and "always playing the piano." What if this is more
than a childish hobby? What if Fiona was good—really good? I
throw the idea out to the WhatsApp group, hoping more than
anything that Jake will respond.

> **JAYNE:** Where might you study if you were a gifted musician?
> Anyone have any thoughts?

I can hear Meredith moving around upstairs, making herself
comfortable, so I brew a fresh cup of tea and wait for a response.
Carina is the first to reply.

CARINA: My niece studied music. I'm pretty sure all the big schools were on her long list: Bristol, the Royal College of Music, Manchester, maybe a couple of others. She ended up at Royal Holloway and loved it. Does that help? What are you thinking?

JAYNE: Brilliant, thank you. I'm just trying to piece together some of the items in Meredith's apartment with the occasional reference she has made to Fiona. I'm wondering if she might be a musician, a pianist.

DAVINA: I think there's also a Royal Academy of Music in London too?

JAYNE: Carina, can you focus the graduation gown search around those universities and let's see if it gets us anywhere? A long shot probably but you never know.

CARINA: I'm on it!

There's no response from Jake despite the blue ticks that tell me he's seen and read the messages.

It's like stepping into a giant jewelry box. The entire room glows gold. The air is thick with the scent of roses.

"Welcome to the drawing room of Mayfair, ladies." We are greeted at the entrance to the Promenade and shown to our table, which is unlike any table I have taken tea at before. We both sit on a high-backed sofa that's covered in a plush floral olive green fabric.

"Brocatelle!" announces Meredith.

"Sorry?"

"The fabric, how exquisite." Meredith runs her fingers along it. "And goose down cushions too. This really is very fancy."

And I have to admit, it's a civilized way to spend an afternoon. Every table in the place is full. Everyone is dressed up. No one has dared risk denim. Meredith is wearing a neat skirt that sits tight on her waist and then flows out gently at her hips. It has a matching jacket in pale pink that's flared slightly at the bottom with a white collar that brightens her face, making her look younger.

"You match the roses, Meredith," I tell her. "Look."

Carefully positioned urns stuffed with roses are thoughtfully placed around the room to create maximum privacy for each table. Gold-framed mirrors and coral-colored silk drapes make the huge space somehow feel intimate, while the gentle background tinkle of the pianist, the palm leaves, and the low lighting take us all away from the madness of London outside.

The tea is a work of art. A slim china tray of perfectly cut crust-free sandwiches alternating between white and brown bread arrives scattered with colorful fresh pansies and herbs. Scones are identically browned on top, warm juicy raisins pushing their way out through the cracks in the side. A rosebud is carved from a soft white mousse. A perfectly peaked meringue kiss sits on a circular biscuit base. The layers of peach, vanilla, chocolate, and pistachio slices are precision cut, finished in a glossy icing the color of egg yolk and decorated with a single fondant daisy.

"William would appreciate the exactness," says Meredith as the tray is placed in front of her. "Remind me to take a doggy bag home for him."

She drinks her Darjeeling tea from a gold-rimmed white bone china cup and saucer but doesn't touch any of the food. She looks detached. Something is wrong. I let her sit with her feelings for a few minutes before she finally voices her concern.

"There are so many roses in here." She's shaking her head. "It's the wrong flower. She isn't wearing roses tonight. It's tulips. Purple, not pink."

Meredith starts to rise from the table.

I know I won't be able to stop her now that she has decided she needs to be somewhere else. And neither do I want to. I tell a passing waiter that we will be back and follow Meredith to the main hotel reception.

"We're at the wrong entrance and I can't be late," she says, pushing through the revolving doors. She turns right and walks quickly out onto Park Lane, yanking us both from the calm hotel interior and into the roar of black taxis and red London buses. I speed up to ensure I am alongside her. "We need the ballroom entrance." She doesn't look at me, her focus is on her new destination.

I follow her through another set of revolving doors and up a small flight of stairs onto a marble floor, where she pauses. We're surrounded by a disorientating wall of mirrors and glass double doors that would confuse anyone. Meredith spins, unable to get her bearings, so I take her arm and lead her forward until the space opens out into a circular room with a shiny silver ceiling.

"The caged bird," says Meredith, looking up to a chandelier that I can see has glass birds perched inside of it. "Horribly ironic."

Then we move onward into the vast ballroom.

"So many people, all staring at her. I feel so proud of William, but he should be here to see it with me." She looks to one end of the room. "Every time she moves, the white silk chiffon gently lifts around her. Meters and meters of it in the skirt. But it's the streamers that fall from her neck down her back I have to keep my eye on, so easy to catch on something. You see, I told you it's purple tulips and green leaves, can you see them?" She smiles at me, then looks back to the head of the room as if she is seeing Diana there, in front of her. "Hasn't he made her look beautiful. None of them can tell, can they?" She shifts her gaze around the room now, encouraging me to do the same. She leans in closer to me, not wanting anyone else to hear, oblivious to the fact we are alone. "All those weeks of construction, like an architect with his instruments. All that engineering but none of it visible, which is exactly as it should be. She wears it more than once, which is the greatest honor. To dinner with the Queen and all those prime ministers: Major, Thatcher, Heath, Wilson, and Callaghan. What a lineup!"

"And where are you, Meredith?" I step a little closer to her.

"There are five hundred for dinner tonight. They seat me on a table close to hers, with the security. The food is out of this world. The softest partridge. Buttery potatoes that just melt on my tongue. But I could be eating a stale cheese sandwich. It doesn't matter. All I can think about is William. My William. The way he holds me. The intensity between us. And I just want so much more of him." She pauses and I watch the faintest flicker of concern cross her face. "We're closing in around each other. No one else matters anymore." She shakes her head and I recognize the sad shade of regret in her eyes.

TWENTY-FOUR

❧⟡❧

Meredith looks tired. Her face a little grayer this morning. The lines around her eyes more prominent, her movements sluggish. She hasn't spoken since she joined me at the small white kitchen table where I'm sitting, listening to the radio.

"Would you like some of the lovely bread Jake left for us?" I ask. "And there is some marmalade in the fridge, too, if you fancy it?"

"I don't know a Jake." She sits with her hands clasped in her lap, looking at the empty plate in front of her like she has no idea how she got here. I think yesterday has drained her.

"Jake lives in the building with us, Meredith. But no matter, there are eggs. I can do you some on toast. Or chop some fruit if you prefer?" I'm trying to sound upbeat, but I know the Meredith who was so keen to come on this trip has not joined me yet this morning.

She remains silent, her head lowered like she doesn't want me to see her upset. Like she's ashamed.

"Did you sleep okay?" I shuffle my chair closer to her, forcing her to make eye contact.

"I couldn't find my memory room." Her eyes have filled with tears. "All of my pictures and cuttings are gone. William is gone.

He won't be able to find me here. Where is he?" she asks, anguish in her voice.

I take Meredith's hands, so desperate to offer her some comfort. There is fear in her eyes this morning and more than anything I want to take it away. I want to give her the gift of some peace. To pass through just one day without the gnawing doubts and unanswered questions that scramble her mind with little respite. Then I remember the quick film I recorded of her memory room.

"I have some film footage of your memory room, Meredith. Why don't you have some breakfast, get washed and dressed, and then we can watch it together if you like?"

That seems to make her feel better. She nods and I start to cut some bread to toast for her. She keeps her eyes on me the whole time while I move about the kitchen, making fresh tea, washing my own breakfast plate, and wiping down the work surface. Her expression shifts. Her eyes narrow and she folds her arms protectively across her chest.

"Who are you exactly?" Her tone is firm, confrontational even, and I feel every muscle in my neck tighten.

"It's Jayne from upstairs." I try my usual introduction, still keeping my tone light. "I bring you the forget-me-nots and I walk the dogs. Remember Margot?"

"You've never brought me flowers. Only William does that." She shakes her head. She looks angry because she thinks I'm lying to her. "Are you always going to punish me, is that your plan? We are working so hard, things get missed, too many things, but you . . . you *abandon* us." She is sobbing now, her hands raised toward the ceiling, emphasizing every word she says. "I love you with all my heart. I always have. Why isn't that enough?" She shakes her head, confused, then narrows her eyes, and I see a determination to confront some deep buried hurt. Without any further warning, she stands and shouts at me, "Why can't you see the bigger problems? Why won't you help me?"

I take a couple of steps back away from her. Her eyes are wild, like she's shocked at the volume of noise that just came out of her.

I freeze, too stunned to respond to her. I give the moment time to subside and the air around us a chance to settle. I think of Davina, how brilliant she would be in this situation. Of Jake, how might he react if he were here now? Would he stand back or step between us?

Meredith slumps back into her chair, allowing her arms to drop heavily beside her, and I know we are over the worst of it. When she speaks again her words are soft and delivered with such tenderness.

"I will always love you. I will always find you fascinating and brilliant. There will never be a day when I regret that you are mine. But you make me feel like such a failure. All that bitterness, I'll never understand it, but I can accept that at least part of the blame must be mine, if you will too."

We sit together, neither of us speaking, me feeling my heart rate begin to slow in my chest until finally she lifts her head.

"Oh dear, I think my tea is cold." My Meredith has returned. I reach for my phone, feeling it is safe now to share the film with her. I smile as the pictures of a childish Fiona appear in front of us both. Meredith taps the screen, pausing the moving image on one of Fiona frowning over her birthday cake.

"We celebrate so late. A month after her actual birthday because the deadlines won't have it any other way," she says. Then she takes my hand, squeezes it tightly, and leans toward me so our shoulders are touching.

"It's Leicester Square today, isn't it?" She beams. "I'll get my essentials bag." Then she's off again, humming her usual tune.

"Why is there so much traffic?" We are standing on Bayswater Road waiting for a break in a continuous line of black cabs and red buses. "It's never *this* busy." No one is stopping for us at the pedestrian crossing that will take us into the park, and it is unnerving Meredith. She shuffles from foot to foot. The thrum of unbroken engine noise. The suffocating cloud of traffic fumes. The shouts from cyclists weaving dangerously in and out of the cars is stressful for me and disorientating for her. Finally, we make it across four lanes of traffic, her gripping my arm, onto the wide path that forks right through the park leading us down toward the Serpentine with its blue-bottomed paddleboats.

The lake is busy today. The tourists are out in force soaking up the rare London sunshine. We walk across the broad stone bridge and bear left, remaining in the park, walking parallel with Knightsbridge, where I plan to hail us a cab.

I first notice the crowds clustered around the Diana memorial when we are halfway across the bridge. I don't know how I could have forgotten it's here. I should have diverted us left earlier so we walked on the opposite side of the lake. Meredith may find this upsetting and then our whole day could unravel.

"What are they all here for?" Meredith points toward them. "What are we missing?" She seems excited about the prospect of an impromptu performance that we may have stumbled upon by chance.

I have no idea what the correct response is, but she seems determined to find out. She takes the lead, hugging the footpath

between the water and the crowds, then comes to an abrupt halt
in front of the curved concrete walkway and reads the sign aloud:

WELCOME TO THE

DIANA, PRINCESS OF WALES

MEMORIAL FOUNTAIN

She gives herself the time to take in the view. Mums with trouser legs rolled up to their knees enjoying the cool of the water
they're standing in. Abandoned buggies and clothing strewn
about. Lunch boxes and bags scattered along the walkway. The
occasional child in nothing but their underpants. Builders and office workers taking a break, heads angled to the sunshine. And
the light, joyful sounds of laughter and screams carry on the air,
mingling with the refreshing splash of water.

"She would have loved it, I think," says Meredith, smiling. "Just
like you do." She has caught me smiling at a young mum trying to
keep herself upright in the water, each hand gripping a bouncing
toddler. "What a shame it ever had to be built."

It's nearly one o'clock by the time we get to Leicester Square and
I know Meredith will be asking me for an egg sandwich any minute now. I scan across the top of the crowds for somewhere to buy
one when the time comes.

"Well, I'm very happy to see William Shakespeare all cleaned
up." Meredith looks toward the stone statue in the center of the
square. "The gardens look neater than usual too. Everything looks
brighter. Less brick, more glass." She takes a seat on one of the
wooden benches and pats the space next to her, encouraging me

to do the same. "Oh, it's so exciting. I'm a little used to the hysteria now. But this is the premiere. Charles joins her on the red carpet and they walk the line, shaking hands with all the cast and crew, some of the representatives from the Prince's Trust charity. Shirley MacLaine's bright red hair! Julia's endless smile. I love the smart porters in their gray capes and peaked hats that line our route." Meredith scans the cinema building, looking peaceful, like she's reading a longed-for postcard.

"Would you like to go inside?" I ask. "I'm sure they won't mind if we take a quick look."

She glances up at its shouty advertising hoardings and shakes her head.

"I don't think I need to." She smiles. "I can see it all perfectly."

We walk toward the entrance and the familiar toasted scent of warm popcorn reaches us. We're jostled by children not prepared to wait for their tickets to be checked. Then Meredith seems to change her mind.

"I'm needed! This is the night. They are all about to go through and take their seats." Her eyes flick off to the left. "I've just started to relax, knowing she will be sitting down soon." Meredith closes her eyes and I stay perfectly still, hoping nothing will distract her now, just as the images are returning to her. "I'm given the signal and whisked into a nondescript back room. I think it's the staff room or the manager's office. It's very small, windowless."

She pauses again and her eyes drop to the black bag at her wrist that has accompanied us every step of the way so far. "It's the gold stitching, one of the flowers at the wrist of her tailcoat. They look so dramatic on the burgundy silk velvet. Bouton Renaud. The best."

I'm not entirely following but I allow her to continue uninterrupted.

"The pearl embroidery must have caught on something with all that hand shaking. It's very small, barely noticeable, but she feels it tug and she's worried it will unravel further." She lifts the black bag higher now, clutching it to her chest.

"Why don't you open the bag, Meredith. Perhaps what is inside will help?" But I sense her mind has moved on. The contours of her face have shifted slightly. The strain of concentration has eased, replaced by a softness, a longing.

"I cry quietly all the way through the movie." She sweeps her fingers under her eyelashes now as if the tears are still waiting to be wiped away. "But not for the reasons everyone around me is crying. The acting is good, it feels so real. I feel the pain of their sorrow. But it is easily canceled out by him." She closes her eyes and sighs deeply, as if she has lost something that might never return.

"I know now that he loves me. And that we are going to be together. That my life will never be the same again. I'll never have to doubt it. I have found my other half."

I feel my own mouth drop open and I know this powerful sentiment is what has bonded me to Meredith in a way that has been hard to articulate to others. This need for another half, a missing half for both of us. Hers I pray we will find, somehow. Mine, lost forever. I wipe a tear from my cheek before she sees it.

"That's it, isn't it?" she continues. "The feeling of total certainty. From the moment we meet, we are never really apart. It's like we were put on this earth for each other."

I swallow down the sadness for everything that should have been and may now never be.

"And how wonderful, Jayne, can you imagine it? A man who doesn't shower his love and affection around freely, aiming it all at me, only me."

Is this something I can find for myself? Might I have found him already? Not to replace a lost sister who will always remain missing. But who can enrich my life in other ways? Is this what Jake might do? Is it what he wants to do if I give him the chance? If I could trust him with my heart? I think again about his garden parties, the lack of one consistent person by his side but also his confession that he didn't want to be alone the other night. Is he looking for the same closeness I'm looking for but too afraid to take the leap to find it?

"Certainty is a gift. To be certain of yourself and of each other. I think it's impossible to be any happier, we are together and I believe it's enough."

I absorb Meredith's sweet recollections, attaching my own hopes to her wise words. Standing in Leicester Square, surrounded by a swarm of tourists and reliving this beautiful love affair of hers, feels like a privilege. I see it in her face like it is happening afresh. Like she just fell in love for the first time right in front of me.

TWENTY-FIVE

꧁ঔৣ꧂

We eat our egg sandwiches in Green Park, slumped in two of the green-and-white-striped deck chairs for hire. It took us thirty minutes to walk the route back along Piccadilly to the park entrance, a journey I can do in half that time, but Meredith was lingering, staring into the shop fronts of every business that wasn't here when she was last.

Now as soon as she swallows the last mouthful of her lunch, her eyelids grow heavy and droop. Very soon they are closed, and she is lightly sleeping. I gently brush the crumbs from her lap and use the time to update the WhatsApp group, sharing this morning's frightening outburst from Meredith but also the wonderful progress we are making, the closeness that I feel between the two of us, the trust that seems to fuse a little stronger with every hour we are together. Davina is the first to respond.

> **DAVINA:** I have so much respect for you and what you are doing, Jayne. You are helping her so much.

> **OLIVIA:** I know it's hard not to defend yourself, but letting her get there slowly in her own time is better. It will probably just confuse her more if you try to correct her mistakes.

JAYNE: Thank you, everyone. Is there any update on the Fiona situation?

CARINA: YES, THERE IS!

I hold my breath. Carina is not easily overexcited. This sounds promising.

JAYNE: Go on!

CARINA: The graduation hood Willow spied matches the colors worn by students at the Royal College of Music. I emailed the admissions department the image of Fiona and they are almost certain it is one of theirs. That's the good news.

JAYNE: But there's bad news too?

CARINA: I'm afraid so. They have no record of a Fiona Chalis graduating from there in July 2017.

JAYNE: Really? But it's got to be her, hasn't it?

CARINA: It feels like we're missing something. I don't think Fiona would have got the date wrong, unless it's the date she sent the photograph to Meredith and not the date of the ceremony, but that doesn't seem likely.

JAYNE: So, we're no further forward?

CARINA: There is hope . . . Their head of admissions, a fanatic for detail apparently, who has run the department for over thirty

years, is on holiday, but the lady I spoke to said she will show her
the image when she returns, and if Fiona studied and/or
graduated from there, she will know.

DAVINA: Well done, Carina! Just keep doing what you're doing,
Jayne, and we'll take care of the rest here. Oh, and a message
from Maggie for you, and I quote, "The fairies say yes, don't give
up." I promised I'd pass it on!

Lovely Maggie. She has been back to the woods and read a
letter someone has put in place of my original one, presumably
thinking they were answering a child.

Even with the lovely notes from everyone else, I still can't help
notice there's no word from Jake.

I look at Meredith, her eyes fluttering under the glare of the
sunshine, and it makes me smile to think she isn't missing William
now, he's right here with her in her subconscious, being pulled
slowly forward, hopefully every bit as keen as she is to be re-
united. Then I think about how cruel this situation is. That Meredith has spent a lifetime gathering and guarding her precious
memories, only for them to be stolen when she didn't even realize
it was happening. Not content with that theft, Meredith's tormentor
teases her with glimpses, has her believe every single day that her
craved-for normality is returning, before it's snatched away again,
leaving a trail of confusion, sadness, and exhaustion. Every day
she goes through this, and if there is anything I can do to ease her
suffering, then I will.

But what is the final destination on this journey of ours? Where
am I taking us both? The map and her dress sketches might spell
out the logistics, but will she be happy once she arrives? Is finding
William and Fiona the right thing to do? I have little idea of what

has passed between them. When all this is done, will she wish she'd never left the safety of her memory room? And will any of it mean anything? Will she remember in the long term what we are rediscovering together today? Olivia said if her memories and recollections are genuinely felt then they are more likely to stick but we also have to accept that we can't make her better. Any improvement, if we can even put it that way, may be short-lived.

But I've already gained so much from my time with this wonderful woman. The tiniest window into her rich world. A life so well lived that it stubbornly clings to her, fighting to be remembered. If she really did make these incredible gowns for Princess Diana alongside her William, as I now feel sure they did, how is she going to feel if she fully remembers that? When she opens the black bag she's clutched tightly since we left Bath, will she instinctively understand that the contents are hers, that they played their own special part in the history books?

She starts to stir, and I rest my hand on her right arm, letting her know she's not alone.

"Shall we get going, Meredith, when you're ready? It's Launceston Place next, back toward the palace."

She blinks, her eyes darting around, trying to place her surroundings. She waits for the trees above us, the passing people, and me beside her to return to focus. Then she turns to face me.

"Is William meeting us there?" And I know for sure that she has been dreaming about him. I recognize the momentary elation, when for a few brief seconds she believes her dreams are reality—until the hollowing realization of her whereabouts tells her they're not. For a moment she believed she would see him but it's the sight of me that confirms she won't.

Her body seems to slump a little deeper into the deck chair, her eyes are lost in the distance, finding the park bandstand way off to our right. It's more than disappointment that settles into the creases of her face, she is sad about another thought that has arrived uninvited.

"So many missed chances. All those deadlines we can't ignore, so we sacrifice the things we can, when really it should be the other way around. We let the wrong person down. I make a promise I can't keep." The realization causes her eyes to cloud and her lips to squeeze together, a hard swallow.

"They will understand, Meredith." I'm not entirely sure what she is confessing to.

"You're right." She nods her head like she is accepting whatever wrongs she feels she has committed. "Some things can be forgiven, but not all. There's something else, isn't there?" She lowers her head into her hands, trying to force a thought to the surface. "Something I said. Why did I say it?" She's getting agitated, squirming in her chair, trying to sit herself more upright. "I ruin everything."

"What did you ruin?" I keep my voice calm, despite the thump of my heartbeat.

Meredith's lips part and I think for one glorious second she is going to get there, whatever it is, she has found it, the piece of information swimming around inside of her just out of reach, she's made a grab for it and this time she is close enough. But then the energy seems to drain from her face and her arms, and she relaxes her weight back into the chair.

I smile and reach for her hand. I don't want to push her. It's more important that we arrive at our next destination with her feeling positive, not stressed and frustrated with herself.

"Why have they changed the seats?" asks Meredith. "I much prefer them facing each other, with the draft screens. And the lovely wooden floors have gone too. William always lets me face the way we're traveling. I don't like going backward. No one does really, do they?"

Meredith wanted to get the Tube to our next destination "because we always do," so we've hopped on the Circle line at Victoria for the three stops to Gloucester Road.

"The doors between the carriages have gone too. This isn't right at all." I can see it is unsettling her, but the fact she's remembering how the carriage used to look can only be a good thing, I hope.

As we arrive at Launceston Place, I decide to let Meredith take the lead. All we have is a street name, the only information that was scribbled on the sketch in Meredith's memory room aside from William's hint that *Soon we will be three.* It's a lot less clear why Meredith or Diana may have been on this pretty residential road. We start to walk slowly past bright white three-story houses, each with a broad flight of stone steps leading to a glossy black front door that's recessed into an arched porchway. I notice some have huge circular golden doorbells that glow in the sunlight—a hint at the wealth that sits behind them. Meredith smiles up at the last of the cherry blossoms, the tree of choice in most of the front gardens we pass.

Every front door is black. Every house sits behind black iron railings and is framed by a black window canopy. The roofs are black slate as are the old-fashioned lanterns dotted along the pavement. It must be the most monochrome street in London. Surely the most stylish. Some of the houses are separated by perfect box hedging, others have shaped olive trees potted on either side of the doorway. First-floor balconies are filled with flower boxes, ivy trailing down toward the basement windows below.

"We need to walk right to the end," says Meredith, "on the right-hand side." She seems to know exactly where she's heading.

As we pass a house about halfway along, the door opens and two women about Meredith's age appear. They are dressed smartly but comfortably, expensive-looking fabrics, dark sunglasses, their hair flatteringly blow-dried off their tanned faces. I notice the discreet but expensive gold jewelry. I pause and glance in through the large first-floor window to the antique furniture beyond. This is not an address for first-time buyers. There is an air of civility but also watchfulness. These ladies know on sight that we don't live on this street and I can almost sense them silently questioning what we are doing here.

"How do you keep the exterior of a house so spotlessly white?" I ask Meredith. "Every one of them."

She chuckles to herself knowingly. "These people don't live as you and I do. There is no messy day to scramble through. There are staff and rotas and order—ways of doing things." There is a bounce in her step this afternoon; she is happy to be here.

Right on cue a middle-aged woman in gym gear and a full face of makeup walks past with a small white dog obediently at her heel.

"See, even the dogs are clean," laughs Meredith.

We are almost at the very end of the street and I fear we have missed whatever it is we came to see when Meredith finally stops and turns right to face the largest house we've passed.

"She suggests I sit on the small soft blue sofa at the back of the room. Maybe I look paler than usual." Meredith's hand rises to stroke her left cheek. "She's so kind, just like you. She doesn't have to be, but she is. She asks someone to get me some ginger tea." Her hand rises to her forehead as if checking her own temperature. "Then I watch her. So poised and relaxed in his company. They know each other well. He's taken her picture before."

"Who lives here, Meredith? Whose house is it?" I shouldn't force her, but she seems so confident in her storytelling now.

But she ignores my question.

"He is making magic. Taking something exquisite and capturing it forever. All those pearls and golden glass beads, the way the soft pale pink chiffon seems to mimic her ease in front of the camera. It all works so well with her complexion and hair color. A different shape this time, draped like a sarong." She lets her hand move across her own body from her waist down to her lower left hip.

When the shift in Meredith's expression comes, I am ready for it this time. I know her memory will go only so far before it fails her again. She knows there is more to tell but she can't find the images or the words she's suddenly grasping for. Perhaps they are there but refuse to line up in the correct order. Her body starts to tense, her fingers curl inward. I sense her rising panic at the loss of control.

"This is where the problems start. Right here. In this house. It's such a wonderful day, it reminds me how much I love my life, despite the hard work and long hours." She is visibly upset now, on the edge of tears, speaking quickly, spitting the words out before they desert her. "I love it *so* much. But things are changing. How will I keep my promise?"

I'm nodding furiously at her, ignoring all passersby, determined to keep her talking as long as I can.

"And he hides things. Later on, he hides things that he shouldn't." She's stuttering now, the clarity is leaving her. "Oh no, I encourage him, I think. At least, I never stop him. But then it is too late to tell her, to fix things. Something awful that I can't stop. I make the phone call. It isn't enough!"

I rest my hand on her shoulder to try to reconnect her with the present, to show her she is safe here with me, but she is beyond comfort now.

"I started it, but I can't stop it!" Meredith bellows the words up at the house and I know we need to leave. It's only a matter of time before someone comes out and questions us. "What is it? What don't I stop and what can't he tell her? You stupid, stupid woman."

TWENTY-SIX

꩜

I make sure Meredith is tucked into bed with everything she needs before I head back downstairs and collapse onto the sofa. It's been an exhausting day and I feel confident she will sleep well tonight, even if I won't. It's just gone nine o'clock. Meredith wanted only buttered toast for dinner. I haven't eaten yet and although I'm hungry I can't summon the will to cook anything.

It's our last night in London. Tomorrow morning, we will visit Spencer House in St. James's and then we will be catching an afternoon train back to Bath. Has it been worth it? Honestly, I don't know. I'm more confused than I was before we set off. But is Meredith? She's been able to share so much but every recollection, every detail, seems to come with another question attached.

I open my purse to check the tickets for our visit to Spencer House tomorrow and my eyes find the business card for the Live Well Center Olivia volunteers at. The prospect of unloading everything and how I feel about it to a faceless stranger who can't see me is enormously appealing. So, before I have time to talk myself out of it—and encouraged by the suspicion that I'll be at the end of a very long queue—I call the helpline.

The man's voice is soothing but not patronizing. He delivers just enough verbal affirmations to reassure me he is listening as I speak, uninterrupted, for twenty-five minutes. And I can feel the weight of the day physically drain from me. I say everything I'm thinking, without the gloss of hope, optimism, or encouragement I use with the others. There is no layer of false capability I might add for Mum's benefit. None of the apologetic, don't-mind-me dismissiveness I might include if it wasn't a total stranger who has taken my call. What starts as a progress report on Meredith soon diverts to my growing feelings for Jake and my concerns for Davina, Olivia, and Carina, even little Maggie and Willow. I speak about my grandmother, all my unresolved guilt, my mum and Sally, questioning if I am a disappointment to both. I unload the lot of it, unedited, so keen to hear a neutral take on it all.

When I finally stop, he says very little, but asks me two questions: "Do you ever let other people care for you, the way you do for them?" and when my silence answers him, "Do you think maybe it's time to try?"

I'm going to miss sharing our cozy London refuge. I'm scrolling through the list of terrible TV choices, trying to ignore the deep rumble of my belly, when there is a gentle knock at the door. My instinct is not to answer it since obviously they'll be looking for Jake. But the knock comes again a little louder and I decide to see who it is before Meredith is disturbed.

I open the door to find Jake standing there holding a large brown paper bag and wearing a smile that I instantly mimic. He's dressed casually, but there's a hesitance in his demeanor.

"Jake!"

"Hello, there. I thought you might be ready for some different company. A late supper?" He raises an eyebrow hopefully. "I have wine, cheese, some cold meats, bread, of course. And a determination to make you see all your secrets are safe with me, just in case you've been doubting yourself—or maybe doubting me." Obviously, he knows I have. But he looks tentative, not quite holding my eye contact, unsure if this is the right idea or not.

Neither of us speaks. But I am so pleased he is here. I feel a deep excitement stir low in my belly and I want him to know it. The significance of the effort he's put in—driving all the way here, organizing dinner for two—settles on me and I feel a surge of adrenaline drive up through me. Even I can recognize he hasn't done all this because he was bored and fancied a change of scenery.

"You really didn't have to knock, it's your place." I force some composure, while trying very hard not to let my face reveal that this might just be the most wonderful thing anyone has ever done for me. Then I think better of it and smile broadly. "I'm glad you came. I've missed you these past few days."

"Are you sure? I don't want to intrude if you and Meredith are busy." He glances over my shoulder.

"She's already in bed. It's been quite a day. Sorry, come in." I step aside to let him through, but he hesitates, reluctant to occupy the small space between me and the doorframe.

"I'll tell you what, grab the tablecloth from the drawer next to the sink, and let's eat outside. I don't want to risk waking Meredith up." He nods toward the small picnic table on the cobbles. "It's still warm out." And I honestly can't think of a single other thing I would rather do right now.

I lay out the cloth, and while he's arranging the food, I grab some cutlery, plates, and wineglasses. The effort he has gone to makes my heart feel too large for my chest. The wine is chilled, the meats and cheese wrapped in wax paper. There are four different types of bread, which he pulls apart with his hands, sharing them between us.

"Okay, just one final thing missing." He smiles. "Hang on." And then he disappears toward his car, which is parked farther down the narrow cobbled mews.

I watch as he opens one of the rear doors and bends inside, reaching for something. The next thing I see is Margot racing full pelt toward me, her tail high, her mouth pulled back over her teeth, her entire body wagging from side to side almost knocking her off course as she runs. I barely have a chance to say her name before she launches herself onto my lap and sets about licking my neck as Jake joins us again, laughing loudly.

"Looks like I'm not the only one who missed you!" I am so grateful there is no hint of awkwardness between us after everything that was said on Friday night. He has made sure of it.

"What is she doing here?" I can't contain Margot on my lap. She is frantically jumping on and off me like we haven't seen each other in years, not just a few days. "Is Davina okay?"

"Yes, everything's fine. She just needed some extra help. The usual story, demanding clients, last-minute dramas, and the school holidays have started. Willow has done a great job keeping on top of all the dog walking but I offered to bring Margot so they'd have one less thing to worry about. Margot and I have been having a great time together, haven't we, girl?" He ruffles the top of Margot's head and she diverts her attention back to him, finally settling down on the bench beside us. I feel a growing swell of gratitude expand through me at the way everyone in our pretty town house is pulling together, that they are beginning to naturally help one another without me orchestrating meetings and updates.

"Olivia has been great too. She actually took two days off work and spent the whole of it cleaning Meredith's apartment."

"She took time off work?" I am genuinely shocked to hear this.

"Yes. I think your enthusiasm—your love for Meredith—is infectious."

This makes me almost as happy as the fact Jake is here with me tonight, but then I remember the warning Olivia delivered the first time we all got together to discuss Meredith's needs.

"Hang on, I thought we weren't supposed to tidy Meredith's place? Won't it just confuse her when we get back tomorrow if everything has been moved?"

"That's why it took so long. She cleaned *around* everything. She's left everything exactly where it was but got rid of all the grime and dust. The kitchen was pretty appalling apparently."

I think of the number of times Olivia has barely paused to say hello to me properly when I've arrived to take Teddy off her hands. I know she will have worked through the night to make sure her job didn't suffer from her rallying around Meredith like this.

"But listen, even better, she came across some old school reports, sheets that seem to have been torn out from a larger book. They are dated between 2001 and 2006, so they must be Fiona's, not Meredith's. There's no cover sheet so we can't see the name of the school unfortunately."

"Oh, okay. Did they provide any further clues, anything at all that might help the search?"

"Not exactly, but they do seem to confirm your thinking about Fiona's education. All the pages are from her music teachers. Meredith hasn't kept any reports from any other academic subject, as far as we can see. But all the teachers agree Fiona was 'gifted' and 'an exceptional talent' and 'destined for great things.' Let's just hope we find out more when the head of admissions at the Royal College of Music is back from her break."

It's good news, undeniably. Another hint that we are looking in the right places for Fiona, even if we are not there yet.

"Thank you, Jake, that does sound really promising. We're getting there."

"And how are *you*, Jayne?" Jake spreads his elbows wide on the table, leans in, and listens patiently while I update him on everything from the past couple of days. He nods, makes encouraging noises, but says very little. His eyes never leave mine. He leans in a fraction closer to me across the table.

"I've been thinking a lot about our chat the other night." He maintains eye contact. His tone is soft and encouraging, as always. "I just want you to understand that I know how it feels. To believe you are not enough, that there should be more. I spend a lot of time feeling that way, that I've somehow missed expectations, even if they are only my own."

This is so far from the image of Jake I have constructed in my head. The man who fills his garden and his coffee shop with people who always seem happy to see him, who can alter the temperature of the room just by walking into it, who is infinitely kind and generous with his time and resources. How can he possibly be lacking?

"People don't see it. I suppose I've made sure of that. I've become very good at it." He shares more of the food out between our two plates, offering Margot a scrap of some expensive ham. "But I didn't build that beautiful home just for me. I always imagined I'd be sharing it with someone by now. The fact I'm not, well, it feels like a failure that's hard not to take personally."

"But the parties and all this confidence you have, I just don't understand . . ." I'm missing something, there is a real disconnect between the Jake I see and the one he is describing.

"Well, that's the easy bit, isn't it? Fill your garden with people who like to dress up and drink good champagne. Anyone can do that."

"Can they?" I know I couldn't. "People still have to *want* to come." He's drastically underestimating the pull he has over people.

"They don't come for me, Jayne. I'm not arrogant enough to believe that. They come to feel good about themselves. To mingle and make connections that will benefit them in some way." He shrugs, accepting of the small part he believes he plays in his own popularity.

"Okay, if that's true, what's the hard bit you *can't* do? What's missing from this seemingly very comfortable life of yours?" I laugh as I say it, because I can't believe any of this is actually true.

"It's all surface level, Jayne, there's no depth to any of it, and that's not what I'm looking for. There are parties and people, but it's all about self-validation, people making themselves feel good. But I'm not sure either have ever really made *me* feel good. I'm just surprised it's taken me so long to realize it." Jake looks at me, hoping, I think, I'll bring my usual enthusiasm to solving his problems, too, but I can't. I'm stunned that he feels this way.

"I'm not sure I could call on any of those people in a crisis. And after a while I started to question, What's the point of it all? I just didn't have a better idea, so it carried on. I've never been very good at understanding how you move a relationship on. When you feel a connection with someone, how do you make it more?"

"I think you might be asking the wrong person." I smile. "I'm hardly an expert on that one."

"I think you are. I've been on plenty of dates, but I've never really opened up to any of those women, not like I did with you the other night—not like I am now." He laughs a little at himself then, maybe a little at the both of us. "Being good company comes much more naturally when that's all it is. It's the next bit, *this*"—he opens his arms to indicate what we are doing right now—"that's much harder."

"But you are good at this too." I can't help but sound incredulous.

Jake looks at me then and smiles, takes my hand. "Maybe. Or perhaps I'm only any good at it with you. Did you consider that?"

"Nope, I definitely did not." I am immensely grateful that Margot has wedged herself between us now. Perhaps she senses I need her, and I run a hand over the top of her head.

"What you're doing for Meredith is incredible, but I've seen how patient you are with Maggie. The way you make extra time for Davina. I know you worry about Olivia and if Carina is coping with everything on her plate with running the business. You have this hardwired need to help people. You've helped me to work out a few things too."

I look at the food spread out in front of us. "I'm just happy you came here tonight, that I didn't scare you off with my own history."

"I'm here because I care. Too much, I think. I care about *you* too much, Jayne. Do you understand what I mean?"

I nod.

"I don't want to be friends. Not *just* friends. I don't want you to be confused about that."

I'd love to put my arms around him. Instead I do my usual trick and exit the situation.

"I better just go and check on Meredith," I say, pointing behind me and rising from the table.

"Jayne, please." I don't even make it to the doorway before he reaches for my arm, stops me, and guides me back toward him. "I just need to hear whether it is okay for me to be here with you. That you don't want me to leave?"

How can I have made him believe that? How can this incredibly generous and kind man even question himself? I feel awful for placing this doubt in him.

Still I say nothing.

"But I need to be honest with you too. I didn't drive two hours to check on your progress with Meredith. I care, of course I do, I hope I've made that clear, but I came for *you*. I don't want to pretend otherwise. I can't keep hiding it from you because I'm worried about how you'll react."

He reads something on my face, my need for him to dispense with any more words, which are clearly not my strong point, and just kiss me.

Then his lips are on mine, both his hands reach up from my lower back to hold me close to him as the kiss deepens. And I'm kissing him back, letting every drop of doubt pour out of me, every awkward exchange we've ever had blissfully forgotten.

A glass falls to the floor back inside the kitchen and he snaps away from me, and for a moment, I consider pulling him back.

"Can I check on Meredith?" he offers.

"No, let me, she's not expecting to see you and it may unsettle her."

Meredith is picking up the pieces of a broken water glass, placing the shards into the palm of her hand.

"I'm so sorry about the glass," she says when she sees me. "I woke up thirsty and needed some water."

"It doesn't matter, it's only a glass." I help her with the rest of the pieces.

"William is the only man to ever kiss me like that." She looks at me like I'm the luckiest girl alive. "I remember the feeling of weightlessness. My entire body hollow like I might just float up and away. No one else ever makes me feel that way."

I blush at the accuracy of her description.

"There were other men, then, before William, I mean?" There must have been but I'm curious if she can recall any of them.

"My goodness, yes, so many wrong ones. I could probably write a book," she says, giggling. Then when she sees the surprise on my face, "I hope you're not imagining that I just landed in this perfect love affair without any of the pain that preceded it? This isn't some sort of sweet-smelling fairy tale." Her tone becomes more serious. "If you want to find a man like William, you have to get out there and hunt for him."

The idea of Meredith hunting William down does not fit at all with the image of their romance I've constructed.

"Are you hunting, Jayne? I sincerely hope you are." She glances back over my shoulder to Jake outside.

"Not really, no."

"Whyever not?"

"There may not be any need, Meredith. I think he may already have found me."

For a fleeting moment she looks immensely proud, then her mouth collapses and she is sad again.

"We will find William, won't we? You won't give up on us?"

How do I make her believe and remember that I never could?

"No, I won't," I say, giving her hand a squeeze to show her I mean it.

"Thank you." She walks across the kitchen, heading back to her room. "I would give everything to have my time again. To be back where you are now with it all ahead of me. To relive those glorious days and nights and make right the things I got wrong."

Then she smiles, encouraging me not to waste the opportunity, I think, and disappears up the stairs.

Jake is waiting for me, refusing to intrude on my time with Meredith despite the fact it's his house. Margot sits next to him, her head cocked to one side, like even she can't work out why I don't just get on with it. Margot loves him. Meredith loves him. Maybe it's time I allowed myself to. He's refilled our wineglasses and moved so he is sitting astride the bench on my side of the table. He takes my hand and pulls me down next to him, then moves closer so his legs are on either side of me.

"I've booked a hotel room for the night, so I'll head back there. I know you've got a big final day tomorrow. But I could give you both a lift back to Bath if you want to avoid the stress of the train?"

"No, it's okay, she seems to like the train journeys. She might not be as comfortable in your car. I'm not sure I should risk it. But thank you for the offer."

"Okay, understood. I'll get going but, well, hopefully we can chat some more when you get back?" He isn't giving up, not just yet, it seems.

I nod and he leans in to kiss me, on the cheek this time. "I'll leave all this for you and Meredith to finish up, shall I?" He's being so kind and cheerful, not pushing me for anything. But I know he wants more—and so do I.

He picks up his phone and car keys from the table. "I hope tomorrow goes well. Come and tell me all about it when you get back?"

"Or you could . . ." I don't want to regret these next words.

"I could what?" His eyes travel from my lips down the length of my body. I know we are both thinking the same thing, wanting the same thing. "I could what, Jayne?" He takes a step closer to me.

"You could stay?" I whisper.

I hear his keys hit the cobbles beneath us before his mouth is on my neck. I close my eyes and melt into him as his hands wrap around my waist. Margot stretches out on the bench. I think she understands she's staying the night too.

TWENTY-SEVEN

❧

Meredith
1992

There is no time to plan a wedding. It's a simple ceremony in the anteroom at Chelsea Old Town Hall. Two witnesses are pulled off the street and asked to spare them half an hour.

Meredith doesn't care. Why would she? She has her William and the gift of an incredible piece of dove gray silk embroidered in French needlepoint lace from Catherine. There will never be another dress like it.

They spend the afternoon sipping champagne, eating spaghetti with lobsters and clams at a Kensington bistro, just the two of them. After dessert comes a heartfelt promise from William that as long as they are together, everything else can be figured out. "I know this was sudden, but I'll sacrifice everything I can for you and our baby, Meredith." He wants to say more, she can tell by the way he's shifting on his chair, stopping midsentence like he's unsure of himself. Should he go on or not?

There is no honeymoon. Not even a long weekend. Deadlines demand their presence in the workroom. Overtime is mounting up. Weekends off no longer exist. Private commissions have pushed William to the very edge of what anyone can feasibly achieve in the course of a day and night—but still he won't say no, determined to save for their future.

And now last-minute changes are needed to a dress that was finished a week ago. A fleeting moment of relaxation when they thought they were ahead of the deadline.

"The venue has changed. It's no one's fault, it's just one of those things and we have to be able to respond to it," explains Catherine. It's not quite eight thirty a.m. and William is surrounded by the design team. "The scale of the event demands full-length, the proportions of the dress are now inadequate as it stands. What are your thoughts, William?"

He looks at the finished dress, back on its stand, all the detailed embroidery that sits across the bust, perfectly aligned bands of simulated pearls and glass beads that took several days to finish. The flattering outline of the sleeveless bodice that cuts in low under the arms. To change this would mean more hours than they have available to them.

"We could keep the bodice as it is and simply add a longer skirt, but I think we might like to find a way to ensure the shape is defined. If we drop the skirt from the existing bottom of the bodice, it will lack definition, the silhouette may be too fluid. Meredith? Do you agree?"

"Yes." She has to, even though she can see the hours of extra work ahead. "It feels like it may need something that sits between the two elements, to soften the join, the movement from one to the other. The bodice silhouette feels quite daring—is there a way to elongate this into a longer skirt?"

The design team disappear to discuss the options while William and Meredith await their instructions, too tense to pick up other tasks in the meantime.

"Are you okay, William? You came to bed so late last night." Meredith rubs her hands across the back of her husband's shoulders, watches as he closes his eyes, melting into her touch.

"I'll manage," he says. "It's just my eyes are tired, so I'm having trouble focusing on anything."

"Well, let me cook you something special for your birthday dinner tonight." She smiles. "I haven't forgotten."

"My birthday?" He looks at her quizzically for a moment. "Oh my goodness, it is, isn't it? So, is this what I can expect from my fifties? Forgetfulness and extreme tiredness. Not much to look forward to, is it?" He smiles. William is not the sort of man to feel low. He always rallies and pushes on. But it's the first time Meredith silently wonders how much of it is for her benefit. William protecting the woman he loves, the mother of his only child, from any need to worry. He hasn't spoken much about the baby, but the situation is obviously weighing on his mind.

In the end, the dress is a success. The pale blue-gray chiffon is newly ruched from the waist to below the hip before the fabric falls away into the full-length skirt they all know is needed. It's the perfect solution, conceptualized and performed in under twenty-four hours. A success, if you discount so little time for sleep and a canceled birthday dinner.

But it's the last one, Meredith reminds herself. Soon she can relax. She'll be at home and she can catch up on all the sleep she needs. But when will William rest? She's praying the baby will hold on. Let them have a couple of weeks' grace before the sleepless nights begin and shatter what little energy the two of them have left.

TWENTY-EIGHT

❦

Jayne

When I wake the next morning there is a note by the side of the bed.

> *That was wonderful. You are wonderful. I'll see you when*
> *you get home. Jake x*

It truly was but I am pleased not to have to explain his presence to Meredith this morning. She is already dressed and having breakfast in the kitchen when I get down there. One of the great advantages of helping her pack for this trip was that I was able to influence the clothes she brought. What she's wearing, a light cotton olive green shirtdress with white anemones printed around the hem and across the waistband, is, I'm happy to say, entirely appropriate for a wander around an eighteenth-century aristocratic town house, a *center of entertainment in London*, according to the website where I booked our tour tickets. I'm slightly less impressive in a navy polyester skirt and a pale blue scalloped-edged blouse I must have bought five years ago.

"So, it's our last London location today, Meredith. Are you excited to return to Spencer House?"

Her response surprises me. "No, I don't think so."

It's a foreboding start but there is no backing out now. We finish our breakfast together, then take a taxi to Marble Arch, zipping down Park Lane toward Hyde Park Corner and on to Piccadilly. Meredith is very quiet and the break in conversation allows me to revisit my own memories of last night. Did it really happen? The flashbacks of Jake are making me crave more of him. I think about his hands, the warmth of his skin against mine, his tenderness, the way he touched me so gently, his eyes trained on my face for any sign it wasn't right, until we were completely lost in each other. I'm not sure how I'm going to face him after the things I did, the things I said in the throes of it all. How he encouraged me to go somewhere freer where all my inhibitions disappeared.

"You seem different today. Happier, I think." Sometimes Meredith misses nothing and I can't help but smile at the fact. "Is there someone making you happy?" She seems to have no specific recollection of Jake being at the house last night.

I think about her question, turning to look out the window as the tempting shop displays of Fortnum & Mason flash by.

"There is someone," I say. "But it's also you, Meredith." I turn to face her again. "For trusting me to help you. For allowing me to see and feel the things I need to. I think you're teaching me far more than you know."

She doesn't answer but reaches across the seat of the cab, takes my hand, then places her other one protectively on top of it.

We enter Spencer House on an unassuming backstreet off St. James's Street, meet our guide, and are taken into the library.

"This is where I wait," Meredith announces as soon as we step in through the huge double wooden doors. "So many beautiful ballerinas floating around, but I sit here." She points to a stiff high-backed armchair next to a glass-topped table with a huge display of white orchids and another beautifully inlaid with a chessboard.

"I'm very uncomfortable." She reaches her hand around and rubs the small of her back. "Listen for the ticking clock on the mantelpiece." She closes her eyes in an attempt to drown out all other noise.

She's right. I can hear its rhythmical click over the sound of other visitors' footsteps entering the room.

"I find it very calming . . . for a while at least."

Our guide starts to talk through some of the artworks on the wall—the Kissing Duchess, Lord Nelson, William Pitt—then we hear how many of the original features were removed from the house and taken to Althorp, before a huge restoration project began in 1985.

The group has started to move on, through a door in the corner of the room, but Meredith seems reluctant to follow.

"Of course, I can see it now, a shorter dress would be all wrong. Just look at the height of these ceilings. The location changes, so the dress must too." She rises from the chair and we pick up our place at the rear of the group.

"Everyone is worried about me. I am getting to quite a size, but we are busier than ever."

"Busy doing what?" It's the first time I've asked her a direct question about her involvement with the dresses.

She looks down at her hands as if she might find the answer there, rubs an index finger across her wedding ring.

"I have to wash them every hour but . . . but William's missing." She shakes her head in frustration.

I shouldn't push her. The fact that William is missing is preventing her from completing the circle of facts. She can't push the burden of his absence far enough aside to see the rest of the story. It's a warning we need to take this slowly today.

"The pale blue-gray chiffon is so delicate it gets tired very quickly when it's handled. Time is running out and Fiona isn't going to hold on for much longer. She's impatient from the very beginning. This is my last event before I am off with her."

"You are pregnant at this point, Meredith, is that what you mean?" I'm having to whisper so I don't interrupt the guide, who is standing in the center of the dining room under a huge crystal chandelier, directing people's gaze to the original wine tables and the eagle-and-lion symbol of the Spencer family.

"Yes, and very ready not to be. But I wish I knew what little time I'd have with her. It would have changed so much."

We pass through a heavily gilded room, the Palm Room, our guide explains.

"There are lots of photographs in here," chirps Meredith. "The men stay for drinks and cigars and the women move upstairs to the Music Room."

I take hold of her arm as we climb the stone steps upward under a domed ceiling and past what our guide tells us is a Venetian window and lantern. I feel Meredith's grip tighten on my arm.

"Everyone is worried about me," Meredith tells me as we reach the top. "But I'm worried about William. He's taking on lots of extra private work, saving up for the baby. It's too much. He's tired and stressed in a way I haven't seen before."

We enter the Music Room, which feels calm and less formal with its pale blue walls. The furniture seems to fit the dimensions of the room better, it's not overly grand.

"But don't be fooled," our guide announces, reading my

thoughts. The group forms a casual semicircle around him, drawn in by the intriguing tone he has adopted. "Spencer House has many very valuable and important works of art and one of the very finest is in this room. Can anyone spot it?"

Everyone starts to scan the walls, keen to impress the guide with a correct answer. I do, too, and it's the gold-framed painting of a large building that my own eye is drawn to, positioned above a central fireplace. There is something familiar in the depth of its coloring and style that I can't put my finger on, and before I have time to voice an opinion, a middle-aged man next to me shouts, "The Canaletto!"

"Spot on!" returns our guide, and I instinctively snap my head toward Meredith, remembering her reaction to the Canaletto poster back in Bath. Before I have a second more to predict her reaction, she cries, "No!" toward our guide. "Not Venice!"

"Uh, well, no, actually," he responds nervously. "Rome this time, but of course Canaletto is famous for his depictions of Venice." His eyebrows pinch together. He scans the other visitors for any clue as to what could have prompted such a strong reaction. Everyone is silently staring at Meredith with a new suspicion.

"I never should have gone to Venice," she shouts up at the painting. "Someone should have stopped me. Why didn't anyone stop me!"

"Er, I'm not quite sure what you mean." The guide fumbles for the right words to calm the moment and looks urgently at me for a solution to this interruption. I place my arm around Meredith and try to steer her into the next room, Lady Spencer's Room, with its bloodred walls and heavily swagged drapes. The rest of the group back away from us, unsure of what's coming next, then a security guard places himself in our path, not keen to let someone in the grips of a panic attack get any farther into the State Rooms.

"It's okay, Meredith, I've got you," I say, leading her back out onto the staircase and away from the gaze of everyone else. I sit her on the top step and let her catch her breath.

"I don't want to fly home alone," she sobs.

"You don't have to," I say. "I'm taking you home. We'll go and collect our things and we'll travel home together, right now."

She nods slowly and I watch a single tear slide down her face. It rests on her cheek, and she seems completely unaware of it, so I lift a finger and brush it away for her.

TWENTY-NINE

Meredith
1992

She doesn't like watching him leave alone in the early morning before first light. They always did the walk to work together.

William doesn't like it either. He's the cheerful one first thing, the morning person who'll have the coffee ready, the radio on, pulling them both out of their sleepy state, forcing them to get beyond what the clock on the wall is telling them. Now he rolls out of bed at the very last moment—Meredith will hear the alarm clock sounding over and over before there is not a minute more to spare. Only then does he rise, dress, no time for breakfast. He'll stuff his feet into the shoes he left by the front door late last night and be gone with barely a word spoken. The euphoria and delight of having a newborn baby in the house—the feelings everyone promised were coming—are nowhere to be seen or felt. There's just a body-numbing exhaustion that makes merely acknowledging each other feel like an effort some mornings. Meredith's not sure she can cope alone, and yet she feels she cannot burden William with any of the work at home, not when he's already stretched so thin.

Fiona refused to wait. Perhaps she could sense the change of routine, too, the lack of it defining Meredith's day. She arrives in a flurry of panic two weeks early and nothing is ready. The freezer hasn't been filled with homemade meals. Her tiny wardrobe of clothes hasn't been washed and folded as Meredith intended. Half the baby kit remains unboxed in the corner of the nursery. Neither of them has banked the hours of sleep everyone said they'd need.

But Meredith finds some order in the chaos. It's what she's good at. She lets go of the tight structure that once surrounded her day. Fiona dictates everything now and she has no choice but to let her. Meredith sleeps when she sleeps. She leaves the apartment only once Fiona wakes from her naps. Mealtimes are missed, dinner is rarely ready by the time William arrives home. The two of them spend hours curled up together on the sofa under a cozy cotton blanket. How on earth will there be time for any of this when she returns to work?

Fiona wakes continually through the night, so Meredith makes a temporary bed on the floor of the nursery, that way William won't be disturbed, and she can be closer to this precious bundle, right there the second she is needed. William raised a mild objection to her leaving their bedroom but was too tired to turn it into an argument.

"I'll never see you," he sighs. "Between my hours and Fiona's nocturnal habits, when will there ever be time for you and me again? I miss you."

"It won't be forever. She needs me more right now. Soon she'll be sleeping through the night and I'll be back in with you." She places a kiss on William's cheek, noticing the deep fatigue in his eyes, the drained grayness of his skin. He can't even raise a smile.

"We're newlyweds" is all he adds before he drops heavily onto the sofa.

It's months before Fiona comes close to sleeping through the night, and as hard as he tries to hide it, Meredith feels the resentment softly radiating from William. He starts to work later, hoping the baby will be in bed by the time he gets home. He eats dinner there, too, sometimes goes to his own bed without nudging open the nursery door to check if either of them is sleeping.

Meredith misses him, too, but she is swept away by her love for Fiona, shocked by the strength of the bond already welded between them. There will be plenty of time for William and me later, she thinks, years and years of us to come. I will be back to work before I know it, I need to devote this time to my beautiful Fiona.

THIRTY

≈⊰⧳⊱≈

Jayne

I'm sitting in one of the pretty private gardens that fronts one of the crescents north of the city center with Fitz, a mature Labrador whose bouncy days are behind him. He lives in one of the houses behind us and so we have the key that allows us access to this beautiful patch of green. I've chosen one of the wooden benches that circles a tree trunk in the center of the park, so I can just see the very tops of the buildings of Bath below, glowing pale orange in the first of Thursday's sunlight.

Fitz and I have been sitting here some time. He's the only dog I walk without actually walking. He's old, fifteen now, and it is company and belly rubs he craves, not exercise. So we've been sitting together for a very companiable hour, but today is different. Someone else has joined us.

"What a stunning view. You are so lucky to see this part of the day, every day, Jayne. It's so . . . calming." Jake pauses before adding, "Was it a deliberate choice today?" He looks toward me, trying to read my face for a reaction, and I realize he remembers today is my birthday.

"I think maybe it was." I smile and he understands. "Mum will call soon, and I'll drive back to her place later. We'll do what we always do, sit together, just the two of us, in the memorial garden she planted thirty years ago, when flowers were one of the few things she said could bring her peace." I let my fingers find Fitz's belly, and he rolls over, offering the softest part of himself up to me.

"Has it got any easier over the years, for your mum?"

"She's learned to live alongside it. But I know the length of time that took baffled some friends. It was as if somehow they felt the number of minutes Mum held my sister in her arms should equate to how long it should take to move on with her own life, to be grateful for what she *did* have. But that was to ignore the impact of my sister's loss *and* my grandmother's grief and how hard those combined forces hit my mum. In many ways, Mum was so strong, she found a way to put her other children before her own grief. But watching her own mother fall apart at a time in her life when she should have been surrounded by happy, beautiful granddaughters and not have a care in the world? It was too much. They should have been her golden years. Mum lost a daughter and then her mother."

I feel nothing but enormous relief saying this aloud to Jake, knowing that he won't look for a way to fix something that won't ever be mended.

He nods slowly. "And how about you? Is there any part of you that feels you can celebrate the day?"

"No. I haven't told anyone in the house. I wouldn't feel comfortable with the attention. The day will just slip by, unnoticed. That's what always seems to work best." Later, when I'm alone again, I know I'll contemplate the same quiet questions I always do. But there are fresh thoughts to ponder, too, now. What is worse—to have been denied the joy of growing up as a fiercely protective twosome, or to be lucky enough to find it for yourself, to live deeply within it and then be forced to watch as it slowly seeps away, gently enough for you to see, fast enough that you cannot reach out and pull it back? Isn't the fresher agony of Meredith's burden far greater than mine?

Jake looks at his watch. "I wish I could stay longer, but I need to get to the shop. I wanted to give you this before I go." He pulls a small package from the inside pocket of his jacket, neatly wrapped in yellow-and-white-striped paper and tied with twine. "It's not from me. Olivia asked me to give it to you. I have no idea how she knew but . . . I said I would."

I haven't been given a birthday present from someone who isn't family for a very long time. Probably not since school. The view of Bath beyond the park starts to swim away from me. My throat dries, making it impossible for me to say anything.

"She would have given it to you herself, but she worked at the Live Well Center until late last night and knew she'd need the lie-in, I guess."

I pull the paper from the package and inside is a beautiful hardback book, *The Language of Flowers*. Olivia has written a short note on the opening page: *Give yourself the time to enjoy it*.

I know I will treasure it forever.

I haven't said a word to Meredith about the fact we are all trying to find Fiona and, now that it seems we could be getting closer, it feels dishonest not to. I need to see how she reacts. But I also selfishly want her company today. I want to feel that unconditional kindness and trust, her lack of judgment. Is it wrong that I want to say things to her with the safety net of knowing they will probably be forgotten? I knock quietly on Meredith's door. I haven't seen her today. It was Davina's turn to check on her this morning, and when she opens up, I am relieved to see she is wearing a cool lemon dress with a light coffee-colored cashmere cardigan draped over her shoulders. She looks lovely. As our eyes connect, I see the slightest flicker of hesitation, then she smiles at me and says, "Jayne," and the lump is back in my throat again. I have to drop my gaze to my shoes.

"Hello, Meredith. Have you got time for a cup of tea?" I ask, blinking away the tears that are threatening to come.

"I don't know, you tell me!" she laughs.

"Maybe just a quick one, then, and a biscuit if you have any."

The place is spotless. Olivia has done an amazing job, because all the dust and grime are gone. The entire apartment feels larger, brighter. But every fiber of Meredith remains, exactly as she likes it. We take a seat in the drawing room, overlooking the sheep outside.

"Are you sad, Jayne?" Meredith's question takes me by surprise.

"Sort of but, well, it's a long story. But I shouldn't be. It's my birthday today." I force a smile.

"Happy birthday, darling." She stands and leans over me, planting the faintest kiss on my forehead. "Definitely not a day to feel glum. I've stopped counting mine now, obviously. Shall I see if I have some cake? Diana sent me a birthday cake," she announces.

"Really?"

"Yes, I've no idea who told her, but I was working very late. It was just William and me. There was a knock at the door, and when I opened it, a motorbike courier handed me a large white cardboard box. It was vanilla sponge with fresh cream and English strawberries. And our dinner, as it turned out, since we didn't have time to stop and make anything else!"

"What an incredibly kind thing to do for you."

"Yes. It made me feel very happy and valued." She looks at me then. "Everyone deserves to be happy, including you, Jayne." A weak smile plays across her lips and I feel sorry that I have to end her playfulness with talk of finding Fiona.

I'm working out how best to phrase what I have to say when she adds, "I wonder if I will ever get to sing 'Happy Birthday' to her again."

"To Diana?"

"To Fiona."

"Would you like to?"

"Oh yes, very much, but . . ." She understands there is more, but it sits just out of her grasp.

Now is my chance.

"How would you feel if I could bring Fiona here, to see you again? Would you like that?" I stumble slightly over the name and it rattles her.

"No, I don't think so." There is a nervousness in the speed at which she responds. "She doesn't know anything. William keeps a lot from her. She's too busy and too angry."

"Do you think she might like to know what's going on, Meredith? How you're doing and the help you need? If you like, I could help her to understand?"

"No, you mustn't do that." Her eyes look confused again. "William won't like it. She's not supposed to know."

She shifts her weight back into her chair and sighs loudly, crossing her legs and hugging her arms across her chest. I think about how to rephrase the question, how I might convince her finding Fiona is for the best. She senses I'm going to have another go and cuts me off.

"I understand that I can't stop you." She looks defeated. The sadness of Meredith making her feelings known while predicting that they will be ignored sends a fresh wave of guilt crashing over me. That if I do as I am suggesting, then her situation is being managed *around* her, not *with* her. "There's no need to worry," she says, smiling sadly. "You've done more than enough for me. William will be home soon, he will look after me." The chair seems to swallow her small frame. "Oh gosh, now look, I've forgotten to get you a cup of tea." All the natural ease Meredith was displaying when I arrived has gone. The mention of Fiona has made her agitated and tense and I follow her into the kitchen to help. But as soon as she steps into the room, her nervousness soars.

"No! What has happened! What have you done! This isn't right." She's spinning around the room, unable to focus on one single thing. Her voice is rasping in the back of her throat, her eyes wild, full of anger. I want to reach out and touch her, to ground her again, but for the first time I fear she might strike me.

"It's okay, Meredith, whatever is wrong, we can make it right." I raise my open palms to indicate I will do whatever she asks. "Just tell me what's upsetting you so much?" If only I'd left the door to her apartment open, one of the others might hear and come to help. But I know there is little chance of that. I'm on my own.

"William made these cupboards. He drew out the design, sanded the wood, painted them himself! Who has destroyed them? How could anyone do such a thing?" She's sobbing hard, with no sign that her distress will run out of steam. It's not the first time she has seen the kitchen cupboards since the others—we thought helpfully—removed the doors, but it's the first time she's reacting to their absence.

"Okay, we can make it better again." I hope Jake did what he originally suggested and stored the doors in the basement. "Please don't worry. I can—" But I don't get a chance to finish my sentence. Meredith picks up a bag of bread from the work surface and hurls it at me, scattering slices across the floor. I bend and start to pick them up, which only angers her more.

"Get out! Get out!" she yells, and I have no alternative but to leave her, my legs heavy beneath me. She is sitting on the floor of her kitchen, her knees drawn up to her chest, her head buried between tightly folded arms, like a child so blinded by anger that she can't make any sense of her own emotions. I realize, despite the promise I made her to never give up, I don't know if I can go on. I can't keep doing this to her.

As I leave her apartment, I bump straight into Olivia, who looks shattered, and it reminds me that I am due to walk Teddy for her this afternoon.

I try my hardest to push the emotion back down inside me, to mask how flustered I'm feeling, but I can't fool Olivia. She sees the stress in my face and looks beyond me to Meredith's door, immediately understanding the cause.

"Are you okay, Jayne?" She takes a step closer toward me.

"Yes, yes, don't worry about me. A tough night?" I ask, because I see the exhaustion hanging in her shoulders and I want to shift the focus away from me.

"It really was, yes. Not that I would change it." She exhales and leans the weight of her body into the wall. "I know people think it's good of me to do it but, honestly, it's a lot less altruistic than that. It probably helps me more. This job has taught me how people hold on to their problems and the damage that can do. I'm not sure how some of these callers would cope if we weren't there to listen—but I'm also not sure how much longer I could have coped either."

"Really?" Is my face giving me away? Does Olivia know I have called the number myself?

"We're all the same, deep down, aren't we? We all have these emotions held inside of us and they stay that way, sometimes for years, still feeling true. Until finally we start to talk about them. I suppose I can't listen to other people's problems night after night without sharing a few of my own."

"That makes a lot of sense. I wish Meredith had had access to something like this earlier, when it may have helped."

"We can't reach everyone but, yes, those we do are incredibly fortunate. Me included." She smiles at her own fragility, a recognition that she needs help, just like the rest of us. "It's forced me to confront how I use the endless deadlines to mask the pain I still feel about Mum's death." She lets out a deep sigh. "There, I said it out loud."

I feel bad that I've never questioned Olivia's motivations more deeply before but also very touched that she feels able to share this with me now. "You know I am here, if you ever need to talk?"

"Thanks, Jayne, that would be good sometime. And it works both ways, remember. But first, I need sleep."

"Okay, thank you for the book. It was incredibly thoughtful of you and I love it."

She smiles as she heads up the stairs to her front door. "And don't worry about Teddy. We'll curl up together this afternoon. It's a day for cuddles, I reckon."

I spend the afternoon going over and over the scenes with Meredith. What should I have said? How could I have handled it better? Should I simply have never mentioned Fiona's name? I don't knock on Meredith's door again, but I do make several visits to it, standing there for minutes at a time, listening for any sign of distress from inside. By the third visit, I can hear her moving around the flat, humming her usual tune to herself, and finally I can relax a little.

I'm not sure she will ever trust me again. It is William she needs. The one person on this earth she will never doubt.

I wanted to tell her I can't be sure he's ever coming home from wherever he is, to desperately try to make her understand why it's important we seek this extra help for her. Why we really must find and inform Fiona. I thought today was the moment to be cruel in order to be kind. To play on the closeness we have created to make her see that her situation is not sustainable, that she will feel only more confused as the months and years grind on.

I'm holding back the tears as I answer a call from Mum on my mobile.

"Oh, Jayne." She hears the sadness in my voice and wrongly attributes it to the day. "Come over. Let's sit in the garden and chat. I want to hug you and tell you how much I love you."

I hang up and call the helpline, saying everything I know would upset Mum. The freedom to let it all out, completely unfiltered, is the gift I decide to give myself today—and it is wonderful.

By seven o'clock Jake and I are sitting at Davina's kitchen island, while she's throwing different-shaped crisps into random bowls, Jake comfortingly close to me while Maggie, who is wearing a black catsuit, fluffy cat ears, and a clip-on black-and-white-striped tail, plonks herself down to my left.

"What are you dressed for, Maggie?" I ask.

"Isn't it obvious?" She curls her top lip up at me, pulls her chin in like I am the greatest fool she has ever been forced to suffer.

"Oh, um, not to me, no." I glance around the room. Everyone else looks equally confused.

"Jeez. Halloween, dummy." She tosses her eyes skyward.

"But . . . it's July. Halloween's not until the end of October." She's so confident, I am actually doubting myself.

"Who says it has to be the end of October?" She looks genuinely confused by this.

"See what you've started," laughs Davina. "Do not try to reason with her, Jayne, it will get you precisely nowhere. Go on, Maggie, the adults have things to discuss." Her eyes keep flicking to the door and I wonder if Willow is due home too.

"But what time can we go trick-or-treating?"

Davina looks mildly horrified. She glances at the clock on the wall.

"I'm not sure that's going to work, Maggie, since no one else on the street is expecting Halloween visitors tonight. Help yourself to some sweets from the cupboard if you must."

We all watch Maggie's shoulders slump, let down again by unimaginative adults who are slaves to something as pedestrian as the yearly calendar, not driven by their own creative force like Maggie is.

"I reckon I've got some treats I can rustle up"—Jake offers her a conspiratorial wink—"come and trick-or-treat at mine later."

"Thank you, Jake"—she sneers at the rest of us—"at least someone understands me." Is there a female alive, I wonder as Maggie sashays off, who is immune to Jake's charms?

"Jayne, there is something very exciting we need to show you." Davina's attention is back with me. I feel them all bristle with excitement. They're trying to contain their smiles, especially Davina, who looks like she might burst at any moment.

She pulls a laptop out of her bag and taps away, locating a file.

"I had the idea while you were both in London after a conversation with Olivia about her mother's life story," explains Davina. "It's a technique used in the study and care of dementia patients where they bring together lots of different elements from a person's history into one place. It could be something as simple as a photo album. Or, in this case, a collection of newspaper cuttings, old film footage, voice recordings, music that means something. It becomes a wonderful point of reference for the person who might be losing their grip on who they were and who they are now. I've made a hard copy, too, so Meredith will always have it on hand, she can access the images anytime she likes. I think you're going to love it. I hope it will really help her."

I have to say something. I have to cut through the collective excitement, because we can't continue with our plans after Meredith made it crystal clear this morning that she does not want Fiona to be found. I can't risk any further escalation of her outbursts and the emotional damage they may be doing to her.

"Before you show me, I think you both need to know something."

The room falls very quiet because they instinctively sense this isn't going to be good news.

"Has something happened? She was absolutely fine this morning." Davina's mind has jumped to the worst conclusion.

"Physically, she's fine. At least she was when I saw her late this morning. But emotionally . . ." I take a deep breath. "I'm sorry, but I don't think we can keep going with this. I asked Meredith today if she would like us to find Fiona and she made it very clear that we can't because William wouldn't like it. She was also incredibly upset about the removal of her kitchen cupboard doors. It turns out William made them."

"Oh no. It never even crossed my mind that might be the case." Jake looks crushed by the realization that in trying to help, we have made matters worse, just as Olivia predicted we might.

No one says anything. We just look at one another, perhaps accepting this has to be it now. We've gone as far as we can go.

"I'm really sorry, because I'm sure you've gone to a lot of effort with whatever it is you were going to show me. This is my fault. I shouldn't have pushed so hard for everyone to get involved. But clearly, she doesn't want Fiona's help, she doesn't even want her found. This morning, when I introduced the subject of Fiona, her reaction wasn't good. It was really upsetting to see and—"

"Upsetting to see?" Davina's attitude has shifted. She looks motivated by the setback, not defeated by it. "Well, imagine what it's like to live through then! We can't just abandon her, Jayne. This isn't about us and how we feel, it's about helping a woman who currently has no one else."

"Davina, just let Jayne explain, I'm sure that's not what she means." Jake tries to throw a calming influence over the room, and me a lifeline.

"She says Fiona's too busy and too angry and that William kept things from her," I say, trying my best to defend my rationale. "There must be a reason for that, and it's made me question our cause. Are we treading somewhere we shouldn't be? At the very least are we completely disrespecting Meredith's wishes?" I'm not offended by Davina's response to my doubts. In fact, I love her for it. She cares. Deeply, by the looks of it. Watching her now, fighting for what she feels is best and right for Meredith, is more than I could have hoped for when I first delivered flowers to her door.

"Listen, none of us were in London dealing with what you

were. I have no doubt it was hard, and you had to manage it all alone."

My eyes flick to Jake. Not entirely alone.

"Can I suggest you watch the film we have worked so hard on? If you still feel the same way afterward, then we will have to respect your wishes and Meredith's. Can we all agree on that?"

Jake nods, and I'm compelled to as well because I can't imagine it will make any difference to the conclusion I've reached.

"Okay, gather round," she says, hovering her finger over the play arrow on the laptop screen. But she pauses as there's a loud hammering on the door, which no one other than me seems surprised to hear.

"I'm here, I'm here!" It's Carina's voice from the other side. The others must have invited her, because I had forgotten to with all the emotion of the day.

She edges carefully through the door, carrying a large frosted cake covered in multicolored fondant icing petals, and candles that she must have paused in the hallway to light.

"Happy birthday, Jayne!" everyone is shouting and cheering, and a bottle of champagne is pulled from Davina's fridge. Then Olivia appears. "There better be a slice for me too!"

Maggie flies in astride a broomstick and starts to sing me "Happy Birthday." My face is frozen.

Then Jake is at my side. "I hope this is okay?" he whispers to me, looking suddenly nervous that it might not be. "We couldn't let it pass without letting you know how very special you are." He kisses me gently on the lips, lingering long enough for everyone to see we are no longer merely neighbors.

"Well, thank heavens for that!" bellows Davina, unable to help herself.

"CAKE!" yells Maggie.

"Yes!" shouts Carina, and Jake takes the cake from her before she drops it.

I feel a rolling swell of emotion build somewhere low in my belly. It travels up through me and I try so hard not to let it reach my throat, but I can't stop it. I cover my mouth with both hands to muffle the sound but it's no good. I stand in Davina's kitchen, surrounded by these wonderful people, and gently sob, for so many reasons. But maybe tonight, for once, they are the right reasons. I feel loved by people whom I am slowly allowing to see the real me. Who are slowly becoming the dearest friends.

"Jake, please cut Maggie a slice of cake or she'll never leave us alone." Davina's eye catches mine and I know she senses there is more to this than my being a little overwhelmed by a surprise birthday cake. I know there will be a time in the next month or two when I will sit down with her. Maggie will be in bed. Willow will be doing her homework or out with a friend and Davina will ask about tonight, its deeper meaning. And I will tell her.

But for now, Davina waits until her daughter is back on her broomstick and heading for the sofa before she clicks on the play arrow and a beautiful sepia shot of Meredith and William fills the screen.

THIRTY-ONE

It must have taken them hours and hours of research. There is old film footage and photographs of Diana that they have cleverly interspersed with the sketches of the gowns we have been following from Meredith's memory room, so the dates coincide. Meredith's personal story is intertwined with her professional one. The theme tune from *Steel Magnolias* plays as we see Diana walk the red carpet, before a slightly out-of-focus shot of Meredith and William posing on the steps of Chelsea Old Town Hall. The physical likeness between him and Fiona is clear for everyone to see.

The film pauses then on the image of Meredith surrounded by her coworkers, Diana, and Catherine Walker at Kensington Palace. I see the dresses we have been following come to life, followed by more of Meredith's treasured sketches. A flurry of headlines fills the screen. Record-breaking sums of money, charities to benefit, women posing alongside dresses they now own. Computer consultants, real estate brokers, couture collectors. And one final headline that asks: "What Happened to the Missing Dress? 79 When There Should Have Been 80." Then a close-up shot of the heavily embroidered floral gown in Meredith's apartment that remains thrown over the back of a chair in her bedroom where I found it weeks ago.

The film closes with a photograph I haven't seen before. It shows Meredith and William standing side by side just in front of the main front door to this building. She looks happy and relaxed, as if it's a new beginning. She has her arms wrapped around his waist and she's leaning into him, her face lifted up toward his. But there is a vacancy in William's eyes that doesn't seem right. He's disengaged from the moment, like he's smiling because someone pointed a camera and told him to. He looks shattered but also a little relieved. Maybe the move out of London came later than it should have done. Maybe having a young daughter to run around after meant he wasn't about to get the rest he desperately needed. I look more closely at Meredith and change my mind. It's not happiness expressed in her wide eyes. It's hope.

The screen goes black and every pair of eyes is now on me.

"What do you think?" Davina finally asks. "She's lived a very special life, hasn't she?"

"She certainly has. What a shame she can only remember snatches of it." I want to sound jubilant, to reward them for all the effort they've made, but I just sound sad. "She has the missing dress from the auction." I shake my head in disbelief despite knowing for sure that it is true. "She was thought so highly of that it was gifted to her by Princess Diana herself. The fact she can't remember this . . ." I can't finish my sentence because I feel the sadness threatening to overwhelm me and ruin what feels like it should be a celebratory moment for us all.

"Maybe this will help?" prompts Carina.

"Maybe." I try to think, which isn't easy when they're all looking at me expectantly. How will Meredith react to seeing this? "Maybe not."

"We can add to this film anytime we want to, whenever there is something we think might help. Think of it as a work in progress. There may even be suggestions that Meredith asks us to add." Davina's presuming the film will make it that far.

"What you've all done is wonderful, really, I mean it . . ." Davina senses the *but* coming and tries to head it off.

"It's got to be worth a try, hasn't it? A few weeks ago, she had no idea what that dress was doing in her apartment. But, while you've been away, she's been able to recall a staggering amount of detail about where she was at the time all these dresses were worn."

"Exactly, Davina. That's my worry. She has remembered a huge amount of detail about the dresses and, perhaps more important, about what was happening with her and William and Fiona, but she has yet to tell me explicitly that she *made* these dresses with William. She always falls short of making that connection. It's become obvious to us, but it isn't to her, not yet—and it may never be. I'm not sure why and I am worried about pushing her too hard and where that might take her. We need to be careful."

"Jayne does make a very good point," adds Carina, trying to shift the balance so I am not left alone on this side of the debate.

"Okay. Let me put it this way then. What do you think she would say to that dilemma, if she were here now and had clarity of thought? Would she want to risk it, if it meant even the slightest possibility that it may bring her closer to William?" Davina knows the answer to this before I deliver it.

I look at Jake, hopeful of some steer. What is the right thing to do? But he simply smiles and says, "It has to be your decision. You started this and it is entirely up to you if you want to end it. We are all here to support you—and Meredith—whatever your decision."

I feel Davina squirm in her seat, she wants to try again to

persuade me but feels she can't after that—and not when my giant birthday cake is sitting between us all.

I try to reason my way through the problem aloud.

"If I was going to continue with the road trip, to follow the path of the remaining dress sketches, then that would take us to Sandringham and Althorp, which I guess could both be done in a day trip each. That would give us a little longer to see if the leads we already have on Fiona amount to anything. But then it's Venice and New York. Not exactly easy—or affordable—options, are they? And a much bigger time commitment—and given how she has reacted to Venice up until now, I'm not sure she would want to go. I couldn't risk it."

"Don't worry about that for now," suggests Davina. "You could plan for the first two and see where that leads you. Who knows what will come to light while you are there? And we can let the Fiona inquiries tick along. We don't need to make that decision right away."

"What about work? I can't expect you to cope without me forever, Carina."

She simply waves a hand across her face, like the problem is barely worth raising. "I've told you before, it's not an issue. Don't let that be the thing that stops you going."

"We can easily plan the trips for days when you're not scheduled to work there," adds Davina. "Dog walking isn't a problem either. Willow has loved helping out. We can make sure Meredith's place is kept clean while you're both away and get her fridge restocked too. And those kitchen cupboard doors back on. We'll simply take pictures of the contents and stick them on the outside. That should help."

"I can take care of that, no problem," offers Jake.

The mood of the room has lifted. They all sense they are turn-ing me.

"I can't make any promises beyond these next two trips," I say with a weak smile.

"Absolutely, yes, of course." They're all talking over one an-other. Davina's smile has returned.

"But there is one slight problem. Earlier today, when I raised all this with Meredith, it was very clear she wanted me to leave her apartment. I'm not entirely sure she'll come with me after that."

No one responds, but Davina sighs and her reaction seems to travel around the group, even making it as far as Olivia.

"What am I missing?" I ask.

"The obvious this time, I'm afraid." Olivia cocks her head to one side and forces a rueful smile. "She's not likely to remember, is she? The question is whether you can pretend to do the same, Jayne, just to see where this next stage of the road trip might get us—and more important, where it may lead Meredith."

Put like that, it suddenly doesn't feel like a difficult decision to make, and my smile reassures them all that I'm still in.

"Ugh, someone pour me a glass of that fizz, for goodness' sake," laughs Davina. "We've got more plotting to do. Isn't it your turn in with Meredith first thing in the morning, Jayne?"

"Yes, it is."

"Great. You can share the film with her then. I'll email it to you now."

THIRTY-TWO

❦

It's eight forty-five a.m. when Meredith, looking completely disheveled, opens the door. There is toothpaste on her chin and her cardigan. Her hair is unbrushed and she is barefoot. She stands perfectly still waiting for me to introduce myself. We have taken a massive step backward.

"Morning, Meredith, it's Jayne from upstairs. Are you okay?" I wish I'd had the foresight yesterday to get her some forget-me-nots. They would have helped.

"William is missing." She hugs her arms around herself, rubbing her hands up and down, trying to comfort herself. "He didn't come home last night, and he's missed his breakfast this morning. I made him bacon, but it's all gone to waste."

That explains the unmistakable smell of charred meat that immediately takes me back to cold school camping trips.

"Shall I make us a warm cup of tea and you can tell me all about it?" I smile, trying my best to reinstate some familiarity between us.

"That could be nice," she says, and steps aside. I'm reminded again of how vulnerable she is, how easy it would be for the wrong sort of person to gain access to her apartment and her life.

The oven grill is still on and the remains of the bacon are now just a brown crisp of rind. I turn off the grill, scrape the lot into the kitchen bin, push a window open, and put the kettle on. Meredith looks on. "He prefers it well done," she offers as an explanation.

We settle side by side on the sofa in the drawing room and I pour the tea, already doubting if this is really the best day to play Meredith the film. But I know the clock is ticking over us all, and will there ever be a perfect time?

"There is something I was hoping to share with you this morning, if that's okay, Meredith?"

"Oh, what's that?" she asks, balancing her teaspoon on the edge of the bone china saucer.

"It's a film."

"*Steel Magnolias*? I love that one." She nudges forward, excited at the thought of it.

"Not exactly. It's about you, actually."

She laughs. "Why would anyone want to watch that?"

"I was hoping you might enjoy it. I thought it might remind you of some of the important and special times in your life. Make them seem real to you again."

"Oh. Well, all right then, since you put it like that. Let's watch it. We may even learn something we didn't know before."

I place my laptop on the low coffee table in front of us, propping it up on a stack of books so the screen is balanced higher. I'm nervous. There's very little predicting how this next fifteen minutes might go. My phone screen lights up and I see it's a message from Olivia.

OLIVIA: Good luck this morning. I'm just upstairs if you need me.

My finger hovers over the mouse. I watch it shake before I tap, and the film starts. I sit back, subtly shifting my body weight on the sofa, so I am facing Meredith and not the screen.

The second it starts I hear her intake of breath. Then she places her cup and saucer back on the table.

She doesn't say a word. The images flash and fade, the music starts and recedes, her beautiful dresses cross the screen in all their glory. I watch her face closely as they do. How her eyes widen and contract, fill with tears the moment the image of her and William on the steps of Chelsea Old Town Hall appears. She raises her right hand to her heart on seeing the pushchair, and when Fiona's graduation shot fills the screen, she says, "Oh, look at her, all grown up." There is no hint that she is anything other than immensely proud of her daughter. The only time her focus leaves the screen is when the image of the dress in her bedroom appears. Her eyes cast off in the direction of her room, then snap back again.

The film finishes and I hear her exhale, like she's been holding her breath throughout, but she's calm, her face looks soft, not tense.

"I have the missing dress, don't I." It isn't a question, she knows. I nod. "I think so."

"She knows I love it. It's 1992, the India tour. Such a sad time for her but a very exciting one for William and me. Fiona is on her way. I feel like I am on the start line of the happiest years of my life." I watch her shoulders slacken, perhaps with the knowledge that she is no longer living those days.

"I'm not sure she decides to give me the dress until that day at Kensington Palace, when we all had our picture taken together. We chatted a little. I had a chance to explain that I worked on the dress while I was pregnant, that it was truly a labor of love, as all her dresses are—*oh*." I can almost hear the penny drop. I think she can too.

She takes a breath. "Did—did *I* make that dress for her?" She raises her fingers to her lips. "Did I make *all* the dresses for her? With my own hands? With William?"

"I believe so, Meredith. I think that's why your recollections of those times have been so vivid. Because you were there."

"*We* are there. We do it together. We always do it together." Before I can prompt her any further, she shouts, "My essentials bag!" She shoots off the sofa and across the room, toward her bedroom. When she returns, she is holding the black bag in her hand. She sits back beside me and slowly unzips it to reveal its closely guarded contents to me for the first time: steel pins, a tightly rolled cloth tape measure, a pair of very small, sharp scissors, a thin paper pocket of needles in varying sizes, and identical spools of different-colored cotton.

"Can you play it again, please?" she asks.

This time she watches it with the laptop balanced on a cushion on her lap, so she is much closer to the screen, greedily absorbing every image and sound.

"Again, please," she says as soon as it finishes.

By the third viewing, her mood has shifted. The elation of the surprise discovery has left her. She passes me the laptop and then collapses over into her own lap, sobbing. This is exactly what I was worried about, it's too much in one go. Nearly a decade of missing memories, all firing back at her at once.

"Oh no, I am so sorry, Meredith, I genuinely thought this might help." I shouldn't have let the others persuade me. I should have trusted my instincts. Who knows what the longer-term effect will be on her now, how much it may set her back?

When the intensity of her sobbing subsides, she reclines back on the sofa, drained, wiping the last tears from her face.

"You don't understand. It's the relief. It always has to be me, you know? William makes sure of that from the very beginning. I think she trusts my discretion. I am great at slipping into the background. Going unnoticed. Disappearing when I have to."

I sigh because this is exactly the problem, why Meredith has lived unseen, right under our noses, for so long.

"Of course, I need the skills to do the job. But they need someone who understands the spotlight is not theirs to seek. It is always made clear that I shouldn't talk about any of it."

"But . . . it's your *life*, Meredith. You can talk about it as much as you like now. I hope you know that?"

"I do, thank you. Watching this beautiful film is like watching my memory room come to life. You've made all my favorite people and places real again. I feel like *me* again." She bites down on her bottom lip to stop it quivering. "I can't believe you've done this for me." Then her arms are around my shoulders and she is hugging me harder than I have ever been hugged before. I feel her fingers press into my shoulder blades. Still she squeezes tighter. My hand finds the back of her head and I cradle her there, my mind tripping back through all the steps we have taken to get here. Right back to my grandmother's sitting room, her lap, all the hugs I should have given, being channeled into this very special one now.

Finally, she releases me.

"I can't take all the credit. I had a lot of help. Davina, Carina, Jake, and Olivia, they all put this film together while we were in London. Do you remember Davina? You met her before we went to London."

"And her little girl, so full of life."

"Maggie, that's right. So, the question is, How do you feel about rejoining me for the second leg of our trip? There are two more dress sketches in your memory room that I think we should explore. If you'd like to? One was worn to Sandringham."

"The Big House. That's what she calls it."

"And the other is Althorp. Tomorrow is Saturday, so if you feel up to it, I think we should travel to Sandringham, stay overnight somewhere, and do Althorp on Sunday on the way back home. How does that sound?"

"It sounds wonderful! I better get packing."

THIRTY-THREE

❧

William
1993

I always knew she was the talented one. I suspect everyone does. You have only to look at her table to see it. No matter what time it is, she will never leave for the day unless it is spotlessly tidy with everything in its rightful place, ready for her the next morning. That never changes—not even when she was heavily pregnant with Fiona. I miss watching her work, tuned out to everything that is going on around her. If I want her attention, I have to leave my table and physically touch her, only then will her brain disconnect from the movement of her hands. She smiles when she is sewing. No matter the pressure or the closeness of the deadline.

Now that she's at home and we are forced to spend our days apart, I can feel the absence of her talent in the room. There's a lack of surety in the air that wasn't there before. I wonder if the others feel it too. Maybe it's just me? Maybe the shape of the person covering for her is just a daily reminder of my own shortcomings, ones I worry will be discovered now she is no longer here to cover for me.

It's not that Eliza, her replacement, lacks ability, but my

Meredith is missing, in the small details of the day, all the glorious things I love so much about her, like the way she handles the fabric. The tautness of it between Eliza's fingers isn't the same. The invisibility of Meredith's stitching, the extra sprinkle of brilliance that is hers alone. This dress is technically sound, I have made sure of that. Professionally it's a complete success and yet . . . Meredith is missing from its layers.

It's simple. A clean, defined silhouette. One I have shaped many times before. Minimal embellishment. It relies on the precision of the stitching. The perfect partnership of lining and fabric, so not even the faintest crease can ruin it. When it is finished, I step back and examine it on the stand. I can tell from three meters away that it isn't Meredith's work. No one else will notice but the sections of velvet are fighting each other. This fabric can't be pressed, it has to be steamed over a needle board, so it won't mark. It's like a delicate fruit, the softest nectarine, Meredith would say, it bruises easily. She always insists on doing the job herself, never trusting anyone else to reach her same standard. She has her own way of doing things and this isn't it. She's just the same with Fiona, her patience far exceeding mine. Is it wrong of me to say that despite how much I miss her during the day, I am glad she is doing the job I know I couldn't do?

Maybe I also have to admit that it is her brilliance that has made my work shine brighter these past years. Why else would I question my own ability now in a way I never have before? Is it good enough? Did I prioritize speed over precision? I wonder how many more errors I missed, Meredith spotted, and dealt with discreetly so no one else in the workroom knows? I can't ignore the evidence in front of me. Two dresses this year, so similar in style to our own work but created in another designer's workroom. Silhouettes, textures, and detailing that we are known for. The midnight blue columnar halter-neck evening dress, simply trimmed with black satin crossing over at the back and the waist, the skirt sharply slit at the side. Then the ruched asymmetrical bodice of the black silk crepe cocktail dress, with its low cap sleeves that attracted so much comment, as I'm sure she knew it would, bought off-the-peg from another designer. I obsessed about those dresses, studied those images of her at the Serpentine Gallery parties, rolling the same question round and round in my head for days until it almost drove me mad. Was it my fault that she chose to wear other designers while Meredith was off? Am I not what I once was? Am I, in fact, nothing without Meredith?

THIRTY-FOUR

※❧❧❧※

Jayne

I let Meredith get to packing, slip out the front door, and start to race back up to my apartment, then halt halfway. Her latest recollections are great news and I want to share them with someone.

A minute later, I'm knocking on Jake's door.

"Well?" He beams the second it swings open.

"She loved it. It worked. It's going to help. For the first time, she realized *she* made the dresses, Jake. I think seeing them all together with the footage and coverage, it connected it all. Who knows how much of it she will remember beyond today, but . . ." I throw my arms around him, he's not ready for it, and we both clumsily collide.

"That's such good news," he says. "I am so happy for you."

"Isn't it! We're heading to Sandringham tomorrow, leaving early. I feel so much better about all this now. It feels like we may have taken a major stride toward finding out what's happened to William."

I pause as I see he is gently laughing now.

"Oh, sorry, Jake, I'm blathering on and you're probably in the middle of work."

"Yes, I am, but it's absolutely nothing I would put before seeing you so happy." He hangs back, keen to see how I will respond to that.

"This does make me happy," I say. "All of it. Meredith, everyone in this building, and . . ." I leave the sentence hanging but he isn't going to finish it for me this time.

". . . and you. You make me happy, Jake." I don't shy away from the words.

A gentle, beaming smile lights up his face. "Glad to hear it," he says as he grabs my hand and pulls me in through the door, "because I have a birthday present for you. It's not the kind of thing I could give you in front of everyone last night, so I'm sorry you've had to wait."

The mischievous look on his face says it all. This is not something I'll be unwrapping but undressing.

I really should have taken at least a cursory look at the map before I offered to drive us both to Sandringham. It's going to take four hours, goodness knows how much longer by the time I've factored in all the loo stops. But the train was a nonstarter this time as there's no direct route.

Remarkably, Meredith is ready and waiting for me when I tap on her door at eight a.m.

"Have you packed toiletries, Meredith? Remember we are staying overnight."

"Yes, yes, I have it all."

"Are you sure? I can take a quick look through your case if you want me to."

"No need, it's all packed," she chirps back cheerily. "I made a little list for myself yesterday, after you left, so I wouldn't forget anything."

"Excellent, okay, where's your case? I'll get it into the car."

"It's there." She points down the hallway to a suitcase that is the size you might reasonably expect for a family of four taking a week away.

"That is a very large case for one night, isn't it?" I try not to think about the number of random items that may have made their way inside.

"It's the case we always take away. It has all the brilliant internal compartments so I can make sure our things don't get muddled up. I can't travel without it. That would just be odd." She smiles at me like I'm the one lacking common sense.

The one thing she hasn't got with her, I notice, is the essentials bag that she always insists on carrying, unless that, too, is stuffed into her case.

"Okay then, let's get going." I grab hold of it, then struggle to move it across the carpet it's so heavy. Everything I have packed is in a backpack that's slung over my shoulder.

Davina, Willow, Olivia, and Jake all appear to wave us off, accompanied by Maggie, who is loudly complaining about the fact she's not invited. Carina's message wishing me "the very best of luck" pinged onto my phone screen at seven this morning.

I've placed a cooler bag between us in the front of the car, filled with egg sandwiches, a couple of ripe bananas, some digestive biscuits, and a handful of the individual cheese portions I've noticed in Meredith's fridge before. That should keep us going.

We are about an hour into the journey, happily coasting in the middle lane of the M5, Meredith humming her own version of every song on the radio, when suddenly she stops.

"Oh no." She clasps both her hands to her cheeks. My foot instinctively eases off the accelerator.

"What is it, Meredith?" I try to keep my voice level and calm.

"I've just realized what I've forgotten." She looks at me side-ways like I'm going to be really unhappy when I hear what it is.

Whatever it is, surely we can cope without it?

"Oh gosh, it's the kettle. I'm so sorry."

"The kettle? You were planning to pack a kettle?"

"Yes, the travel one."

I sigh audibly with pure relief. "Well, no need to worry, I'm sure the cottage I've booked will have a perfectly good one."

"Ha! I thought that last time, though, didn't I? Do you remem-ber? And then I couldn't have a decent cup of tea. Awful!" She chuckles to herself, then reaches across and gives my thigh a pat.

"Where was the trip, when you forgot the kettle?" I nudge.

"Oh, um. Where were we going now? Salcombe, I think. Yes, a girls' trip. Do you remember all those tiny tucked-away shops, all squeezed together? You loved exploring them all, buying pretty boxes covered in seashells and postcards to write to school friends."

"Did I?" She's speaking to me as if I am Fiona, and I'm really not sure how to react, so I simply play along.

"Do you remember our walks down to the waterfront? Hilly, wasn't it? Fine on the way down, not so good on the way back up. The fudge shop! Salted caramel, that was always your favorite. Do you remember the day we got the little boat across the estuary?"

I look at her quizzically, encouraging her to remind me.

"Far too cold for the tourists—wasn't it?—so we had it all to our-selves. Our own personal water taxi. As we tried to get out of the boat it bounced off the harbor walls and you leaped off the little bench seat. D'you remember? We both got soaked to the skin as the water emptied into the boat. We were still laughing about it when we got back to the B and B. I made us a cream tea and we sat in front of the fire. You said it was the best holiday you ever had." She pauses for a moment, giving the images in her mind time to sharpen. But then her head dips and she looks so incredibly sad.

"Then I got a call from your father and we had to cut the trip short. My goodness, you were so angry with me . . . it felt like you'd only just got your bucket and spade out of the boot and I was telling you to put them back in again. You cried all the way home. How could I have been so cruel?"

I try to ask Meredith more questions, but she doesn't want to speak after that. She turns her head away from me and stares out of her window, watching a sudden rain shower pelt the glass. I sense her embarrassment. That the fleeting moment she thought she was sitting next to her daughter has passed and now she feels foolish for ever believing she was here. Or is it because she remembers the great disappointment Fiona felt and that she was the cause of it?

I've booked the last unrented cottage on the estate, despite the fact it's excessively large for just the two of us, and paid for the minimum two nights though we need only one. But its exterior, with its high arched windows, looks impressive, and I hear Meredith sigh loudly in appreciation as we approach it.

"Oh, look at this," she whispers. "We are going to be very happy here."

The red-and-brown brick house is double fronted, covered in dense ivy, and sits close to the estate's formal walled gardens. It has its own private walkway leading directly into them. There are only a handful of cottages within the grounds—all owned by the Queen—that can be rented, and I'm hoping I've struck lucky and Meredith stayed in one of them, maybe even this one. It's the closest one to Sandringham House itself so there is a certain logic to this being the best choice. All of the furniture and pictures inside, I've read, have been borrowed from the royal residences, so who knows? Perhaps Meredith will see something that she has seen before that may help resurface some important detail. It's optimistic, but that's what I feel we need.

None of the bedrooms on the first floor are en suite. Meredith chooses one on the south side, overlooking the well-stocked flower beds and borders below, and I take the smaller one next to hers. I throw my bag onto my bed and then return to her room to help her unpack.

She has pulled the case open and is starting to remove items of clothing. It takes me a few seconds to realize what is so wrong.

There is a small packet of pocket handkerchiefs with a *W* embroidered on them. A compact shaving set, a comb, some chunky woolen socks, several jumpers and trousers, tartan pajamas, three dark woolen suits. Then a large box of aspirin and a packet of earplugs. With the exception of a handful of Meredith's items that she seems to have tossed on top of the already full case, everything here is William's.

"Are these William's things?" I prompt. It would explain why there are so few of them in the places I'd expect to see them at their apartment.

Meredith begins to pick up each item and turn it over lovingly in her hands, tracing where William's fingers were before hers, before setting it neatly back onto the bed, apart from the shaving set, which she holds and studies further. "He has the softest skin, always so meticulous about shaving, never leaves any bristles because he doesn't like to think they'll scratch my face when he kisses me." I watch her slowly swallow down the pain of the recollection. Then she stands back from the bed and stares at the belongings, frowning.

"Did you pack them, Meredith?"

"I think so." She remains staring at the items lined up on the bed. "But not for this trip. They must have been left in the case from before."

I decide we could do with stretching our legs and getting some fresh air after such a long journey. I give Meredith some space to sort through the few things of her own she has brought, and we arrange to meet downstairs when she's ready. We decide on the shorter of the two mapped walks, which is a mile and a half circular route, and head off in the direction of the main visitor center. From there we pick up one of the broad woodland paths, both greedily absorbing all the sights and smells that nature gifts us, following the yellow arrows that mark our route. I point out all the trees I recognize: the Corsicans, Scots pine, oak, sweet chestnut, and birch. The trails are peaceful, and by the sounds of it, everyone has headed for the kids' adventure playground, shrill screams are carrying through the tree branches above us and it reminds me of Maggie.

Meredith is very quiet and, I notice, there is still no sign of the essentials bag.

"It's supposed to be one of the Queen's favorite residences, isn't it, Sandringham?" she eventually asks.

"Yes, I believe so. The house and formal gardens close to the public every autumn and winter when she comes."

"It reminds me of Richmond Park. The same earthy smells, the same sense of wide-open space. Families having fun together, forgetting that there is work to do tomorrow." She lifts her nose and inhales another lungful of ripe woodland air. "I walk for miles with her around that park at weekends. Sometimes that's what it takes to get her to stop crying. She's always crying."

"Is Fiona a difficult baby? Do you find it hard being a new mum?" I follow Meredith's lead, sticking to the present tense. "I know lots of women do."

"I knew it would be tough in the early months, we both expected it to be, but I feel the extra pressure of making sure William is getting the rest he needs. I try to take her out a lot so he can catch up on his sleep. Sometimes the crying gives him terrible headaches. He needs silence. His brain needs complete rest. To totally switch off."

"Why is that?" I ask.

We walk on a little farther in silence. Either she hasn't heard my question, or she is choosing to ignore it. Perhaps she is unsure of the answer.

"Would you like to go up to the main house, Meredith? I think we still have time to go inside if you'd like to, before it closes."

"Would you mind terribly if we head back to the cottage?" She seems disconnected from the day. Her gaze more vacant than usual. "I feel quite tired. I may have a little nap before dinner, if that's all right with you?"

Maybe it was the early start, but Meredith lacks enthusiasm for this trip so far. Her usual keenness to explore is missing. Sandringham isn't having the same effect on her that other locations have had, and I can't work out why. While she heads to her room, I start preparing some vegetables to go with the lamb shanks Davina has supplied for our dinner. But as I'm peeling and chopping the carrots, I'm wondering if this trip may be a waste of time after all.

"Pureed carrots, they're always a winner," she announces as she enters the kitchen and sees ours in the saucepan on the stove. "She won't eat most things, but she will always eat carrots."

"Are you hungry yet?" She's slept for far longer than I thought and it's nearly six p.m.

"Starving actually. Can I do anything to help?" She bends down to take a peek through the oven door, keen to discover what's on the menu tonight.

"Why don't you lay the table and I'll dish up," I suggest.

"I suppose I have it easier than them," she says to herself as she is placing cutlery onto the table and folding some napkins that she's found on the sideboard.

"How's that, Meredith?"

"Well, I'm at home with a tiny baby that I adore more than anything, but William is learning to work with someone new in my place." She's picking up the conversation we started on our walk, like the sleep she's had in between hasn't happened. "And Fiona, well, she's discovering the world around her, having new experiences every day, working out what she likes and what she doesn't, and I am so lucky to be witnessing it all. Everything's changing." She says all this with a lightness and ease, like it is no big deal at all, but then, as is so often the case, there is a shift in her tone. Suddenly she's more serious.

"The problem is, things slip through the net when life is that busy, don't they? Or maybe that's just an excuse."

Of course, how could I have missed it? The fact that Meredith must have been on maternity leave with baby Fiona when this dress was worn by Diana to Sandringham. She wouldn't have ac-companied her here that night.

"Am I right in thinking you never came to Sandringham, Mer-edith? You didn't follow the dress here with Diana, as you have with the others? You've never been inside the main house?"

"Oh goodness, no. There is no way I could. Fiona's tiny. I need to be at home while William works."

It explains why she has been so reticent since we arrived. None of what I am putting in front of her means anything because she never experienced it the first time around and I could kick myself for not pausing to work that out.

I try not to let the disappointment show on my face by loading our plates with the lamb and some creamed mashed potatoes. And all may not be lost. Perhaps other details will surface.

My mobile is on the table and I notice a message from the WhatsApp group illuminate the screen.

DAVINA: Jayne, call me when you can. x

I make a mental note to respond to her when we have finished dinner. It's Meredith I want to give my full attention to right now.

"I guess it must have been difficult for William, without you by his side every day, like he was used to?" I try to pick up the conversation again.

"He doesn't complain but he's not looking after himself." Meredith frowns. "He used to enjoy the walk to work and back but that's stopped. He catches the bus, which isn't really like him. He always used the walk to clear his head, to prepare himself for the day ahead, or to unwind from it before dinner. Being that sedentary can't be good for anyone, can it?"

I shake my head, pleased it's one thing I don't have to worry about with all the dog walking miles I rack up in an average week.

"Then the empty wine bottles started to appear outside by the dustbin. I shouldn't complain, it helps him to relax."

"Did you miss working together?"

"Very much. But I try to follow his example. I get on with whatever needs to be done. If William is prepared to, then I must too." She raises the small glass of red wine that I have poured for each of us. I lift mine to meet it.

"What are we toasting?" I ask.

"To William," she says with a beaming smile. "I think you're going to love him when you meet."

I scrape the last of our leftovers into the kitchen bin and decide to deal with the washing-up in the morning.

"Come on," I say, "it's been a long day. Let's get to bed." I make sure she has everything she needs. "You know where I am if you want anything. I'll keep my bedroom door open so just come in and ask."

I lie back on the bed, every limb feeling leaden, like the mattress isn't strong enough to support me. All my random thoughts from the day start to replay. Snatched moments from the car, Meredith unpacking William's belongings, the food we ate, Davina's message. My thoughts sharpen again. I didn't respond, I didn't call her back. I try to ignore the oversight, but it has started to burrow into my brain, making it impossible to let go of the day and welcome in sleep. I reach for my phone. There is a second message from Davina. She has moved our conversation to a private thread.

> **DAVINA:** I'm sorry to drop this on you, Jayne, but I saw something in Meredith's apartment today while I was having a quick clean. I thought you might want to ask her about it while it's just the two of you there. It's a letter from Bath Crematorium and dated July 2017, a year ago. It's unopened, Jayne. I've been racking my brain and I can't think of a single reason why a crematorium would write to anyone, beyond the obvious. Can you?

I stare up at the ceiling, willing a possibility to come to me. But it's a fruitless exercise. There is no other explanation. Except we checked the records. There is no recorded death for William. So, what could be in the envelope?

Sleep will be impossible now. We all accepted at the beginning that this outcome was a possibility, but we had struck a confident line through it. What have we missed? Surely Meredith cannot be a widow and have forgotten it? And even if she had, her daughter would not leave her alone to deal with it. What if the possible contents of this letter don't relate to William at all? What if it's Fiona? What if we are jumping to entirely the wrong conclusion? Couldn't this just as likely be a circular letter to the local community, appealing for fundraising? Volunteers to weed the grounds and rose gardens?

As I lie here listening to the pounding of my own heart, I see Meredith out of the corner of my eye cross the landing and head for the stairs.

I catch up with her just as she is about to start her descent.

"Everything okay, Meredith?" I ask like it is perfectly normal for her to be wandering about in her nightie late at night.

"I shouldn't be here. It isn't my turn to come this time. I need to get home, I think. William will be wondering where I am."

She looks so fragile. Maybe it's the sight of her in a thin nightie, her hair unbrushed, her face makeup free, a thin veil of fear visible in the whites of her eyes.

I loop my arm through hers.

"You're right, Meredith. It's my mistake. I thought you would like it here, but I was wrong. We can leave straight after breakfast in the morning. How does that sound?"

"I don't know what I will do until then. That's not my bed, so I can't sleep there." She nods back toward the bedroom she came from. "Whoever's bed it is might come back."

I think for a moment. It seems too odd to suggest we share a room for the night. She may wake later and find it even more confusing when it's me and not William beside her.

"Why don't I make us both a warm drink?" That raises a smile. "Then how about you come into my room? I know a great movie we can watch together."

As *Steel Magnolias* is reaching its awful, tragic conclusion and Sally Field is desperately hoping a collection of treasured photographs will raise Shelby from her sleep, the magnitude of the future conversations I may have to have with Meredith weigh heavily on my mind. What if the absolute worst has happened to William or Fiona? What if she has lost the only man she ever loved, or the daughter she so clearly misses? Who will tell her?

Who will care for her?

THIRTY-FIVE

∽୧ℒ୨∼

William
1994

Meredith is away and I am looking after Fiona. But she's restless, has been all day. I know what lies ahead and the thought of it is making the stress bridge tightly across my shoulder blades. I didn't think it was possible to feel any more admiration for my wife, but on nights like this, I know she is unquestionably the better half of us both. The pureed food that Meredith left out for Fiona is already on the kitchen floor. She refuses everything, getting increasingly red in the face. Angry with herself and with me, I think. And now hungry too. If I can't get her to eat anything, she'll wake in the night again, then my last hope is some warmed milk and mashed banana. If she rejects that, then we'll see every hour together until dawn. And I have to finish drawing a new pattern for the Althorp dress tomorrow. There is no more time. It shouldn't have taken me as long as it has, and we are up against the wire. Any more delay from me and it will place the extra burden on Meredith and I just can't have that.

At midnight, in desperation, I bring Fiona into bed with me. I place her across my chest, hoping the warmth of my skin, the familiarity of my smell, will lull her to sleep. It doesn't. She naps for minutes, perhaps twenty at the most. Then the crying starts again. I am out of ideas, incapable of logical reason now, my thoughts crashing between a desperate longing to sleep and a fear of rolling on her and hurting her. At around two a.m. she finally gives in to exhaustion, falling asleep with one arm and one leg pressed against me. I cannot move. I'm willing myself not to need the toilet. Trying to force the thought from my head. The harder I try not to think about it, the more I need it. I move her as slowly as I can, feeling my bladder will explode if I don't get there soon. I make it. The relief surges through my entire body. I sit, my head in my hands, I could fall asleep right here. If I close my eyes for one minute, I think it will happen. Then I force myself up, back across the landing. I am almost to the bedroom door, my body craving the luxury of being horizontal, when the crying starts, and I want to throw open the windows and rage out into the dark night. Instead, I pick her up and she immediately calms. We go into the lounge. She wins again. I place her on her play mat, make some strong coffee, and pick up my pencil, turn my focus to a private commission that is due back with the client next week. Perhaps I can achieve something tonight, when I can count the sleep I've had in minutes, not hours.

You can't be a good pattern cutter sitting down, you just can't. It's like asking an orchestral conductor to do his job without standing. His work would suffer for it, and I know mine is too. How long can Meredith keep hiding the fact for me? It's the raw, bone-deep tiredness. I try so hard not to feel resentful but the feelings seep into me and I can't deny them.

The Althorp dress should be straightforward. We are simply using all her latest measurements to alter a favorite dress that she has worn before. As she's not available to come into the workroom for a fitting, I am drawing the pattern again, ensuring it's perfect. It sounds so easy. But this dress is all about straight lines. The only way to keep them straight is to get above them. But I don't seem able to do that anymore. Not for as long as I need to.

I wonder if people are starting to notice. They must be. That I need to rest so often. Are they aware that I am constantly marking and remarking the lines? Rubbing them out, starting again, shaving off fractions of measurements to correct my own mistakes. I no longer trust my own eyes.

THIRTY-SIX

～⁕～

Jayne

The house is vast. I park in a field opposite the west gate entrance and immediately see its outline dominating the landscape. The unbroken green of the surrounding fields and trees, the glossy black railings, an endless cloudless sky. Then the immovable gray stone walls sitting centrally in their picture-perfect surroundings. There is a beautiful simplicity to it that belies the sadness of the story that seeps from Althorp's walls and creeps unnoticed out into the woods.

We left Sandringham by eight a.m., arrived here by ten a.m., and already it's hot. I hand Meredith a bottle of water as we start our twenty-minute walk up the tree-lined driveway, the essentials bag now swinging from her right wrist, the biggest clue that today holds the promise of further answers. There is no breeze and I can feel the heat radiating from the stone beneath our steps.

"Everything is so still, so peaceful." Meredith's pace slows as she casts her gaze around us. "Not like before. It's a private cocktail party for one of her charities, the driveway is a constant stream of cars."

We are early, ahead of the first coachload of tourists, exactly as I planned.

"Shall we walk the grounds first, Meredith, before the heat gets too much?"

"A sensible idea, yes."

We follow the driveway, bearing left, then right, through a courtyard and converted stables that now house a café and gift shop, before we are alongside the more formal lawns surrounding the house itself, looking even more imposing close up. We pass deep stone-walled flower beds packed with neatly trimmed laven-der bushes, a sea of purple alive with the thrum of industrious honeybees, then pick up a path at the rear of the house that will lead us on toward the lake.

"It's the dress I am most worried about seeing her in," says Meredith, trailing her hand along clouds of white hydrangeas. "It's an old favorite, and there are mistakes."

"Oh?"

"I don't say anything, of course, I just deal with it. It's the small-est margin of error that William hasn't spotted. Sections that should be identical aren't. I make the corrections as I go. I keep it to myself. He is looking after Fiona tonight. He has a lot to think about. Maybe I should . . . ask more questions." She trails off.

"What questions, Meredith? What more could you say?" I don't slow my pace, I don't look sideways at her, I try to convey that my questions are nothing more than polite chitchat.

She stops on the gravel path and glances left, along a grassed walkway, planted symmetrically with two identical rows of fruit trees.

"Is it my chance to stop something and I miss it?" She looks at me, waiting for an answer she believes I can deliver.

"I don't know, Meredith," I sigh. "I'm sorry, I can't help you there. Is there anything else you remember, even the tiniest detail?"

"Everything is good again and it's forgotten. He is very persuasive, William, that's the problem. If he wants you to believe something, then you will. Fiona is so small. When he says he's tired from the disturbed nights, I believe him. Why wouldn't I?"

The path begins to widen out, forking around the lake. We are the only ones here. We walk left toward one of the wide wooden benches. The reeds bordering the lake stand motionless. The water is glass. Even the ducks are respectfully mute. The grass circling the lake has been immaculately cut. The only sounds are the gravel crunching beneath our feet and the lightest whistle of playful birdsong. We take a seat and I feel an unexpected hit of emotion as I notice the columned temple at the bottom of the lake, Diana's unmistakable black silhouette visible from here. And the words Meredith quoted that day to Maggie: "Whoever is in distress can call on me. I will come running wherever they are."

Meredith's sigh is full of sorrow.

"Such a ridiculous waste," she says, looking toward the small rowing boat that is tethered by a rope to the central island.

"There can't be anyone who would disagree with you on that, Meredith," I say softly.

Then we sit there like that for the next half an hour, both contemplating the tragedy of the loss, until I spot a trickle of tourists filing toward us, picking up speed as they realize they are reaching the finale of the tour, raising their cameras and phones, the irony of the intrusion completely lost on them.

I look at Meredith to see if it annoys her, but she is smiling broadly. "I know what she is wearing, her last beautiful outfit," she says, "and it makes me feel so very proud."

"My goodness. What a precious secret to have kept for all these years. I won't ask you what it looks like. There would be no point, would there?" I smile at her.

"No." She shakes her head determinedly. "I'd never tell."

We start to walk side by side back toward the main house. "Time for a quick cream tea?" Meredith suggests.

I nod enthusiastically.

"Then I will take you inside and show you the beautiful portrait of Lady Georgiana Carteret that is said to have inspired Diana's wedding dress."

THIRTY-SEVEN

～∞～

William
1994

It should have been one of the easiest dresses to make. I have made it before, in fact. The blueprint was there. But this one is for Diana, she personally selected it after a visit to the studio some weeks earlier. It shifts the balance in my mind, making the pinch of pressure a touch more intense. I know immediately the newspapers will love it. The coverage will be extensive. It's a much sexier dress than she's used to, the way the black velvet wraps at the waist, draping toward the hip and held at an embroidered pocket. It skims her body, elongating her shape. I'm nervous before I even start. I pause over the table, almost not wanting to begin. Then I look toward Meredith, bent over her own table, her shoulders contracted with concentration.

Inspiration can strike from the most unlikely places. The idea for the embroidery on this dress is taken from an antique picture frame, one finished with exquisite marquetry and edged in lead shot. The black bugle beads and small boulle work perfectly in re-creating it. It is designed to frame her face and neck. But that's the problem, I just can't get the line right and I don't know why. I refer back to Catherine's sketch constantly, drawing line after line, rubbing out those that seem furthest from the original idea. Time is running out. I finish the pattern, giving the go-ahead for the fabric to be cut. The finished dress is perfect. It leaves for Venice and so does Meredith. She will be gone for two nights this time. I envy her the hotel room. The large uncreased bed. The coolness of the sheets. The space to breathe. The spotless cleanliness. The order and the service.

I wish I could take a pause. The hours have been long and drawn-out. The sleepless nights the same. I just want to clear the backlog of private commissions. I promise myself that when Meredith returns, I will take a long weekend, maybe suggest that she does too.

There are only a handful of us left in the workroom tonight. I am working on the pattern for a poppy-red silk crepe dress that is mercifully simple, its fluid shape forming easily on my tabletop, my hands gliding across the paper, the instruments feeling instinctively a part of me again.

It's getting late. Too late to bother with a dinner break now. I will have whatever is left in the fridge when I get home. Some cheese and a glass of red again, probably. Maybe Fiona will even be asleep by then. Leonor, our brilliant Portuguese neighbor, will have settled her. She raised four children of her own, and I sometimes feel she is raising ours too. What started as a few hours here and there when we needed it has stretched, bleeding into every corner of our lives so that now I feel we rely on her, we couldn't cope without her.

I'm not sure at first why the wall is suddenly pressing into my back. I think for one disorientating moment I have fallen asleep standing up. Then the nausea hits me, and I know it's because I haven't eaten. No one notices at first, so I just stay here for a minute, waiting for my center of gravity to right itself. But it doesn't. I try to move to sit down but my legs feel at sea.

"William?" Peter is approaching me. Is he moving in slow motion or am I just seeing it that way? "Are you all right? William?"

I can't answer him. I feel out of myself as if I am watching this happen to someone else in the room. All I can think is how much I would love someone to turn off the harsh strip lighting above me. I can't look at it.

I'm helped into a chair and someone puts a glass of water into my hand. Someone else is making a phone call. I can tell from the way they are looking at me that I am the subject of it. I look at my watch and notice it's seven fifteen p.m. exactly, the day has got away from me again. I can hear them discussing the dress, who will finish it, like I'm not going to be here. Their voices sound muffled, like we are all underwater. I want to correct them. It's poppy red, not russet. The whole thing lasts just a couple of minutes, but Peter insists on driving me home.

Fiona is already in bed. I vaguely remember saying goodbye to Leonor, paying her. Then I sleep so soundly that when I wake the next morning, I know I wouldn't have heard Fiona if she cried out in the night. I sit bolt upright in bed, listening for the slightest sound that tells me she has been awake, calling for me. I look at the clock on the bedside table. It's gone nine a.m. I planned to be at work two hours ago. Then confusion pours over me again. Meredith is sitting in the armchair in the corner of the bedroom. She is wearing yesterday's clothes. She's smiling but she looks so terribly sad.

THIRTY-EIGHT

❦

Jayne

Meredith seems pleased to be home. But I'm not. As she lets us both in, she heads straight for her memory room and I feel an overwhelming sense of foreboding. What will the following few days hold for her? I texted Davina before we set off so she knew what time to expect us, and within a couple of minutes she joins us.

Meredith is listening to a beautiful piece of music while I make her a cup of tea.

"There it is." Davina points to the unopened letter she has placed on the worktop. It could be mistaken for a beautiful invitation on first glance. There is a pale pink watercolor of a cherry blossom branching across the front of the envelope and across the back where it has been sealed. It looks cheerful but I'm not sure the contents will be.

"We should open it." Davina's tone is grim. She's expecting the worst.

I sigh heavily. "We can't. It's private. We don't have the right to open her personal post."

"Jayne, if something has happened to William or Fiona, we

really need to know about it, don't you think? It makes sense to open it. We need to know. And so does she." She nods in the direction of the memory room, where we can hear Meredith cheerfully humming. "Or we can show it to her and suggest *she* open it. If she doesn't, well, let's worry about that then."

"Okay, I'll ask her to open it."

"I'll leave you to it. It might be better with just the two of you. But let me know if you need me and I'll come straight back. Good luck and keep me posted." Davina senses the doubt still lingering on my face and adds, "It's the right thing to do, Jayne, really it is."

I stand in the doorway and watch Meredith sifting through some old photographs in her lap. One of her holding a newborn baby in her arms, another of Fiona riding a bike, a bright red rosette with the number six at its center stuck to the handlebars. What is the worst news this letter could deliver? I wonder. That a missing husband will always remain that way, with no time for goodbyes? Or that Meredith's broken relationship with her only daughter will never be fixed, that Fiona will forever remain a teenager, pinned to a corkboard?

If she opens this letter in front of me, will she be able to process what the contents mean? Will she accept it? Will she have any memory of it tomorrow? Then I think about how she might react. Like she's hearing the news for the first time, when the shock will be its most visceral.

I take the armchair next to hers and settle myself in, holding the letter in my hands. I feel stiff from so many hours driving over the past couple of days. I need to get out for an early-evening walk and some fresh air. I miss my dogs.

"Meredith, I have something to show you. I'm not sure if you've seen it, but this letter came for you, quite a while ago by the looks of it. Perhaps you ought to open it?" I hold it toward her.

"Oh, thank you, darling." She doesn't look up, too absorbed in the photographs.

"It looks important." I try again and she looks toward me, smiling. I don't want to be the one to remove that smile from her face. "Here, it's addressed to you. It must have got missed."

She takes the letter from me and places it in her lap, returning her focus to the photographs.

"Would you like to open it now, while I'm here?"

"All right then."

She picks up the envelope and traces a finger across the cherry blossom, then turns it over. She's going to open it. A deep sense of dread sits low in my stomach and I hold my breath, almost willing her to put it down again.

"You know what I'd really like to do?" She starts to shuffle forward in her chair. "Go for a walk before we miss the last of the sun. Shall we go together?"

Relief washes over me. I've got to swing by the flower shop to answer a couple of Carina's queries, and Meredith could come with me. I imagine she'd love to see it.

"Yes!" I snap straight back. The letter can wait. If it contains the worst kind of news, I don't want her to know it today. Not when the sun is still shining, and she looks so peaceful.

"Give me fifteen minutes to change my shoes and grab some water for us both," I say, heading toward her front door. "I'll be right back."

Meredith is a little quiet, but I feel a renewed bounce in my step as the steep hill sweeps us down toward Bouquets & Bunches.

Poor Carina looks shattered when we arrive. It's still hot and she is wearing a tiny slip of a dress under her usual thick cotton apron. Each time she bends down, she has to raise a hand to her chest to stop it gaping open, exposing her bra. I can see how much it's annoying her.

"Oh gosh, Carina, do you need some help?" I offer. "I'm sure Meredith won't mind perching with a cup of tea if you need me to wade in for an hour or so?"

"Absolutely not. It's Sunday; I'll be closing soon anyway, and I feel bad enough for dragging you in here as it is. I just need to ask you about the two new corporate accounts you placed in the system before you went away. They're both due to start this week and I want to make sure we get them right. Meredith"—she turns toward her—"can I get you something cool to drink? Some elderflower? Or an iced tea perhaps?"

"Just a water would be lovely, thank you." She is staring at Carina's dress and I can tell she is going to comment on it. "The neckline . . ." She hesitates and looks away, not wanting to finish her sentence, raising her own hand to her collarbone.

"Oh, I know, I've got it all wrong this morning, Meredith. But it's so hard to find something to wear under these aprons when it's this hot." Carina laughs it off.

"The neckline isn't right. It's sexy, not formal. More mistakes again." Meredith is shaking her head, not disapprovingly but like she is trying to wrestle some thoughts to the fore.

"Blimey! I hope it's *not* sexy," laughs Carina. "That's not the look I'm going for at all. Sexy would be wasted around here!"

"Here you go." I hand Meredith a glass of ice water and nod to Carina that it's okay for us to head out the back to check through the orders together on the computer. Meredith seems agitated and I don't want to leave her too long. "Just shout if you need anything, Meredith, we'll just be through there." I point toward the small archway that leads out to an even smaller office space. "If anyone comes in, the bell above the door will sound so one of us will come straight back out, don't worry."

The phone rings, loudly. Carina always has the volume turned up high so she doesn't miss it if her head is buried in a delivery. The noise makes Meredith reel back on her stool, and for one awful moment, I think she is going to topple right off it. "The phone!" she yells.

"It's okay, Meredith, it's just someone calling through an order. It's loud so we don't miss it." I try to calm her, but her hand is visibly shaking now, splashing water out of the glass and onto her lap.

"I'd only just put my suitcase on the bed."

"We unpacked you this morning, Meredith, remember? Everything is where it should be." I take the glass from her and place my hand on her shoulder, trying to bring her back into the room.

"The phone. It's so loud, it makes me jump. I'm not expecting it." She's whispering now.

I sit with her for a minute and wait until her breathing shallows again. Whatever the panic is, it seems to have subsided. "I need to help Carina now, but I will be as quick as I can and then we'll head for one of the parks, shall we? Get some fresh air?"

She nods slowly and so I rejoin Carina. I can see immediately why she has called me in. I haven't entered half the information I needed to, or at least not saved it properly, so she would have no idea how to make the orders up and what to include.

"I'm so sorry, Carina. I think I was so distracted planning the trip with Meredith. I'll check back through the order book for the notes I took at the time." While I do that, Carina starts to reenter the information as I find it, me dictating aloud, her tapping the keyboard.

The bell sounds in the shop. "Just one minute," shouts Carina, and I speed up, we're nearly done. I'm reminded again how wonderful Carina is. Most bosses would have taken issue with this silly mistake, but not her. It's hard to imagine what would make her lose her temper. "Are you worried about Meredith?" she asks gently, quietly so there is no chance of her overhearing us.

"I am, yes. I'm also worried about my ability to help her. What if I'm not enough? She's relying on me and what if I let her down? What if I miss something crucial or make a wrong decision about what's best for her?"

"I'm still plugging away on Facebook but everyone I have messaged so far doesn't know Meredith, although there must be at least twenty who have yet to respond to me."

I feel horribly guilty that Carina could be wasting her time looking for someone who can't be found, but it feels too soon to share this information when it's so incomplete, and I would hate to undermine all her hard work so far.

"Even if you do find her, that still leaves the question of whether we should tell her what we know. Meredith has asked me not to, don't forget."

"I know, but we don't always want what's best for us, do we? Even when we are thinking straight." She clicks save and we're done.

We step back out into the shop and I feel all my blood drain through me.

Meredith is gone.

I throw the door open and look both ways up and down the street. She is nowhere to be seen and tears are starting to blind my vision.

"Carina! It wasn't a customer. The bell ringing was Meredith leaving." I race back into the store. "She's got a good head start on us."

Carina hurries to the door, flicks the sign around to **CLOSED**, and sits me down. "Breathe, Jayne. It's all right, we'll find her. Just think. Where is she most likely to be heading? Home? Or is there somewhere local that has any sort of resonance with her? She was clearly a little agitated about something today."

"I need to message the others," I stammer, reaching for my phone.

JAYNE: Meredith has given me the slip. She's left Bouquets & Bunches without me and I don't know where she may have gone.

DAVINA: OMG, OK, she hasn't turned up here yet but obviously if she does, we'll let you know straightaway and look after her.

JAYNE: Can you do me a favor, Davina? Can you go into her apartment and double-check what the next dress is in the sequence on her wall? After the one Diana wore to Althorp. What comes next?

JAKE: Don't worry, Jayne, she can't have gone far. I can come and help you search for her if you need me?

JAYNE: I think I'll be fine but please hurry, Davina, I need to catch up with her.

DAVINA: On my way up there now.

There is an agonizing wait, while I picture Davina belting up the stairs from her place. Should I leave the shop? Pick a direction and just go? Carina reads my mind.

"Just wait, Jayne, it's better to have an idea where to head. She could have gone in many different directions from here. This is a time to be measured, not panicked."

DAVINA: I've got it. It's the full-length dinner dress with sequins at the neckline. Diana wore it in 1994, according to this. To Venice. But Jayne, there's more.

My mind races back to Spencer House in London, the huge upset the Canaletto painting caused Meredith, even though it was of Rome, not Venice. Then the poster of the Canaletto Venice exhibition right here in Bath. The very first step we took on piecing Meredith's story back together. She had such a strong reaction that day, I wonder . . .

JAYNE: She may have gone back to the Holburne Museum, where the Canaletto exhibition has been on. I've no idea if it's still running, but I'm heading there now. It's going to take me fifteen minutes.

OLIVIA: Good luck, Jayne, please keep us posted.

JAKE: Please call if you need me.

My phone rings then and it's Davina.

"Davina, I really need to get going, I can't talk." I try not to be short with her but I'm struggling to suppress my own panic.

"Listen, while I was in the memory room checking the order of the dresses for you, there was something else."

"Can it wait, Davina?"

"It was the letter, Jayne. From the crematorium. I saw it on the floor of her memory room. But it was out of the envelope this time. Did she read it while you were with her?"

I freeze, my hand hovering over the door handle. "No. She said she would but then never did. We came straight here, so she never had time. Unless . . ."

"Unless what?"

"She must have opened it while I ran back upstairs to change my shoes. But she gave me no indication that she had. She seemed fine when I returned. What does it say?"

"I haven't read it. You were so adamant that none of us should see it before her, so I left it on the floor by her armchair."

By the time I reach the Holburne Museum, I am bathed in sweat. I sprint up the stone pathway toward the entrance, praying that Meredith is somewhere inside. If she isn't, I have no idea where to head next.

I am stopped at reception by a member of staff.

"Can I see your ticket, please?" she asks.

"I don't have one, but I really need to get in." I watch as her eyes scan me. I realize I must look a mess.

"I'm so sorry," she says, "it's the final day of the exhibition, and we're fully booked for the last entry." Her eyes shift over my shoulder to the next visitor, one helpfully holding a printout of her ticket.

"Please." I allow my tone to be firm, I want her to know I'm not going to give up easily. "I think my friend is in there and she's not well. I need to go and fetch her. I really won't be long." I'm hoping Meredith had more success than me at slipping unnoticed through the crowd.

The staff member is obviously used to dealing with difficult customers and hardens her tone too.

"I can't let you in without a ticket, I'm sure you understand. This has been a very popular exhibition and in fairness to those who have paid"—she looks again to the women waiting behind me—"I'll have to ask you to stand aside."

"She has dementia, for goodness' sake!" I raise my voice, attracting the attention of the security guard at the staircase leading to the exhibit. "She's *lost* in there, and I'm asking you to help me. *Please*."

She sighs loudly and then directs me toward the ticket-booking counter. "If you don't want to take my word for it, then please join that queue and ask to speak to the manager, but we are closing very soon."

The queue has at least fifteen people already waiting in it. I can tell from the slumped body language, the bags scattered around feet, that this queue is not moving quickly. I glance at the staircase I know will take me up to the exhibition and seriously consider making a run for it. Then I catch the eye of the security guard positioned on the bottom step, who is watching me. I guess I'll have no choice but to sit it out and hope Meredith appears.

Then he tilts his head toward the top of the staircase. I frown back at him, not quite sure if this subtle communication is intended for me. "Quick," he mouths, and tilts his head again. It's all the invitation I need, and I move swiftly toward him. As I draw level, he gently touches my arm. "My grandmother lived with it for years. Absolutely heartbreaking. Don't be too long or you'll get me into trouble." Then he moves off the bottom step toward a young mum who is struggling to keep an overstuffed pushchair upright.

I take the steps two at a time and rush through the halls, the artwork a blur as I race by. I search frantically for a familiar head until, suddenly, there she is.

Someone has been kind enough to get Meredith a chair and she is sitting in front of a painting entitled *The Grand Canal with Rialto Bridge and the Fondaco dei Tedeschi*, oil on canvas, 1731–1736.

As I move to her side, she looks up at me and I feel the pain spread through my chest at the sight of her tearstained face.

"I never should have left him," she sobs. "As soon as I arrive at the hotel it's time to go back. I don't even unpack."

"Oh, Meredith," I say, dropping to my knees and taking her hand.

"The neckline is wrong, it's uneven and I have to fix it. The pocket is in the wrong position, too high at the waist, and it needs to be lowered to the hip. Of course, the dress is perfect in the end, no one would ever know, least of all Diana. She loves it so much she wears it to the Palace of Versailles that year too." Meredith allows herself a small smile at that memory.

A guide approaches us then. "One of my absolute favorites, this one," he says, looking toward the painting in front of us. "At the time Canaletto painted it, the Rialto was the only bridge to cross the Grand Canal, although it inspired plenty of others, including our own Pulteney Bridge right here in Bath."

"The detail is just staggering," I say, leaning in closer to the canvas.

"Well, that is one of the great distinctions of Canaletto's work," he says. "He often painted what he wanted to see. Accuracy came second to his idea of what was pleasing."

He steps away, leaving Meredith and me to draw our own

conclusions about the painting's validity. But my thoughts are elsewhere, just as I'm sure hers are.

"Perhaps you should find Fiona," she finally says, rising from her chair. "I'd like to go home now."

I just hope that I can.

THIRTY-NINE

Meredith
APARTMENT 8
KENSINGTON PALACE
1997

William has been looking forward to this day for weeks. They all have. Nerves are running high. With the exception of Catherine of course, Meredith is the only one among them who has spent time in Diana's company, but today they will all get a chance to shake her hand, to have their contribution acknowledged, and to be personally thanked for it.

A butler shows them through the apartment into a large drawing room and asks them to wait. Catherine is already here. So are the dresses. All evenly spaced on rails with identical silk hangers. Meredith takes in her surroundings. The cheerful yellow walls, a piano where the princes are said to have learned to play, covered in framed family photographs, treasured cuddly toys nestled underneath a formal painted portrait of the princess—the private and the public colliding right in front of them.

And then Diana arrives, and it is as if the entire room stands to attention, holds its breath, no one—with the exception of

Catherine—quite knowing how to stand, what to say, what is appropriate. Then comes the release, the exhale. Diana bustles through the room, embraces Catherine, showers them all in praise, and the tension and expectation deflate. Faces ease, smiles return as she moves to the rails. As her hands touch each dress, she wants to know "Who made this one . . . and this one?"

Meredith takes a seat in one of the deeply upholstered armchairs while Diana speaks to William. She keeps her distance but their hushed tones and the glances her way suggest they may be talking about her. William's eyes shine. She wants him to enjoy this moment for himself. He shows Diana the pale pink, wild silk dress with its detailed floral embroidery. The one he knows is Meredith's favorite. Created when she was blossoming too.

Later they pose for a group photograph before the dresses will be packed up and sent to America. The auction is Prince William's idea, Diana tells them all. "William is missing, he should have been with us today. He would have loved to meet you all. I miss him terribly. I miss my William."

Meredith's eyes find her husband. Is he as moved by this as she is? But William has made his way to the door they entered through, his eyes cast down to his feet, trying not to be noticed by anyone as he ducks out of the room.

FORTY

Jayne

"There is only one dress left in the sequence of sketches," I say to Meredith. The two of us are nestled in her memory room, a pot of morning tea and a plate of custard cream biscuits keeping us company. She has said nothing of the letter from the crematorium, but I can see it on the floor where she left it, face down. "It's the one that Diana wore to New York, according to the handwriting. To the CFDA Awards. I looked it up, it stands for . . ."

"Council of Fashion Designers of America," Meredith says, finishing my sentence. "I don't enjoy making this dress."

"That's the first time you've ever said that," I point out, and wait for her to elaborate, but she falls silent. I give her the time she needs, just as I have learned to. She shuffles up a little straighter in her chair. "Everything is changing. Things are being done differently. It doesn't suit me anymore."

"At work do you mean, Meredith? How is it different?"

She stands and pulls the sketch away from the peg it's attached to. "This dress makes them all sit up and take notice. It has a built-in corset and is lined in blue silk. It feels like butter in my fingers. It's flawless, *she* is flawless. I don't think I've ever seen her

look so sculpted." She raises a hand and tucks her hair back behind her ear. "Her hair is different, too, slicked back, more modern. More beautiful than she has ever been, if you can even
imagine it." She traces a finger across the neckline of the dress.
"Do you remember the pearl choker?"

"Incredible, wasn't it?" I say despite the fact I have never seen
it before.

"Then five matte blue satin rouleaux that cross at the back."
She turns the sketch over expecting to see them on the reverse of
the card, but there is nothing there. "Incredibly difficult to get
right." She smiles then, more mischievous this time. "'The been
there, done that New York fashion crowd stopped dead in their
tracks,' that's what the press says. I must have read the cuttings a
hundred times. They'll be in this room somewhere." She casts her
hand around. "Along with that beautiful picture of us all at the
palace before this dress and all the others are sent on their way."

Then her face falls again. "It should be a career highlight, but
it isn't."

"Why, Meredith? Can you remember what's wrong?" I keep my
gaze on the noticeboard dominating one of the walls. I don't want
her to feel watched.

"Everyone is worried she won't come back."

"Is that why you're sad? You think you might not make any
more dresses for the princess?"

"No. I don't like James. He's so different from William." She
starts to fidget in her chair, putting down her cup and saucer, then
picking it up again. "Loves the sound of his own voice. Why can
I always hear his voice above everyone else? He never consults me
like William does."

"What is James's job, Meredith?"

Her eyes glass over and I can see she is visualizing something that is far beyond the four walls surrounding us today. "He insists on using shorthand, it's always RSU and SA and CF. William always took the time to write his notes in full. How much sweeter the memory of this dress may have been if he had worked on it with me."

"Oh, I see. And why didn't he?"

She shakes her head. Her eyelids look heavy and I stop asking questions, knowing she needs to rest. Just as her eyes are closing, she mutters, "I've read those articles so many times. It's the next best thing to being there, I suppose."

While she sleeps, I dig a little deeper into the memory room. There is so much here, none of it in any discernible order, although I know it all makes sense to her. I find a stack of old newspaper cuttings. Wealthy-looking women with big, stiff hairstyles are pictured alongside some of the dresses I now recognize as the ones Meredith made. It doesn't seem right to me. That they get to enjoy these incredible gowns with no appreciation of the sacrifice that was required to make them, the couple who devoted at least ten years of their lives together to bringing this fantasy to life— and at the expense of what?

There are other dresses too. A short pale blue cocktail dress embroidered with scrolls of glass beads is dated 1995, when Meredith and William were still juggling busy lives in London with a small child. I wonder how close they were to making their decision to leave the capital by then. Had they started to discuss it? As these gowns were bought and sold across the globe, new more wealthy women outbidding one another to step into the same slip of silk that walked the halls of Buckingham Palace or traveled thousands of miles on foreign tours—how then were Meredith and William settling into their new lives in Bath? As Fiona grew up, how much farther did their dresses scatter? Who was wearing them by the time Fiona disappeared from Meredith's and William's lives? Is this how Meredith traces her life, when she is looking at her newspaper cuttings and the faded photography that charts her own journey?

I read how another long-sleeved ball gown changed hands several times before it was eventually bought in 2016 by the Fashion Museum, right here in Bath. The very one Meredith and I saw that day, back at the beginning.

I pick up the wonderful framed image of the Catherine Walker team at Kensington Palace in April 1997, pictured together a couple of years after Diana wore the last dress in the sequence to the awards ceremony in New York, an event I now know Meredith did not attend herself. And just a precious few months before Diana's own death. I swallow hard at the horrible, unknowing innocence of the image. All those proud, smiling faces with no idea what was to come. The thought makes my stomach tighten. My eyes settle on Meredith then and I notice for the first time that her gaze is not directed at the camera. It is on William, when you might assume it would more likely be on the princess. She is the only one in the picture not quite smiling.

Why didn't Meredith make that trip to New York when I feel sure she would have wanted to? Fiona was old enough to be left by then, and Meredith had trusted William to care for her alone before. I wipe the glass of the picture frame, releasing a plume of dust into the room. It doesn't bother me like dust in my own apartment might. Everything in this room feels like it is a cherished part of Meredith and William, that it belongs here. To disturb it is one thing but to remove it would be unthinkable now.

I place the photograph back where I found it, spying a Christie's catalog just underneath. I lift it and start to thumb through its pages, seeing again some of the dresses that feel so familiar to me now. I find a sheet of paper lodged inside the back cover. It charts every one of the dresses sold at the auction and the sum of money that each lot raised. I scan through the numbers and feel a swell of pride. The very first dress that Meredith ever worked on, the one worn to the fashion awards at the Royal Albert Hall, has raised a staggering six-figure sum. One dress is notable for its absence. Lot number 19, the dress that was gifted to Meredith and lies, still, in her bedroom. What might it be worth now, I wonder?

There is a small antique trunk on the floor, its catches sprung open. I gently lift its lid with my index finger, not sure what I'll find hidden inside. It's more dresses, tiny this time and made in playful colors for a special little girl. As I lift them from the trunk, they grow in size, some of the larger ones so pristine it's as if they've never been worn. Each one has a sketch pinned to its collar or neckline, a loose outline of the dress that it became and the girl who would wear it. My eyes move back to the noticeboard, the photographs of Fiona there, transforming from a baby in her mother's arms to a young woman, then nothing more, as if she is frozen in time. It's subtle but I can see her in the sketches. The way the pencil has captured the determined arch of her eyebrows, the straightness of her back, and the slim contours of her body, the desire to impress in her face. It's definitely her. I lift the first dress and hold it up to the window. Meredith did not save all her skills for Diana. The stitches are tight and neat, the hem perfectly folded, the scalloped edging on the collar carefully picked out in a contrasting color. It's a wonderful show of love, captured forever without the need to say a word.

I replace it and my fingers find the glossy cover of an estate agent's brochure for this apartment. It is dated with the year 2000, which I'm guessing must have been when William and Meredith viewed and then bought this place. I look at the images inside, the personality-free rooms, styled to sell. Nothing like they are today with their layers and layers of life. Decades of history and memories, the light and shade of a love affair and marriage that we have been trying so hard to piece together again.

"Ahh," says Meredith, cracking her eyes back open. "I thought that was the answer to everything." Her eyes fall on the apartment brochure. "A solution to all the worry." There is no bitterness in her words, more a sad resignation that she was wrong about something that I simply don't have the time to explore right now.

While she shuffles off to return our plates to the kitchen, I quickly google an email for Christie's sales department and drop them a brief note, explaining the dress Meredith owns and asking how we might go about getting a valuation for it. It would be useful to know at least. I follow her into the kitchen. "Did you get a chance to read the letter I gave you, Meredith?"

She looks at me blankly, like she hasn't got the faintest idea what I am talking about. I could fetch it now, we could read it and face together whatever the contents may be, but it will take time and sensitivity and much more thought, and I feel the pull to be with someone else. I want to put my own needs first today. Maybe I'm finally comfortable with the idea of that.

I briefly wonder, as I watch her rinsing the plates without using any soap, if I should stay and keep her company. Would she prefer me to?

No, actually, I don't think she would. Not if she understood why I am cutting short our time together today. So, I say goodbye and leave because I want, more than anything, to spend the afternoon with Jake. And I think she'd approve.

FORTY-ONE

❧

William
2010

We will lose her soon, I'm sure of it. Fiona has outgrown this apartment and her parents. Perhaps Meredith feels it too; maybe that's what's unsettling her.

It was barely noticeable at first, I'm not sure Fiona has noticed it at all, she's so rarely here. It's the constant questioning that's so unlike her. Are we making our usual trip into town on Saturday? What time are we leaving? How long will the drive home take? Have I made the egg sandwiches? This isn't Meredith. She's always been fanatically organized but never needy or indecisive.

Is this the empty-nest syndrome she feels is coming? I don't think so. She's so proud of Fiona. She's ready for her to make her mark on the world. Maybe she's been like this longer than I realized. Has it all been hidden by the routine of her working day? Two months into her retirement, is it the excess of time that's exposing her?

More than twenty years after she first walked through the doors of the Catherine Walker workrooms and changed my life forever, Meredith has closed her essentials bag for the last time—professionally speaking at least. Finally said goodbye to her remaining private clients who come to the apartment for alterations and when they want something special made for a big family occasion. Is this the cause? Is she questioning everything because she's unsure what life means for her now? It's hard to believe when we have been looking forward to this, excited for it. We've talked about planning a big trip abroad as soon as we can.

She calls me through to dinner and I take a seat opposite her at the table, studying her face a little more closely tonight. She seems calm, content. My Meredith.

"It's just us two again tonight," she says. "Fiona is eating with friends."

"Perfect, because I'm starving and there will be more for us to share." I start to slice into the chicken leg and watch the meat fall effortlessly from the bone. She's always been a wonderful cook. "Maybe we can take a walk down to Henrietta Park after dinner, just the two of us? It's still light."

"Do you really think we have time?" She looks confused now, like I've made a bizarre suggestion, something totally out of the ordinary.

I glance at my watch. "It's only just gone six, Meredith."

"But this one is taking a lot longer. It's the wild silk, such a delicate shade of pink. I'm having to wash my hands very frequently so I don't spoil it." She looks down at her own hands and huffs.

I lower my cutlery and look directly at her. It's like she's not really talking to me but someone else in the room.

"I'm not blaming you, of course, the pattern is complicated, I know, and all the beautiful floral embroidery, the jacket too." She shakes her head, struggling to finish her point. "I just need it finished before the baby comes."

I feel my mouth drop open. She's referring to a dress and jacket we made for Diana back in 1992, when Meredith was heavily pregnant with Fiona. The race was on to get it finished before she arrived.

"Meredith, what's going on? You're talking about a dress from a very long time ago." I laugh because this is madness.

"No, I'm not." There is a stubbornness to her tone that I don't recognize.

I go to contradict her but change my mind. Instead, I turn my attention back to dinner, how can I argue about something so nonsensical? I scoop one of the carrots up to my mouth and feel the hard coldness of it on my tongue. They're not cooked.

"Meredith, you forgot to cook the carrots!"

"What? No!" She tries to stick a fork in one of her own and realizes it is rock-hard. We look across the table at each other, there is a moment of stunned silence, and then we both laugh out loud.

"I can't do everything, you know!" she shouts across the table, still laughing. "It's okay for you, you disappear every day. I'm juggling everything on my own."

I'm surprised by this, even if she is joking. She's never accused me of not pulling my weight before. "That's not fair, I do my bit."

"Then again, you never wanted a baby, did you? That's what you said, so I can hardly complain!" She tosses the comment casually across the table at me. How can she say something so callous with such a lighthearted tone?

"Meredith! Where is all this coming from?" I want her to stop. No one wants to hear their wife say such unkind things.

"You said it. You never wanted children! I'm—" She sits there then with her mouth open, hopefully a sign that she's about to apologize. But her eyes are fixed behind me. She's stopped laughing.

I hear gentle sobs and I know immediately what they mean. I turn sharply and there is Fiona, standing in the doorway, shock and pain written all over her face. She runs straight back out the door before I have a chance to reach her.

When I look back at Meredith, appealing for an explanation, her face has softened. She is completely calm, as if the past five minutes never happened.

"Would you like cream or custard with the crumble? Or both?" She smiles.

I don't know what to do. So, I do the only thing that comes naturally—that has always come naturally. I walk to Meredith's side and wrap my arms around her shoulders, wanting to protect her. Thank goodness there are no guests at our table tonight. We can keep this to ourselves.

"I'll have whatever you're having."

These are the mistakes I made. Believing Meredith was having some awful off day, sparked by her retirement and the impending departure of our daughter. And that her foolish, meaningless words, shouted into the air, could be explained and forgiven. That covering them up—just as she had my own mistakes—was the right and best thing to do.

A month later, Fiona leaves home without saying goodbye to either of us.

FORTY-TWO

❧❧❧

Meredith
2015

So many people all buzzing around in one place. Meredith feels their excitement, she shares in it. She and William have arrived early, she likes it that way. Valet parking is quick and easy. They dispense with their luggage and now they have a little time to wander the shops, grab some last-minute suntan lotion before boarding their flight, and by tonight, they will be dining overlooking the Amalfi Coast. It's their favorite hotel. William has been talking about this trip for weeks.

"I want to buy a book for the flight," Meredith tells William. "Let's meet at the gate in half an hour, shall we?"

"I'll come with you, let's go together." William loops an arm through hers.

"No, go find a quiet spot and have a coffee. Honestly, I'll be fine. I'll be back before you know it."

William lets her go, but Meredith recognizes that face. He looks just like he did when Fiona started meeting friends in town alone, declining his offers to drive her in and pick her up. It's been so long since they've seen her, despite William's attempts to make contact.

But she won't let that thought take the shine off this trip to celebrate her sixty-eighth birthday. True, she isn't as sharp as she once was, but she's never done anything to make him feel she can't be left alone for half an hour to buy a book.

"Okay, please don't be late. We don't have that much time until the flight will be called."

Meredith wanders off in the direction of Waterstones, relieved to see him head to the upper floor and the small Italian coffee shop he prefers.

She runs a finger along the display of bestselling paperbacks, all competing for attention. What was the title she was looking for? She can't remember the author's name. Never mind, she'll know it when she sees it. She picks up three or four, hoping for some recognition. The shop fills with people—stressed parents, excitable children, impatient businessmen. Pushchairs blocking the walkways. Carry-on wheelie cases clashing with the back of her ankles. Confusing announcements repeated over and over on the loudspeaker. The incessant beep, beep, beep of the tills. Someone crying. An argument about where the queue begins and ends.

Why did she come in here? What is this place with its fluorescent colors and plastic wrappings, its overstuffed shelves? Meredith wanders back beyond the entrance, into an even busier throng of people. She spins, trying to focus on something, anything that will tell her where she is and why she is here. She will remember soon, she knows she will. She raises her head and looks at the signs. The words are bleeding into one another, making her feel dizzy. Only one image seems familiar: the outline of a woman in a dress, an arrow pointing right. She follows it to a room full of mirrors, several closed doors, an astringent smell. She has been here before. The loud gush of hot air tells her so.

"Are you in the queue or not?" A woman in low-slung jogging bottoms that expose her hip bones can't be bothered to wait for an answer and jumps ahead of Meredith, disappearing behind the one open door.

Meredith spins and sees herself in the mirror. She walks toward her own reflection, tries to relax her features. Then there is a woman beside her, wearing a pretty white cotton dress, its hem and cuffs edged in beautiful turquoise stones.

"Your dress is beautiful." Meredith reaches out to touch the sleeve.

"Oh, thank you. It's one of my own actually. I own a small boutique in Richmond, lots of this sort of thing, easy-to-wear pieces that are perfect for a flight. I can see you're a fan of a good dress." She nods toward Meredith's pale green shirtdress, belted at the waist.

"You're right. I do like dresses, yes." Meredith nods slowly. Perhaps this woman can help her. "Do you sell anything like this?" Meredith opens her arms, giving the woman the chance to fully examine her outfit.

"Absolutely. Shirtdresses are probably our biggest seller in fact." The woman finishes drying her hands on a paper towel and pulls her phone from a straw bag. "Lots of different lengths too." She holds the phone toward Meredith, who watches as the women clicks through to another screen and a fresh series of dresses appears.

"The sale starts in two weeks, and look, I shouldn't but I'm going to show you which ones will go in at seventy percent off. They'll all sell out in the first few days, so you'll have to be quick if you want one." The woman guides Meredith to one side so they aren't blocking others from using the sinks. "You're lucky, my flight has been delayed by two hours so I'm in no rush."

Meredith suddenly feels uneasy again. She shouldn't be in here. She needs to be somewhere else. But the woman is talking, talking, talking, and she feels rude attempting to cut her off.

"I'm going to give you my card." Now she's pulling all sorts out of her bag, searching for her purse.

"I think that's me, isn't it?" Meredith suddenly asks.

"What d'you mean? Oh, there it is." The woman hands her a business card that Meredith can't remember asking for.

Meredith raises a finger in the air, appealing for the woman to listen.

"This is the final call for Meredith Chalis. Please proceed immediately to gate 43, where your flight is boarding."

"Oh no, you better get going. Come on!" She takes Meredith's arm and then the two of them are back in the main shopping concourse. "Gate 43, look." The woman points to the signs above their heads. "Go!"

"She was wearing such a beautiful dress and we just got chatting." Meredith can't understand why William is so cross with her.

"You've been gone nearly an hour. Do you realize how close we were to missing the flight? They are about to close the gate. What on earth took so long?" William looks at the bundle of books in Meredith's arms, the lack of a carrier bag.

"Meredith, did you pay for those books?"

Meredith looks at them, not remembering how she came to be holding them. "No. I don't think I did."

FORTY-THREE

❧

Jayne

I promised to keep an eye on Willow and Maggie for a few hours this morning. Davina is at work, and all of her usual childminders are booked, despite sky-high rates because of the school holidays. I can't sit with them all day, so Willow is officially in charge. But I'll be popping my head in every now and again to make sure they're not burning the place down or destroying the contents of Davina's expensive work wardrobe.

I want to spend some time with Meredith this morning, to have another go at getting her to share what's in that letter. I'll head down there as soon as I can.

My phone pings with a new email and I'm floored to see the word *Christie's*—I only sent my email yesterday, but I've already got a reply from a man called Stephen Glover, the head of private sales. My eyes fly over the words, struggling to take it all in. I have to stop on the first floor and read it again from the beginning. Mr. Glover explains that the accompanying handwritten letter, the well-documented provenance of the dress, the personal connection of its current owner to the original one, the romance surrounding the fact it was pulled from the auction back in 1997, and the fact that Diana is now sadly deceased make this dress *incredibly attractive*. There is a *significant global network*, he goes on, of collectors who would want to know if it came to auction.

Then, at the very bottom of the email, he says that assuming all is as it seems, if we were going to sell this item—without even seeing or verifying its condition himself—he would expect to allocate a six-figure reserve price.

I grip the banister a little tighter and read the whole thing for a third time, convinced it must be a hoax. But logic would absolutely dictate it's not. I contacted Christie's, I remind myself. I've seen what the other dresses fetched at the original auction. Comparatively, this is not an outrageous sum of money. In fact, now I think about it, it seems like the perfect honor to bestow on Meredith. After all the years she devoted to making those beautiful gowns and this one in particular has actually increased in value. The question is whether she would ever consider selling it.

My thoughts are cut abruptly short by the sound of a piercing scream filling the air. Olivia immediately appears out of her door on the second floor having heard it too.

"Meredith!" she shouts, and we run the stairs together to the first floor. But when she answers the door her face is a picture of calm vagueness.

"Oh, Meredith," I stutter, slightly taken aback. "It's Jayne from upstairs. Is everything all right? I thought I heard you call out?"

She shakes her head, completely unflustered. "Oh dear, was I humming again?" I feel the relief flood through me.

"No, no, don't worry. I'm so sorry to disturb you, Meredith. Go back inside and I'll come and check on you later."

"Okay." She smiles and obediently closes the door.

Olivia and I stand for a moment, looking at each other, confused.

"Can you hear that?" Olivia asks. "I think it's coming from downstairs."

I start to shake my head but then stop. I do hear something. A child crying.

"Oh no. Maggie." We head down to the ground floor and Davina's front door this time. Willow throws it open and I see immediately that something is seriously wrong. She's flushed and clearly panicking.

"She wanted to see if her fairy wings would make her fly, so she climbed up on top of Mum's wardrobe and jumped off." She's tripping over her words, her breath snagging in the back of her throat. "She's done it a million times before and been fine, but she didn't put the pillows down to land on this time. She isn't moving!"

My own heart is banging as we race through to the bedroom to where Maggie is lying in a crumpled heap, her left arm horribly bent outward from the elbow at an unnatural angle. She is pale and quiet, which is the most worrying thing of all. All the life has been knocked out of her.

"Don't attempt to move her," I say, trying desperately hard to remain calm. "We need to call an ambulance."

"I've done that," sobs Willow. "It's on its way. Is she going to be okay, Jayne?" Her voice quivers and I sense the guilt she is feeling because this happened while Maggie was in her care. But it's me who should be feeling guilty. I should have come straight here this morning.

"She's going to be just fine," I say, gently lowering myself down onto the floor next to Maggie. "You've done brilliantly, Willow." I run my hand gently from Maggie's forehead back across the top of her head, barely touching her, but wanting to let her know I am here. Her eyes flicker open, but she doesn't speak. It's not like Maggie at all.

"We need to let Davina know," says Olivia.

"Oh God." Willow starts to sob louder, the child in her not wanting to confront the seriousness of what has happened.

"Sit with her, will you, Olivia, while I call Davina? Just keep an eye on her and hopefully the ambulance will be here soon." I step outside of the room to make the call.

"Jayne! Listen, I am about to go into *another* meeting. Is Meredith okay? Has she mentioned the letter yet?" I feel my throat constrict while I try to find the best words.

"I'm so sorry, Davina, but you need to come home." I try to blink away the tears filling my eyes.

"What's wrong? Are the girls okay?" She already senses what's coming.

"It's Maggie. She's hurt herself. Willow's called an ambulance."

"Oh God. What happened?" I picture her then, throwing items into her handbag as she walks to the door. I don't want to say too much and worry her further.

"She's had a fall and her arm doesn't look great but she's conscious. Olivia is with her and Willow now."

"Okay, all right, I'm on my way. Stay with her, please, Jayne, will you, until I get there? She adores you."

"Of course I will. See you soon."

"Oh, and Jayne, tell Willow this is not her fault, please? It's mine and I'm not cross at all. I know she'll be worried."

I end the call and head back into the room. I can hear the rise and fall of an ambulance siren a few streets away.

"Olivia, will you go and open the front door so they can come straight in?"

In the following minutes the siren reaches a deafening volume, paramedics in green overalls and heavy black shoes fill the hall-way, carrying a collection of equipment and a stretcher. The sight of them is going to frighten Maggie. Then Davina comes flailing through the door, dropping her handbag and blazer on the floor. Her mascara is bleeding under her eyes. Jake appears too. It's all getting too chaotic and I'm pleased Maggie isn't seeing all the fuss. I decide to stay in the hallway, giving the paramedics and Davina some space to examine her.

"It looks like she's heard all the commotion too." Jake nods toward the staircase, where Meredith has appeared, rubbing her hands frantically up and down her arms. I watch as she hugs her arms tightly around herself and rocks back and forth on the top step. The ambulance siren has stopped but her face is illuminated by the blue flashing light that is pouring in from the street. I move quickly to join her, but before I can reach her, she begins shaking her head frantically back and forth.

"They're here. They're with him now. He's unconscious!"

I take hold of her with both hands and force eye contact, trying to help her recollect who I am and where she is.

"Take a deep breath, Meredith. It's Jayne, from upstairs. Every-thing is fine. Come on, I'll walk you back to your apartment."

"I can't go in there!" she bellows. "They're working on him now. They don't want me to see." She drops her face into her hands. "I begged him to get those headaches checked, but he never did."

"The ambulance is here for Maggie, Meredith. The little girl who lives on the ground floor?" I take hold of her hand. "She's had a small fall. Nothing to worry about, I promise."

"His arm won't work. He can't tell me what's wrong. They are asking me lots of questions and I can't remember the answers." She's casting her eyes around, and when they finally settle back on me, it seems to soften her. She releases a long slow breath and allows me to guide her back into her apartment and sit her down on the sofa.

"Did William need an ambulance, Meredith? Did the siren and the flashing lights remind you of that?"

"He opens his eyes briefly and I kiss him." She smiles at me, lifting her fingers to her mouth. "His lips are so soft, but I'm not sure he can see me. I lower my face close so I am right there in front of him, and I hold his face in my hands and I kiss him again. My wonderful William. Then . . . then he leaves."

Meredith's breathing has calmed. She's reclined back into the sofa and her body has slackened with relief or exhaustion, I'm not sure which.

I know what I need to do. I tuck a woolen blanket over her lap and switch the television on, lowering the volume so it is barely audible but enough of a distraction. I make her a hot, sweet tea that she probably won't drink. She'll need a nap, while the adrenaline dissipates and allows her body to relax again. I wait for her eyes to close, for the frantic flickering of her lids to subside, then I head for her memory room.

The letter is there on the floor and this time I don't hesitate to pick it up. My eyes scan the words, my entire body stiffening as I read and understand them. I read them again. I check the date at the top of the letter: 13 July 2017. Then I feel the thump of disappointment and sadness drop through me like a dead weight.

He's gone.

The crematorium has written to Meredith as his next of kin to advise that she has yet to collect his ashes. The letter explains that if it isn't done within six months of the cremation date, then his ashes will be scattered in the memorial garden.

We are too late.

Meredith is too late to say her final goodbye. She has spent an entire year waiting for her husband to return, waking every morning, believing this would be the day that he would, and it was never going to be. How will I ever find the words to tell her this?

I take a seat in her favorite armchair and sit there silently for I'm not sure how long. Long enough to cast my eyes back over the wall of photographs and to briefly step back into Meredith and William's lives. The smiles, the milestones, the achievements, the expressions I'll never understand, the cracks that it's now too late to heal.

I shake my head and sigh at the realization that we were never going to find him. We were looking for the wrong William. The letter confirms that while they shared a life, William and Meredith never shared a surname. He was William Hatfield.

I step back out into the drawing room, where Meredith is stirring.

"He will get better, won't he?" she asks as soon as she sees me. "How is he now? Can I go and visit him yet?"

FORTY-FOUR

William
23 MAY 2017

Meredith is getting worse. I worry all the time about leaving her on her own now. I tell her where I'm going and when I'll be back, but she behaves like I've been gone for a week when I return from buying my newspaper. What's worse is she'll try to hide her concern and I can see the stress that performance causes her. I know she's in there but reaching her some days feels so terribly hard. How can this be us?

How did we get here when we have shared so much and loved so much? And when we still feel so much for each other? I'm holding on as tightly as I can but every day I feel she is falling away from me. It's slow and drawn-out, making me question if fast and brutal might have been better, if I had the luxury of choice. I doubt she has any idea she is losing me too. I'm hopeful it's a pain she will never know. I'm not a healthy man. I haven't been for a long time. I don't need a doctor to tell me that. Borrowed time, that's what I'm on. Too late now to go back and reverse the decisions I made or face the ones I chose to ignore.

She always was the brains. I was always the legs. One half of each other. She could reason a problem away. I would force my way through it. Now I feel her burning frustration in every forgotten conversation and misplaced belonging, in every word left hanging because she's no longer sure why she said it, where it may have been leading. The only medicine I can offer her are my kisses. When I see she is struggling, I pull her close, shut everyone else out, and soothe the panic away until she softens in my arms.

I used to look at her face and see pure contentment. It's the same face but it's static, like she no longer trusts the world around her. She bears the expression of someone who has suffered a great hurt or loss and is too frightened to step back into the woods, into the clinging darkness, to search for her happiness again.

I did take her to the doctor, under the ruse of getting our flu jabs. She never would have gone otherwise. She played it all down, just a silly, isolated mind blank, something that happens to all of us. She even managed to make me feel stupid, as we left fifteen minutes later clutching a handful of leaflets on everything from depression to menopause. They sat unread on the kitchen table for a couple of days before she discreetly placed them in the bin. Neither of us mentioned their disappearance. I decided to do what I always do. I protect her—from her own embarrassment at first, when she returned home empty-handed from the supermarket again and I couldn't be sure if she had even made it there. Or when chatting to friends and the name of our road or a favorite restaurant would escape her. Then, more dangerously, I protected her from her own exposure, just as she had done for me. I closed ranks around her, covered up her mistakes so no one else would know. It felt kinder. I felt reassured it was what she would want. That I was following her lead.

Fiona was the exception. I did briefly try to find and enlighten her. But she ignored every one of my approaches and I never had the heart to explain that to Meredith. I foolishly held on to the hope that Fiona would talk to us when she was ready. Then Meredith got worse and I kept Fiona shut outside of our pain just as easily as I silently nudged closed the doors on our social life. This was our secret and we would manage it. I would look after Meredith in whatever way she needed me to and pray this worn-out body of mine would outlast her failing mind.

Should I try to find Fiona now? Or leave Meredith with the older, fonder memories that she believes are more recent than I know them to be? Is the game up? Am I kidding myself to think that the strength of our love will keep her with me? I've read enough to know dementia is what this is.

That a woman with so many treasured memories should be robbed of them is a cruelty beyond my comprehension most days. I ask myself these questions over and over, weighing the pros and cons. Fiona was always so efficient and organized, but is that what Meredith needs? Would she thank me for letting our daughter build a plan around us? I have never once doubted her love for Fiona, but it still surprises me how the same cells can split and divide and create something so different from the original.

There is a softness to my wife, an inner depth that can be reached only with kindness and consideration. She responds to gentleness and understanding. She warms only to those people who share it. She hates to be rushed. Fiona is governed by a world Meredith knows nothing about. I can see it, even if neither of them can. Fiona's world is constructed around the necessity to succeed, to be nothing less than brilliant. It rarely pauses to consider people's feelings. It wraps itself convincingly in the cloak of creativity but it's ambitious and calculating and strategic. I admire her for having the gumption to stomach it. Talent is not easily defined in Fiona's world. Perhaps it can't be when you find your-self in a room with so many equally talented people.

Meredith is the opposite of Fiona. She loves glamour and ro-mance. There is goodness running through her. It's why I worry she will last longer than me. It's why I have to make my wishes clear now. She hasn't allowed the rot to seep inside of her, to twist and turn her into something she was never destined to be. She is a woman who will always turn her face to the sun. So, no. My letter to Fiona is written. I have left it where I know it will be found. My planning is in place. The map of our lives is drawn, I only hope she will recognize it. She just has to follow the dresses. I know my darling wife will be okay when the time comes. I have no choice but to believe that.

She sleeps in today, not waking until well past ten o'clock. I take a breakfast tray to her in bed and she jokes that I must be guilty of something. Then I watch the flicker of doubt cross her face. She's asking herself if she has forgotten something. A birth-day? An anniversary? I reassure her quickly that I do it simply because I love her, and her cheeks flush, not with embarrassment but with the warmth that naturally lights her from within.

It's as I am placing the tray back in the kitchen that the nausea grabs me, like the very worst kind of motion sickness. I recognize the feeling but not the intensity. The room spins away from me at a speed I cannot fathom. I make a grab for the kitchen work sur-face but miss it and the tray clatters to the floor. The shower is running. Meredith doesn't hear it. I collapse forward, feeling as if I will vomit, but nothing comes. Then I am on the floor, the tiles cold beneath my cheek. The temperature is momentarily comfort-ing but panic takes over. I can't move my right arm to force myself up. Half of me is already dead, lifeless, like someone has drawn a line down the exact center of me from my head to my toes. I lie there, useless, stunned, waiting for the second impact that will finish me off.

I try to call her name, but my lips won't respond to my desires. I am locked inside myself. Panic rises. I need her. I've always needed her. But I don't want the imprint of her panic to be the thing I take with me. I close my eyes. She's with me now, back in the workroom, her lap covered in precious silk, doing what she loves. I feel her kiss and I pray harder than I ever have before.

Dear God, let it not be the last.

FORTY-FIVE

Jayne

The solicitor confirms what we now know to be true. He is holding the will for William Hatfield and a letter to his daughter, Fiona Hatfield, expressing his final wishes.

Davina has more than enough to contend with today—Maggie's arm, broken in two places from her fall, will take at least six weeks to heal in its cast—so I sit on my roof terrace, alone in the late-afternoon sun with a notebook and pen, and make the call to the Royal College of Music. Mrs. Osman, the head of admissions, is back, and she has good news.

"I recognized the image of Fiona as soon as I laid eyes on it. An exceptionally talented concert pianist. I am only sorry you didn't get me immediately when your neighbor called the first time. I could have saved you a lot of confusion."

"Thank you," I say, smiling at the depth of satisfaction in Mrs. Osman's voice. "Could I ask one more favor, please? I was hoping you could put me in touch with Fiona? I suppose the college must have her contact details. I need to speak to her about her parents, William and Meredith." I have to assume at this stage there is a good chance Fiona does not know about her father's death. If she

did, wouldn't she also understand more about Meredith's life and
be more present in it?

"I can't give you her email or phone number, I'm afraid. That
would be a breach of our privacy rules. However, if you are happy
to share yours, I could email Miss Hatfield right away and ask her
to get in touch with you."

Before the sun dips below the chimney pots that punctuate my
view, Fiona has emailed me back. It feels remarkable to see her
name sitting there in bold in my inbox, nestled between requests
for last-minute dog walking bookings and a reminder that my
iCloud storage is full and needs upgrading. All these weeks of
trying to track her down, everyone devoting their spare hours to
the cause, the dead ends and the false leads, questioning if we
could or should, when of course the answer was in Meredith's
memory room all along—just as she said it would be, just, I suspect, as William planned it to be. This is not a conversation I can
have over email and so we arrange to meet. Without hesitation,
Fiona agrees to come to Bath tomorrow. On Jake's suggestion, we
arrange to talk at the coach house. I think it's best if I share everything I know first, before she sees Meredith.

Jake has left the place comfortably tidy for us. Not so immaculate
that I feel I can't touch anything—but considerately so. There are
fresh irises in a vase on the kitchen island, the radio has been left
on because he knows a shared silence makes me twitchy, and of
course the place is filled with the exquisite smell of freshly baked
bread. It makes me smile, because I think Jake truly believes that
any situation can be made better by the simple act of sinking your

teeth into a slice. Everyone has sent messages of good luck, but it is Carina's that forces me to take a seat and a deep breath.

> **CARINA:** You did it, Jayne, and I couldn't be any prouder of you. Whether she realizes it or not—and I believe she does—Meredith is the luckiest woman on earth. The day you turned the key in your lock for the first time was the day the course of her own life changed for the better. You've helped her, not because a family tree dictated you should, but because you are a good person. That says so much about you and Fiona will understand that immediately when she hears what you have to say. And don't be afraid to let her know how much you love her mother. I am here and can close the shop at a moment's notice if you need me. Much love x

It will just be Fiona and me today. We all agreed this meeting doesn't need an audience. We don't know how much or how little Fiona already knows and how painful the conversation may be for her. She arrives bang on time and I take my steps to the door unnaturally slowly, bracing myself, allowing my lungs to fill and expand.

I see immediately she has William's smile. Soft and genuine. A mop of glossy hair the color of a varnished pine table falls about her shoulders. I hadn't noticed it from her graduation picture because it was pulled back. There are freckles sprinkled across her nose and on her rosy cheeks—nothing like Meredith and everything like him. She hasn't blended the concealer under her eyes into the skin properly and it catches the light, making her seem more human, less composed. She's tired. Like me, she probably didn't sleep much last night.

"Hello, I'm Jayne. Thank you so much for coming, Fiona," I say, extending a hand. "I'm not sure if Mrs. Osman explained but it took us some time to find you." I release her hand and step back out of the doorway, so she knows to enter.

"Yes, she did. I'm sorry, Jayne, the different surnames wouldn't have helped, I'm sure. Mum has an old address for me, from when I first moved back to London, but, well, not the latest one and certainly not my email. She could have given you my mobile number but that obviously never happened."

The idea that Meredith would remember the number, or where it might be written down, is wildly improbable. It's my first indication that Fiona is unaware of the way her mother is living.

"Would you like a tea?" Jake has helpfully left everything out on the counter so I don't have to rummage around for it.

"Just some water would be great, thank you." She slips onto one of the high stools and I hear her take a deep, calming breath. She's nervous, too, and it gives me the push I need to get to the point. I sit facing her.

"Can I ask, when was the last time you saw your parents?"

"Not since 2010. I moved back to London to enroll at the RCM, the earliest date I could. I haven't spoken to either of them since then." The fact she can recall the dates so easily says a lot, I hope. This is not insignificant for her.

"No contact at all?" I say, stunned.

"To be fair to him, Dad tried, several times at first, but I wasn't ready . . . I didn't want to talk to either of them back then." She forces a small smile that seems loaded with regret. "By the time I was ready, the two of them had clearly moved on. I didn't get any response." Her smile remains fixed in place.

I suspect this is not a subject she has discussed much until now. She's choosing her words carefully, just giving me the facts as she sees them.

"I sent plenty of concert invites that went unanswered. And I came by once. It was April last year. I wanted to give them both a recording of my work. It was one of my final exam pieces—Chopin—and I was so proud of it. I hoped they would be too."

"Piano Concerto Number 1 in E Minor, by any chance?" I smile deeply as I recall all the times we've heard Meredith humming softly to herself, a tune none of us could identify.

Fiona pulls back from me slightly, clearly stunned by my guess.

"Well, yes, but how on earth did you know that?"

"Meredith is always humming it. Sorry, please go on."

She takes a slow deep breath, trying to give herself the courage to continue. "I stood outside on the pavement and Mum appeared at the window." She smiles then at the memory of seeing her, before it quickly fades. "I waved up at her and . . . nothing. She ignored me." Fiona shakes her head. Even after all this time she hasn't been able to make sense of this encounter. "I stood there like a fool smiling until eventually she moved away from the glass. I pushed the recording through the letter box and left, thinking she couldn't forgive me for the lack of contact for so long. It was a four-hour round trip and I didn't even get to say hello." The recollection hurts her. She drops eye contact and reaches for her water. I recognize the deflection tactics and I also know her tears are hovering just below the surface. This would have been her last chance to see her father before . . .

"Your mum listened to the recording, Fiona, many, many times, you can be very sure of that." I nod slowly, trying to convey that I am not judging anyone's actions.

"Maybe there was just too much bad blood." Her eyes cloud. "Maybe they were ashamed. Maybe they just didn't care. I have no idea. Sending the graduation photograph was my last attempt. I told myself if I didn't hear anything after that, then it was time to walk away for good. And I had accepted that, but then I got Mrs. Osman's email and here I am, still hoping to be loved." She chuckles sadly.

Her honesty floors me. She doesn't speak with self-pity but a weary acceptance that there is little more she feels she could have done. But with every word she says, I feel sure she has no knowledge of Meredith's situation—and why would she after so long apart? She can see only the rejection and none of the complications behind it.

"There is so much I need to tell you, Fiona. And I'm sorry if it's not in the order it should be, but I think a lot has changed since you returned to London."

"Dad." She nods, swallows hard, then pinches her lips together.

"Yes . . . he's passed away. I'm not sure if you knew that?" I try to soften my body language, leaning toward her slightly.

"Not until last night." She reaches for the water again and I can see her hands trembling. "I guessed there had to be a specific reason why you were getting in touch now and not before. I also knew if one of them had died, there was a good chance it would have been talked about in some way. They were both exceptionally good at what they did—it was their absolute passion in life beyond each other—I felt sure the moment would not have passed without some acknowledgment of that and I was right. There was a memorial, organized by the team at Catherine Walker. Even some film footage. It's not how you imagine you'll discover the loss of a parent, is it, on YouTube?" I see the performer in her then. The way she is using her breath to steady herself, to hold in emotions in a way that most of us would be incapable of. Her long fingers, probably so used to moving with fluidity, are knotted tightly around one another.

"I don't know if anyone at Catherine Walker ever attempted to find me, but the chances are, like you, they wouldn't have known where to look. And anyway, wouldn't they assume my own mother would invite me?"

"I'm so, so sorry, Fiona. For your father's loss but also that this is the way you had to discover it. And I am so very sorry we didn't get to you sooner. We've been trying, I can promise you that."

"I think it's probably Mum who needs to apologize to me. Hopefully she will find it in herself to do that. She said some awful things before I left that she has never said sorry for." Her tone firms, and as much as she has my sympathy, I also can't bear the thought of her being cross with Meredith when they see each other.

"What do you mean?"

"She was there, Jayne, at the memorial. I could only bring myself to watch it once but she's clearly visible in the footage, surrounded by all her former colleagues. She had that moment to honor him, to praise him if she wanted to. But she denied me the chance. She never called me. I was never invited. Why? He was my father, and despite everything, I loved him. I deserved the chance to say goodbye. Or to at least have a choice about whether I wanted to." The part she has been playing crumbles now. Tears start to stream down her face, and she loses control of her voice, her words pitching higher than she intends them to. I reach for the box of tissues Jake has placed next to the flowers, another small act of kindness that I love him for.

"I can't speak about the memorial, Fiona, I knew nothing about it until just now. But I know there is a letter waiting for you from your father. It's at the solicitor's office that holds his will. That may have some of the answers you are looking for."

"A letter?" Her face recovers a little. She likes the practicality of it, I think, and maybe the prospect of hearing her father's voice again.

I allow my lungs to fill.

"Fiona, we believe your mum is living with dementia."

There's a long pause before Fiona weakly says, "Dementia? How do you know? Has she been diagnosed?" Her back straightens, her face twists with concern. I can see love there—she cares, despite her attempts over the years not to, perhaps.

"Not formally, no. But one of the other residents in the building has a little experience with it. There's been a lot of trial and error by everyone, trying different intervention methods to help your mum, some of which have worked well, others less so."

"Everyone?"

"We've had a bit of a rota going so the residents in the building check in on her at least twice a day. We make sure she's getting dressed properly and that she's eating enough. Everyone thinks very highly of your mum." I'm trying to decide whether to come clean about the road trip, me dragging Meredith off to London, twice, then Sandringham and Althorp, but Fiona looks so crushed, I hold back.

"It should have been me. I should have been here helping her. I'm so sorry you had to shoulder all of this. What must you all think of me?" She cradles her face in her hands. "I don't know where the time has gone. How the days have somehow turned into years."

"You don't have to explain anything to me. Families are complicated, I know that."

"I don't want you to think I don't love her. I do, of *course* I do. But they were both so devoted to their careers, I often felt as a child that I came a poor third, after their work commitments and each other. Even when we moved to Bath and they scaled back, I spent most weekends at the university having music lessons with the children of other parents who were too worn out to entertain them on their precious days off. At least, I remember that's how it felt. They gave me this huge opportunity to nurture a skill I never knew I had until the first time I was put in front of a piano. Financially, my father made sure I had everything I needed. He covered all the cost of my tuition at RCM, but he never once attended a concert. Neither of them did. I wasn't wanted, Jayne. I was a mistake. Mum told me as much."

I shake my head. I know this cannot be true.

My mind travels back over some of the conversations I've had with Meredith, the more lucid ones where she has smiled deeply through her recollections of Fiona. How proud she is of that graduation photograph. The regret she confessed that day at the Royal Albert Hall of never hearing the piece of Chopin played live. I think about the trunk of small dresses in the memory room, the late nights she must have spent making them. Then I think about Meredith's references to William protecting her.

"You have lots of time to talk now, to try to really understand each other, that's the positive in all of this, isn't it? If you want to?" I will my face to convey this is exactly what Meredith would love.

She traces her fingers under her eyes, wiping the tears away. "I'd like to very much, if she would? I feel like I need to get to know my own mother all over again."

The fact she is keen to see Meredith is great. I don't think any of us had ruled out the possibility that whatever pushed this family apart may have been too insurmountable to bring them back together again. But I also need to warn her.

"I just want to prepare you for what you're going to see when you enter her apartment."

"Okay." Fiona straightens on her stool.

"Seeing it for the first time, you'll think it looks incredibly cluttered. But it's not messy to Meredith. She likes to have her things around her. She has built a memory room, a space that charts her life in a way that makes little sense to the rest of us, but it comforts her. We think your father may have helped with it, when he realized she may need it."

"I could have helped with that too." She brushes away fresh tears with the tissue I hand her.

"You still can. Also, we've made some changes that might seem odd when you first see them. Like putting pictures of what's inside her kitchen cupboards on the doors so she knows where everything is. And we've signposted a lot of things, like her morning wash routine. There are also headshots of us all just inside her front door so she knows who to let in and who not to."

The shock is visible in the wideness of Fiona's eyes.

"It's a lot to take in, I know. We've had a lot longer to absorb it all than you have. The important thing, I think, is that she has been doing so well, with a little help. It derailed a little last week when the ambulance . . ." I pause, thinking how best to phrase this. "She heard a siren and panicked. We don't know any of the details around your father's death, how it happened, but she seemed to connect the sound of the siren to William needing medical help."

Fiona lowers her head while she processes that thought. "Do you think she may have been the one to call it, that he might have died at home here and she had to deal with it all alone?" I see the guilt cling to her. It settles heavily on her shoulders, hangs in her jaw, making her head appear heavy. I don't want to dwell on the negatives, but neither can I lie to her.

"Sadly, I do think it's possible, yes. There is rarely anyone at home here during the day except Olivia, and she often works wearing noise-canceling headphones. Her kitchen, where she works, is at the back of the house, she probably didn't see the flashing lights. Plus, it's a busy city, there are sirens going off all the time. Even if Olivia had heard it, she wouldn't necessarily have thought to investigate it, I'm afraid."

Fiona nods. She understands. Anyone who lives in a city would. I think about how I've learned to block out noise, barely registering the scream of a car alarm anymore.

"What's clear is Meredith needs more help. We are here, of course. But we can see she needs a formal diagnosis of her stage of dementia and professional help that is tailored specifically to that. The apartment could become very difficult for her to manage otherwise."

I immediately regret saying it, because the way Fiona slowly nods and starts to punch notes into her phone suggests it might be Meredith's living arrangements that she'll prioritize, when her mum needs her to first understand her wishes.

"There's no rush, obviously, but I'm sure you'd like to go and see her."

"I really would."

I open my mouth to deliver my usual "Hello, Meredith, it's Jayne from upstairs" but I don't get any further than the first part.

"Fiona!" beams Meredith. "Gosh, your hair has got so long. I need to book you in for a cut."

Fiona and I exchange a quick glance but it's Meredith who takes the conversational lead.

"Come in then. You'll want tea and crumpets for breakfast, won't you?" As she turns and moves away from the door, I see ladders in her tights running up the backs of both legs, one so bad her heel is exposed.

I look at my watch. It's long past lunchtime already.

"Don't worry, Mum, I'll grab something to eat later."

"After your lesson with Mrs. Tims?"

I'm guessing from the horrified look on Fiona's face, Mrs. Tims is a teacher from many years ago.

"I'm not having a lesson with Mrs. Tims today, Mum, I haven't had one for . . ." Fiona looks to me for guidance on how to finish her sentence.

"Hang on," Meredith shouts over her shoulder. "Just let me get the kettle on."

We perch on one of the sofas, listening as she clatters around the kitchen.

"I'm going to leave you to it," I say. "My advice, which obviously you don't have to take, is to just go along with the conversation, rather than trying to correct her. She'll be more comfortable that way and the alternative might tie you up in knots."

"Are you sure you wouldn't like to stay?" She grimaces, but her eyes are bright, anticipating what the next hour or two may bring.

"I can if you'd like me to, but I think you will be just fine without me. This way she only has to concentrate on you. I'll be upstairs, and you have my number if you need me."

Meredith steps back into the sitting room carrying a tray of tea and a plate loaded with biscuits, most of them broken.

I say my goodbyes as she's setting the tray down on the low table.

"Are you sure you wouldn't like a biscuit before you go?" She lifts the plate toward me. "Just not the custard creams. They're William's favorites. He won't appreciate it if we eat them all, will he, Fiona?" She chuckles and the effect the sound has on Fiona makes my heart ache.

Her face seems to droop with the relief of being accepted back into her mother's home, like she stepped out only a few hours ago to visit a friend. But she is also seeing the struggle that lies ahead, the difficult conversations, the frustrations, the altered reality that's now the norm. The fragility of a mother she might once have thought unforgiving and single-minded and how her own hurt has robbed them both of the precious time that is cartwheeling away from Meredith at a rate none of us can truly understand.

As I open the door to leave, I also see the unguarded happiness on the face of an older woman, my friend, who for the first time in eight years will spend the afternoon with her only daughter. One she clearly never stopped loving.

Meredith raises her hand to Fiona's cheek and traces her fingers across her skin. "You look so much like your father," she says, smiling. "I'm so lucky to have you both."

FORTY-SIX

❦

William
JANUARY 2017

Dear Fiona,

I hope this letter finds you well and happy. The depth of my sadness at writing to my daughter with no knowledge of where to send this note is shameful.

How did it come to this?

How did I become this man, the kind of father who could be so neglectful?

I have questioned myself many times over the years. Did I make the best decisions? Did I properly care for the women I love? Will I leave this world knowing that I did everything I could?

I know now that the answer to all of these questions is no. It can't be when I am writing this letter to my daughter, whom I haven't seen for eight years, to tell her she is losing her mother when she has already lost her father.

I see now that in trying to solve one problem, I created another, and I can only hope it is not too late to fix that. If

*you are reading this letter, I'm afraid it means it will be up
to you to fix it without my help.*

*I'm not sure, as I look back on the time between us
arriving as a family in Bath and your decision to leave,
where the fault line appeared, where it cracked, spreading
in all directions like a piece of intricate lace. But the point
is, I never stopped it. I could have hit the brakes before we
went over the edge, but I didn't, and I want to explain
why—not because I think it absolves me, but in the hope
that you will come to understand the impossible decision I
had to make.*

*I think I knew for a long time that I wasn't well. It seems
ludicrous to admit that now. All that wasted time when I
could have acted, and I didn't. Raw fear is the only
explanation I have. There can only be so many headaches, so many dizzy spells before you can no longer deny
what is beating down on you. But I would recover, months
would pass. I convinced myself, surprisingly easily, that
was the last of it. Don't waste the doctor's time, don't give
your mother anything else to worry about. This was the
precise moment when cowardice crept into the room,
encouraged by my fleeting symptoms, like the sun blazing,
then fading behind clouds on a windy day.*

*Self-diagnosis is a dangerous thing, but I read enough
to make an educated guess. Some ministrokes can be so
mild they are barely registered. They can pass in an hour,
almost undetected. The big one, if it is coming for me,
should, according to the experts, have come by now.
If you are reading this, then perhaps it's come for me
at last.*

I'm glad I'm able to write this first. I need you to understand not just the practicalities but also the one fact we never shouted loudly enough. You are so very loved, my darling girl. And it was always so. That awful night, when your mother said what she did, we were already losing her, I just didn't know it. There was a stranger at our table for dinner that evening but I was too stupid, perhaps too scared, to confront her and act.

In the years after you returned to London, I started to see the signs that your beautiful, talented mother was not herself. But I write this with the benefit of hindsight, when I was already in the thick of hiding my own deficiencies.

When she was well, she cared for me, sometimes at the expense of you. And when I knew she wasn't well, I followed her example, I closed ranks around her, again at the expense of you. What a truly awful thing to have to admit. But now is the time for honesty. I always imagined you would return when the rejection had lost its sting. Or perhaps when I could no longer keep her secret from the world. I hoped for a knock on the door. A surprise phone call. Is it completely crass to say I hoped the fact I was paying for your school fees showed you I cared? I worry now that it merely showed I could afford to.

I didn't come for you, Fiona, because I was afraid to face the potential consequences. I was afraid to show you how I was diminishing and afraid to expose your mother.

Only now I have no choice. Your mother is losing herself. The very fabric of her life is unraveling around her. She is beginning to doubt herself and everyone else. The one solitary thing she never stitched together well enough is, ironically, life itself, or at least her memory of it.

I've watched it come loose, worried that the harder I try to pull it back together, the more it unravels. How long until I am afraid to look at it at all? What horrors might it still have to show me?

It is my final wish, and I know it would be hers, too, that she stays in the apartment. Her life has always been vivid, so full of color and texture and energy. The end of it can't be a sanitized box with smooth, clean edges, where the days bleed into the nights. Don't let her be packed off somewhere she'll never be able to see the sunlight. These are the thoughts that haunt me in my darkest moments.

I have signed the apartment over to you. Legally, you now own it. Even as I write this letter, I believe Meredith is incapable of managing her own affairs without help. That help will need to come from you now, Fiona. Can you find it in your heart to do that for me and for her, please?

I cannot for one second imagine a world in which Meredith wakes and I am not lying there beside her. If the tables were turned the loneliness would take me in no time. She deserves so much more—and so do you. Take the chance to discover her all over again—and let her enjoy you for however long you both have left together. It is too late for you and me, but not for you and her.

With all my love,
Dad

FORTY-SEVEN

Jayne

Jake places a warm sourdough between us all. He rips it open with his hands, allowing the steam to escape and rise. It's Saturday evening, the city below us is teeming with the excitement of a long balmy bank holiday weekend—and I am in the company of a man I find so attractive I have to remind myself not to sit and stare at him. I watch as the butter melts into the pockets of the bread and he expertly fixes a round of gin and tonics in heavy glass tumblers, one large ice cube in each, topped with a spiral of orange zest. The whole gang is here, filling Davina's kitchen once more. I only wish Meredith was completing our little family but there are things to discuss first.

"Make mine a strong one please, Jake. It's been a shitty week, but Maggie is asleep in bed, Willow is FaceTiming friends, and I have the weekend off. Tragic as it may sound, that's all the excuse I need."

Me too. I want to lift the glass, arch my head backward, and drink deeply, to loosen my joints from the heaviness lodged in them.

"Well, your lovely mum has been doing brilliantly, Fiona." De-

spite the appraisal of her week, Davina is fizzing with energy tonight, her arms thrown wide in excitement. "She has remembered
so much. It doesn't always stay with her, but it's been like she's
living it all over again in vivid detail. It has been a privilege getting
to know her." Davina raises her glass aloft and we all do likewise.
"To Meredith."

"Thank you." Fiona's cheeks flush a little at the compliment.
"Sorry. That sounds so inadequate. What you all have done for
Mum is truly humbling."

Davina bats away the praise with a flick of her hand.

"And actually, thank *you* for sending us the memorial footage,"
adds Davina. "We've incorporated it into Meredith's digital life
story, along with some of the early photographs you sent from
before she and William were married. It works wonderfully together, I think, but you can see for yourself."

"I would love to watch it." Fiona's response is genuine, but I
wonder how hard it will be for her to revisit times when she didn't
feel as loved as I believe she is. After one quick trip back to London to gather some more belongings, she's been in Bath a few
days now, spending most of them sitting with Meredith in her
memory room and absorbing the contents of William's letter—the
details of which I hope she will share with us all tonight.

"I brought some fabric swatches back with me too. Some are
from the very dresses Mum has been revisiting. She always kept a
small piece from each at the time. A memento I suppose. She'd
bring them home and I'd tuck them away, fascinated that I owned
a small scrap of a princess's dress. Even after all this time, I
couldn't bring myself to throw them away. Maybe they might be
useful now? Something more tactile?"

"Yes! Show them to her. It's one thing to see film footage but
quite another to hold the very fabric that she worked with again.

It could work wonders." Olivia beams as she takes up her place in front of the laptop. We all squeeze in tighter, as close to the screen as we can get without blocking one another's view.

"My goodness, they were so in love," Davina says wistfully as the first image fills the screen.

"They adored each other," whispers Fiona. "I never imaged a time when they wouldn't. Even then, as a child, I could feel the force of it, the way they gravitated to each other. If one of them wasn't in the room, the other couldn't be fully at ease. It's staggering really that their paths crossed because, honestly, I don't think either of them could have lived a happy life without the other."

Except that's exactly what Meredith will have to do now, and the collective knowledge of that forces a thoughtful silence to descend over us.

I feel Jake's hand slide into mine as the film reveals a collection of new baby and toddler pictures that Fiona has supplied. Two exhausted parents on a brown leather sofa, Fiona wedged in between them. The family resemblance between Fiona and William is clear for us all to see. Then a vast bouquet of pale cream roses that would require two arms to lift, its stems stripped and covered in a thick band of finely stitched lace. Meredith in a small brimmed hat, black gloves, holding a handkerchief that bears William's initials. I feel my jaw lock, my teeth clench together. This is the end. How is Meredith going to react if she is shown it? Fiona's eyes don't leave the image of her mother, her eyebrows twitching as she leans in a fraction closer to the screen, absorbed by what she's seeing.

A framed image of William appears, taken in the workrooms of Catherine Walker. He's wearing the long white overcoat. It's unbuttoned to reveal a smart navy suit beneath. He looks focused, leaning his weight forward onto the table on one elbow, his head

tilted in concentration, like he's listening intently to someone just out of the shot.

The image is held on-screen, giving everyone time to read the inscription below.

William Henry Hatfield
Born April 1942
Died May 2017

Husband to Meredith Rebecca Chalis and
father to Fiona Caroline Hatfield

A quiet perfectionist. A modest gentleman.
An admired talent.

As his portrait fades, the camera shifts to people in sharply tailored suits and monotone dresses as they rise from their seats and begin to exchange kisses. Men wrap arms around each other's shoulders or deliver hearty handshakes. Champagne flutes start to move through the crowd. There must be two hundred people present. Then I see Meredith, her eyes impassive, quietly receiving a swirl of people who make no genuine impact on her expression. I notice how she sets her smile, lets it drop momentarily between one well-wisher and the next, then quickly resets it. Her essentials bag is bobbing from her right wrist, rising and falling with every handshake, like a security blanket she cannot detach herself from.

"She's not right," Fiona says as the film ends.

"It must be hard to watch," says Davina, "but I suppose we have to remember that she had recently lost her husband. She was grieving."

I know everyone experiences the death of a loved one differently, but it looks nothing like the grief I've seen—where there

was no place for well-dressed women with immaculate hair and a ready repertoire of polite conversation.

"No, that's not it." Fiona's voice is flat.

"None of those people look close to her," I add hesitantly. "Maybe they weren't. It's a memorial, not a family funeral, so they would have been professional colleagues and clients presumably rather than close personal friends?"

Fiona nods her head in agreement. "Her eyes are vacant, she looks detached from what's going on around her. She never made a speech. Even from that short clip, I can tell she wasn't personally involved in organizing the day. It's someone else's idea of how my father should be honored. And I don't mean to say it wasn't wonderful and I am so glad they did it, but . . . it's just not her."

"What do you mean?" asks Jake.

"She was already struggling to understand what was happening. That Dad . . . that he wasn't coming back."

Davina rewinds the film and plays that section again.

"It might also explain why you weren't there, Fiona. If Meredith hadn't fully grasped the finality of William's memorial, then she wouldn't necessarily connect the need for you to be present."

Fiona nods slowly. "His death certificate shows that he had a fatal stroke. I checked the records before I left London. And I know from the letter he left me that it wasn't his first. There were other, milder ones preceding it. Surely Mum would have been aware of that?" She sighs, shakes her head. "I always thought she knew his health wasn't the best. I remember him being tired. They both worked so hard. The hours were long but the job so rewarding that he stayed in it longer than perhaps he should have. It must have been very stressful, all those deadlines, all that visibility. I remember them discussing Dad having one of his headaches or dizzy spells. But his symptoms were always relatively mild, easily

dismissed, I suppose. I'm concerned that Mum has lost all knowledge of that."

"She has talked about long hours and William not looking after himself, his headaches, and how he never bothered to get them checked out." I try to recall anything else she may have shared. "But I don't think she has ever specifically referenced an illness."

"The letter my father left for me with the solicitor was dated January 2017. That's six months before his memorial took place. He makes it very clear she was already declining. I don't understand how she could have attended this day without anyone questioning her behavior and whether there was more to it?"

"Because they weren't looking for it and it would have been easy to miss in the circumstances, wouldn't it? This was a woman supposedly grieving for her deceased husband." Davina starts to make everyone a fresh pot of tea.

"Perhaps no one thought it was their place to question her, on this of all days," adds Carina. "They assumed that someone else was taking care of her. At least some of them knew she had a daughter, presumably? The inscription says as much."

"Yes, you're right, of course." Fiona understands that Carina's words are not intended to hurt her. She wants to help, to offer possible explanations, just like the rest of us. "But it does make me wonder if Dad's final wishes are really the right ones. If it's for the best. He says in his letter to me that he wants her to stay in the apartment, not to be moved to a specialist care home. He has signed over the legal ownership of the apartment to me. It seemed perfectly reasonable when I first read it but now . . . I'm not so sure."

I close my eyes slowly. I feared this would be her reaction. Jake's eyes settle on me. Even with her back to us, I register the slump of Davina's shoulders, she looks to the ceiling in exasperation.

"Surely there has to be some recognition on her part that my father, her husband, is gone and he's not coming back? I've seen no sign of that yet. And if she can't even recall him being unwell, then what are the chances of that? I don't want her to continue waking every morning to the same awful feelings of abandonment. She needs professional help to understand that he didn't *choose* to leave her but also that he's not coming back."

Everyone exchanges a look of deep concern, collectively understanding that these decisions must be deferred to Fiona now, no matter how much we may all disagree with them, but Davina isn't so easily silenced.

"Meredith's done so well these past few weeks but that day with the ambulance arriving seemed to push her a little further," she offers. "She seemed to understand then that there is an ending to this story—to her and William's story."

Jake's eyes fix on Davina, appealing to her not to push this too far.

"But she's made no mention of it to me at all," Fiona says. "I don't think she remembers the incident. I've spent the past few days slowly and gently trying to take Mum back over everything that happened in the months and weeks leading up to my father's death and afterward. To see if there might be some level of acceptance, or resignation even. But there isn't. I think it's why she struggled initially with any clarity around her working life. He was so entwined in it that the pain of losing him wiped out everything else, until now. Until you all started to help her. But she still can't accept that he's gone." She shrugs her shoulders as if resigned to the futility of the situation that has led us all here.

I can't speak. Meredith isn't a spreadsheet, preprogrammed to respond a certain way. An equation that will logically complete itself once the correct information is inputted. I know Fiona needs time to work this out for herself, just as we have, but the clock is ticking.

I realize then that Fiona sees that future plotted along one straight line, when the truth is more a network of roads branching off from one another—disappointing and confusing dead ends, ways in with no ways out, but also beautiful views from the top of Meredith's chosen hills and the mountains she will climb.

Carina starts to clatter the teacups around in front of us, asking Jake what he's baking next. They're trying to break the conversation, to signal to Davina that we have taken this as far as we should today. She registers what they're doing and ignores them.

"It's going to take me a while to work out what's best for her." Fiona's voice drains of confidence. Panic is creeping in. "She's going to need lots of intervention as the months and years go on, isn't she? How will she manage in that apartment? It would probably be too large for someone on their own even without the dementia."

"Look, Fiona . . ." Davina's voice is too hard.

"Wait." Jake raises a hand to cut her off. "Fiona has a very valid point. We are already organizing her food shops. She will need someone to manage her utility bills, her medical appointments, all her financial affairs. It's not a small thing. Which means it won't be an inexpensive thing. How far off might she be from needing full, around-the-clock care, even if it's here at home?"

"It's going to cost a fortune. My career will start to demand I travel more and how can I?" Fiona swallows hard. "She isn't going to get better, is she? Only worse. Selling the apartment would mean I could get her the best care she needs. But it's not what Dad wanted. He says it's not what she wants either."

"She won't want to leave." I force some softness into my voice. "I'm sorry, Fiona. This is your decision to make. I just want to make sure we've told you everything we know before you make it, that's all."

"Jayne is right, she really won't," adds Davina, more measured now, "and, honestly, neither would I, if it were me. She's become . . . well, she's become a very dear friend to us all. We don't want to let her down. We all remain ready to help."

Fiona smiles, like she appreciates the offer, but I can see the doubt in her eyes. She doesn't know us. We met for the first time only a few days ago. I'm sure she's asking herself what there is to stop us reneging on this arrangement at any point—and where that might leave her. Having to abandon a busy work schedule? Sacrificing a loved career—something she's already explained her parents never did for her?

"As you know, Mum has very little concept of time. Dad's disappearance doesn't feel like it happened more than a year ago to her, it feels more like last week. She truly believes he is coming home, and I have started to wonder if it is better to allow her to believe that, rather than fighting it."

I feel Olivia bristle beside me. I look at the others and it is the saddest sight. Not one of us is unmoved by this.

"Our goal has always been to bring her some peace," I say. "I'm really not sure how this would achieve that."

"She remembered those dresses, Jayne," Davina reminds us all. "Because of you and the time you gave to her, she remembered all the magic she created with William. You took her all the way back through their story to the night the ambulance was called. That's not a failure—that's an enormous success."

She's right. What we have all done for Meredith and the effect it has had on her can't be understated.

"We're not experts, Fiona, but what does that mean anyway? Everyone will experience dementia differently. There isn't a tried-

and-true method for this. It takes kindness and time and patience. We have taken the time to get to know your mum." I look around the room at my friends and see the pride and passion in their faces, their absolute determination not to give up. It gives me all the courage I need to say what needs to be said, not just for me but for them too.

"We know that when she travels she feels more comfortable if I take a flask of tea, that she will never say no to an egg sandwich, that she knows every word to every song in *Steel Magnolias*, that she boils her eggs in the kettle and sleeps with William's scarf on the pillow next to her because it still holds his scent. We have played her life story to her every single day, and for the hour or two afterward, she is more alive and energized than at any other time. She loves Davina's leftovers, especially the lamb because she cooked it for William, and even though after all these weeks I have to introduce myself almost every time I knock on Meredith's door, names don't matter. It's how she feels in our company that makes all the difference. There has been great honesty in the way we have all supported your wonderful mum and, forgive me, but I'm just not sure we should alter the truth to suit her. Doesn't she deserve more than that? Could we just take some more time to think it through?"

Fiona's face has visibly dropped. She's worn down by us, baffled by the decisions she has to make—and it's our fault for making her feel cornered by our experience versus her obligations.

"I will never be able to thank you all enough for everything you have done for my mum when you could so easily have looked the other way. I also know you might disagree with some of the choices I have to make but I hope you can respect that I have to take responsibility for them." She stands and picks up her handbag from the floor.

"Maybe Meredith should experience death and grief, just like we all do?" Olivia has said very little until now.

"Sorry?" Fiona is at the door but pauses. "What do you mean?"

"Why shouldn't she feel the hurt? The crushing emptiness that comes with losing someone irreplaceable. Feeling it will only confirm how right she was to love William as hard as she has all these years." Fiona doesn't know it, but Olivia is revisiting her own hurt. Her face has crumpled. She doesn't want to talk about any of this but for Meredith's benefit she is willing to enter the fight.

"Do you really think she could cope with that?" From the look of skepticism and doubt on Fiona's face, her raised eyebrows, it's clear she's already made up her mind.

"She's human. She has a right to her own feelings, and who are any of us to deny her them? As the months wear on she's going to feel less human, less sure, less of everything. Let her feel as much as she possibly can, while she still can. Let her be as much of herself as possible. It's the greatest gift you can give her right now." I watch as a single tear slides down Olivia's left cheek.

"You know this?" Fiona has placed her bag back at her feet. I think she senses that Olivia is speaking from a position of true knowledge.

"I wish I didn't, but yes."

Jake hands Olivia a glass of water, then Davina is at her side, a firm arm wrapped around her shoulders.

"Hang on." Carina slides off her stool. "We're losing sight of what we know. We have a clear way to connect Meredith to William's death. She was at the memorial. The film footage places her there in the same way the dresses and all the locations they were worn to placed her back into her professional world and closer to William."

I place my hand on Fiona's arm, keeping her still for a second longer.

"Let's at least try it, shall we?" I smile, I need her to know that I am on her side. This is not us against her.

This is what we all wanted. We are within touching distance of everything we hoped we might achieve when we came together that first evening and promised to help a woman find her husband and daughter.

"Okay, but honestly, from what I have seen of Mum since I got here, I'm not expecting it to work. She's spent such a long time believing one thing. I'm not sure we can hope the footage will easily reverse that."

As I watch Fiona leave, I think about the dress in Meredith's apartment, where this all began, the email from Christie's still sitting in my inbox, everything we have done together, the lessons she has taught me, the confidence she has filled me with, without even realizing it. I think about Meredith's warmth, the truly happy times we have spent together, and the times she's unleashed her fury on me, and I silently ask myself, Is it just too much to hope that her love for William will triumph over everything?

FORTY-EIGHT

～～⚬～～

Fiona opens the door to Meredith's apartment with a face that is the polar opposite of optimistic. It's not a great start.

"Oh, hello." Meredith rises from the sofa and greets me like we've never met before. "I didn't know we were expecting company."

"Morning, Meredith, it's Jayne from upstairs." I take the seat next to her. "How are you feeling this morning?"

"I'm okay, but I think someone is a bit stressed-out." She nods toward the kitchen, where I can hear Fiona banging cups around. "I don't like it. It doesn't feel good and William won't stand for it." She's getting agitated and I wish it was just me and her. But this can't be about what I prefer. Fiona needs to hear whatever it is Meredith says when we watch her life story again.

Fiona places the mugs of tea down in front of us. "Sorry, I've been away from London longer than I said I would be, and I've got some catching up to do today before I go back tomorrow."

"Look what she gave me this morning." Meredith looks at me excitedly. "My fabric swatches!" There is a large drawstring bag on the table that's stuffed with scraps of material. She looks at Fiona and I know she can't remember her name.

"Do you have anything from the dress that Diana gave you,

Meredith? The pink silk one in your room with all the beautiful floral embroidery." I'm keen to introduce the subject of the dress to see how Meredith might feel about selling it, when and if the time comes.

"I gave *her* the dresses, she didn't give them to me," she laughs, and I catch Fiona frowning, more evidence that what we're here to attempt today isn't going to work.

Meredith reaches for the bag, pulls it open, and starts to spill the contents into her lap. There are beautiful bright silks, tiny swatches of intricate beaded lace embroidery, satins with a luxurious glossy sheen, and a pale pink chiffon I think might be from the Launceston Place dress.

"Shall we?" Fiona takes the armchair adjacent to the sofa.

I push the memory stick into the side of the laptop, wait for it to upload and the play arrow to appear.

"I thought we could watch that lovely film of your life again." I turn to face Meredith. "We managed to add a few extra photographs and film footage that I thought you might like to see, if that's okay?"

Meredith is all smiles, running her fingers across the fabrics now covering her legs and spilling onto the floor and the sofa beside me. I pause. She looks so innocent, childlike almost. There is something so unfair about the knowledge Fiona and I hold, which isn't shared by her. I don't like the unasked-for control it gives us. Is what I'm about to show her going to be more than she can cope with?

I think about Olivia's words last night and how they apply to Meredith today. About her need to be seen, by others but also by herself. To recognize the woman she is in the world around her. How, in her own way, she has fought for that right, and who are we, when the journey reaches this difficult fork, to stop her because she might feel a depth of emotion that we deem too strong? That *we* might find upsetting. I also think about the enormous gift she has given me, how I would be facing another week of solitude— how I may never have forged my friendships with Davina and Olivia, different as they are, or enjoyed more of Carina's company, never laughed with Maggie, and never felt the closeness and the thrill of Jake—if not for her. More than that, she's made me realize that there is great skill involved in listening to someone, really listening. Not everyone can do it or wants to. Olivia said it, too, maybe it is my superpower. It's thanks to both women that I will be meeting Olivia later outside the Live Well Center, only this time we will be going in together and she'll be taking me through my first shift. Maybe there will be more Merediths I can help. And many others besides. I hope it will remind me that it's okay to take a step back at the end of the day and enjoy the new pleasures in my own life, with Jake and these wonderful new friends. That sometimes I need to be my own priority. It could be the beginning of something special and fulfilling—something I have needed for a long time.

Meredith has no idea what she has done for me, and so I am going to press play and whatever happens next, I will be here for her, just as she has been for me.

The film starts. Meredith shuffles forward in anticipation. She smiles along at first, just as she usually does. She's on safe ground, seeing again all the dresses and the photographs that are familiar to her. Even if she might struggle now to name a place or retrieve a date, she is comfortable that these images are known to her, that they are part of her story. And she remains relaxed until the framed image of William in his white coat and navy suit fills the screen. Then her tears come. They are quiet tears, nothing like the panic I have witnessed in her over the previous weeks. I think she is finding some comfort in the fabric, still in her lap. She is passing pieces gently through her fingers, but she is calm.

She will speak when she is ready to. I hold a hand up to Fiona, encouraging her to wait, to say nothing and let Meredith speak first.

Finally, she looks at us both. "I chose the portrait of him." Her voice is barely more than a whisper. "The one they framed. He always liked it. I think because it was one of the last times he was in a place he loved, doing what he loved, wearing his favorite suit. Looking smart on that day"—she nods toward the laptop—"of all days, was important. My darling William."

Fiona won't know it, but it's the first time I have heard Meredith speak about William so firmly in the past tense.

"You made an excellent choice, Mum"—Fiona takes her hand—"and I think he would have been grateful for that."

Meredith nods. It's a small step, tiny, I know, the subtlest acknowledgment of what that day was about, the part she played in it, but it's more than she has ever said before.

"Can I watch it again, please?" I hit play while Fiona and I head to the kitchen.

"It's not much, I know," I say as soon as we are out of earshot, "but at the same time, hugely significant."

"I honestly didn't think she would connect herself to Dad's memorial in any way," admits Fiona, glancing down at her watch again. "I'm sorry, Jayne, I have to go, but maybe we can talk again later?"

I temper my excitement—and, risky as it is, her acceptance of what she's seen. "There will be more setbacks, steps forward, and then huge ones back again but I truly believe we can make it work if you decide it is best for your mum to stay here."

"Thank you, Jayne. The fact you care as much as you do means a great deal to me, and to her."

Fiona returns to the sitting room and gives Meredith a quick kiss on the forehead. She turns to leave before looking back at her mum again. She slowly asks, "You like living here, don't you, Mum?"

"Where else would I live?" Meredith doesn't remove her eyes from the screen. We both watch as Meredith gently sways to the sounds of the *Steel Magnolias* soundtrack we included on the film. Fiona allows herself a small smile before continuing out of the apartment. I close the door behind her and let a huge rush of breath escape me. Then I take my seat back on the sofa next to Meredith.

We watch the final scenes together again. There are no tears this time.

"Would you like to get some fresh air, Meredith?" I ask as the film ends. "I have no plans until later so we could take a walk to one of our favorite parks if you like, maybe let Maggie and Margot tag along if they both behave themselves?"

Her face brightens. "That sounds like a lovely idea. Will we pass a dry cleaner's on the way?"

"Yes, I'm sure we will. Do you have something that needs to be dropped off?"

"Yes, that navy suit of William's. It's a favorite. He'll want to wear it again soon."

EPILOGUE

SUMMER
2019

We are all huddled around the laptop. Me, Meredith, Fiona, Jake, Davina, Olivia, Maggie, and Willow. Carina has closed the shop for an hour and joined us too. Jessie is here as well. She is Meredith's new carer. Someone we can all rely on to be here when she is needed the most. Someone who can respond to Meredith's needs as they arise, who can have fun with her without having to press pause on other commitments. She's young, her energy levels only topped by Maggie's and, most important, Meredith instantly warmed to her. The two of them spend hours every week buried in the memory room, rooting through all the chapters of Meredith's life, in the unrushed way I know she needs.

They can't see us, but we can see all of them. There must be three hundred people packed into Christie's in New York. The auctioneer is already at his lectern, the gavel poised in his right hand. And there is Meredith's dress, expertly displayed on the mannequin next to him, the handwritten letter that Catherine sent to Meredith back in 1997 framed next to it. We all listen intently as he retells the very personal story of this incredible dress. I know them, of course, but I listen to the facts detailing the fabric and decoration and then I think about everything else this dress represents that today's audience will never come close to appreciating. The period of time in which it was conceived and made along with all the others, and how those days and months and years have remained so special to one woman—the one sitting beside me now enjoying all the fuss, if not perhaps entirely understanding why her dress is an ocean away.

Fiona and I discussed the rights and wrongs of it at length with everyone else, pulling Meredith into the conversation at every opportunity until we were confident she was giving us every indication the decision to sell was the right one. It's a beautiful, meaningful dress, the starting point of our whole adventure together, but I can't allow my own sentimentality to swerve the story in the wrong direction. What this dress can gift back to Meredith today is far more valuable than if it had stayed thrown over her bedroom chair where I found it. Perhaps exactly as William planned it.

As I look at her now, struggling to contain Maggie on her lap, I know not even Meredith could have guessed the impact that period of her life would continue to have on her, how it would come to be so vital in connecting her past, present, and future. How the stitches she made back then would help weave her own world back together in a positive way that makes sense when everything else around her suddenly didn't.

The one thing I can't bring myself to think about is what may have been—if Margot hadn't darted into her apartment that morning, forcing us into each other's company. Everything that would have remained lost to her and the friendships I never would have made. The changes I may never have made. How I had no idea back then how much good would come from going back. Making peace with everything that I had left unchallenged for so long and the rewards that bravery would gift me in return.

Meredith never wanted a life without William. Theirs is a love so strong that her heart and mind simply refuse to let him go. I have had to live my life without my sister, never getting to feel that depth of connection with her. And it is only now that I have traced Meredith's story with her that I can see the good that can come from my own experience. A young woman called the Live Well Center last week and it was Olivia who took the call. She managed to grab only snatches of her story between her sobs. A lost sibling. Tragic. Unexpected. No chance to say goodbye and now a weight of grief she doesn't feel able to share with her family. Olivia, even with all her experience, can't help this woman. Not like I can. We don't often schedule calls. The whole point is the lines have to be kept clear so that those who need us the most can get through. But this young woman will call again tomorrow night at six p.m. and I will be waiting to listen to her, but also to speak, to share my own experience, in the hope that it helps her realize there is always a way back.

The bidding starts and there is a fevered response to the auctioneer's directions, to every movement of his hand from one side of the room to the other. The numbers climb quickly, sometimes with an almost imperceptible nod of a head. Our cheers follow the rise upward. It's impossible to keep track of who has the advantage. There are telephone and online bidders competing, too, probably from every continent in the world. No one moves from their spot and twenty-five minutes later comes the loud whack of the gavel on wood. It's done. There is a winner and the price they have paid far exceeds anything we might have hoped for. The relief brings tears from most of us. A champagne cork pops. I feel a special poignancy at the fact this dress waited all this time before it reached its original intended destination. There would have been no benefit to Meredith if it had made it to Christie's back in 1997. The fact it is there now will be life-changing for her. Just as she has been life-changing for me.

"Did someone really just pay all that money for a dress *you* made?" Maggie is stiff with excitement.

"I think so," laughs Meredith.

"Well, then, you're *mega* rich. The richest person I know!" She starts to dance around the room as only Maggie can. Then she sits, thinks for a minute while we are all hugging and kissing one another. "Can you make me one?" she asks, her eyes firmly on the prize.

"You'd like me to make you a dress?" The question causes a swell of emotion in Meredith that sends both her hands to her cheeks.

"One hundred percent I would, yes, please!" Maggie shouts. "It will need sparkles."

"No one has asked me to do that for a very long time. I'll need my tape measure." She disappears in search of her essentials bag.

I know who I am hoping has won this auction, and there is a chance because the commentary tells us it has gone to a phone bidder. If they get it, I know they will let Meredith see it whenever she wants. She'll be able to touch it, to cast her hands across the same fabric that William once did but knowing that this time others will be able to appreciate his work too. They will both get the recognition they richly deserve. Their full story will be told and preserved forever, safe from a decaying memory. Somewhere dementia cannot touch it.

As summer starts to draw to a close, Meredith, Fiona, and I have a very special day planned. We're heading to the Bath Fashion

Museum to see the dress, something I dearly hoped I may be able to say. It feels like William is finally coming home. Then we'll be heading to the memorable garden where his ashes are scattered. Fiona has arranged for a rosebush to be planted there in William's memory. We'll be able to sit in the late-afternoon sunshine on one of the benches and chat through some of Meredith's favorite stories. I can ask her to tell me again about some of the dresses she's made and how much she loved working with William. Some days her clarity is breathtaking and on others she is empty and wordless, but we have all learned not to see those days as failures.

The two of them are so at ease in each other's company, I sometimes wonder if it's not only Meredith but Fiona, too, who has forgotten about the years when they weren't together. The physical likeness between father and daughter helps, I think. Perhaps it is William whom Meredith sees when she looks at Fiona. Either way, they seem to have reached a place of deep understanding and love. Fiona has been a more regular face at Lansdown Crescent. She's managed to negotiate more time away from London so she can see Meredith every week, not just a handful of times a year. I am taking a step back, giving them the space they need to reconnect with each other. The space I need to focus on my own life too.

Jake has asked me to move into the coach house. I spend most nights there anyway, but I don't want to let practicalities squash romance, so I'm thinking about it. Oh, who am I kidding? My mind was made up the minute he said I can choose where the dog bed goes. There's the most adorable French bulldog joining our home in three weeks and I've got a walking rota to plan.

It's time to go. I grab the packet of egg sandwiches I've made, add them to my tote bag with the red flask of tea, and head downstairs to Meredith's apartment.

She answers the door and I smile as I see her essentials bag swinging from her right wrist. Her face is wonderfully calm but slightly puzzled. She's forgotten who I am.

"Morning, Meredith," I say once again, a smile overtaking my face. "It's Jayne from upstairs."

ACKNOWLEDGMENTS

Thank you to my brilliant editor, Sareer Khader, who took a very rough first draft of this story and turned it into something I now feel proud of. You always bring a brilliant new perspective, and I am so very grateful for your patience and expertise; thank you. And to the wider Berkley team for caring as much as you do.

Thank you also to my US agent, Kristyn Keene Benton, for your wisdom and enthusiasm. And to my UK agent, Sheila Crowley, for your brilliant editorial input.

Enormous thanks must go to Dr. Karen Harrison Dening, head of research and publications at Dementia UK and an absolute lifeline while I was researching and writing this book. Thank you for making yourself available, despite your own enormous workload, and for ensuring the accuracy and the tone of this book were where they needed to be.

A huge thank-you also to Emma Askew-Miller, creative pattern cutter and lecturer in fashion design at Bath School of Design. Your insight into the couture process was absolutely invaluable.

Thank you to the florist Marcia Wood for sharing your stories with me, and to Katherine Raderecht for introducing me to the best of Bath and connecting me with the people who made this story come to life. At your suggestion, I loved lingering in Berdoulat on Margaret's Buildings, an emporium of local products that was to inspire Jake's business. If you are lucky enough to find yourself in Bath with an hour or two to spare, do not miss it.

Thank you to Rebecca Derry-Evans, a woman I had never met before my first research trip to the city. I was walking along Lansdown Crescent, wondering if this might be the setting for Meredith and Jayne's town house, when we passed each other and exchanged a few words. I explained why I was there, and she invited me in for a full tour of her home, pulling out old photographs of how it had been transformed over the years. We walked through her garden together and to the converted coach house that was to become Jake's home. Without realizing it, Rebecca revealed the starting point of my story. It's these serendipitous meetings that are one of the most joyous things about being a writer. It means you cross paths with warmhearted people you may otherwise never have spoken to.

Writing this book provided so many fabulous opportunities to lose myself in fashion history. From the *Royal Style in the Making* exhibition at Kensington Palace, where I stood in front of Princess Diana's wedding dress; to tours of Althorp, her childhood home; to going behind the scenes at the Royal Albert Hall to view the private staircase and rooms that only the royal family use; and to wandering the drawing rooms of Spencer House and studying the visiting *Canaletto* exhibition at Bath's Holburne Museum (which you will recognize as Lady Danbury's house in Netflix's *Bridgerton*)— everything played its part in fusing this story together.

To the big legal brains—and friends—Seanin and Graeme, for helping me to work out the tricky intricacies of how you lose someone and find them again.

And to all the readers of *The Palace Dressmaker*, wherever you may be, thank you for taking the time to read this story. I hope Jayne, Meredith, and all the gang provide some escapism and entertainment and perhaps some comfort, hope, and optimism that everything can feel a little better with a good friend by your side.

My grandmother lived with dementia, something I expand on more in the Readers Guide at the back of this book. We lived in different cities by the time it got hold of her, so I didn't witness the daily challenges in the same way my mum did. But I saw enough to know that it can be heartbreaking, exhausting, and frightening, yet can also tighten family bonds and offer moments of humor at the most unexpected times—at least it did for my family.

It seems only right that my final thanks should go to the late Catherine Walker, whose exquisite work is, I hope, celebrated across many pages of this story. Having the opportunity to look back at those incredible dresses never once felt like work to me.

And on that point, I know Diana has a global network of loyal fans, some of whom may read this book and enjoy revisiting the incredible gowns she wore by Catherine Walker. These dresses are at the heart of this story. Please forgive me for the adjustments I sometimes needed to make to their original timeline. I didn't want the months and years to overly restrict the choice of dresses I was writing about.

I read some wonderful books during the research for this one, which included:

London's Number One Dog-Walking Agency by Kate MacDougall
The Diana Chronicles by Tina Brown

Dresses from the Collection of Diana, Princess of Wales by
Christie's
Catherine Walker (an autobiography)
Elizabeth Is Missing by Emma Healey
Somebody I Used to Know by Wendy Mitchell

The

PALACE
DRESSMAKER

JADE BEER

READERS GUIDE

BEHIND THE BOOK

❧

I stumbled across a copy of the Christie's catalog *Dresses from the Collection of Diana, Princess of Wales* online one day and decided to order it for no reason other than that I found it intriguing. As I waited for it to arrive, I began to read about the auction. There seemed to be an inconsistency in the number of dresses being reported for sale at this auction. Articles referred to eighty dresses, but only seventy-nine sold. Why was that? I wondered, since I couldn't imagine one went up for auction and didn't sell, given its royal owner and the obvious investment value.

Looking at the breakdown of sales figures that arrived with the Christie's catalog, I realized that there never was a dress number 13. A superstition perhaps? Would no one bid on the unlucky number? But it didn't matter. I was already imagining other possibilities. What if there were eighty dresses originally but one was pulled from the sale? Why might that have happened? And where would that dress be now?

Enter Meredith and dress number 19 in the catalog, casually tossed over the chair in her bedroom and forgotten about. This dress sold at the 1997 auction for over $60,000. I named Meredith (the character) after Meredith Etherington-Smith, the editor in chief of *Christie's* magazine and the curator of the Princess of

Wales auction. Sadly, I never met her, but I did read her brilliant eulogy written by Nicholas Coleridge describing a woman who "was incredibly zeitgeisty, with her bejeweled finger on the pulse of fashion and style and society." She had, Nicholas said, "a love for her husband that was deep and profound. She liked to present their union as one of the great love stories of the century." I wanted my Meredith to have this too. It gave me the very glamorous premise I love all my stories to have. But it also needed to be grounded in something more real and relatable. For that I looked a little closer to home.

My last surviving grandmother was an incredibly independent woman. Her husband died when I was five years old (I remember being taken out of school to hold his hand and say goodbye), and she never remarried. So to me, it feels like she always lived alone. There were boyfriends, but never one she liked enough to invite in permanently. She embraced life single-handedly, with the safety net of unconditional love from her daughter, my mum.

I remember her house was always spotlessly clean and tidy. She had two sitting rooms. One for casual TV watching after a day in the garden. And another that was more formal. If it was your birthday, you'd probably blow your cake candles out in this one. She always had a well-tended arch of roses over her front gate, a vast wardrobe of soft pastel-colored suits and floral sundresses, and a dressing table carefully laid with hairbrushes and mirrors, little lace doilies sitting beneath them. She never left the house without her hair done, lipstick applied, and wearing a very good pair of shoes.

When the house eventually got too much for her, she moved to a smaller one-story bungalow, where she quickly seemed happy and settled. Life carried on just as it had for a few years. But then things started to change. She began to wave out of her kitchen window to a man who would always wave back from the row of houses behind. Except there was no man waving back, despite her insistence. She'd tell stories about visitors who never came and outings that we all knew logistically could not have happened. She might have introduced you to someone who was not in the room and never had been. Sometimes they were historical figures who lived in a different century. We never corrected her. We joined in and let the conversation gather pace. But inevitably we got to the point where my parents felt she needed more around-the-clock care. Considerations for her safety outweighed everything else.

But my grandmother, through the fog of dementia, made it clear she did not want to leave her home. On the day she moved into cared-for accommodation, I was there to try to help ease the transition. When we pulled into the driveway of what was to be her new home, she wouldn't get out of the car. I tried to coax her. I said how excited I was to see her new room, and that seemed to cheer her up. I asked her if she would show it to me, and she became more animated. But once we were inside, her mood darkened. Despite several earlier conversations, she seemed only then to realize that she was there to stay. Very little of what she said by this stage made logical sense—something we never highlighted to her.

It was an afternoon of forced jollity and strained conversations, but when her moment of clarity arrived, it was fueled with anger. She looked me in the eye and demanded, "How would you feel if someone did this to you?"

In the years since her death, I've thought about that day from time to time, acknowledging that it's a decision that countless families have to make: Should you prioritize a loved one's safety and well-being over their own strongly stated wishes, or not? It's the central issue that Jayne, Fiona, and the community of new friends on Lansdown Crescent—including Meredith—have to face.

My mother continued to visit my grandmother every day until the very end. It was the same love, but delivered in a place where the smells, colors, and people felt unfamiliar to her.

I would sometimes take my children to see her, and when my youngest daughter held her hand and sang to her, the confusion and bewilderment seemed to ease a little—just as it does for Meredith in Jayne's company, or when she is reliving her cherished moments with William through the magic they created together during their time at Catherine Walker.

Perhaps the tune my daughter sang took my grandmother back to her own childhood, to happier, simpler times. I hope somewhere in there, deep down, she remembered the love we all felt for her.

DISCUSSION QUESTIONS

1. Was Jayne right to intervene in Meredith's life in the way she did? How might you have acted differently in her situation? In what ways was William's decision to hide his wife's dementia an act of great love? In what ways could it be considered cowardice?

2. Should Meredith have been told explicitly of William's fate?

3. Is Jayne and Meredith's friendship equally beneficial? In what ways did each woman help the other?

4. Which of the female characters goes on the greatest emotional journey: Jayne, Meredith, Olivia, Fiona, or Davina? Why?

5. Who is the more romantic: Jake or William? Why?

6. What are some of your most cherished memories? What or who would feature in your own memory room?

7. Which of the locations featured in the book would you most like to visit? London's Royal Albert Hall or Spencer House?

Sandringham, Althorp, Kensington Palace, Bath, Venice, or New York?

8. If you could own a piece of fashion history, what would it be?

9. Lady Diana's dresses are still bought and sold around the world today. Do you think it's right that people can still buy her dresses? If you had the opportunity, would you ever buy one?

10. Which of the ten Catherine Walker dresses featured in *The Palace Dressmaker* would you most like to own?

11. What significant moments in time and which people do you think will define your life story?

WHAT I AM READING FOR WORK AND PLEASURE RIGHT NOW

❧

House of Nutter by Lance Richardson

Bespoke by Richard Anderson

Making the Cut by Richard Anderson

The Savile Row Story by Richard Walker

Such a Fun Age by Kiley Reid

The Square by Celia Walden

Piglet by Lottie Hazell

Maybe Next Time by Cesca Major

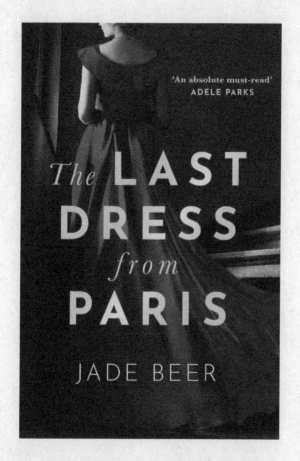

'An absolute must-read'
ADELE PARKS

The **LAST DRESS** *from* **PARIS**

JADE BEER

Each Dior dress tells a story . . .

Discover this unforgettable tale of fashion,
family and romance from Jade Beer.

Available now!